The Chronicles of Amerista: Griefold

A Novel

Richard M Wagner

eBook ISBN: 979-8-89795-088-1
Paperback ISBN: 979-8-89795-089-8
Hardcover ISBN: 979-8-89795-090-4
Fawcett Publications

CONTENTS

CHAPTER 1

Four hundred winters, four hundred winters, and I still have to grease this dusty old wheel, thought Patrallin as he added more auroch grease to the secret source of his clan's steel. The Minnertalla Clan had used the water wheel for centuries to forge the strongest and finest steel in Amerista. The wheel worked the pulleys and belts that pumped the bellows beneath the crucible used by the Talla to melt the raw iron ore into steel. The pulleys and gears also worked the forge's bellows, aiding in the weapons they produced. The old wheel had had many repairs over that time and bore many scars from the idle hands of young boys and girls. Children like him should have been paying more attention to their work.

Patrallin was tired of smearing the old gears with grease and could not wait until the coming winter, even though it was only the first breath of spring. That would be his thirteenth winter and would be a special one for the young boy. He would finally be allowed to shave his head and begin his braid. The braid would show his entrance into adulthood and the leaving behind of childish chores. Patrallin could barely wait, and the greasing of the gears for the water wheel seemed to be a never-ending task. It bored him, but he had to do it.

"You would think, being the only child of the Tallanta of the Minnertalla, I would not have to do this kind of work!" Patrallin muttered just a little too loudly.

A large glob of auroch grease fat fell on top of his head from above; Patrallin looked up just in time to catch an even bigger one right in his upturned face. A tinkling laugh drifted down to him, and his mother's throaty voice soon followed, "You should know better by now, little bull, that all in the Talla share in the work to keep the wheel working. It does not matter who you are or how old you are! We all do our fair share of the work to keep the steel flowing, and greasing the gears in a very important part of that work. Now, why don't you go and see what is keeping your father while I finish greasing the wheel? After that, you may clean up your face and hair...not before!"

Patrallin immediately dropped his bucket and brush. He knew that he was lucky and that a head full of auroch grease was a light punishment for what he had said about being the only child. It was not his mother's fault that she had lost the last child she carried during the Zealot raid five winters ago. He felt bad for what he had said; it may not have sat well with her, but at times, it was hard to control his annoyance.

Those were some of the weak moments he had experienced in his life.

The Tigre' the giant red and black feline with a bobbed tail, had gone insane because its handler had killed himself after the battle. If Tenara had not jumped on the back of the wild animal, it would have killed all of the children in the crèche winton. She killed the animal by repeatedly thrusting her daggers into its thickly muscled neck, swiftly ending the life of the giant feline. During the Tigre's death throws, it clawed Tenara across her abdomen, killing the baby she was carrying and nearly killing her as well. It was fortunate that a Priest Pair had showed up the next day, and the two men were able to save her life from blood loss and infection.

Even though the twin priests were able to save her life, they were not able to save the unborn. Tenara would never be able to bear another child. Patrallin hung his head in shame as these thoughts ran through his mind. It was hard enough on Tenara as it was being the heart-mate of the clan leader, but not being able to provide him with more children made things even worse. Patrallin ran through the small village, dodging the occasional crafter as he searched for his father.

The Talla had not recovered well from that Zealot raid and the damage to the young children was felt most keenly. Nearly every adult member of the Talla died in that raid, leaving many of the young parentless. Yet one of Amerton's tenets is to *"Follow the way of the herd and always protect the young."* So now the few remaining adults had children who were not their own, and many of the children now called someone else mother or father.

Time would heal the Talla. If only the Priest Pair had arrived a day earlier, then they could have prevented the raid. Still, the pair of old men had arrived in time to save many lives of the wounded, Tenara included. The pair had foreseen the Zealot yet had been slow in arriving because one of the old men had injured his ankle while hurrying to the village.

When Patrallin finally reached the village's edge, he prepared himself for an ambush. The young man used all his senses to prepare for the attack he felt was sure yet again to come from his father. He checked that his low-top boots were laced tight and his leather clothing was not too loose to hang up on some underbrush.

Patrallin promised himself the last time that he wound up with bruises across half his body that it would never happen again. Almost counted as a man and a warrior of his people, Patrallin still could not ambush or even sneak up on his father. This was one of the last tests he had to pass before he could be counted as a man, and he was determined to do it before summer was entirely on them. The young man knew he could do it if he could figure out his father's tricks and use them against him.

The boy crept through the forest, paying careful attention to where he placed his feet and slowing his breathing as much as possible. This was the first step taught to him to keep himself ready for his potential attack on the old bull that was his father. Patrallin moved as silent as the wind through the forested hillside to the area of the fallen star that had struck sometime during the winter.

His father was sure that something could be made of the stones that had destroyed the village's one source of root crops. Petralis often spoke about a story from his grandfather's time, something about stones left behind by falling stars.

Convinced that this was the way to save the Talla and to show the other Tallas that the Minnertalla were still strong, Petralis checked the stones every day to see if they were cool enough to handle to move the soil to reveal the sky stone. Petralis hoped that having something special to trade at the next Winter Meet would make the other Tallas more willing to share their sons and daughters. Patrallin felt that his father was dreaming too much. It would take many winters to rebuild the Talla, but the fallen stars would not do it. Also, the soil was so deep that it would be several winters before Petralis could get the skystone out of the ground as it was.

The next shipment of iron ore from Dentalla was due to arrive at the end of the summer that year. Patrallin eagerly anticipated that since it would mean Aristian's return with the wagons of iron. By that time, summer would be fully on them, and then maybe he could persuade her to come into the woods with him again like last year.

Last summer, he was only able to kiss her before her bratty identical twin sisters found them and interrupted. This summer, he hoped more could happen. During the winter gatherings, the older boys always made vague hints about some great secret they knew about girls. Well, he was thirteen now, braid or no braid, he was a man. He thought it was time to find out what that secret was. Patrallin found where the snow patches ended and the scorched trees and undergrowth began. Here was the edge of the area that was destroyed by the skystone. This stone destroyed a large field of tubers, and the Talla was going hungry, waiting for more food to come in with the warriors, now turned hunters.

If this stupid stone hadn't fallen this winter, then father would be helping grease the waterwheel, and I could be out learning more about Velocity, Patrallin thought as he began to stalk his prey. He amused himself with his thoughts for a bit longer.

Patrallin could make out his father's shadow from a distance while walking around the impacted place near the heart of the destroyed area. Patrallin was in luck! Today, Petralis had a deep look of concentration on his face. Patrallin knew so well. He saw that look every time Petralis began to work his forge and was focused on his work with intense concentration. It made the Minnertalla steel valued and made his father forget everything else around him. One time last summer, Petralis had worked two straight days like that. It was only when Tenara had stood in front of him with her daggers drawn and offered to castrate him if he did not rest that Petralis stopped.

Patrallin knew he had his father this time and would finally get the old bull for the first time in his young life. As he stalked closer to his prey, he drew the weighted training sword and dagger all the Ameristan children carried at their sides. Patrallin ran through the attack in his mind as he crept closer to Petralis. A quick slash across the hamstring on the left leg, followed by a return slash across the right side as well. Dagger was drawn, a fast slash across the top of both shoulders to disable his opponent, and finally, a stab through the heart to finish him. He must remember to use extra effort; auroch hide leather was tough, and he had to hit hard enough to cut through the leather that his opponent wore. His father had driven this attack plan into his mind for the last several winters in the training circle.

Just as Patrallin entered striking range, Petralis spun around and lashed out on his own! A painful slash across the chest with a sheathed Xiphos hit Patrallin right over the heart, an instant kill right there. Patrallin froze on the spot and nearly dropped his training sword from a suddenly numb hand. He could not understand; his stalk was perfect, his father was so busy concentrating, and he even approached from what he thought was downwind.

Before Patrallin could utter a word, Petralis growled out in his deep voice, "If you cannot control your tongue around your mother any better than that boy, you will find yourself on a long journey this winter! With my belt across your backside the entire way to The Holy City!"

Patrallin looked at his father in shock, then said, "How did you know what I said?"

Petralis spun away on his heel from his shocked son and began pacing around the impact site yet again with an intense look of concentration on his broad, scarred face.

There was no response from him.

Patrallin had no choice but to follow his father silently around the site and try to figure out how his father knew what had happened. The boy kept wracking his mind, running through all the possible solutions and then quickly eliminating them. By the time they had made two complete circuits of the crater, Patrallin was as confused as he had been. He could see that the tension had finally left his father's shoulders as he was finally ready to talk to him again.

The broad-shouldered smith turned so quickly again to face his son that his waist-long braid wrapped around his neck and landed across his massive chest. Patrallin knew that all Ameristans were broad across the chest, although he was much larger than the Iristian youths who traded with his people. Yet his father was massive in comparison to other Ameristans.

Patrallin studied the scars that spotted and crisscrossed those arms that had just so short a time ago delivered the bruise to his chest. Those same arms could make the hammer and red-hot steel seem to sing on the anvil in the family forge. The scars that covered those arms came from a lifetime spent working on the hot steel and iron that the Talla was known for and the many battles he survived. Patrallin had to fight down the urge to touch the bruise forming on his chest under his leather shirt, wondering at the control his father had with his blade.

Easing his eyes up to meet his father's face, Patrallin looked into the flaring blue eyes beneath the short fringe of blonde hair. For a short time, Patrallin looked up more to the finger-length hair and then let his eyes travel to the braid still hanging around his father's neck. The steel chain intertwined through the blonde braid, glinted tauntingly at Patrallin the entire time. Letting his eyes drift back to meet his father's again, the older man's blue eyes radiated the forge's heat back.

Finally, Petralis took a deep breath and slowly let it out. He said, "You had to mention being an only child in front of your mother again?! What were you thinking? I know you feel that the work on the waterwheel is boring and that you should be doing greater things with your time! I know you would rather be running through the woods chasing Aristian. Well, that will not happen at your age, and until I say that you are ready for more, it will not change." Petralis took the one step separating him and his son, resting a large work-scarred hand on Patrallin's shoulder, "And by the way, don't ever try to sneak up on anyone when you have auroch grease all over your head. YOU REEK OF IT!"

Patrallin's jaw dropped open in shock, and he began to splutter out an answer to this revelation from his sire. Before the young man could answer, Petralis began to laugh at the hearty booming sound that had been so rare to Patrallin's ears for the last few winters. Turning away from his son, Petralis looked over the crater again before he answered Patrallin's unasked questions.

"I knew you were coming before you even cleared the trees because of the grease your mother left on you, Patrallin. It has a distinctive odor, and you absolutely reek of it. Now follow me and learn something important for a change instead of trying to advance beyond what your Tallanta feels you have earned." Taking on a lecturing tone that was far too familiar to his son, Petralis led him into the crater site. "Watch your step here. The skystone shattered when it hit, and there are small fragments all over the ground; it is dangerous. I don't need my journeyman to slip and hurt himself before he even has a chance to begin his work."

On hearing this, Patrallin again froze in his tracks, this time even faster than when his father had hit him in the chest. He started to splutter at his father about this sudden revelation. The normal flow of teachings to be a weapon smith said that Patrallin should be an apprentice for at least another year at the very least, normally two more than that. Again, before the boy could come up with the question, Petralis laughed at his great booming laugh.

Petralis continued to the center of the crater, saying, "Believe it or not, you were not that far off last fall, but I wanted to see if you were ready before making the decision. The journeyman status will only be conferred upon you if you can accomplish one very difficult task. Before jumping into it, you must know what this sky stone can do and how to forge it into something useful. I also want you to forge something out of the skystone that can be useful for trade. To do that, *you* are going to smelt the rock, make the ingots, and then forge something from them."

Patrallin continued to be stunned by his father to this day and spoke to his father in barely a whisper, "But, aren't I too young to be considered for this yet, father? Most boys my age are barely allowed to work the forge in the Himlatalla, let alone become a journeyman weapon smith."

Petralis knelt to the scorched earth and once again crossed his scarred arms as he looked off into the distance. He looked as if he were seeking guidance from another source to answer his son, maybe to their god Amerton or even closer.

"Son, listen, you need first to understand some things now that you will have to learn as a father in your own time. A day will come when your child shows you they are ready to take on more responsibilities than you may even realize. This will be an eye-opening experience for you and make you realize your mortality. Your actions today were that for me. Let me explain before you say anything.

"Your stalk today was flawless; if not for the grease, you would have had me more easily than you realize. Kiital told me this past winter at the Gathering that he had no more to teach you about Velocity and that only time and battle would make you a better warrior; to that end, you are going to take on one of the first steps in the correct direction. Tomorrow morning, you will start gathering the sky stone and smelting it for use in the forge. Ensure that you gather enough to make your first weapons as an adult and a warrior of the Talla. From the looks of the site here, there should be more than enough to make various weapons depending on what weapon you choose to follow."

Patrallin decided to think before answering his father this time. He spent several minutes following his father's tracks around the crater, looking over the material at hand and doing the equations in his head about what he would do. Petralis observed his son's silence, which was an obvious sign that his son was making a conscious decision about what he would say and do. An improvement over his actions from earlier in the day was the sign of growth that was becoming more evident in Patrallin. This was one of the last signs that all Ameristan parents looked for in their children before preparing them to take the Blood Oath to the Talla and Amerton.

Petralis felt his heart begin to swell with pride for his son because his only living child was showing signs of adulthood. It was about time to speak with Aristian's parents and their Tallanta about a marriage very soon. If Patrallin did a good job with the skystone, he could show them his son was a good match for her. Some new fresh blood in the Talla would be a welcome change after the last few winters of loss.

Patrallin broke into Petralis' thoughts, saying, "Father, some of the smaller pieces seem to have cooled enough for me to collect them now. I will take them and work my first dagger from them as soon as I can get the materials together. I will work on mastering Velocity, becoming a master in his own rite, and being another weapon smith for the family. When I am ready to take your place as Tallanta and at the forge, I will prove to you and Mother that I am ready to be a warrior and a man. I am not ready now, but I know time will tell."

Petralis suddenly burst out in tears. It was not a moment of weakness but a warrior preparing to say goodbye to his son and greet a new warrior to his Talla. Patrallin was shocked by his usually stoic father's sudden outburst of emotion.

Typically, the Ameristan people showed no outward signs of emotions outside the family winton. At first, this sudden display of emotion startled the boy, and then he was scared when Petralis swept him up in a rough, rib-bruising embrace. It was all so sudden; the poor boy didn't have time to process that the embrace was meant as a gesture of affection. Patrallin still did not know what to do when his father suddenly cried out the Minnertalla war cry and then squeezed him even harder, cracking a couple of ribs in the process. Patrallin was so distracted that he did not even react when his father began to draw his razor-edged dagger.

CHAPTER 2

A ten-day had passed since Patrallin began the work on his first weapon, one of his first steps in becoming an adult Ameristan of Minnertalla. The sweat kept rolling down from his stubble-covered head into his eyes since the hair he was used to having was now long gone. Patrallin had to keep stopping his work to wipe the sweat from his eyes as it became annoying. He thought that he would have to take Tenara's advice; a strip of cloth tied around his forehead would make him feel silly but serve the purpose of keeping his vision clear. Stopping yet again to wipe the sweat from his eyes, Patrallin went back to work. It annoyed him, but he continued to work on his bellows, using the rhythmic pumping that allowed the greatest amount of air to flow across the flames under the crucible. It was taking a greater amount of time than normal for the larger pieces of ore to melt. This was what kept the stubborn young warrior working for so long. He could tell by the color of the molten metal and the heat coming out of the crucible that it was almost ready.

After nearly an hour more of hard work, Petralis finished his own work on the main forge and came over to his son to see how Patrallin was progressing. Petralis was impressed and showed it by saying, "That is some of the purest and finest work to enter my crucible in many winters. Once you begin to add the coke to the mix, the material will be ready for the ingots and then the forge, my son."

Patrallin began shaking his head as he replied, "No, father, I have a feeling that to get the best possible material from this sky stone, I am going to have to use it in the purest form possible. This is something that I cannot explain, and that frightens me because I cannot explain this feeling. This feeling came upon me last night as I was working here at the crucible."

Petralis immediately wanted to pass off this statement from his son as just a heat-induced fantasy of his son's. It was common for youngsters to see things that weren't there or imagine the worst-case scenarios that undermined their abilities.

Yet, the looks of certainty on his young face made the elder Ameristan hesitate and think before he spoke. Petralis walked over to the crucible and gingerly looked into its contents. The molten metal had the bright orange-red color of well-formed steel and appeared ready for the ingot molds.

Petralis turned back to his son and said, "You may be right, young bull, but next time, I want you to talk with me before you make those decisions in my forge. You are still my journeyman for now, and that means that you still answer to me. On the better side of things, I want to get some of the children to help us get your materials into the ingot molds."

Patrallin smiled up at his father and was hard-pressed not to stop his work on the crucible to pump his arms up in joy. Father and son carefully changed places without breaking the careful rhythm, so Patrallin could run and gather up his former playmates and cousins. Now that he was out of the forge for the first time in days, Patrallin stopped to take a deep breath of the fresh, clean air. Before his father could call him back to his task, the young warrior began to lope through the village of wintons. Patrallin ran three circuits around and among the village, calling for all the young to gather at the forge to help. When he finished this, all fifteen of the children, all of the children in the village, were ready and waiting for him.

Before Patrallin could make his announcement, Tenara's voice cut through the chatter of the gathered children, saying, "Children, you all know the drill by now. Get ready to move the ingot molds once they are filled. The youngest gathered all the water buckets to prevent any fires and burns on the others. The older ones, you know your positions and prepare to change the molds out as they are filled. Patrallin, your father is waiting for you with the crucible, and you must also get to work. If you want to get your work done anytime today, you must get in there now and get to work, little bull."

Patrallin hung his head a little to try to hide the smile that came to his face. It was not his place to put the young of the Talla to work like that, and he knew it. Getting his mother to step in like that was a trick that his father used all the time to settle her. Tradition always stated that the mate of the Tallanta, man or woman, was the one to set apart the need for labor in the family group. It was up to the mate of the Tallanta to best serve the Talla and determine where the people's most use could come from. The attempt to try to usurp her role would always irritate Tenara and Petralis did all of the time.

It was one of the games that the pair played to show their affection for one another in public. Being able to play the game with his mother like that gave Patrallin insights into what his future should look like. Once he had brought his own heart-mate back to join the Talla, as Petralis had done winters before, they would start their own little games. Patrallin went into the forge to assist and supervise the poring of the ingots. This would be the most important part of the job in creating his weapon; having a pure, strong steel ingot was important to start with. If the ingots were not strong enough, he would waste much time and effort for nothing. Patrallin took up the far end of the handles made to lift the crucible from the heat, just as Petralis did the same. Without speaking, father and son began the process, which had remained virtually unchanged for more than four hundred winters. Parent and child working in unison to create the greatest steel on the face of Tarnara, the skills passed father to son, mother to daughter for generations among the Minnertalla. In the Ameristan way, both sexes were counted equal, and the oldest child, no matter their birth, inherited the role of the senior parent. Thus, another of the tenets of Amerton was obeyed: *Let your people be like the herds; the oldest inherits the herd to protect and guide it.* This was one of the many thoughts running through the young journeyman Smith's mind as he worked. Reciting the Tenets was a technique Petralis had taught his son, something he learned from his mother at this same forge. The two, father and son, worked to pour the molten metal into the ingot form and even into the form needed to create a chain or wire. The last was a special addition by Petralis, who had a special use for this unique metal in mind for his son.

After several hours of hot work, the poring was complete, and the children of the Talla were left to return to the crèche winton. As the children left for their winton, or parents who were calling them, the small family returned to their own small hide-covered dome tent. These dome tents were the traditional homes of the Ameristan people when they were not living within the confines of The Holy City during the Winter Gathering. They preferred the tents. Each winton was covered in auroch hide, with the fur still left on the outside to help repel water and bad weather. Each winton was a family treasure and made by each couple after a Priest Pair joined them as a mated pair. The winton of a parent was shared amongst the children after both parents had passed. The inside of each winton was decorated in runes, symbols of Amerton, and pictures showing the family's history.

When Patrallin entered the winton that night, his mother was adding symbols to the walls that showed his triumph that day, working the forge for himself for the first time. It was a great achievement for him. Patrallin was surprised by this because it was going on the wall of his parents' winton. By all rights, this day's events should not be put onto his parents' walls.

Patrallin asked, "Why are you painting what I did today on your own walls, Mother? Surely it was not that important to take up space on the walls of your winton?"

The all too familiar tinkling laugh of Tenara came from the wall of the dome, soon followed by her throaty voice saying, "My little bull, you are such a darling. You still don't know everything, despite what you want to think that braid your father gave you. I am adding this event to our winton to show everyone who enters who you are and what you have accomplished today. I want everyone to know for what you do, and when you bring your potential heart-mate to greet your father and me, she is going to see what you have done, and how truly good a smith you are. In addition, when you leave us, this will form a part of your winton. This piece will show your children and grandchildren how important this day was. This day you have forged a new metal, something not done by any of our people before. Isn't that something worthy of some space in our winton? Also, today, you have shown me and your father that you are truly ready to become a full adult of the Talla."

Tenara took a deep breath to steady herself, but before she could continue, Petralis shoved aside the hide flap, saying, "And today, the Tallanta and his heart-mate have decided that their son is a child of their winton no more! It is time for you to move into your own winton and to prepare for your own life, Patrallin. I have spoken with the other warriors of the Talla, and it is agreed upon that you are now a full member and that it is time for you to take your Blood Oath. Come outside and bring your dagger with you."

With his son in a state of shock and his mate fighting back tears as she followed him, Petralis turned and left his home. Patrallin stood frozen in place yet again, wondering at his father's sudden moves, much like that fateful day in the field. Patrallin mentally kicked himself into motion quickly washing his arms with a damp towel left out by his mother. Patrallin next checked the edge of his dagger. Finally, Patrallin calmed himself as he moved aside the hanging hide that worked as a door on all wintons. He was not surprised by what he saw waiting for him since he had watched the same ceremony being performed on several occasions.

Waiting for him outside his parents' home were all of the village's adults with both arms bared to the shoulders. On both the men and women, there were at least one, and usually two or more, scars on the inside of the arm running from elbow to wrist. The scars were proof of the oaths each had taken in their lives as adults and how important each oath was to them.

Patrallin knew he was taking a very big step in his life by taking his first Blood Oath to the Talla. Any Ameristan did not count themselves as warriors and adults unless they kept their given Blood Oath. Breaking a given word, especially an oath, were things of the weak and of children. Any Ameristan Warrior would die before allowing themselves to break any Blood Oath. With a slow, purposeful pace that showed reverence for the occasion, Patrallin entered the center of the circle made by his direct and extended family.

Once he reached the center of the circle, one of the men threw extra wood onto the already raging fires surrounding the outside of the circle. Large amounts of light suddenly sprang up around the circle of adults and spying children, giving the solemn ceremony an illuminated aura. Petralis walked into the circle and stood opposite his son.

Raising his arms, Petralis began to address the crowd, "Tonight, we are here for a boy to become a man! My son has proven himself to my mate and me and has shown he is ready to move on to greater responsibilities. Today, Patrallin, son of Petralis and Tenara, becomes a warrior of the Minnertalla! Tonight, he takes up the battle to protect our people from the Iramians, as we all have in our time! Patrallin, come forward and take your oath. Come forward and join your Talla as a warrior ready to defend your people!"

Patrallin stepped closer to his father as he drew his own dagger. The young man wished he had sharpened his blade that morning, knowing what was to come. Patrallin raised his right arm high above his head as he cut a shallow gash along the inside of his forearm from wrist to elbow. He raised his arm high above his head and let the blood flow from his elbow drip onto the ground at his feet.

Patrallin began to speak his oath, saying, "My blood binds me. My words bind me. By my blood and by my words, I bind myself! I will protect my Talla, my family, my people. I will serve my Talla for my life and do what is needed to protect and nurture my Talla." With these words, Patrallin took the final steps to become a full member of his clan and accounted for being a full adult in Ameristan society. This was the one step that every young Ameristan looked forward to throughout their lives. As Patrallin finished his oath, the whole village let out the loudest war cry that they could manage.

As the sound began to die down, Tenara stepped forward to bind her son's arm and prevent too much blood loss. She was openly crying as she bound his still bleeding arm with clean linens, with much-practiced swiftness. Tenara then returned to her place in the circle next to her mate, Petralis.

Petralis then said, "Welcome to the Minnertalla, young Patrallin. I am your Tallanta Petralis, son of Palatine, daughter of Hentan. I welcome you to our Talla, and we all wish you a long, brave, honorable life with us."

As his speech finished, this was the awaited signal for the anticipated speech to begin. Members of the village began to bring out joints of roast auroch that had been cooking all day long. Cooked foul and other wild meats began to join the well-roasted meat and wild tubers and fruits abundant in the early spring. This was a long-anticipated event for the village, giving the people a well-deserved reason to rejoice after such a harsh winter.

Patrallin made his way around the village, greeting each full adult member of the Talla. At this time, he found himself shocked by his newfound responsibilities of adulthood. He decided that he was going to focus on creating his weapons and perfecting one of the daggers as a gift to his mother. As he made his second circuit around the milling group of people, Patrallin heard something that caught his attention.

Two of the warriors who were the primary hunters for the Talla were talking, which caught the young man's attention. "I am telling you, I was raised Himlatalla before marrying Celtania. I know the signs of a griffon nest when I see them. There is a mated pair of plains griffons making a nest deep in the forest west of the village. In a few more days, there are going to be eggs in that nest, and by the time the snow falls again, there will be the beginning of pride in our lands. In a few more winters, we can begin to have watch animals of our own, and our Talla will grow that much stronger. Just think about it, Marten, we could save the Talla and become heroes all in the same move. My wife will not have died for nothing, and our daughter will live free from fear of raids taking her life or the lives of her children to come."

"I know," Marten said, "don't forget that I, too, lost loved ones in that last Zealot raid. Celtania was my sister, and I lost my wife and children during that raid, Zentar! We must share this information with Petralis in the morning; we do not want to ruin the ceremony for Patrallin…. speak of the Raider, and he shall appear. So, young Patrallin, how does it feel to become a warrior and finally join the Talla fully?"

Patrallin smiled as he raised his arm, saying, "Oh, it would feel great if it didn't hurt so much…I should have sharpened my blades." Then the young man started laughing aloud and said, "Working the forge is much more painful than this scratch. What was this I heard about a griffon pair nesting near the village that could help the Talla?"

"Well," Zentar said, rubbing his chin, "first of all, you don't eavesdrop on others when they are talking to each other. Doing so is just plain rude."

Patrallin hung his head in shame yet again, and the smile faded from his face. Again, the young man had failed to meet the standards of his people. Showing that he could not be trusted by others and being so close to his own ceremony would greatly embarrass his parents if they found out.

As Patrallin turned to walk away in shame, Zentar reached out to stop him, saying, "In the Himlatalla as our passage, we are required to work as a group to acquire one griffon egg from a nest. Our entire Talla would go out with the youths preparing for their ceremony to raid one nest each and take only one egg from each nest. After our successful raid, we are counted as having passed our trial and as full adults in the Talla. Much like you having to begin to forge your own weapons for the first time. On the other hand, my daughter has to complete her own armor. Each Talla and each parent has their own tasks presented to their child, and then each must pass that before they can achieve the level of warrior and adulthood. This is one of the many things you will learn when you become a father, Patrallin."

Patrallin listened to this statement with awe and wonder. His own mother was Himlatalla born, yet she had never shared any information about it with him. After becoming a mate to his father, despite all tradition, she removed her Talla symbols from her braid after the bonding. If people did not know any better, they would assume that she was Minnertalla her entire life instead of Himlatalla. Such dedication she had with her partner.

The steel chain glittered in her blonde hair as she moved around the circle of clan members talking with them. Tall for an Ameristan and proud, Tenara never let anything get her down or slow her pace as she moved from person to person. The claws from that Tigre' had greatly damaged her, yet she never let the scars slow her down as she did her duties in the village. Without warning, Tenara turned to look at him as if she had sensed his looking and thinking about her. She smiled and began to walk over to him, something glittering in her hands as Petralis moved to join her beside their son. Patrallin stood still as, without a word, his mother and father undid his short braid and began to add a new steel chain to his hair. This caused the young man to cry in joy as he received this mark of a warrior of his people.

After the chain had been braided into his hair, the young man went to every member of the Talla and personally thanked them for coming. Once it was all over, he walked to his parents' winton to sleep while he was still allowed to live there.

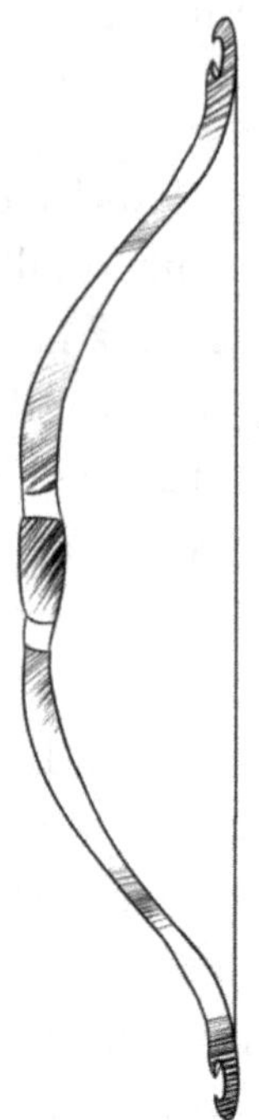

CHAPTER 3

Several days had passed, and the young man worked furiously to forge his weapons and work on a particular project. This metal was far different from the steel Patrallin was used to working with. Because of this difference, he had to develop new and different techniques on the spot, which he had never thought about using before. These techniques and ideas came from his father, as well as suggestions and stories from his grandfather winters ago. These techniques were a remarkable sight and wonder for the young weaponsmith as he worked on creating his daggers. His first dagger was forged after laboring for several days to get the heat just right, as the amount of time in the forge was just right. It was an ugly piece of work, a simple fighting dagger that all Ameristans wore as a weapon or to cut anything. Ugly in looks, it may be, the dagger was perfectly balanced for his hand and fit his palm as if it were never going to fit another hand. The perfect weapon for a Velocity user would give him a dagger to last through many battles.

Later that same day, the finer piece of work came from the flames of the forge and took on a much more beautiful aspect and shape. The second dagger to emerge from the flames of his family's forge that day was truly a work of art in every sense. The young man had worked hard to make a beautiful piece of work to match that of his mother in the way of apology for what he had said all those days ago. The diamond cross-section blade was as razor-sharp as he could make it before tempering the blade. The cross guard had the carving of a griffon on either side so that her Talla could be shown to all who saw it.

At last, he etched the runes of his name and Talla into the blade to show her how much she meant to him. By giving her his name and family name, he proved that she was part of him and that he would always be with her as long as she held the blade. Finally, the young man began the final step of the long-drawn-out process of tempering the blades. This was time-consuming since the process could only be done once, and any errors in the process destroyed his hard work.

Hours later, the process of tempering the blades was done, and Patrallin began to polish the blade he intended for his mother. This would be a special job for her, so he wanted it to shine in the sun any time she had to draw it for all to see. As he worked to polish the metal, the shine of the steel seemed to take upon itself a colored hue unlike that of a normal steel blade. Instead of a mirror finish, he was expecting the blade to begin to show a rainbow of colors running the length of the blade from tip to pommel. This was not what he was expecting, yet what he could do was the blade was forged, it was tempered, and now it was time to begin to finish his work. Patrallin continued to polish the metal, assuring himself that it was just that the metal was not steel; it was something different, and he was going to have to deal with the changes to it. The young man polished and sharpened the blade to a razor's edge with more effort than he thought it would take. Next, he moved onto his blade, and the same properties seemed to show as he continued to work.

Patrallin spent the entire day and night and part of the next day working on the blades and handles so they would never slip in combat. The work was finally done, and the young man was as exhausted as he had never been before in his life. Picking up the dagger intended for his mother, he turned to leave the forge and tripped over one of the tongs he had dropped in exhaustion. Normally, Petralis would have been fuming at him for it and berated him for days for his lack of care with the tools of his trade. However, Petralis had been busy creating Patrallin's first winton so the young man could have his own home. As the young man tripped, his gift to his beloved mother flew from his hands and landed point first on the anvil with a loud clang. Fearing the worst that he had just destroyed the work of art he had worked so hard to create for his mother, Patrallin ran to the far side of the anvil.

Resting on the ground was the dagger, still pristine and as beautiful as when he had just dropped it. He looked to the anvil where the dagger had struck it and found a groove carved through the hardened steel like a plow had cut through the ground. Sitting on the ground, the young man picked up the dagger and slowly pushed it through the anvil to the hilt of the dagger with little resistance.

Patrallin looked at the anvil as he removed the dagger and then started screaming for his father to come immediately. Within minutes, the entire village was running into the forge. Even the children had their training daggers drawn, expecting danger of some kind. Petralis had his Xiphos drawn and began demanding an explanation for the yelling. Then, he saw his son sitting on the ground, stuttering. Petralis knelt down to see where Patrallin was pointing, saw the dagger had penetrated the ancient steel anvil, and immediately ordered the forge cleared.

Resting a hand on Patrallin's shoulder, Petralis said, "Son, tell me what happened here."

Patrallin said, "Father, I tripped over one of the tongs as I was getting ready to present this dagger to Mother, and it slipped from my hands. I heard it clang across the top of the anvil and feared that I had damaged the dagger's edge or even worse. Then I found the groove it had carved on top of the anvil. I could not believe it had caused that damage, so I tried to push it through the anvil by hand, and that is what happened." He pointed to the small hole now in the anvil near its base.

Petralis could not believe that a dagger could have done such damage to his anvil, the anvil that had been in his Talla for over three hundred winters. He snatched up the second dagger intended for Patrallin and rammed the blade at the anvil with all his might, expecting the blade to snap. As the blade struck the anvil, it slid into the anvil with barely any resistance and stopped dead at the crossguard. This was more than he could take. What had happened to his anvil to allow a simple dagger to damage it in such a way? Slowly taking his sword and gently pushing the tip at the anvil, Petralis realized there was nothing wrong with his anvil. There was something dreadfully different about his son's work, and it was not something that he could think of any answer to.

Turning to Patrallin, he demanded, "What did you do differently to make your weapons damage an anvil that has been in our family for more than three hundred winters? What materials, what techniques, what did you do?!"

Patrallin started to cringe and said, "I don't know. I only followed the suggestions that you gave me from your grandfather about how to forge the sky stone, and then I tempered the blades like you taught me. I did not know it was going to be a problem. I only though that I was doing the right thing."

"No, you did nothing wrong. I... I remember my grandfather mentioned tempering the metal when he made the chain for my mother. It was only a small amount of very impure stone, and he thought a special gift for her would mark her ceremony. If he had done the same thing as you, we would not be so surprised right now. Patrallin, do you realize what we have found here in our mountains? We have found a way to end the raids for all time! We could arm our warriors with weapons such as this, but nothing could stop them from destroying all of our enemies. This…this god touched steel. This Amersteel will save our people and allow us to thrive once again. Patrallin, we have to hide what you have already made into ingots, and you must begin to work on new weapons for our Talla. When we find more of this metal, you are going to begin to work on it in the same fashion and begin to save our people."

Patrallin began to think about all of the possibilities about what he had discovered in the metal on which he had worked. This Amersteel would give his Talla unprecedented status among the clans and allow him to do anything. He would finally be free to join with Aristian; even her parents could not stop them. This was all of his hopes rolled up into one great gift in one day. The thirteen-year-old could not begin to think of how this would help him achieve his goals, but then he realized that he had to put his Talla first. The Talla were his family, and the tenets said to protect your family like the herds protected their own. With this thought foremost in his mind, the young smith began to work out which of the weapons that his people used would first be crafted by his hands. This would be an ideal gift for his father, but better yet, a mating gift for Aristian to mark her new status as Minnertalla at the ceremony.

Patrallin set to work with a newfound passion as he worked hard to create the finely woven herringbone chain that all Minnertalla wore in their braids. This work was time-consuming and difficult since it would take many hours of hard work to draw the fine wire through the dies one at a time after carefully heating the metal. It was a ten-day of work for the young man, with not a few mistakes made, before he was prepared to begin the tedious task of weaving the metal together into the chain.

While he worked, Patrallin's parents spent many hours standing together, watching their son hard at work and admiring how he was so determined to win the heart of the young Aristian. Even though he had not spoken about his plans to anyone, they knew what he was doing since what had happened the previous summer.

Petralis one day said, "I guess I am going to have to speak with Aristian's parents this year after all. Well, adding more blood to the Talla is a good thing."

"I was at least hoping to keep him my son for another winter yet." Tenara replied, "But, I suppose you are right, my heart-mate. I will have to see what this girl metal is made of during the ritual combat. Do you suppose I should give her a scar or two for Patrallin to discover their first night together?" she finished with an evil grin.

Petralis' reply was a soft laugh as he said, "Just because my mother made you bleed does not mean that you have to make our soon-to-be daughter bleed as well. It is supposed to be ritual combat, and you know it, my mate. Besides, you should know that the young girl favors Dominance in style and prefers the great axe. You should be careful because her father is the Weapons master of the Dentalla and is originally from Amertalla. He only left The Holy City to stay with his heart-mate; that young man was a sight to behold on the battlefield. I once saw him spar with another Velocity user, and he defeated her within four heartbeats. Together, they are a formidable pair, and their daughters are all just as deadly in the training circles. Oh, well. Whom am I kidding? You are going to try your best to scratch the girl because she will be taking away our little bull from us, aren't you?"

"You're damn right!"

"Just promise me it will be a shallow cut, please. You know that my mother never really forgave you for the cut you gave her, even though it was only an accident."

Tenara's only reply was a sniff as she turned away to her winton to begin to remove the dome tent panels that would be added to Patrallin's. She had a feeling that the two would not wait until the Winter Gathering this year to join, which meant they were going to need more room. She drew her new dagger again, smiling at the beautifully wrought blade, and carefully removed the panels that she felt would show the most important stages in Patrallin's life. Petralis soon joined her in her work by replacing the missing panels with new blank leather sections. He hoped to soon add scenes from his son's joining ceremony and scenes of his grandchildren's birth. The burly master smith set to work with a needle and thread, sewing in the panels with a delicate hand and flair that would have astonished any viewer.

CHAPTER 4

The days slipped by while the young Smith worked and his family prepared for the arrival of the iron ore shipment, which was the lifeblood of the weapon smith clan. Together, all of the Talla members spent hours working on the necessities of life, such as hunting and gathering food, as well as just the simplest things, such as maintenance of the winton. One such day, Patrallin was working on his own winton, preparing it to introduce himself to the love of his life, when he again overheard Zentar talking about the griffon's nest.

"I was in the area again this morning. Marten and the adults were out hunting, so I checked on the eggs to see how they fared in the spring and the wyverns. There are four fine healthy eggs there, and they seem ready to hatch in the coming ten-day. There seem to have been no wyvern raids on this nest, and any day now, there will be four hungry hatchlings for the adults to care for. This will definitely be a summer to remember, Patrallin discovering that Amersteel, the griffons settling in our area, and my daughter entering her ceremony this winter. Yes, definitely a summer to remember!"

Patrallin was suddenly reminded about the nest and his plans from earlier in the spring. It was the height of summer, he still had not made his plans come to fruition about going to the nest, and his time was nearly running out. Also, Aristian and the rest of the Dentalla were due to arrive any day now as well. What was he going to do? To prove himself as a true warrior, he had to do something special, or her fathers' permission would never be given, but to be a true Minnertalla, he had to finish his chain.

Well, Patrallin thought to himself, *I will have to do both at once, and that means that I am going to get into a lot of trouble if I am caught tonight.*

A plan formed quickly in his mind, and he knew how to make it work if he were lucky enough to have a dark night that night. It was nearly the full moon, and the skies promised a clear night. Time will tell.

That night, the entire village was asleep in their wintons, with families happily sleeping and the sentries patrolling quietly as they moved around the village in ever-shifting patterns. Only one of those who should have slept was awake, and the young man was trying hard to slip past the vigilant sentries as they protected their people. This was an old game played by the children of Talla and Patrallin, who had never been able to play it. The game was to sneak past the sentries and then return to the village after sunrise to prove how good they were. Patrallin had never been able to make it past the sentries with his playmates successfully, so this was going to be his only chance.

Time and the weather were on his side; it was late at night as dawn was only a few hours away, and the clouds had rolled in during the early evening, darkening the skies. It was nearly lightless at night, and this allowed the young man to experience a greater amount of stealth as he crept out of the village. Passing one sentry after another, it seemed almost impossible to Patrallin that he was able to do it so easily, surely. Amerton was on his side as well. It took him an hour of slow creeping to crawl a hundred yards that separated his winton from the edges of the sentries' patrols. Once safely past the range of his people, the young warrior nearly ruined his successful escape by whooping with joy as he rose to his feet and began to move through the woods. Keeping silent was the hardest part of his trek through the woods for Patrallin. He wanted to run and shout with joy since he had finally shown that his abilities were truly equal to those of the rest of his people.

The journey to where Zentar had described the griffon nest was a dangerous and nerve-wracking one for Patrallin. He had only the rumors and stories told by the Himlatalla children at the Gathering to go by about griffons. The rumors said they could see in the dark, hear your heart beating for a mile, and breathe fire. Patrallin did not believe the breathing fire part, but seeing and hearing his heartbeat for a mile, he was not so sure. Since this was something he could not be sure about, he needed to take extra precautions in his approach to the nest because he did not want to become some animal's next meal. Patrallin continued to move through the woods with the same precaution and stealth that he had used at the beginning of the spring to sneak up on his father. This stealth and cunning helped him approach the nest just as dawn was breaking over the treetops. Patrallin was just in time to see both parents leave the nest in search of food, he assumed. It was a beautiful sight as the two griffons lifted off from the tree-top nest and winged away into the rising sun in the east. This was the perfect time for Patrallin to scale the tree leading to the nest and to capture an egg. If he waited much longer, then the parents could return and add him to the menu.

Patrallin began to scale the tree the nest had been made among using the skills of the child, who was still in body, if not in mind and soul. The young man quickly climbed until he reached the edge of the twisted branches that made up the nest. Slowly looking up and over the rim of the nest, Patrallin saw the four eggs laying in a neat pile in the center of the nest. With speed inspired by fear, he scrambled across the nest and grabbed the nearest egg, which he quickly stuffed down the front of his leather shirt. Patrallin started to climb down the tree again as fast as he could, dropping several branches at a time and making good speed as he went down. As the young man neared the bottom of the trees, an ear-splitting shriek nearly made his bowels loosen themselves. Looking up, Patrallin saw one of the wyverns from the southern mountains of Dracolia begin to soar toward the unguarded nest. These wyverns were known for eating the eggs and young of any animal that they could find unprotected, including humans. In addition, their hide made a fine, strong leather strongly sought after by the armorers for its resiliency and strength. Hitting the ground just a few feet below him, Patrallin fell to his back, praying, deeply and silently, that he did not damage the egg stuffed into his shirt simultaneously. Sorely climbing to his feet, Patrallin drew his own Amersteel dagger and prepared to defend himself, the wyvern, should it decide to attack.

Just as he drew his dagger, another screech could be heard, yet this one seemed to echo upon itself and then stopped with a loud crunch. Looking up again, Patrallin saw that the adult griffons had returned and were beginning to attack the wyvern to protect their nest. Taking this as a sign from Amerton, the young man turned on his heels and ran away as fast has his feet could carry him. Normally, the Ameristan people hunt the wyverns as the animals enter Ameristan territory. Yet, on this day, the young man figured that the adult griffons would be taking care of this particular type of raider when he returned to his home.

***

As the young warrior was stealthily making his way to the nest of the griffons, another hunter was stealthily making their way to the Minnertalla village. He was one of two hundred men sent by their God Emperor to find the Minnertalla and wipe them off the face of Tarnara. He may be a ship's captain and a noble in his nation. He even controlled his own small island. Yet, when your God spoke to you, you obeyed, especially in Iramia, where the God Emperor's word was law, and the captain's entire family could end up as slaves if he did not obey. On the other hand, even worse, they could receive a visit from the dreaded Blood Death Assassins. That thought alone had driven the captain and his crew so far from his beloved ship and the ocean. Having to bring the High Priest and an extra hundred Royal Guards did not help the captain feel any better about the situation. The captain had planned to bring some Ameristans back as slaves to add to his holdings, but the orders were clear. All men, women, and especially the children were to die, or the crew's families would join the slaves of the islands. For the crew, this was no choice at all. The unsuspecting village would die with the dawn of this day. The nameless captain was certain that neither he nor the rest of his crew would ever return to the islands as it was. The captain had already arranged with his best friend to take in his sons and save them from the slave brand. The family slaves could wear the brands of another from now on. His sons were all that mattered, even though his family would end with him.

As the Iramians reached the village's eastern edge, a Minnertalla sentry nearly discovered them when the priest struck out with the steel rod in his hand. A spark of light flew from the end of the rod and struck the sentry right over the heart. The woman just froze on the spot. Calmly and with an evil smile, the priest approached the sentry. Without a word, the priest took the same rod with the end suddenly glowing red hot as the day it was forged and slowly shoved it into the sentry's chest. A look of sheer agony appeared on the young woman's face as the smell of burnt flesh filled the air.

With his face breaking out into a look of sheer ecstasy, the priest forced the rod through the sentry's heart. The poor woman was conscious throughout the whole ordeal until the tip of the rod burst her heart. Sighing with pleasure, the priest turned to the waiting men and said, "Go! Kill them all, and let none survive! Let your tilltons drink deep of the blood of a people that think they could kill our God Emperor!"

In near total silence, the Iramians descended upon the still-sleeping village, and the slaughter of the innocents began. The first few winton walls were not strong enough to stop the razor-edged, slightly curved blades. Within the first few seconds, the occupants of the small dome tent were dead in their sleep, with none knowing any better. The slaughter continued for only those first few wintons before the cry of warning went out, and the Minnertalla reacted. The doomed people showed the tenacity and the fighting ability that made the Ameristans so feared in Tarnara. The eighty-three adult warriors, all still wearing little to no clothing, swept into battle with a ferociousness that slowed the attackers. The eighteen youths all drew their daggers and jumped into the fray, killing the wounded attackers and attacking where they could. The Minnertalla was doomed to fall from the beginning and knew it from the time the first blow was struck in their defense. The adults quickly formed a protective circle around the surviving children, now numbering only ten. Once the adults formed the circle, the fighting stopped for a minute as the priest made his way to the front of the fighting. He motioned his men to clear a path so that the Minnertalla could see his approach and fear him even more.

When the way was in the clear, the priest said, "I am Tona Deltin, High Priest of the God Emperor of Iramia. For the crime of daring to believe you could one kill our God, we Iramians are here to exact our punishment from you! Your people will die, you will die, and you shall never raise the weapons foreseen to kill the God Emperor. Lay down your arms, and we will make this fast. Continue to fight us, and your children will suffer the most!"

In answer to this, Zentar threw his javelin at the priest with all his strength. The spear flew straight and true until the priest raised his steel rod, and the javelin froze in midair, as did Zentar. The priest chuckled as he walked to the spear, gingerly touching the razor-sharp tip. He smiled even bigger. Tona Deltin grabbed the shaft, plucked the javelin from the air, spun it in his hands, and threw it. The weapon flew unerringly to strike the abdomen of Zentar's young daughter. She screamed in pain as she died on her father's weapon. Zentar was so angry that the waves of emotion were almost palpable to the people crowded around him. With a distracted wave of his hand, Tona Deltin sent his warriors back to killing the encircled Ameristans.

Even though the Minnertalla were outnumbered two-to-one, they fought to the death, with Tenara and Petralis being the last two survivors. The fight was short and brutal, yet the Minnertalla killed over half of the Iramians before succumbing to their fate. As the last two surviving adults of the Talla, Petralis and Tenara had the worst job to contemplate, the last surviving three children knew what was coming.

With tears streaming down their faces, the Tallanta and his heart-mate took their daggers and swiftly killed the children in a painless way. Turning to face their attackers,

Petralis kissed his heart-mates blood and tear-stained face, then ran into battle, killing himself on his enemies' blades. Tenara wished her son well, seeing as how his winton was empty and his body not among the dead, prepared to do the same. Before she could do so, Tenara found herself frozen in place, much like the first sentry and Zentar before he died. Struggling to move, she did not know what to do.

Tona Deltin appeared before her face again with the evil smile on his face that was there when he killed Zentar's daughter. Laughing, he said, "So, you think to kill yourself like your owner had? Too bad, slave, I would rather have had him under my rod for the questions I must have answered. You will have to do!"

***

Patrallin was smiling as he began to make his way back to his village, anticipating a hero's welcome from his people. For the hours that it took Patrallin to reach the griffon's nest and return, his entire world was turned upside down. As he approached, where one of the sentries should have stopped him, Patrallin knew something was wrong. There was no challenge to his approach, and at least two sentries should have been confronting him by now. Patrallin removed his leather jerkin and woolen undershirt to use as wrappings to protect his hard-won prize. After all the hard work that he had put into acquiring his newfound treasure, he was not about to let it get damaged or destroyed. He then placed the egg in the hollow at the base of a tree among its roots and covered his prize with leaf litter and loam to disguise it better.

Next, the young warrior drew his new dagger as he prepared to enter his village. It was an eerie sight to Patrallin. At this time of day, the village should have been busy with the families preparing for the day. Children should have been herded to the crèche' winton as their parents left for patrols or hunting to feed the Talla. The forge should have been ringing with the sound of his father hard at work, creating the weapons needed for the Winter Gathering. The more devout members of the village would be gathering on the east side to greet the rising sun in worship of Amerton.

Yet the young man could see no worshipers moving through the village nor hear any sounds of work being done anywhere. As he approached his own winton, Patrallin got his first indications that something could be truly wrong with his village. Along the side of his dome tent nearest the village, he could see a neat slash made along the side that faced the village. The slash that was made in the winton was made with a razor-sharp weapon, and it cut through the last scene his mother had painted onto the panel before his ceremony. There were signs of someone hastily searching for something in the winton as his few possessions were strewn about the area. Since he had placed his winton out of sight of the village, Patrallin could not see what awaited him within the village proper.

The young warrior entered his stalking demeanor as he prepared to attack anything out of the ordinary to be found waiting for him. Stripped to the waste, the young man searched his village in vain for his people. It did not take long for him to find the first casualties of the raid. What Patrallin saw that lonely summer morning was enough to give him nightmares for the rest of his life. Everywhere he looked, there was death and the destruction of his people. Here lies the infant Alana, born during the last Winter Gathering, just outside her parent's winton with her skull crushed. If that were not enough, the most secure place in the village, the village crèche, was a smoldering ruin. It was here that Patrallin stopped this pile of ash and charred wood that was home to his earliest childhood memories. It was in this place he was raised until the age of five, like all Ameristan children by the whole village. Here was where Patrallin first met Aristian when her Talla had come to trade iron for weapons. It was here where he had shed his first blood in the Zealot raid. Now, the place of safety from all the dangers in the world was destroyed, and with it, all his family. Surely, that could not be Zentar. He was one of the strongest fighters in Talla. How could he have died by a single thrust in the heart and have no other marks upon him. Moreover, why is Petralis there among the Iramians that lay dead all around the circle of the villagers? He would have stayed in the center, directing the fighting and protecting the young as tradition demanded. Where was his mother? Surely Tenara would never have left his side while she was still breathing. This scared Patrallin more than anything else he found that day. How could he lose both of his parents in one day?

The warrior was in shock and could not help but be afraid that the worst had happened. His family was all gone and here he was all alone in this village-turned-charnel pit. Patrallin continued to search the village and tried in vain to find any survivors. The attackers were a race unknown to him, and they appeared like the Iristian traders that came to the Winter Gatherings, yet they did not. The facial features of the two races were very much the same, but the coloration of the Iramians was much lighter. Patrallin searched the bodies of the slain Iramians, looking for anything that could identify them to try to discover who they were. All that Patrallin could discover from the bodies was that they were all male and that none of them bore any weapons. The weapons had obviously been carried off. In addition, all of the dead men were tattooed on the left side of their necks with a trident-shaped tattoo. Only one of the men had another type of tattoo; instead of a trident on his neck, it was the tattoo of a sword. Patrallin had never heard of this before and marked it in his memory to try to find out who these people were. Finally, Patrallin turned to the one place he had dreaded to go near the most.

While the village lay in near-total ruins around it, the forge still stood untouched, as if observing the Talla's destruction. Fearing what may lie inside, Patrallin took slow, heavy steps to the one place that still held his most fond memories. What lay inside would scar the boy for life and send him down the path of vengeance for the rest of his life as well. Before he could even finish opening the stout oaken door, the smell of burnt flesh and drying blood assaulted Patrallin's nostrils. With a great war cry, Patrallin threw the door open to the horror that was left of his mother, spread the eagle across the anvil, and tied it to its base. Tenara was exposed to his eyes. With tears stinging his eyes, Patrallin rushed to her side, knowing she had to be dead after the evident torture that had been done to her. The beautiful woman's entrails were piled at her feet. In addition, one of her eyes lay next to her blood-soaked braid across the room from where her body lay. Screaming in outrage, Patrallin ran to her side, hoping beyond all reason to find her still alive. The warrior laid a trembling hand on her exposed chest to try to convince himself that what he was seeing was only a horrible nightmare. As he laid his hand upon the body of his mother, the shocking reality of it all came crashing down upon him. Yet before the boy-turned-man could collapse from the grief, he felt a slight rise to his mother's ruined chest.

Despite obvious torture that should have killed her, Tenara still lived, and she was trying to say something to Patrallin. She took a second struggling breath as she opened her one good eye to look at him.

Upon seeing Patrallin, she gasped, "Son…, Patrallin…please…kill me. Iramians…don't forget…Tona Deltin…. KILL ME! *Please…*" With the last word, barely being above a whisper Tenara once again fell silent, but the spirit of her will keep her heart beating. Patrallin stood back from his mother in a set of emotions too complex to name.

Love for his mother warred with shock at what had happened to her, alongside pity for the pain she must be in. knowing what he must now do, the young man, the boy no more in anyone's eyes, ended his mother's life swiftly and painlessly. Patrallin tried to think of any of the Tenets of Amerton that fit this situation and could only come to one conclusion: *Sometimes, a man had to do what Amerton would not.* This was a new personal Tenet Patrallin adopted on that fateful day in the late summer of his thirteenth year.

It took Patrallin all day and most of the night to prepare his people for a funeral pyre. This was following his people's beliefs and the only way he could care for his dead. He also gathered and cleaned the braids from all of the adults and the locks of hair from the children. All of them had died in battle, as warriors, so he would return the braids to the Minnertalla longhouse in The Holy City as soon as he could. This task was the hardest for him to do, as each member of the Talla had died a gruesome death. As for the remains of the Iramians, Patrallin dragged them as far as he could from his home and left them there.

Let Amerton deal with them as he sees fit, he thought during this task.

As Patrallin worked at cremating his people, he also worked at restarting the forge and began to create something from the ingots of Amersteel. Revenge for what had happened to his people burned foremost in his mind. With that thought in mind, Patrallin created more weapons from his remaining ingots. The first item he set about creating was the head of a bearded axe. Patrallin felt he needed to create a great weapon of destruction in memory of his people who were slaughtered. The memory of Zentar rang loudest in his mind since the man had done so much over the winters to help him. Because of its simple construction, the bearded axe head only took him a few hours to complete. After hammering out the shape, he sharpened the blade with a file. This was going to be the most labor-intensive part of the work for this particular weapon. It would take days of work for him to sharpen the bearded axe blade enough to be ready for the tempering process.

By the time a ten-day, had passed, the lone warrior had barely left the forge to eat; he slept in the forge itself. He worked as a man possessed, speaking little and then only to the griffon egg he had worked so hard to acquire.

"Here, see the file shapes the edge of the blade itself while it sharpens the axe. You have to have a good file for this, especially with Amersteel."

"See now. Tempering is the most important part of firing hardness from simple iron into true steel into the blade. You see, my great grandsire did not know about Amersteel's tempering; he did not know how strong it could truly be. Now, by quenching it in the oil just so…and now we have a bearded axe ready to be polished and fitted with a new handle. Now, egg, we are going to start on a great sword. My father only showed me once how to make one; he preferred the Xiphos himself. Yet, for what I have in mind, I feel two great swords and a few Xiphos will have to do instead. Besides, I could use the trade goods, but I will have a hard winter at the Gathering this year. I have to supply myself, and that is going to be very hard for me to do. Well, back to work. I have to get this done now, or I will starve this winter."

The lone weaponsmith continued his work, creating weapons he intended to use to avenge his people and to survive. All Patrallin could think about while not working were his mother's last words to him and how he had ended her life. He felt that he had murdered her, and this weighed very heavily on his conscience.

He kept asking himself, "What kind of monster killed his own mother, especially when she is unarmed?!"

Patrallin had searched the village many times and could not find the dagger he had created for her. It was now obvious to him that the Iramians had taken it. They had taken everything from her, but her life, and they took away from her his gift. Patrallin did not know what to think about that fact, so like his other thoughts, he pushed it aside to think about it later. Now, he had to complete his great swords and begin to work on the creation of another weapon. Here, he saw that he was beginning to run low on his ingots, so Xiphos was all he was going to make. His great-grandfather was said to have used a pair of Xiphos. Well, someone among the clans was sure to do so as well.

During the tempering process of the third Xiphos, the Dentalla arrived a ten-day ahead of schedule. The iron mining people were at least a month early, and they came into the Minnertalla village with weapons drawn, expecting a fight. Another Priest Pair had brought the Talla on their rounds early this year because of the raid. Even though the priests had assured them the danger was long past, the warrior people were ready for battle. Leading the search of the village was a pair of burley men, both carrying great swords drawn and looking for enemies. Hartinnia was the dark-haired one of the pair and led his heart-mate through the empty village carefully. The weapons master could see no signs of life except for the careful stacking of personal clothing and items. Here and there were signs of a none-too-recent battle to his trained eyes. This battle was distinctly one-sided, and the largest concentration of dried blood was near the village's eastern edge. Whoever had attacked had done so at the break of dawn and sought to use the sun to their advantage. This had not boded well for the Minnertalla during the raid. Hartinnia was about to report this to his Tallanta when his heart-mate Kiital stopped him.

Kiital was slightly slimmer than his heart-mate in build but more deadly for all that slight difference. Where Hartinnia was dark, Kiital was light, with the blonde hair and light-colored eyes normally found among the rest of the Ameristans. Kiital exuded a dangerous feeling of impending violence and was one of the deadliest men with a Xiphos among the Dentalla, yet was the gentlest of all the warriors.

Hartinnia looked to where his heart-mate pointed and saw the faint trails of smoke coming from the forge. With a rueful grin, he said, "I should have looked there first. Let's go see if we have any survivors or Iramians just trying to hide."

Kiital only nodded grimly in response; his oldest daughter had planned to join the Minnertalla very soon. Well, that was not going to happen anytime soon now, was it? Kiital was very angry about this, Aristian was the daughter of his heart, and now he would have to break her heart with this horrible news about her love of Patrallin. She had been in love with the young warrior all her life and would never consider another as her potential heart-mate. It was going to destroy her, and if she did not run off into the wild, he would be surprised. The warriors made their way towards the forge, where the rasping of a file on metal could be heard. The fire and the rasping could mean only one thing, either Petralis or Patrallin were still alive. This Talla boasted of having many weapon smiths at one time, yet the raids had nearly destroyed them. If one of them survived, there was hope that the Minnertalla could survive as a people. Kiital and Hartinnia stalked towards the forge, still on edge and ready to fight to the death. What the heart-mates found inside astonished them, causing the weapons master to drop his great sword suddenly from numb fingers. There inside the forge, where the men had anticipated finding Petralis, stood a figure out of a nightmare. Still stripped to the waist and covered with ash and soot stood what looked like a young man. He worked the file tenaciously across the finished edge of a Xiphos. From the looks and smell of the forge, the young man had not left the building in several ten-days at the least. In one corner looked to be a pallet of blankets and winton leathers, nestled among which could only be a griffon egg.

Slowly, the demon before them completed his work and turned to the egg, saying, "You see, egg, by filing it before tempering the blade, it gets a much better edge, and the blade is sharper and stronger in the end. Once I temper this blade, I will finally be finished, and then I just have to wait. You see that during the Winter Gathering, I will trade these weapons for supplies to let me find the Iramians. It is obvious that these Iramians are not from near us, and I have to search for them, no matter where they are. Don't worry, egg, you will be coming with me on this search, so I have a companion. I will need a watch animal, at least, to keep me safe at night. You will soon hatch, and I will have to start training you myself. I would have asked Zentar how to do it, but with him gone, it is just me now."

As the young man spoke, he began to prepare the smaller forge that was used for the tempering of the blades. Kiital slowly lowered his blade to the ground in preparation for entering the forge. The pair could tell that Patrallin was close to collapsing from sheer exhaustion. If they did not do something soon, he could seriously injure himself in the forge by collapsing. Carefully, the heart-mates approached the oblivious young man to try to help him. Hartinnia gently laid his hand on one of Patrallin's shoulders and felt the heat of fever burning within the young man. Illness from the lack of sleep and food had set in; they had to act quickly, or the boy could die from this. Hartinnia went to move to stop the young smith from his work, but a fist suddenly landed right on his chin. Before the weapons master knew what was happening, the young man had a dagger out and was attacking. Using all of his skill, he was able to avoid the attacks, if barely at that, coming from a mere boy. Hartinnia was afraid he was going to die beneath the snarling boy's strange-looking dagger when his heart-mate struck. Kiital used his own sword's pommel to render the boy unconscious. Patrallin collapsed at both men's feet like a felled auroch and barely stirred once he was on the ground. By his signs of breathing, it was obvious to the men that the boy had fallen into a very deep sleep. They left him where he fell to await the Talla's Priest Pair, who were waiting to come and help any survivors found in the village.

Kiital whistled loudly and long for his wolf, Lobo, to come to him. The trained animal ran to his master and waited for his next command. "Go find the girls and bring them here now, Lobo!" The large black wolf turned and ran off into the trees in search of the most current Priest Pair of the Ameristans.

The Priest Pair had recently come into their full powers and was still learning how to control them. Iriena and Aralla had been begging the Tallanta for a ten-day to hurry and save the Minnertalla. It was first thought that the girls were only trying to help Aristian get to spend more time with her love. It was only after they had demonstrated the rare duel talents of being able to heal as well as see the future that the girls believed. After Iriena and Aralla had predicted an attack by a feral wolf pack and then healed the injured defenders of the Talla, were the girls believed at all?

These signs were what finally forced Tallanta Carolus to send a fast party to the Minnertalla. At the same time, he sent runners to every other Tallanta, calling for an emergency meeting at the Minnertalla summer village. He now knew it would be too late to save the people as a whole, but one or two could have survived the raid. Every Tallanta, as well as the Talla's Priest Pairs, were all on their way and should be arriving anytime now as well. If only Petralis had accepted, the Priest Pair offered to help them, yet the Tallanta was stubborn, especially since that last Zealot raid.

While Carolus was pondering these thoughts, three young girls apprehensively watched the edge of the empty village. The features of the girls were so much alike that a casual observing man would think they all came from the same mother. Even though the girls all shared the same father, they had two different mothers from two separate Tallas.

Kiital's tamed wolf, Lobo, came trotting up to the trio and woofed at them to get their attention. The overlarge Grey Wolf then began tugging at the hems of the girls' shirts, each playfully. Obviously, to the girls who were familiar with these antics, Kiital had found something and wanted his daughters to come to him. Motioning silently, Carolus led his remaining best warriors into the village, weapons drawn. Even Aristian had picked up her bearded axe, letting the leather cover fall to the ground. As tall as she is, the razor-edged weapon could be devastating in combat if used properly by an expert. Given that her father was the weapons master for the Dentalla, she was such an expert.

Aristian tried to force her way to the front of the warriors. She wanted to be first into the village proper. Carolus reached out a hand and silently stopped the advance of the dark-haired girl.

He waited until all of the others were out of hearing before whispering to her, "The only reason you are here, *child*, is that your sisters insisted upon it. You are not to go through the ceremony until this Winter Gathering *if* you learn to act as an adult and obey your Tallanta. We always let the best of us lead the way into a dangerous situation for a reason, Aristian. The best warriors are best able to deal with the problems that could arise, and we do not need to risk the lives of our young people for no reason. I know that your fathers have prepared you well and that in many other Tallas you would be acknowledged as an adult by now. I also know that in those Tallas, you would be on your way to the Holy City to test as a weapons master. While I am Tallanta of the Dentalla, we will follow all traditions, and that means that you are a child until you perform your ceremony with the others in your age group." Carolus said this with the exhausted air of something that had been repeated many times over the winters to many a young person. He started walking with Aristian towards the commotion at the forge as he continued, "I know that your blood-father wants you to move through the Ceremony before this winter, but that is not how it is done. We are one of the oldest Talla, and that means that we have to ply ourselves to the traditions all that much more. In time, you will understand that when you have achieved your adulthood and brought your heart-mate back to the Talla, you will see."

This part of the lecture was a new one for Aristian, and it did not sit well with her at all. With a look that was pure venom, she turned to her Tallanta and said, "I will mate myself to Patrallin of the Minnertalla or no one at all! I have given my heart to him and him to me, Tallanta Carolus. You have no right to deny me the choice to join his Talla and leave the Dentalla, which is no shame to anyone. Just because you insist that we remain one of the largest Talla and that the others should suffer for strength, for it is ridiculous. With or without your approval, if Patrallin lives, I will join him and join the Minnertalla!" After saying this in a voice just short of a growl that would have made a bear proud, Aristian began to storm off to join her sisters in the crowd around the forge.

Lying on the ground with her identical twin sisters working the innate magic that they carried within them Aristian could see a young warrior. As Aralla and Iriena moved their hands along the prostrate form, they also worked to clear the soot and ash from the man. He was small for being accounted a man, yet there was something that was familiar to him at the same time. As the dirt was cleaned from, the young man's scars from the work of a forge were evident along his arms. On the inside of his left forearm was a scar that was still healing from his Blood Oath Ceremony. It would have been long healed if he had been acknowledged by Tallanta Petralis this last winter if he had been one of the three. This scar was still raw, as if it had been only ten-days instead of many moons old. There could be only one person who had not been acknowledged at the last Gathering. At his youngest daughter's direction, Kiital slowly turned the boy over, and a sight that was heartening to Aristian's eyes appeared. Much thinner and more worn than she had ever seen him, it was definitely Patrallin, alive and obviously in need of the healing ability of her sisters.

The young, untrained Priest Pair worked to heal the fever and the exhaustion that had so damaged the young man's body. The young girls were unsure of what to do and let their newly awakened abilities guide them to do what was needed to help Patrallin. While the members of the Dentalla looked on, the hours slipped by as the twins struggled to save the love of their beloved sister's life. As the sun began to set then the twins were exhausted from using so much energy to try to save the young man. It was obvious that he was going to be fine now and needed rest more than anything else.

Just as the twins turned to reveal this information to the awaiting crowd, a pair of voices spoke out as one. Dry with age and as rasping as the leaves of the fall, the voices were still clear and powerful, and they demanded respect when heard. "The young man is ready for rest now, girls. You have done well for two untrained and untested High Priestesses, and you must come with us back to The Holy City for proper training. You shall be our replacements in time to come, and you will be more powerful than you ever realize. Carolus, you are too close to the traditions we set out all those centuries ago. It is time for change. We are here to make those changes begin."

Walking into the crowd was a pair of wizened High Priestesses who wore their age as a cloak. The braids of the two women were as white as snow and long enough to trail on the ground behind them. A pair of warriors followed the High Priestesses, holding the elders' braids from the ground. The female warriors looked grimly at any who came to close to the pair and looked ready to draw their Xiphos without notice. While it was uncommon for there to be full-on bloodshed among the Ameristans, these two women looked ready to do so without a second thought. There were many legends among the Tallas of this particular Priest Pair, who were said to have lived for more than four centuries and started the Tallas themselves. These pair could only be the legendary Deana and Eldora. These two were thought never to leave The Holy City anymore, and among the young, they were thought to have died a long time ago. The Dentalla as a whole fell to their knees in honor of such a venerable pair of High Priestesses who were the founders of the modern-day Amerista. If not for these two, there would never have been the formation of the Talla, let alone the fighting for their freedom or the discovery of steel.

With a smile that many an elder has bestowed upon the foolishly young, the pair approached the prone Patrallin. As they had done for more winters than they cared to count, Deana and Eldora spoke as one, saying, "This young man needs to be placed into a winton that is still standing and given time to rest; he has had a very hard time recently, and the shock of being healed will wear on him more. Carolus, you are the senior Tallanta here for the moment, and we want you to prepare for this unprecedented Gathering. Have your warriors gather food and wood. There is going to be much talked about before the ten-day is out, and the need for food and fire is going to be dear. Aristian, do not think about going to your young warrior right now. He needs rest, and not you are hovering over him like a mother auroch over her first calf. He will recover before the ten-day is out, and when he does, Patrallin will need as much help as all here can give him. He is the last of the Minnertalla for now, and that is something that the young warrior has not faced yet. Aralla and Iriena, before you two sneak off to look at his egg, you both will come with us and help our great grand-daughters set up our winton. They won't admit it, but this is the first time they have ever left The Holy City and all the men around here scare them and some young women to talk with will help them. Now, you two quit glaring daggers around and help get the winton set up. We are tired and we demand a place to rest for a while before the other Tallantas begin to arrive for the Gathering. When they get here tomorrow and the next day, we will greet them, and then we will hold the Gathering until let the boy sleep!" With that, the two ancient High Priestesses turned to where they wanted their winton set up and walked to that area.

In the next several minutes, a winton was put into place, and the High Priestesses entered it with a swish of the leather door. The two bodyguards took up positions outside the door to prevent anyone from coming near it for any reason.

For the two days, that it took for the Tallantas of all of the Talla to arrive, the ancient High Priestesses never left the winton and their guards did not either. It was during those two days that the special properties of the weapons that Patrallin had created were discovered. This discovery shocked the Dentalla to no end since this new metal was something that could change their world. The High Priestesses were told of this discovery through their guards and kept their own counsel on this situation. As the other Talla trickled in, each Tallanta was told of the discovery as well. It was immediately decided that this discovery should be kept secret between the Tallantas only.

While the other Tallas trickled in, Patrallin slept in his winton with the constant supervision of Aristian. She would not leave his side at any time for any reason, and this began to worry her fathers'. Yet, they could understand Aristian's fears about her love and how he could never wake from his fevered sleep. While the young man slept, he muttered and talked in his fever-induced dreams as he constantly relived the last moments of his mother's life. The constant muttered screams that scared Aristian so much also caused Patrallin great amounts of fear. The young warrior had changed so much in his life over the last few ten-days that he feared waking up to find that it all was true and that he had no family left. Patrallin feared what the other Talla would think of him and how he was the only one to survive the death of the Minnertalla. Patrallin felt that he should have died with them at times, yet at other times, he felt that if he had, what would have happened to the egg he had taken? Also, he thought about what would happen to the discovery he had made about the Amersteel and how it could change the future of his people. Little by little, Patrallin began to come back to himself from the fevered sleep and knew that someone was in the winton with him. Over several hours, Patrallin came back to himself and worked to figure out who was hovering over him during his sickness. At first, the young Tallanta thought that he was being watched over by his own mother, and then he realized once again what he had done. When this realization came over him, Patrallin again sank into unconsciousness. It was less than a day before the last Talla arrived before Patrallin came back to himself more fully and knew that it was not someone he immediately recognized hovering over him.

Reaching carefully beneath the blanket covering him, Patrallin searched furtively for his dagger, intending to defend himself, if necessary, from this person. As he grasped the handle of his dagger, the person sitting next to him shifted just enough for Patrallin to strike out suddenly. With the skill of a man who was a master at his art, Patrallin stopped his strike just short of drawing blood as he realized just who his care giver had been. Patrallin had stopped just short of killing the love of his life and worked hard to control his quavering hand at the point of contact with Aristian's neck.

With a quavering voice and a weak smile, Aristian said, "It is nice to see you too, my love. I hope that you are not angry with me for sitting here in your winton without your permission, but you were sick. Also, the High Priestesses, Deanna and Eldora, wanted to speak with you when you woke up. They are across the village. Before you get too far, though, you need to check your griffon egg; it has been making some tapping sounds for the last few hours."

Patrallin threw off the blankets that were wrapped around him without realizing until too late that he was naked. Blushing from his head and down his neck, Patrallin quickly picked up one of the blankets again and leaned over the busily rocking griffon egg near his feet. The egg was rocking back and forth across the winton floor with a loud tapping sound from the inside, indicating that the occupant was ready to leave. As he looked at the egg, a crack began to appear near the small end of the egg, and very quickly, the tip of the beak could be seen. Unsure of what to do next, Patrallin could only sit there and wait to try to see if the animal within could find its own way out of the egg.

A rustling and a bar of fresh light in the winton made Patrallin turn around to see the Himlatalla Tallanta enter his winton. Tallanta Hrodebert said, "I had heard that you had captured an egg and that it was near to hatching. I ask your permission to enter your winton and to give you advice on how to go from here with your new charge, Tallanta Patrallin."

Retreating to the familiar aspects of the society he had been raised in, Patrallin turned to Hrodebert and said, "Tallanta Hrodebert, please enter my winton and make yourself at ease within my home. Please, help me. I do not know what to do now. I was planning to have Zentar help me when it came time to hatch the egg, and now, he is gone. The egg is hatching and the hatchling has made a small hole. What do I do now?"

Hrodebert smiled at the young man and the scared look on his face before he gently said, "Don't worry, this part of the hatching is where the young take a few hours to catch their breath and rest for a while. When they start to peck at the shell again, you are to come in and help them get out of that shell. You see, normally, the parents would be working from the outside to help break the shell at this time, but since you have it here, you have to help. After you see the High Priestesses, come back to your winton, and I will be waiting here for you and will help you with the process." With that, Hrodebert began to work his way around the naked young man and set himself to watch the egg. Without admitting that he was watching, the young woman who was not really allowed to be alone with an undressed young man Hrodebert put a look of discontent on his face.

Aristian knew what the look on Hrodebert's face was about and decided to take that moment to say, "When you are ready to meet with the High Priestesses, I will gladly escort you there, Tallanta Patrallin. I will be waiting for you outside of your winton when you are ready." Then she turned and quickly left the winton with the feeling of having been scolded by her fathers without words. Aristian quickly scurried out of the winton as fast as she could and then stood outside, trying to look as if she had left the dome tent by her own choice.

Patrallin searched his winton for clean clothes and was glad to find them cleaned and laid out for him to wear. The leathers were freshly scrubbed and showed signs of being carefully dealt with, showing the signs of someone caring for him while he lay unconscious. He worked slowly to get into his clothing, knowing that Aristian had worked hard to care for him while he was sick. Also, he knew that the two most important women in the history of the people of Amerista were These High Priestesses, who brought about the creation of the Talla and established the current way of Ameristan life. Why would the two most powerful women in the known world wish to speak with the boy who was the last of his line and now alone in the world? Would they order him to leave Amerista as an exile to wonder the face Tarnara alone with no person to call friend? On the other hand, would they force him to join another Talla and have the Minnertalla fade into history as a footnote in the stories? Well, if they were going to do that, then he would face it as a warrior and as the Tallanta of the Minnertalla should. With renewed determination, Patrallin began to stride towards the winton guarded by the two female warriors.

He stopped short of the fierce-looking woman, saying, "I am Patrallin, son of Petralis. I am Tallanta of the Minnertalla and present myself before the High Priestesses as requested."

"Tallanta of nothing but yourself, you mean." The guard on the left said with a smirk across her face.

Before either side could respond, the twinned voices of the High Priestesses spoke out, saying, "Girls, you show respect to the Tallanta, or we will see you guarding the privy trench until we depart for The Holy City. Now, Tallanta Patrallin, come in here and meet with us now that you are well enough to try and tumble your girl in your winton."

His face burning and his ears turning red, Patrallin entered the winton respectfully and bowed deeply to the High Priestesses in a very uncharacteristic show of deference. Before he could raise his head again, the twinned voices broke out in a tinkling laugh that had the effect of calming the young man while also easing the tension in him. The tinkling laugh reminding Patrallin so much of Tenara first put a smile across his face, followed by a wave of grief.

The memories of that evil day began to come back as well, leading up to the memory of how that day ended. It was too much for him. Before he could close himself off again from the pain of the loss of his family and shut himself off from the world, Patrallin felt a soft pair of hands gently resting on his lowered head. Tears that Patrallin had fought so hard to keep hidden broke free and began to flow down his face.

"Let yourself grieve for your people, and especially for yourself. You are not to blame for what happened here. It was an evil deed done by evil men who would be punished at the right time. You are going to be a part of that justice, but for now, you must learn how to prepare yourself for what is to come, and part of that is to leave your summer village behind. No, you are not giving up your Talla. The Minnertalla are not going to die out any time soon, nor for any time that we can foresee. You are going to return to The Holy City with us, and from there on, you are going to begin to learn many new things. To begin with, you are going to begin to learn to let yourself grieve and to find that you do not have to be as strong as the steel that you forge."

Patrallin stayed where he was as the voices moved across the winton. He looked up and, for the first time in his life, looked upon the faces of the two most important people in his nation. The bemused smile on their faces was a shock to Patrallin. He was expecting two old women covered in wrinkles who were barely able to hold themselves upright. Instead of that, he met the identical eyes of two women who were of an age with his mother in spirit. The eyes were those he had seen in his memory of Tenara, the eyes he would never see again in this life.

As if reading his mind, the High Priestesses said, "Yes, we remind you of your mother, especially around the eyes and the chin a little. She did not know it, and many still do not, but she was one of the last of her line and our great-grandniece. You are a distant nephew of ours as well; you are the last of our original family and carry the great hope of our entire people in your blood. Long ago, we had a vision of a Minnertalla warrior defeating the God Emperor of the Iramians and ending the raids. This warrior is one of your lines, meaning that you or one of your children will be the ones to destroy this curse upon our people. To do this, you are going to be the one to lead our people to the next new way of life. You, Patrallin, are the Tallantanar, the High Tallanta of the Ameristan people. The Tallantanar will unite the Talla in a way like never before; a Tallantanar will create a new class of warriors to help destroy the raider threat to our people. Now, you are going to work on a few things for us in the next few days while the other Tallanta gather. The first is that you and your love are going to comport yourselves properly until we say you are fully ready to become mated in the eyes of Amerton. Next, you are going to finish your mastery of Velocity. Also, you are going to leave your Talla's summer lands to come to The Holy City permanently. The Iramians now know your Talla's summer grounds are no longer safe for anyone. Finally, you are going to have to hurry back to winton right now. Your griffon egg is hatching, and you need to go learn about one of your new tasks."

Patrallin stood there in shock for a moment. The High Priestesses were changing his entire way of life, and he was all right. He was just stunned about how this was going to affect him. Having to leave the summer grounds and live in The Holy City year-round was going to eliminate any chances of seeing Aristian again. How was he going to ask her fathers' permission to have her become his mate if he could not show he was able to survive? Then, what else had been said to him sunk in, and Patrallin's jaw began to drop. Before the High Priestesses could admonish him any further, Patrallin spun around and rushed from the winton and back to his own.

Inside Tallanta Hrodebert was waiting for him with a rapidly rocking egg resting on the ground in front of him. Hrodebert said, "You got here just in time. The egg is about to hatch, and you need to make some decisions about it before the young comes free. Are you going to be the parent to this young animal, or are you going to let it go, exposed to the elements?"

Patrallin was taken aback by this question. He was shocked by the fact that he would have to consider leaving the young animal to die. How could he even consider leaving the helpless youngling to die when he himself had been the reason for it to be here? Patrallin shook his head in the negative, and upon seeing this, Hrodebert grunted his assent.

Hrodebert said, "This is the first time that I can remember that an Ameristan was the one to hatch a griffon's egg. The normal course we follow is to let the Talla griffons hatch and raise the younglings for us. When the young hatches, they bond with the first animal that they smell. In Talla, we train the older animals to guard and protect us in the wild, and the parents and the rest of the pride look after and teach the young. You are the last of your Talla, so you will have to train and raise the youngling yourself. My oldest grandson will help you with that from time to time as much as he can. His name is Barten, and he is ready to begin his Task. By working with you, he will be addressing his passage and will teach you about your mother's people. Now, you have to work at helping the youngling out of its shell and be ready to spend days feeding it. I don't envy you the task." Hrodebert left the winton with a small smile on his face as Patrallin focused on the task at hand.

The egg was rocking hard on the winton floor in front of him, and Patrallin could hear a tapping coming from the egg. As the tapping got louder, the egg rocked that much harder. It was evident that the egg's occupant was working hard to escape from the egg while Patrallin waited. He was unsure exactly what he should do and watched the egg closely. A small crack began to appear on the smaller end of the egg, and Patrallin was encouraged by this sign of life. As the crack grew, the tapping slowed, and Patrallin tapped back to see if the occupant was all right within. As he tapped on the egg, the hatchling tapped back harder again, obviously encouraged by Patrallin's tapping. The harder Patrallin tapped, the harder the egg rocked in response; this gave him the idea to try something new. Patrallin ran across the mostly deserted village grounds to his forge to retrieve his smallest, lightest hammer before returning to the egg. Immediately, Patrallin set to gently tap along the crack, gently adding to the size of the crack along the way. The occupant added their own strength to the process and worked from within to match the work from without. Little by little, the shell broke away from the animal, and the wet fur and down started to come into view. The animal inside looked so weak and soft that Patrallin had a hard time believing that someday, this very creature could grow into one of the most dangerous animals on the face of Tarnara. A full-grown plains griffon could carry off an adult bull auroch. How such a small animal could grow into such a large and dangerous creature stunned his mind. Gently, Patrallin began to dry the animal's fur and down it with an old woolen undershirt. Patrallin's smooth stroking motions seemed to calm the creature into sleep and relax him at the same time. Once the top of the youngling was dry, Patrallin gently worked another undershirt under the animal to remove it to a drier part of the winton. Next, the young Tallantanar cleaned up his winton and collapsed into a deep sleep himself. He did not realize that he had spent the remainder of the daylight hours and most of the following night working on freeing and caring for the youngling. It felt as if he had only just laid his head down when the youngling had begun a high-pitched squawking that Patrallin could not ignore. Rushing to his feet and barely remembering to pull on his legging, Patrallin lifted his charge and gingerly carried it out of the winton into the daylight for the first time. Once the young griffon was on the ground, it began to mewl loudly, and a laugh rang out across the village grounds. Tallanta Hrodebert was watching Patrallin's efforts to try to deal with his young charge unsuccessfully.

"You have to feed her," he said, "By this time of day, the parents of the griffon would have brought back enough to feed themselves and the younglings in the nest. You need to do the same."

For the next four ten-days as the other Tallanta finished gathering with their most trusted and finest warriors, Patrallin was a nursemaid to his new companion. At the same time, Aristian was constantly patrolling the immediate area to prevent her from accidentally finding herself in Patrallin's winton once again. This change in circumstances, along with his new occupation as a griffon parent, left Patrallin with little time for his love. When the last of the Tallanta and her warriors arrived, the High Priestesses called for the council meeting. It took only a few short minutes for the Ameristans to gather round the ancient, powerful women who stood next to a blazing fire. As Patrallin was relieved of his duties by one of Hrodebert's warriors for a short time, he ran to be the last of the Tallanta to join in the gathering. The High Priestesses raised their hands to silence any questions in perfect unison as they began to speak.

"We gathered the Tallanta here for very grave reasons, and it was a very great revelation for the Ameristan people as well. You all know by now that Tallanta Patrallin of the Minnertalla is the last of his Talla and the last of his line. We are here to reveal to you parts of the prophecy that we first spoke about over four hundred winters ago but never revealed in all. In our seeing, we saw the rise of a Tallantanar, a High Tallanta, and the person who would lead all of our people to destroy the Iramians. This you all know. For this Tallantanar to come, certain parts of the following circumstances had to be met. Tallanta of the Hentalla, do you have any former members of the Minnertalla among your people anymore?"

"My daughter's heart-mate was of the Minnertalla, and he was killed last spring by some unknown disease. My grandchildren from him also died from the same disease at the same time. All of my Talla who had any Minnertalla blood died over that summer."

Again, the High Priestesses pointed to another of the Tallanta with the same question and received the same answer in response. Any warrior who carried the Minnertalla blood had died over the last two winters either from fights or from some disease. This was taken in by the gathered Tallanta with a very dark heart among many of them. Most of them had lost good friends or family. Such a waste of life, and then the decimation of the Minnertalla was more than they could have imagined. How could so many of their own people have died so swiftly, and yet they seemed to have missed this coming?

With a heavy heart-wrenching sigh, the High Priestesses said, "We see you are all realizing the true danger that our people have been facing and none have been seeing. Even we, the High Priestesses of Amerton, have been blinded by this in some way that we do not recognize. From now on, listen to the young ones, those who are not fully bonded as a

Priest Pair yet are somewhat free of this blinding of our Seeing. Now, what we are here to discuss will be fully revealed to all of the Tallanta. Those of you familiar with our personal history will know some of what we are about to reveal in full."

For the first time in four hundred winters, the identical twin High Priestesses began to speak as individuals, something that was unheard of in a Priest Pair. "He will be the one to create a new way to fight for our people." Came from one, followed by, "He will be the last blood of his people." from the other.

Then, at the same time, once again, "He will be the Tallantanar, the Tallanta of Tallantas, and the leader of our people. By his words, the law will be written, and by His Will, the Iramians will find their final destruction. Patrallin of the Minnertalla is the Tallantanar, and it is through him that our people finally know true freedom and peace."

Tallanta Hrodebert was the first to speak out, "We have seen the weapons he has made with his own hands, and he has also been the only person in any Talla's history to capture a griffon egg on his own. Patrallin has been able to bond with the griffon youngling. In our past, they almost entirely rejected the presence of humans after hatching every time it was tried. We of the Himlatalla will acknowledge him as the Tallantanar. Any who wish to challenge this will face my blade!"

Each Tallanta stood forward in turn, giving his or her support for Patrallin as the foreseen Tallantanar. Only Patrallin was left to step forward and unsure of what to do.

Slowly, he moved into the center of the circle until he was as close to the roaring fire as he could stand and looked to the High Priestesses for guidance. There was no formality to fall back onto at this point, and Patrallin decided to just do what felt right.

"I take this responsibility from your hands and ask that each of you please take the time to teach me what I will need to know." Patrallin quickly decided to bow to each of the other Tallanta, in turn showing them deference to their age and experience.

With a chuckle, the Tallanta of the Amertalla said, "Well, he has potential at least. I have met some of those Dantorin merchants, and I know he has the right mind set to show them how to be humble. Now, I think that the Tallantanar should be prepared for any situation and come learn from the Weapons Masters at The Holy City."

Tallanta Hrodebert immediately spoke up, saying, "His mother was of Himlatalla, and he already has bonded with a griffon. He should stay for a winter with us first."

At that, the Tallanta each began to state the reasons why the new Tallantanar should come to stay with his or her Talla first instead of another. Patrallin began to fear that weapons would be drawn and bloodshed before he could say anything. The High Priestesses spoke up.

"The Tallantanar is the one who has the choices to make, and it is his word that is now the law! We all must ask him what he wants us to do and how he will handle the situation. It is the Tallantanar who will change our future, and we must let Tallantanar Patrallin decide. Tallantanar, what is your first decision for our people?"

Patrallin looked around at the gathered Tallanta and warriors surrounding him and almost began to shake in fright. At the thought of Aristian waiting for him near his, winton gave the young man strength. He stood straighter and looked down at his feet, collecting his thoughts before speaking.

Patrallin said, "I believe that I need to begin by going first to The Holy City and learning all that I can from all of our people. It pains me not to destroy the Iramians who destroyed my people and my family, yet I have to think of all Ameristans. We need to stand against future raids so that this never happens again. We need to work together to defend our people instead of just protecting our individual Talla. If there were warriors working together between the summer grounds looking for Iramians, we could stop them from doing much or any harm. According to what I have heard from the Dentalla, ships can only come to our lands in one area. If we protected this area at all times of the year, then we could completely stop the raids by sea. We would be safer from those raids, at least. The Zealots will still attack, but they are so rare and only attack us, never destroy our villages and carry off our people as slaves."

The High Priestesses interrupted Patrallin, speaking in unison again, saying, "So he speaks as the Tallantanar, the good of all the people is what come first to him. He sees to his herd. As the great bull protects his herd, so does the Tallantanar. As the people of Amerista are its heart and soul, so is the Tallantanar its body. As the body protects the soul, so then the Tallantanar protects his people from harm."

Immediately, the arguing began again amongst the Tallanta about who would control what areas of the land and how to best supply and protect those areas. Patrallin sank to the ground, listening to the arguing for several minutes before he had had enough. He said so at the top of his lungs.

He said, "*My fellow Tallanta*! Please, we are all here for the same thing and arguing about who controls what is going to hurt our people instead of helping them. Why can none of our people share equally in the safety of the whole or our people and lands? Why does not every Talla send a handful of warriors to share in the burden every spring? Then, when the Winter Gathering comes, these same warriors could follow our elders to The Holy City. Every year, we lose more of our elders to the wolves and the snow since they cannot keep up with the rest of the Talla. If we were to protect them, then all of the knowledge that they have would not be lost with them."

Again, the High Priestesses looked at each other in unison and nodded their heads together, all without saying a single word. This silent approval of what Patrallin was saying carried great weight with the more religious members of the Council.

Patrallin continued by saying, "All of the trails and paths taken by the herds, even those only known to each Talla privately, need to be watched and checked all the time. Even these private trails, thought only known by the Minnertalla, were used by these Iramians to find my poor village. If, as a people, we had warriors watching and following these trails, this fateful raid could have been stopped.

"I am all that is left of my people, and I will speak for all of them when I say *NO MORE!* Tallanta Hrodebert, don't you have a slave who was a Dantorin that your people captured several winters ago?"

Tallanta Hrodebert replied, "No more, my Tallantanar. He earned his freedom and decided to marry into the Talla instead of returning to his people. He is now a son of my own line. Parthenus married my youngest daughter this last spring, and now he fights for my people. Why?"

"Don't the Dantorins build the great longhouses made of stone that they call castles?"

"Yes, he has spoken of them to me many a time about how these *castles* keep out their enemies and protect their families from danger. I do not see what… Oh, I see where you are going with this Tallantanar. You want to build our own villages into these *castles* to protect our people from the Iramians?"

"That is not what I was thinking for the time being. I would not have our people give up the ways of the plains and the trail that soon. If we had some kind of protection around the place where ships can land, then we could forever stop the Raids from the sea.

"Now, this will not stop all of the Iramians; I am sure that they will soon find other ways to get to our people. When the Zealots attacked, they always came from the south of my lands in the past."

"Yes," Wawatam the Centalla Tallanta said, "we see more Zealot attacks than slaver raids every year than the other Talla. If we could turn our eyes to the south more often, then we could do more to turn aside these potential attacks and defend against the Zealots. We could finally put a stop to those damnable Tigre' riders once and for all." He had lost several children to the zealot attacks over the past winters and was very bitter over this.

"On this, we could all agree." Neonilla of the Amertalla said.

It was at this point that a friendly and joyful debate began in earnest among the Tallanta, with each vying to be the one to put the most warriors in the field. Patrallin quietly slipped away at a silent signal from the High Priestesses.

Once outside of the circle of Tallanta and warriors, the two ancient women said, "You have done your work for now, Tallantanar. Let those with more experience in leading and planning make way for the future. It is time for you to return to your own winton and your griffon. We will send it to you again when it is time for you to make your own decisions and finalize the plans." Having said their peace, the ancient twins turned and rejoined the elder Tallantas in their decision-making.

In the following days, decisions were made and agreements struck. Changes were set into motion by the council that would have a lasting impact on the future of the Ameristan people. Runners were sent to every village and every mine with orders for patrols to start immediately. Each Talla was to provide several warriors and enough provisions to see them to the next summer grounds. Once there, the warriors were to gather with that Talla's group of warriors to patrol and more provisions. The plan called for seven patrols of at least fifty warriors to travel the plains on a constant basis. The warriors were not to spend more than one season away from their own people before returning. Patrallin had to join the discussions and planning for the patrols repeatedly to ensure that his wishes were being carried out. As the beginnings of the fall fell across the nation, the Ameristan people began the annual migration to The Holy City for the harsh winter to come. It was during this time that Patrallin grieved for his lost family. It was during this time that none other than the High Priestesses themselves mated Patrallin and Aristian. The Minnertalla longhouse was a lonely place for the two young lovers, and they spent many ten-days together, getting to know one another in every way.

During this long winter, Patrallin left the longhouse only to attend meetings with the council, and he did not reveal anything that was really happening within the longhouse. The young Tallantanar had taken up training his griffon, named Tenara after his beloved mother, in a new and secret way. The members of the Himlatalla who kept coming to check on the young warrior never knew what he was really doing; had they known, they would have stopped him. Patrallin was training Tenara in a most unusual way and did not want anyone to know what exactly he was doing. Little by little, Patrallin was adding more and more weight to a harness he had created for Tenara to wear. The Bostowlians rode the Tigre' and the Dantorins were said to ride something called a horse in their own nation. Why couldn't he be the first to ride a griffon into combat with his fellow warriors? The Council had long ago agreed that Patrallin was much too precious to risk going into combat or on patrols with the other warriors. Their argument had some weight to it, seeing as he was the last of the Minnertalla. This chafed at the young man since he wanted to prove himself equal to the other youths of his age group. Yet while they were preparing for the fighting sure to come with the spring thaws, Patrallin was spending his days learning the ways of the other Talla. This grated on the young man to the point where he was beyond all frustration. To try to find a way around this restriction, Patrallin had thought that if he was above the fighting upon the back of Tenara, then there could be no stopping him.

The one time that Patrallin had broached the idea of taking Tenara into a fight or on patrol with some of the other warriors to Aristian, she said, "If you even consider riding into combat and risking your own life like that, *I will* break your legs myself. There are far too many of our warriors waiting in line to die to defend you at the slightest risk to your life that we are not going to let you risk yours like that."

Having said that, Aristian considered the matter settled and then went on to plan how they would spend the coming summer moons. The female warrior had moved into the Minnertalla longhouse with her new mate as if she had always lived there. She now carried the bearded axe that Patrallin had created during his time of extreme grief everywhere she went. Patrallin only felt that it was right that she carried the weapon since he could not use it as skillfully as she could.

It was after the conversation with Aristian about young warriors being willing to die for him that Patrallin struck upon another idea. If the council did not let him join in on the patrols, and she did not let him either, he could create his own patrol force. With this idea, fresh in his mind, Patrallin petitioned the Council and the now ailing High Priestesses to allow him to travel to the lands. He told the gathered leaders that he would only travel to the well-controlled areas and that he would take twenty warriors with him as well. Reluctantly, they agreed to this since Patrallin used the ruse that he was going there to learn more about his mother's people. As soon as spring began to thaw the ice from the roofs of the longhouses, Patrallin and twenty warriors, within a year of his age, left for the Himlatalla range. To one, each warrior was a friend of his or Aristian's or a blood relative of Aristian's. The fast-moving group traveled across the snow-covered plains that spring.

All the men and women who followed Patrallin that spring were the fittest of the warriors available, and yet by the time they reached the wooded hills of the Himlatalla, they were even more fit. Having had run for more than six days to beat the Himlatalla as the clan was returning to their summer grounds. To accomplish this, the group had to set out each day before the sun had fully risen into the sky and kept going long past the time it died on the Sun Dagger Mountains. The youths thought that they had accomplished something special in being able to move so fast. Patrallin was only glad to have been able to move so quickly that none was the wiser to his true motives.

The group reached the wooded hills on a cold day, which showed that winter had not yet fully given its grip on the plains. It was this morning that Patrallin decided to reveal his true plan to his gathered friends and fellow warriors.

With the sun rising in the east and shining into his eyes as he turned to face them, Patrallin said, "Warriors, friends, Talla. I call you all that since you are going to join me in a new undertaking and allow me to prove to our people that I am still a warrior who can truly lead them as an equal. I know that the Council of Tallanta and the Priests and Priestesses all fear my death if I go into battle at any time. I have come up with a solution for this, and you have all been instrumental in this. I have decided that I need to have a group of people who will fight by my side in all ways so that I can face our enemies and be able to watch my back in battle. By now, you all know that I was able to bond with a young griffon and that Tenara obeys everything that I ask of her. Well, seeing how our enemy, the Zealots, are so fearsome on their Tigre, I ask you why we cannot be more fearsome than they can be?! If they can ride their beasts into our villages and into our Talla, destroying and killing all that they can see and find, why cannot we use our own griffons to come down upon them from the skies and stop them in their tracks? If we tame our own griffons in the same manner that I have already shown is possible why we do not do so. I say that a patrol of Ameristans fighting from the skies will be just as effective as our brothers and sisters on the ground. At the same time, we should be able to see farther into the plains and find anyone who wishes to raid us that much sooner and then call in as many patrols and able warriors as possible. In this way, *we could end all raids in our lifetimes*!!! Think of it, brothers and sisters, our children could live their lives having never to know the fear of a Tigre' tearing them apart or the dawn time raid that kills their entire family!" This short speech was met with a ringing shout of support and pride in the cleverness of their new leader. The gathered young warriors quickly silenced themselves as Patrallin raised his arms again to gather their attention. He then said, "I know how to find the nests of the griffons, and those of you from the Himlatalla know the ways to gather the eggs. Yet, I say this. Let each warrior take his or her own egg by themselves through cunning and bravery. We each will prove to ourselves that we can do this and let this mark those of us brave enough to ride the skies and chase our enemies from our lands from the air."

Having finished his speech, Patrallin turned to those nearest him from the Himlatalla and began asking them to help the others. In a few short hours, the group had already found griffon nests that were already occupied and beginning to form their clutches. These hardy animals were known to lay their eggs throughout the spring and summer and even into early fall. No one really knew why they did this for the group yet. This was a good thing since there would be eggs in the nests that were ripe for the picking and would not be ready to hatch for a ten-day yet. Over the next four days, each warrior was able to accomplish their task of finding their own egg and safely retrieving it from the unsuspecting parents. It was on the afternoon of the fourth day that all of Patrallin's carefully wrought plans came crashing down upon him. He had just finished checking the last warrior to find his egg and return to the encampment, a man two winters his senior named Barten when a familiar voice spoke out from behind him.

"If you thought that you would get away without me finding out about you and this plan of yours, you were sorely mistaken, my mate. I was well aware of what you were going to do long before you left, and I made sure that the Council was aware of it, too."

With a feeling of dread sinking into his stomach while anger fought to rise up in him, Patrallin turned around to face Aristian, who was standing there with her characteristic smirk on her face. She had the Amersteel bearded axe slung across her back and her twin sisters sitting on the ground behind her. Before she could say anything else, Patrallin began sputtering, "How could you have known? I was careful, and you have not been feeling well. You told me that you thought my going to visit my mother's people was a good idea and that you would wait for me in The Holy City. Why are you here, and why are your sisters here too?"

Just as Patrallin finished his questions, he was suddenly bowled over by a large brown and white feathered blur. The creature landed on his chest with such impact that he nearly broke his neck and rolled several feet back before regaining control of himself. The blur turned out to be a very happy-looking Tenara with a very bloody odor on her breath. She must have just finished eating recently. Joyfully, the young griffon romped about his feet, making small hissing sounds and acting like a giant-sized kitten as she batted at his ankles, trying to get him to play with her.

Aristian said, "Well, you can see how I was able to find you and keep track of you during your little jaunt up here. As soon as you left, Tenara went almost wild trying to get out of the longhouse, but it was worse when she could not find you in The Holy City. Finally, I let her free of the harness and followed her as fast as I could on foot. She does not fly too fast as of yet, thankfully, or I would never have been able to keep up. Do not ever leave her like that again! As for why my sisters are here, they have to explain that to you themselves. I don't like to meddle in the affairs of the priesthood."

Standing and turning to face Patrallin as one, in an eerie copy of the High Priestesses, the twin girls spoke out in unison. They said, "We are not the High Priestesses of Amerton, and he has seen fit to give us our full sight so that we may be able to share the future with you, Tallantanar. Our predecessors have passed on just this morning and now sit at the feet of the Bull God upon the Great Plains. Their last vision was that of you becoming the Tallantanar and taking your rightful place among our people. Our first vision to be revealed to you is that you are now ready to become our leader, and it is time for you to come and lead us. You have to give up your childish dreams of revenge for now and accept your place as the protector of your herd. Come Tallantanar, return to The Holy City, and allow your people to help you find the revenge that you want so desperately."

Shaking his head in denial, Patrallin could not accept the fact that these two young Priestesses, girls really, were now the High Priestesses of Amerton. It was only two summers ago that Aristian and himself had chased the two off for interrupting an attempted tryst in the woods. Now, he was supposed to take their orders and obey them as if they were the voice of his god themselves. This was too much for him to take in at once.

It was then that another voice broke into his thoughts and completely sealed his fate, stopping him from seeking his revenge as he had hoped. The young Barten spoke from behind, saying, "Tallantanar. I have been chosen to speak for all of the warriors gathered here because of my youth and the fact that I am closest to your blood. Your mother was my mother's cousin, and we were a close line ourselves, so I feel as if I am the brother that you should have had. We have decided that even if you want us to ride our griffons into battle with you, it will be only if there is no other choice. You are the last of the Minnertalla, and you have to be defended at all costs. We name ourselves the Griffon Riders and choose to place our lives before yours in all things."

Drawing their daggers, the gathered warriors cut their arms from elbow to wrist, just deeply enough to draw blood, as they began a Blood Oath, saying, "We have chosen ourselves to be your personal guard, to protect you and your children in all things from now until we are called to the Great Plains. We shall serve you and your line in all things, even unto our own deaths. Our blood to be shed before yours. Our lives are to be given before yours. We shall protect our Tallantanar and the line of the Tallantanar in all things until Amerton relieves us of our duty." As the blood began to flow onto the ground, the warriors waited without making a sound or moving to bind their arms. Each was waiting for Patrallin to acknowledge the great sacrifice that they were willing to make for him. These youths had done something that had never happened before in the entire history of the Ameristan people. They had sworn to themselves and their descendants to serve and protect Patrallin and his line for the rest of the time.

Patrallin was stunned into silence and did not know what to say until he heard Aristian's response, "I will accept these oaths on behalf of my mate and accept you into service as guardians of the line of Minnertalla." Aristian then walked in front of Patrallin with a smirk lighting up her face. Before he could say anything to her, she said, "You forget about my sisters and the High Priestesses. The last vision that the High Priestesses had was of you heading off to the Himlatalla hills with this group. The old sisters died in their sleep the morning that you left, and my sisters have taken their places as the new High Priestesses of Amerton. It is time for you to lay aside your vengeance for now and prepare yourself for the much greater task, my mate. Let us form your Griffon Riders, and they will protect us and our family while we forge our new nation from the old."

Patrallin stood looking into the face of the girl he had always loved, and many different emotions ran through his mind. Surprise followed by anger replaced with joy and finally acceptance of his situation. As a proper Ameristan Warrior, none of these emotions showed on his face, but Aristian, who knew her mate so well, saw them flicker through his eyes while he thought.

Finally, he gave her a sardonic grin and said, "You and my mother, so much alike that I could never get anything past either of you. I will do as you suggest and lay aside my vengeance for now. It will always be there for our children to take up if need be. As for now, it is time for us to get some griffon eggs and help our new guard take shape and begin their training." Patrallin then turned to the other warriors and began issuing orders to them about how to care for the captured eggs and what to do with them afterwards.

The raid upon the plains griffon nests for eggs went as smoothly as hoped, with only minor injuries and no deaths among the warriors. Since the raid was completed, the group began the long return trip back to The Holy City with as much haste as possible. As the newly formed guard force for the Tallantanar, the Griffon Riders took it upon themselves to have scouts and a rearguard as they moved across the plains. The Riders were more concerned with the safety and welfare of Patrallin and Aristian and took all pains to keep them as protected and comfortable as possible for the trip. The out runners kept a steady stream of information coming into the main party as to what lay along their path home. All of this quickly began to get on Patrallin's nerves, and he became agitated by the protectiveness of his old friends. All of this caused the group to move much more slowly than normal, and a trip that should have taken a handful of days quickly grew into a ten-day.

Two ten-days into the return trip Patrallin's grumbling exploded into yelling and cursing at the new guard, using terms to describe them that would normally be cause for a fight to the death. Once, Patrallin had run out of insults and stood staring at his Riders, waiting for the first move of an attack with his hands on his own Xiphos.

Aristian said quietly to him, "Are you quite finished, my mate? I am sure that those are not all of the insults that you know and that there are more threats that you could make to our friends and guards. Do you have something that you want to say to me? I can assure you that I will not attack you either, no matter what you say. It is time for you to accept that your life is no longer yours alone! As the Tallantanar, you need to be alive as long as possible as well as safe as possible. The Ameristan people will not lose you so soon after gaining you. You *will* accept that fact!

"Now, what do you say about living in the Temple until the Tallantanar's longhouse is built and ready for us?"

The riders took this outburst between their Tallantanar and his mate in stride as they continued to escort him ever closer to The Holy City. For the rest of the long trip, the two young lovers were deeply involved in discussing their future together. Plans were made, and many changed several times before the group finally reached The Holy City for the last time.

CHAPTER 5

It was over the coming winters that Patrallin and Aristian brought three healthy children to life. The children were prospering under the peace so new to the Ameristan people that fate again struck.

The first of the children was a strong young boy whom they had named Petralis II in honor of his grandsire and the sacrifices he made. They also named their first-born son in the manner of the southern kingdoms in hopes of trying to bring their people to greater acceptance in the world.

Their second child was also a boy whom they named Griefold in honor of Patrallin's grandmother who had created the secret of Minnertalla steel. The two oldest boys were as night and day when compared to one another. Petralis took after his mother with a streak of obedience and hard work that was to be envied. Griefold took after his father with his stubbornness and desire to prove himself as his own, even at a very young age.

The third child born to Patrallin and Aristian was another strapping young boy who was a rarity for the Ameristan people with a shock of pitch-black hair. Given his black hair and great strength even in the cradle, they decided to name this son Blackston.

The three boys were born in rapid succession to the royal couple and were the very soul and hope of the Ameristan people. After this, Aristian failed to carry a child to term for three winters in a row; with each event, she and Patrallin both grew more despondent and doted on their sons. It wasn't until Petralis was approaching his thirteenth year and his manhood rights that Aristian began to swell again. It was also at this time that other kingdoms began to take notice of the now fledgling nation that they had once dismissed.

For many winters, these nations had taken advantage of the Ameristan people and their desire for self-isolation. The other peoples of Tarnara had dismissed the Ameristans as backward and ignorant people not even worth the effort to try to deal with them. The first nation to reach out to the Ameristans in peace and friendship were the Dantorin peoples from the south of the continent. The only way to reach the Dantorin people by land was through the treacherous and unforgiving jungles of the Bostowlians. The Dantorins reached the Ameristans by sea and landed at the only safe harbor on the coast of Amerista, now called Patrallin's Fist. This bay was named for the way the harbor was safely enclosed by rocks and stone reefs in the shape of a partially closed fist. This, for many centuries, was the province of the Iramians, who, for long winters, had kept a strong force there to hold the bay. Shortly after his sons were born, Patrallin himself led an attack on this bay, driving out the Iramians and burning their structures to the ground. Some of the freed slaves returned to their homeland of Dantorin, and thus, trade was slowly established.

The first full trade shipment and emissary from the Dantorin people was to arrive on the longest day of the year. This hot summer day saw Patrallin waiting with his two oldest sons at the main gate to The Holy City, waiting for the delegation to arrive. He was wearing his best brigandine armor polished to a high shine and oiled to the point that he glowed. Petralis, as his oldest, was wearing his own brigandine as well, along with a small golden torc showing his rank. Griefold was dressed much the same, except his torc was silver instead, and he was anxious to be out of the sun and inside the city playing with his friends.

As the minutes rolled by and the heat increased, Griefold became more restless and wanted to leave and go play with his friends. Looking at his father yet again he said, "Can I *please* go and find Bernella and Arten? They said that they were going to show me the new items that the Dantorins had sent in the last trade caravan. They told me that there was some kind of new animal sent as a gift, something called a *Pig.* What could that look like? Is it like the aurochs or the griffons, or is it like the bears from the northern ice fields?"

Shaking his head with a smile on his face, Patrallin rubbed his son's mop of dark blond hair and said, "You remind me so much of myself. I remember when I was so eager to see a griffon nest and how…." With a darkening of his face, Patrallin stopped speaking slowly and then was taken back to the turning point of his life so long ago.

Upon seeing this dark look on his father's face, Petralis knew that his father remembered the day of the raid and the massacre of his people. Petralis said, "Grie, I saw those animals; they are loud, stinky, smelly, and super ugly. But if you want to see them after the delegation finally shows up, we can go and see how fast they run."

Griefold smiled at his older brother at the thought of the trouble that they could get into with the new animals sent to

The Holy City. The animals were only the first of many items sent to The Holy City in recent ten-days in preparation for the arrival of the "Emissary" from Dantorin. For a full cycle of the moon, new items and packages had been arriving regularly full of amazing gifts and foods that they had never even dreamed of before.

With his troublesome son now distracted, Patrallin turned his gaze back to the plains surrounding The Holy City and strained his eyes, looking for any sign of the delegation. He was ready to return to the longhouse with his sons and pregnant wife when two messengers interrupted him. One from within the city and one from without.

Barten, the warrior Patrallin had placed as a scout out on the plains to look for the delegation, arrived at the same time as the brother and sister Bernella and Arten came from the city. Turning to the children first, Patrallin raised a hand to his old friend and gave the children a command to speak.

Bernella said, "Tallantanar, your mate has entered labor early! The High Priestesses are with her now and sent us to tell you that your sons need to be by her side during this time of danger for her!"

Like a bolt of lightning fear and shock ran through him while Patrallin quickly barked out orders for his sons to return to their mother that very instant. Aristian was not due to deliver their latest child for at least two more moons. This was not a good sign, and if the High Priestesses themselves had come to help their sister, it was very serious indeed.

Before turning to Barten, Patrallin snapped out, "Bernella, I charge you for ensuring my sons return to their mother and stay with her! Arten, you do not let Griefold talk you into anything and keep him with his mother."

The two young warriors nodded and quickly grabbed the offended Griefold and began dragging him into The Holy City as he struggled. Seeing that the young were out of hearing, Barten spoke before Patrallin could, saying, "Tallantanar, the delegation is approaching now across the plain, and the emissary will be here within the hour. You should be able to see the dust cloud from their approach any minute now. Do you wish me to greet them for you so that you can join your mate at this most dangerous time?"

Patrallin thought this over mere seconds before responding to his oldest friend and leader of the Griffon Riders, saying, "No, my old friend. You go in my place and ensure her safety. Keep everyone away who is not necessary and ensure that her sisters have everything that they need to see her through this safely. I do not think that she could survive another lost babe, and I fear I could lose her as well if we lose this child." Clapping his friend on the shoulder, Barten began running into the city and calling for several of the attending Griffon Riders to follow him.

Patrallin turned to look out into the slowly increasing cloud of dust and prepared himself for the meeting with this emissary. He hoped that by forming ties with the Dantorin people, they could eventually work together to find the source of the Iramians and finish them. As the minutes ticked by, the cloud did not grow in size, and a sick feeling began to form in the pit of his stomach. Patrallin felt that such a meeting would entail more people than what he could begin to see. Approaching the city were a score of women, ranging from wizened crones to girls barely aged to womanhood. Noticing this feeling and the strange group, the remaining Griffon Riders formed a protective circle around their leader and drew their weapons. Upon seeing this large group of heavily armed warriors waiting for them, the group of women stopped.

Patrallin stepped out from the circle of Griffon Riders and spoke out loudly to the waiting women, saying, "Are you the emissaries from Dantorin? I was led to believe it was a man named Lord Haveneth who was to be coming, but if that has changed, it is all right. We Ameristans do not hold one sex above the other and respect all those who can prove themselves. Please be welcome to The Holy City and my people. We wish to speak of trade and alliances with you and your people."

Instead of responding to Patrallin, the women all turned to each other and began speaking together in a hissing language that none present could understand. The hissing speech continued for several minutes while the Ameristans watched on, confused and beginning to suspect something was amiss. The Griffon Riders carefully reached out and drew Patrallin back into their protective circle in an attempt to protect him.

Suddenly and without warning, the women began to sprint at the Ameristan warriors, screaming in the same language with daggers drawn in each hand. The edges of the dagger blades were black with some substance at the mere sight of a collective chill that ran down every warrior's spine. Instinctively, they all knew the blades were coated in some deadly substance and that they were about to give their lives in defense of their Tallantanar. Patrallin found himself being pushed back into the city walls and orders being shouted to close the gates despite his efforts to push to the front. If his warriors were going to die defending him, then he was going to die with them as a true Ameristan warrior.

A Himlatalla warrior, judging by his braid, shouted, "Tallantanar, you have to return to the city and your mate right away. If we cannot stop these assassins here and now, then you will have to protect your family as best you can. We will hold them here and do our best to slay all of them for you. Please, save yourself and your family now while you have a chance to do so."

With a sinking heart and memories of losing his own Talla all those winters ago, Patrallin turned to the city and his family inside it. While he was running into the city, Patrallin also realized that the warrior was Bernella and Arten's uncle. Upon reaching his own longhouse, Patrallin saw that there was fighting going on outside here as well. There were women attacking the Griffon Riders who had gone back to the longhouse with his sons as well. These women were dressed as Ameristans but were still shouting and screaming in the same hissing language he heard from the assassins outside the city gate.

Aristian struggled to bring her child to life and heard her sisters speaking in the way of the Priest Pairs, one starting and the other finishing, "Aristian, sister, we cannot save your life today nor that of your mate. A choice must be made, and we have to make it. In order for your children to live, you both must die, along with a number of our people. This will be the driving force needed to push our people into the future and to finally end the Iramians once and for all. The daughters that you are about to bear and the sons that you have borne will lead us all to a greater future and time of peace. Now, it is time for you to give life to your daughters."

Struggling for breath, Aristian could not respond to the twins, but she focused on the birth of her daughters as best she could. The first of her daughters came forth with a gush of blood and fluids, causing Aristian to nearly pass out from the pain. As the first baby was taken by one of her sisters, the other kept urging Aristian to push and keep trying to give life to her child. The sounds of fighting could be heard outside of the longhouse. Struggling even harder to give birth to her last child, Aristian finally and mercifully passed out as the child left her body.

The High Priestesses took the newly born infants and gave them to the oldest of their nephews just as the two assassins came into the longhouse with their daggers drawn. The two guards who protected the High Priestesses leapt into action. The first charged at the assassins with his Great Sword drawn, forcing the attackers back while his partner took the High Priestesses into the far corner of the longhouse, away from the children. The first warrior fell quickly to the poison on the dagger's blade without even slowing the attackers in the least.

With the war cry of the Minnertalla springing from his lips, Patrallin rushed into the fight and began to stab and slash at the assassins, trying to kill his own family. During the fight, he himself took many small cuts and wounds as he fought his way through the door. Once inside the longhouse, Patrallin saw two of the women who had made it inside and had slain one of the guards of the High Priestesses. He was lying on the ground with a white foam coming from his mouth as his body thrashed in pain. The poison was obviously very deadly, as there was only a small scratch on the warrior's hand to be seen. Patrallin knew he had already received several such small wounds himself and could feel the poison beginning to run through his veins. Falling to his knees, Patrallin threw his dagger as hard as he could into the back of one of the attackers, striking her spine and killing her in the process. As he lay dying, Patrallin saw the last assassin approaching his children as they huddled in the corner. He saw his three boys with Petralis and Griefold holding onto two naked and squalling female babes. Patrallin only hoped that they would survive the oncoming attack from the last assassin.

The High Priestesses then stepped around from their protector and spoke a single word in unison, saying, "HOLD!" The assassin seemed to freeze in place as she was within striking range of the children, weapon ready to stab the unprotected young. Anger and hatred could be seen in her eyes as she screamed in her hissing language and struggled to reach the unprotected children.

Aristian slowly found herself coming back to consciousness and hearing the screaming sounds of her newborn infants. Weak from blood loss and pain, she slowly raised her head to see what was happening and said, "Bring my children to me! I want to see that they are all right; bring them to me."

Petralis and Griefold slowly came to their mother carrying their infant sisters, still covered with their own birthing fluids. Blackston also slowly followed his older brothers, unsure of what was going on and afraid of all of the shouting and screaming that had been going on. The five last survivors of the once proud Minnertalla stood next to their mother and waited to hear what she had to say.

Once all of her children were present, Aristian rallied the last of her strength and said, "Petralis, Griefold, give your sisters to the High Priestesses and hand me your daggers now." After this had been done, she motioned for them to come closer and then shaved their heads, bringing the boys into adulthood long before their time. This done, Aristian then said, "You five are now the last of the Minnertalla and must stay alive to save our people. Petralis, you are now the Tallantanar and will lead our people into the future that your father saw for us. Griefold, it is your job to obey your brother and support him in this future or we shall never see it happen. Sisters, please come to me. I need you to do one last thing for me: take Blackston, Arista, and Aristin somewhere safe and keep them away from harm. Petralis will know when it is time for them to return to us; please keep them safe for me…" and then Aristian, heart-mate to Patrallin, died.

The High Priestesses pushed aside their last defender and approached the five children with much depredation in their hearts. Speaking together as always, they said, "Petralis, young Tallantanar, you must now take your place as leader of our people with your brother Griefold by your side. You must now take the place of your father and lead our people. Blackston and your sisters will be taken by some of the Priest

Pairs into hiding. Petralis, you will know when the time is right to send for them and to bring them home once again."

Straining to keep the tears from falling down his face, Petralis nodded, agreeing with the orders of the High Priestesses and his mother. Turing slowly and putting his arm around Griefold's shoulders, the thirteen-year-old boy took his brother out of the longhouse and into the streets of The Holy City.

Barten was carried into the longhouse as the two young brothers were left by the last surviving members of the Griffon Riders. From a force of over twenty strong, they were now only eight. Barten had a rough bandage across his right eye, showing that he had not escaped the battle unscathed. He said, "Sighted Ones, the assassins are finished along with the rest of the Griffon Riders. The poison that the assassins used on their blades was fast-acting and killed all of our warriors with even the slightest scratch."

"How is it that you have survived then, dear Barten?" asked the High Priestesses.

"This is a mere scratch from some youngling, barely older than our own Petralis, who threw herself at me. She had no blade left, yet she scratched out my eye with her nails like a wildcat. I would have brought her in as a captive if she had not taken up a fallen assassin's dagger and slit her own throat. All of the others are dead as well, mostly by their own hands. Is that another one back there? Riders finish off that creature and make sure that there are no more to be found in the city!"

"Do not harm that woman! She is a prisoner of the High Priestesses, and we shall question her about what has happened here and give you any information that we may learn. Now, come here, brave Barten, so we can look at your wounds and explain to you what has happened. There have been many changes, and parts of a new vision have happened. It is a time of change for our people. The true future of the Ameristan people now rests on the very young and small shoulders of Petralis and Griefold. The remaining Riders must go with the other children into hiding along with their Priest Pair guardians. We have many plans to make and little time to make them."

As the High Priestesses spoke in unison about this, they used their healing abilities to deal with the wounds to Barten's face. It was impossible to save his eye, but they were able to stop the bleeding and close the wounds. This allowed Barten to put into motion his own additions to the plans that Aristian gave out with her last breath. With each Priest Pair, Barten ordered that either a Velocity or a Dominance Master Griffon Rider would go with the children to train them as they grew older. Barten himself would train the two remaining boys in the arts of combat but would not let the others lack training in their culture. The remaining Griffon Riders did not accept this decision. After all, they swore to protect the Tallantanar and his line, not just his siblings. It took the work of the High Priestesses explaining the prophecy and their own visions to convince the other Griffon Riders to leave the protection of Petralis and Griefold to Barten alone while replacements were located and trained.

Training of new Griffon Riders would take many winters, and the two young survivors would join in that training. As a final measure, the Amersteel blades that Patrallin had forged after the massacre were to be sent with the children into hiding. The children of the Tallantanar should not lack education in their culture, nor would they be allowed to forget what had happened to their people.

The moving of the children out of the Holy City was all done in one night under cover of darkness to avoid any prying eyes of the Iramians. Sweep riders went out on their griffons to ensure that the lands surrounding the city were cleared of every living thing. Even the vast herds of aurochs that perpetually surrounded the area were swept away temporarily to ensure that no human being was hiding among them. This was done. The children of Patrallin were bundled up to hide their identities, and their protectors quickly took them off into the night to guard and raise them in secrecy until the time was right for them to return to their homes. Petralis II and Griefold both could not understand why their brother and sisters were leaving, nor why they could not go with them. It would be many winters before the two brothers would understand what had happened and how this was for the best of the family.

CHAPTER 6

Shortly after that fateful day, the true Dantorin envoys arrived, and trade began between the two peoples. Winters passed by, and the Ameristan people grew in number and reputation as they reached out into the world around them. Over the winters, Griefold was taught every aspect of war that could be found; generals and war leaders were invited to spend moons at a time with the youth. These warriors spent the time working with Griefold, teaching him how to lead both from the Iristian and from the Dantorin methods of warfare. At one point during these many winters, a renegade Bostowlian, eager to forge peace with the Ameristan people, came and shared his knowledge of the jungles of Bostowlia. Petralis was not kept idle during these winters, it was during this time that he learned the role of leadership and the art of blacksmithing. While his younger brother was being prepared to lead their people into war, Petralis was being trained to lead his people into a new era of prosperity. All of the Tallanta came to meet with Petralis for moons at a time and imparted wisdom to him at every turn. Any time that there was a decision to be made, Petralis was there to hear the arguments for and against, and his own thoughts were sought out.

The Dantorins were seeking access to the aurochs' herds to increase their food source from the overabundance of swine they were accustomed to eating. Iristia, never a people to follow a single leader, sent a small council of merchants to share their wishes with the Ameristans outside of The Holy City. All of the nations wished nothing to do with the

Bostowlians in trade or any form of negotiations due to the Zealot attacks and rumors of dark magic.

It was about the time that Griefold took up his oath to his Tallantanar that a new Dantorin ambassador arrived in The Holy City. With this ambassador, too, came new ideas to the Ameristan people, and with this ambassador came the lust for the southern nation's fashions and ways of doing things. The Dantorins had appeared as a unified nation for many centuries and had a well-established culture vastly different from the simple lives of the Ameristans. The nobly born would wear the richest of clothes and jewels any time that they went about in public. These nobles would wear such items as silks and fine linens and perfume themselves with heavy and cloying scents that were hard to miss. After half a decade of living this way of life, it began to have an effect on the youth of the Ameristan people. An informal court had found itself forming around the young Griefold, who was beginning to be called a Prince by the Dantorin nobles. This was going to the young warrior's head very quickly, and he began to adopt more of the outlandish ways of the Dantorin people. He stopped wearing his people's leather and wool clothing and began to wear silks and linens. In addition, Griefold was heard on several occasions to talk about forgoing his Blood Oath to be the War Leader to his people as something unstylish and useless. Petralis had come to a decision that this behavior must end. There were even rumors that Griefold was going to try to end the patrols across the nation of Amerista itself. This decision was heavily influenced by the Dantorin desire for aurochs. The nation of Dantor had long sought herds of their own since they were primarily a nation of pig and goat herders. This desire for free, unfettered access to the aurochs went against the very nature of the Ameristan people. Every year, more and more Dantorins were caught trying to steal fertile or pregnant cows from herds while traveling the plains. The Talla were not tolerant of the outsiders attempting this, and many of them were caught and made into slaves. Occasional trade was acceptable to the Ameristan people as a whole, as the old and infirm were slaughtered as Amerton intended to keep the herds strong. The patrols, meant to protect the people from Iramians, were instrumental in stopping the theft of the precious aurochs. This was not well accepted by Griefold's new friends. It was during one night of drinking wine and dancing that Petralis stood with Barten watching Griefold acting as a Dantorin.

Petralis shook his head in disgust, then turned and punched a nearby post in the longhouse-turned-court. A loud crack could be heard at the impact, and Barten turned a sharp eye to his friend, seeing that it was the wood that had broken and not the Tallantanar's hand. Barten hid a smile and shook his head. Petralis II was a huge man covered in slabs of muscle, this coming from family lines as well as his work at the forge. The broken post was not the first, nor would it be the last if he knew his friend. He turned to look at Griefold again as his younger brother stumbled drunkenly from one group to another.

Before Petralis could break another post and possibly his hand this time, Barten said, "My Tallantanar, it is past time for it to be done. He is ready. We are ready as a people for this to be done as well. Now is the time to go forth and to make allies of our neighbors, not just trading partners.

Besides, you will feel better if he is out of The Holy City for a while and away from this influence."

Petralis gave Barten a look that was known to send ambassadors fleeing from his presence and rumored to soften the steel in his forge as well. After heaving a huge sigh of disgust, he said, "I know it is the right time, and it is something that he is more than ready for, but Barten, look at him! Look at the way he is cavorting with and acting as if he is one of the Dantorins with no respect for himself! He is acting as if he is not an Ameristan Warrior but one of those Amerton forsaken Dantorins themselves with the clothes he is wearing. See how he is letting his hair grow out as well. If he had half a mind left to him, Griefold would be showing the proper respect and composure required of an Ameristan instead of acting the fool trying to impress the Dantorin Ambassador. When was the last time that he even took a blade to his face? That silly look of braided beards that the Dantorins brought with them was unfit for a warrior."

"I know how you feel, Tallantanar," a much older Barten said to the young Petralis, "I *am* the one who trained both of you as warriors and taught you the ways of our people as you grew up. It is past time for him to give up his ways and accept his responsibilities to our people and his place as your replacement until you have one yourself."

Petralis turned to look Barten in the eye and said, "That particular problem is going to be remedied soon enough, but as for the problem with Griefold, I think that I have had enough of his foolishness." The young Tallantanar then turned on his heel and walked away into the crowd of people surrounding his brother. As well muscled as any blacksmith,

Petralis easily moved his way through the crowd, yet it was not his size nor the fact that he was the leader of the Ameristan people. Petralis moved with the grace of a hunting cat on the prowl, easing his way through the crowd and towards his target. Griefold was not that easy to spot in the crowd. Being average height for an Ameristan, his head barely reached past the shoulders of the much taller Dantorins.

With a roar of anger over his shoulder, Petralis said, "How am I supposed to trust the lives of our people, let alone what is left our family to this…this…*idiot*!"

At hearing the furious roar, the sound from all of the merrymakers surrounding the other young man stopped. Griefold looked over his shoulder and saw the look on his older brother's face. Heaving a long-suffering sigh of his own, Griefold began to make his own way to Petralis through the crowd, nodding and making motions of platitude along the way. Even though the two men were alike as brothers could be in looks and size, the differences were obvious to the casual observing man. Where Petralis's slabs of muscle from working the forge were clear and hard, Griefold showed that he was going to flab already at a young age from rich food and drink. This appearance, too, was a strong point of contention between the two brothers since Griefold was giving more and more into the indolent lifestyle of the Dantorins.

Barten was finding himself increasingly thrust between the two as a peacemaker. Determined to end the fighting once and for all, he had come up with his plan. As far as plans went, it was not very complicated, yet the simpler the plan, the more likely it was to work.

As Griefold approached his Tallantanar, he exuded the smell of too much wine and unwashed clothes. What he was wearing appeared to have not been laundered in several days, destroying the fine silk it was made of. Shaking his blond-haired head, Griefold said, "Well, if it isn't the peacemaker Barten and my stuffed-up brother, the king. What brings you to *my* longhouse at this time of night?"

Snarling his reply, Petralis said, "This is the Minnertalla longhouse and belongs to all of our Talla, *not you*!"

Stepping between the brothers, yet again Barten gently pushed the brothers apart softly saying, "This *is* the Minnertalla longhouse and does not belong to any one warrior also Griefold, you do not speak to your brother, the Tallantanar, with such an insulting word as *King*. You *must* show your brother respect, if for no other reason than he is your elder and your Tallanta. He is Tallanta of Tallanta, first among many. Why must you goad him like that?"

"Well," Griefold began after taking another long drink from the wineskin in his hand, "I was speaking with my good friend, Ambassador Fanteth, and we got to discussing how in other nations, the ruler is called king and everyone had to obey him. Also, we were talking about how if the current king dies and has no male children, the oldest living brother will take over. Well, that naturally led us to talk about how Mirta has not given Petralis any children yet, not even a girl, and how maybe I should take over."

Before Barten could stop him, Petralis launched a blow into Griefold's stomach, knocking the younger man's breath clean from his body. Seeing immediately that trying to stop this fight was futile, Barten stepped back and made a short chopping gesture. Suddenly the longhouse was filled with the elite Griffon riders, handpicked by Barten himself, known as the Griffonara. These men and women were the finest warriors in Amerista, having to have fought in multiple battles and lived. Not only that, but these warriors were also the surviving children of the original twenty warriors who had gone with Patrallin so long ago. Their parents, having failed once in their duties, had forsworn their very lives to the defense of the Tallantanar. No warrior could gain admittance to their ranks without first having achieved great feats on the battlefield and survived.

The Griffonara swiftly emptied the longhouse of the Dantorins and the other Ameristan youths, then formed a perimeter around the building to keep all other people away. Barten had raised the two combatants along with his own children, and long experience told him they would have to fight this out between themselves in order to solve the problem. As he leaned against the outer door of the longhouse, the grunts and thuds of a full-blown fight between two large men could be heard from inside. This fight was long overdue and it was about time that Petralis took his brother into hand. The time was fast approaching for Griefold to take his place among the Talla, and he was going to have to prove himself as a warrior. While the fight went on, Barten reminisced about the many times he had had to intervene with the brothers to keep them from each other's throats, sometimes with weapons bared. Growing up without parents and the fact that they had to live up to the legend that their own father had become was sometimes too much for the young men. If, on occasion, they had fought with one another, at least they were not doing something to endanger their own lives, like taking on a Zealot attack single-handedly. That had cost more young lives over the recent winters than it had been worth. The Zealots had been quiet as of late due to the treaty with the Dantorins. While the Dantorins put pressure on the Bostowlian people from the south, the Ameristans were safe in the north once more. The need for the Bostowlian Tigre to prey on the great aurochs' herds had always been the biggest problem with the Zealots. If only the Cultists were not in charge, then peace could be had between the two peoples. The Cultist leaders of the Bostowlians wanted all peoples to worship the trees and not kill or harm any animals or something to that effect. Barten did not fully believe the renegade Bostowlian who had come to them some winters back, but something kept the Zealots attacking.

The pounding of fists on flesh, yelling, and grunts of pain went on for quite a while before stopping suddenly. It was minutes after the fight had started and mere moments after it ended when the brothers helped one another out of the longhouse. Both men were covered in bruises with ripped and torn clothing, barely hanging off them in some places.

Griefold said to Barten, "I am sorry for what I said in there to you and if I may have offended your honor in any way. Barten, please forgive me and help me start preparing for my quest as my Tallantanar wishes."

Slightly startled but very pleased by the sudden change, Barten's eye widened as he said, "Of course, I will help you. Why this sudden decision to go on a quest of some sort? I thought that Petralis was merely going to try to talk some sense into you, yet *again*!"

"More like beat," Petralis said, muttering none too softly as he rubbed his already swelling jaw.

"He explained to me the importance of family and the importance of familial responsibilities. I have a duty to my people and to my Blood Oath to reunite our family as well as to seek our parents' killers. Besides, I should help to have our brother and sisters here to meet our future niece or nephew when they are born."

The stunned look on Barten's face was too much for the brothers to maintain straight faces for long. As one, they both began laughing at the man who had raised them as one of his own children and rarely ever was stunned by their actions.

Petralis stopped laughing long enough to say, "I have waited my entire life to get that shocked look on your face, Barten. It was worth all of the pains that you put me through to see that look at least once in my life. Mirta just told me this morning, and my Aunts confirmed it as well; she is with child, and we will soon have a child to carry on after me." Petralis continued saying, "Griefold and I have come to an agreement, he will fulfill his Oath to our mother, and I will allow more trade for his new friends from Dantorin."

Spluttering, Barten struggled to find the right words to say to Petralis in response. He had planned for the two brothers to have it out and then for Griefold to leave on a quest to find his missing brother and sisters, not this surprise. After a minute and several deep breaths, Barten recovered his composure and swallowed back any complaints he might have had. Looking over his shoulder, he considered the gathered elite guards carefully. With a moment of thought, Barten snapped out two, calling the named warriors.

Barten said, "Bernella, Arten, come forward!" as the two shadows separated themselves from the rest of the waiting, Griffonara, Barten continued saying, "These are two of my best, and they will accompany Griefold on this quest to find the others. I will not allow him to risk himself for nothing, especially when he has to go forth to find your brother and sisters. I am sending my own two children with you; they know how you fight, and you have trained beside them long enough to be able to fight with them without having to think about it."

The two warriors appeared out of the shadows, stepping into the firelight streaming out of the longhouse, wearing the dark gray leathers of the Griffonara. Of the two warriors, one was a rarity among the Ameristan people, a red-headed woman, slight of build and whipcord lean. She was one of the most beautiful-looking women that Griefold had ever seen before. Her brother was the complete opposite. This man was larger than even Petralis in sheer muscle alone. The man had the typical blonde hair of the Ameristans, a blonde so pale it was nearly white. In addition, he had to be one of the most handsome men Griefold had ever seen in his life. He had a flawless face with a chiseled chin accompanied by skin any maid would kill for, appearing to be milk-white and as smooth as glass.

As his children stepped forward, Barten said, "Bernella, my daughter, is a Velocity Master that even your father would have thought twice about before facing. She is undefeated in all areas of combat and will one day take my place as leader of the Griffonara someday. My son, Arten, is a Dominance Master and he is just as powerful as Bernella is quick. Neither of them will let anything happen to you on your quest, Griefold."

The two were also wearing the purple cloaks of the Griffonarra as well as leather and steel brigandine armor. Arten had the two-handed hilt of a Great Sword protruding over his left shoulder, with the tip of the six-foot weapon nearly dragging on the ground. Meanwhile, Bernella had no obvious weapons on her person. Still, she exuded even more level of danger than her brother did. Both nodded to Barten at the introduction to their childhood playmate Griefold and then looked to him to see what he would do next. Having grown up with Griefold and seeing how he had changed over the last five winters, the brother and sister did not show the disgust that they were feeling.

Griefold's shoulders slumped in defeat, knowing that he had no choices left at this time. He was going to have to go on this insane quest to find his brother and sisters, and he was going to have to do so with an escort of two people he barely remembered. With a sigh, Griefold went into the longhouse once again and quickly began to put on his brigandine armor and to grab up his father's Great Sword. As Griefold was coming out of the longhouse with the rainbow-hued Amersteel sword, Petralis stepped forward and frowned at his brother.

Petralis looked at the sword hanging from his brother's hand and said, "You cannot take the sword with you. I know it was given to you and that you have long since mastered its use, but the sword is too easy to identify. What you are going to do is going to need to be done in secret as much as possible, for the same reason the Griffonara's griffons are going to have to stay here in The Holy City. I am sorry about that, but you will have to take a normal blade with you to keep yourself inconspicuous. The Aunts have also said that they wish to speak with you before you leave; they have some information to share with you about your quest."

Griefold looked at his sword and then again at his brother before saying, "As you wish, I would not want to make you angry again. I am still sore from the beating that you already gave me this evening and too sore to have you add to it again. I will pick up another sword from the temple armory when I am ready to leave. Are the Aunts in the temple?"

"Where else would the High Priestesses of Amerton be?" Petralis answered with a smile. They hardly ever leave the temple these days. I don't remember the last time that they showed themselves at anything but a council meeting with the rest of the Tallanta. You better hurry and see what they want. The messenger they sent seemed more than a little agitated about something."

Turning on his heel, Griefold began to make his way to the center of the city, thinking about what his aunts would have to say to him. He had not seen nor spoken to them in person for many moons now, not since he had begun to spend more time with the Dantorins. As the young warrior made his way through the city of longhouses and meeting halls, the two Griffonara assigned to protect him followed at a discrete distance.

Bernella spoke softly to her brother, saying, "I don't remember him being so easy on the eyes. If he had only put more time into his training, he would be much better-looking and more desirable. Do you think that he remembers me very well from our time training under father? I used to have such a crush on him and wanted to see him more than just in the training circles. Of course, it has been winters since he has seen me with all the Zealot and Iramian attacks that we have been dealing with."

Smiling back at his sister, Arten said, "I used to have the same feelings for him that you had, sister dear. I only wish that he would work harder. He would be much easier on the eyes than he is now. Griefold has grown soft in his time with the Dantorins, and it shows in the way he carries himself and how he lost a simple fistfight with Petralis. I used to wish that he would show some interest in one of us so that I would know if I was placing my heart in the right place or not. I guess while we are on this quest for the rest of his family, we will have the perfect chance to find out where his heart lies. Either with women or with men. I am hoping for the latter myself; I remember he used to be quite muscular and agile for someone so young."

"Someone so young?! He is barely a winter younger than you and only two winters my senior. What makes him so young?"

"Why experience, my dear sister. Experience. If the stories are true our young Griefold has never known the touch of another person, whether man or woman, and has not shown much interest in either. Of course, those are just stories that one hears around the fire late into the night."

"Leave it to you to listen to idle gossip from others while sitting around the fire. I want to know what he is like in the winton when the nights go long, and there is not one around to hear. He has the build of a Dominance Master, but does he have the hands of one as well."

"Get your mind back to business, sister. We are here to help protect him while he is on his quest to find his family. We must put our carnal desires beyond us for now and hope for something more in the future when the time comes if it comes. Besides, did you see the way he looked at me? I have a feeling that I am going to be the one to find out whether he has the hands of a Dominance Master or not long before *you* do."

Nearing the temple of Amerton Griefold began to wonder why his aunts would want to talk to him. They had always seemed distant in his youth, and now they were wishing to speak with him in person. He approached the sole stone building in the entire city and was awed yet again by the effort that went into constructing it. Entering the temple, Griefold was immediately met by a young Priest Pair and silently escorted to the dark recesses of the temple. Waving for him to follow, the young men walked with slow determination into the back of the building. As the Griffonara moved to follow, the twin priests in training turned and held up their hands, stopping the warriors from following. Knowing that to try and force their way into areas where they were not wanted could lead to problems, the Griffonara stopped where they were and prepared to wait for Griefold's return.

In a matter of minutes, Griefold found himself alone outside the darkly stained door, unsure if he should just enter or knock and get permission to enter. Just as he was about to knock, a pair of singsong voices spoke in perfect unison, saying, "Enter, nephew. We are waiting for you."

Pushing the door open slowly Griefold was astounded by the sight of his aunts, know that they were at least twenty winters his senior the two women before him could pass for youths. The twin blond-haired heads turned in sync to look at him and the smiles that appeared on their faces were so identical was it was scary.

In the way of the priest pairs of Amerton, they spoke in unison and moved as one body as the women stood saying, "We have some information to share with you about what has happened and what needs to be done while you are on your search. We have long kept a secret from the Ameristan people that you will now be privy to." Again, moving as one of the twin priests leads Griefold through the simply decorated sleeping chamber to another door at the back of the room. Opening the door, the twins motioned Griefold through the door and then followed him on silent feet into a room barely large enough for the three of them. The room had an ominous feeling to it that Griefold could not place; it was a brightly lit room in the temple of Amerton, but there was something that he could not quite place. In one corner of the room was a pile of fur that drew his eye, seeing as there was nothing else in the room.

Before he could speak, the pile of fur shifted, and a woman's head appeared from the pile. Her head was completely smooth and there were scars above her forehead that looked to have been burned into her skin. The woman had the look of someone who was weary and afraid yet still had some defiance left in her eyes. She appeared to be about the same age as his aunts, without the youthful look that came with the use of magic.

"Oh, look, the torturers have returned to try to question me yet again about something that happened all those winters ago. What will it be this time? Will it be more nail pulling or hot oil, or will it be the knives again? I love having the knives used on me. You get so inventive with them. Well, who is this? he looks too young to be one of your fighting masters, but he has no twin with him, so he cannot be one of your trainee priests come to heal me after you are done. So, who are you, young man?"

"Speak not to her!" the High Priestesses snapped to Griefold. "She is a vile creature and one who would gladly kill you with her bare hands given the chance if you were to come within reach of her. This is the last survivor of the attack that killed your parents and most of the Griffon Riders. She has been kept here and questioned by us for many winters as we have tried to learn her secrets. We brought you here to show you what to look for while you are on your quest. See the scars on her forehead? They are brands given to her by the Iramians to show her as property. It is given to all those who are slaves to the Iramians. They hail from a series of islands somewhere in the Ocean of Fire and raid us for slaves and for their sacrifices. She has no name and only answers to Blood Death Assassin. We know little more than that she is one of the same assassins who murdered your parents and nearly killed all of you when you were young."

Hearing this last bit of information, Griefold reached for the dagger at his belt and began to lunge forward toward the prisoner. Before he could move more than a few inches, he felt himself frozen in place, unable to move anything more than his eyes. Looking sharply to his left, he saw the twins holding their right hands out with a small smile playing across their lips.

In unison, they said, "You will not kill her. She is our prisoner, and we have many more questions to ask of her before we are through with her. We will release you if you are calm enough to listen to us and learn from this. We will share what information we have about where to find your brother and sisters, and then you will be on your way. We want you to know what to look for while you are on your search. While you are looking to reunite our family, these Blood Death Assassins are hunting for Blackston, Arista, and Aristin. The priest pairs that were sent with them for protection have done their jobs well, and we cannot even penetrate the secrets of where they are hidden on Tarnara. We know that one of them is in the mountains to the south, deep in Dracolia, another somewhere in Dantorin, and the third is somewhere in Iristia. We do not have much more than that to share with you."

A wicked laugh came from the prisoner, followed by her saying, "Do you think that being in those countries will stop my sister assassins from finding and killing them? We are never-ending, and we will never stop-…." She cut off suddenly, reaching her chained hands to her throat. The prisoner smiled at the twins and silently laughed again, looking from one face to another with a hint of panic starting to come into her eyes.

Turning to look at Griefold, the twins said, "It is time for you to leave and go with our blessings. We have more question for our guests, and if we find any more information to share with you, we will send a message to you as soon as possible." The twins turned away from their nephew in perfect unison, reaching for the daggers at their hips that all Ameristans wore.

Griefold quickly spun around and left the room, slamming the door shut behind himself. He realized that the fact that the assassin could not scream meant that he could not know what was happening at that moment. This sent a shiver of fear down his spine as he thought about the powers that the High Priestesses had shown tonight. He knew, as all followers of Amerton knew that the priest pairs were gifted with amazing abilities to heal and foresee the future. But this new demonstration of power scared him senseless. If the priests of Amerton truly had the power to block out sounds like that, how many such prisoners could they be holding in the temple? Now more than ever Griefold was thankful for the beliefs of his people in following peace and fighting only when it was necessary.

CHAPTER 7

Once outside of the temple again, Griefold saw that a new sword made from plain steel was waiting for him, along with a travel pack with his belongings. Barely slowing his pace, he picked up the pack and sword, which he swung around his back and settled into place. Before he could take another step, one of the Griffonara, who had followed him from the temple silently, reached out and gently grabbed his shoulder. Turning his head to see what the Griffonara wanted, Griefold saw Arten holding out his hand. In his palm lay several griffon feathers attached to a leather thong.

Bernella spoke first, saying, "If we are to keep this quest secret, then we cannot have you showing your Talla affiliations by wearing the braid and chain of the Minnertalla. Your mother was once of the Himlatalla; they would not object to you wearing the braid and griffon feathers of the Himlatalla while we search for your siblings. Our father made this suggestion before we left with you, but he was afraid that you might take it wrong if you were asked in front of the Tallantanar to change your braid. We know that for right now, you both are all that is left of your Talla, but secrecy must be kept. My brother and I are to leave our cloaks and leathers behind as well. We will simply be three Ameristans seeking our fortunes in the southern lands. Some of the younger sons and daughters of other Talla have done this over the winters, so we will not stand out at all."

Nodding his head in acceptance, Griefold silently began to unbraid his blond hair and remove the herring bone steel chain that Barten had given him when he reached adulthood. This was a very emotional moment for the young man since he felt as if he was leaving behind a part of himself. Being Minnertalla was all he knew, and now being forced to leave behind his Talla to find his brother and sisters left a hole in his heart. Even though, over the last several winters, he had been growing further from his oldest and closest brother and the ways of their people, this came as a blow.

The trio slowly made their way out of the city as the moon rose into the sky over them. Only Griefold knew their first destination was somewhere in the mountains south of them in the lands of the Dragon Riders. He had only ever met the envoys from that nation and had never seen the fabled dragons for which they were so well known. He would have a chance to see one while he was there and maybe even see the fabled capital city of the Dracolian Empire.

The three warriors walked long into the night, working to keep as fast a pace as they could manage to gain as much distance as possible before stopping for the night. It was near daybreak before they stopped to rest for a few hours, and Griefold felt more sore from the trek than his companions. Moons of inactivity and drinking wine had made him soft in comparison to the two elite warriors who were his traveling companions. They did not even bother to put up the winton that they had brought with them for the few short hours that they were going to rest. Simply falling to the ground where he stood, Griefold fell asleep as fast as his head hit his pack. Waking up with the rising sun, Griefold felt aches and pains in parts of his body that he had not felt since his training days with Barten. Opening his eyes with trepidation, he looked at his two smiling companions and groaned in discomfort, wishing he were waking up in the Talla's longhouse instead.

Arten handed Griefold a strip of dried auroch, saying, "Here, have something to eat and get yourself moving before you start stiffening up too much to move today. We have too much to do and too far to walk before the end of the day; by the way, which way are we headed? Last night, we simply left and started walking south. Are we going to keep going south, or are we going to change direction sometime soon?"

Griefold took the tough, salty meat from Arten and said, "The High Priestesses told me the general areas to look for my brother and sisters, but not more than that. We head south for the first of them since they are somewhere in the Dracolian Empire, another in Dantor, and the third in Iristia. I feel that if we search Dracolia first, we have a better chance of avoiding Zealot raids since the mountains are not friends of the Tigre they ride."

"So south it is," Arten replied as he shifted his pack onto his back again and started to head in that direction.

Griefold groaned as he climbed to his feet and began to walk south once again, his mind wondering over the possibilities of what he would find in the mountains. Since the death of the Minnertalla in his father's youth, he had never gone to the summer grounds of his Talla in the Sun's Death Mountains. No one had gone there in the passing winters, leaving the land untouched and leaving behind anything that was left of the Talla to nature.

It took them most of the summer to reach the foothills of the Dracolian Mountains. After moons of hard travel and countless hours spent honing his skills with Arten, Griefold found himself in peak condition once again. The time was well spent since it showed the young warrior how soft he had gotten in spending his time with the Dantorins. It had also hardened his resolve to find his family and to bring them back together again. Arten and Bernella had spent the intervening ten-days getting to know the young man once again, remembering the times they had shared living under the same winton as children. It was hard for Griefold to realize how he had snubbed his childhood friends once he had grown up and began to spend time with the ambassador and his little court. The shame he felt at his lack of ability to keep up with his training partner was too great to deal with at first. The fact that Arten swore he would not hold back in retraining Griefold was the only thing that kept him going. Only the fact that Bernella did not laugh at his first fumbling attempts to keep up kept Griefold from stopping altogether. After spending the intervening moons with them, Griefold began to remember the reason why he had distanced himself from the two upon reaching adulthood. His conflicted feelings for Bernella were only exacerbated by the time that they had spent together in such close confines of the winton. He remembered how he felt toward Bernella in a way that was far more than that of simple gratitude and of siblings that were shared between him and Petralis. Instead, he felt more deeply for Bernella and wished he could act upon his feelings. He was afraid that if he showed his true feelings for her, he would reject him as a friend. Sharing his feelings was something that he had developed while spending time with the Dantorins, and relearning how to hide them was a trial.

The twenty-five winters he had seen had not prepared Griefold for the sight before him when they came to the foothills of the Dracolian mountains. Having spent his entire life in and around The Holy City, he had never seen anything but the rolling plains of Amerista and the gently rising hills that occasionally broke up the landscape. Upon seeing the vast mountains that seemed to take up all the sky before him, Griefold was in awe. Knowing that somewhere in those mountains lay the hidden valleys and glens that housed the Dracolian Empire, he prepared himself. After a few days of travel, they began to climb into the foothills and still found no sign of other humans in sight. There was plenty of game and fruiting plants to keep them sustained, but the lack of any other people was unnerving to Griefold. He has spent his entire life surrounded by people, either Ameristan or some sort of trader or diplomat, trying to seek his favor. This lack made him uneasy, and the two Griffonara were growing on his nerves since they would not talk about anything other than his training regimen. Griefold was grateful for the time he spent with Arten relearning rusty skills, yet he wished for the diversions that he had grown accustomed to, too. Where was the singing and talks long into the night that the Dantorins had? Where were the discussions over what to do about the price of auroch and steel in trade? Instead, his near-silent companions would only preach to him about the tenets of Amerton, refreshing his memory on them or about how he needed to improve his footwork in this way or that.

It was when they were two ten-days into the mountains that they saw their first signs of human life. They happened upon a small flock of sheep and knew there had to be a shepherd somewhere nearby. Fortunately, they found the young man later in the day tending to some late-born lambs and were able to get some information from him. The trio learned that they were only another day's travel from the nearest village, where they would be able to trade for some goods and get directions.

Since the only clue to find one of the missing family members was somewhere in the Dracolian Empire, they came to the consensus that they should start asking discreet questions about any Ameristans who may have come through here in the past. While his traveling companions were working out ways to find out about travelers who had come before, Griefold was busy trying to think of how he could slip away from them for a while. He was sorely missing out on having the chance to drink and sing with people and was looking forward to finding something of the like in the village.

Such was not to be his luck; the village was tiny, housing barely one hundred people, and all they seemed to care about were the flocks of sheep that were seen everywhere. The only information that the villagers had to share was that all travelers simply pass through and that the next village was a tenday away. The villagers were more than happy to trade mutton and other foods for the spare steel daggers that the trio carried with them. Griefold did not sit well with the young man because of this lack of entertainment, yet he was perfectly fine with his companions. Feeling the lack of drink and entertainment, Griefold began to complain bitterly about everything around him. This did not sit well with his friends, but they allowed it to continue in hopes that it would pass with time.

A ten-day worth of travel and complaints later, Griefold, Arten, and Bernella neared a larger village; this one even had a wall made from wooden poles around it. There was a cloud of wood smoke hovering above the village, blocking out most of the early morning sunlight. Upon reaching the wall to the village, they were stopped by guards wearing simple leather armor shirts demanding to know what their business was within the village. Arten stepped forward and explained that they were simply passing through and looking to spend a day or two in the village before moving on. The guards looked over from their greater height and then let the trio pass into the village proper.

Once in the village, they were assaulted by the smells of massed humanity with the stench of burning wool hanging heavy in the air about them. The streets were mostly empty, with a few vendors hawking their wares to the passers-by, most of whom ignored them in the process. Many of the items for sale were simple ribbons and pins, and the occasional person selling meat on a stick.

Since it did not smell like mutton, Griefold felt sorely tempted to try and partake, but he did not have any currency that would be accepted by the locals. All Griefold had was some Dantorin coins and such from his friend back in the Holy City. This was something that he had not anticipated when preparing for his journey; of course, having less than an hour to get ready did not help either. Thinking back now, he should have investigated getting some more coin of some sort to use on this quest, but since the Ameristans primarily used a barter system, he was not used to them. Growing up using the barter system, he was shocked by the Dantorin use of coins to buy things instead of simply trading goods for goods. Slowly but surely, the Ameristans started to understand the use of coins in trade, and they had been talking about even looking into mining precious metal for themselves in the coming winters.

With his stomach growing and tying knots around his spine, Griefold approached one of the vendors and asked, "How much for a stick of meat?"

The taller vendor looked at Griefold, eyeing his sword and armor carefully before responding, "Six copper pieces."

Reaching into his pouch, Griefold pulled out a handful of coins and searched through them until he found the correct amount. Quickly handing over the coins, Griefold gratefully grabbed the proffered stick from the vendor and bit into it. The meat was not too hot and tasted wonderful on his tongue; it was rabbits or some other small animal that he was familiar with but could not easily place. All he knew was that it was warm, delicious, and not dried mutton. That was more than enough for him at that point in time.

Bernella eyed the stick questioningly and asked, "Did you even ask what kind of meat that was before you ate it? It could be something disgusting like a rat for all you know, Griefold."

"I don't care if it is a rat; it is not dried mutton or dried auroch, and it is fresh and warm, ready for a change. After moons of dried auroch and then a tenday of dried mutton, I am ready to eat anything that is warm and fresh for a change."

Shaking his head, Arten said, "I would rather eat rocks than anything that I could not name. You must be sick; it must come from all the time that you spent with the Dantorins back home. They must have gotten into your head with that meat they eat; what was it again? Pig or stig or something like that."

Smiling around his mouthful of food, Griefold said, "Pig, it is delicious when it is properly prepared. You should give it a try; sometimes, it is so soft that it practically melts in your mouth when you eat it. Ambassador Fanteth has his cook prepare the pig in such a way that the skin crackles when you bite into it. It is the best thing that I have ever eaten in my life. It is even better than fresh bread hot from the oven. That is something that I sorely miss as well: bread. We have been traveling all this time, and aside from the dried meat we brought with us, we have had nothing but wild fruits and vegetables. I would kill for some bread right now and wine. Oh, wine, how I miss having a fine vintage of wine to wash down a meal with."

The two siblings looked at each other behind Griefold's back, rolling their eyes in unison and shaking their heads. These were the same old complaints that they had heard with increasing frequency in the last tenday. The brother and sister shared a silent laugh and continued walking further into the village, hoping to find a place to stay for the night.

Both were tired of sleeping in the winton with the whining Griefold, and both were more than ready for a bath. It had been tendays since the last stream was warm enough to use for bathing. It took almost an hour of asking questions of the other people in the streets and looking around for signs before they found an inn. It was not the most expensive inn to be had since they had limited funds that they had brought with them. At least Arten had had the foresight to bring some coins with him when they had left, and now they were going to have to dig into the small amount he had with him.

Entering the inn, the trio were overwhelmed by the smell of roasting meat and spilled ale wafting through the common room. This was not an altogether pleasant experience for Arten and Bernella, but it was familiar to Griefold in a small sense. He had spent many days in the drinking houses that were sprouting up around the city, and the smells were becoming familiar to him. It brought back fond memories of his time spent drinking with the Dantorins and how much fun he had with them. He was looking forward to spending time in the common room and drinking with the other patrons of the inn tonight. As they looked around the wooden-walled common room, they noticed obvious stains on the floor from spilled ale and food. The tables and benches were roughly hewn from local wood and looked none too comfortable.

While Arten went to find the owner of the inn to secure them a room for the night or several nights, depending upon what they discovered, Griefold and Bernella went to the bar. The serving man, wearing a stained apron over dark woolen clothes, looked down at the two Ameristans and said, "What can I do for you two younglings?"

Bernella looked up at the dark-haired serving man and said, "We would like some food and something to drink to go along with it. Also, some bread, if you have any, would be nice."

"We have mutton roasting on the spit, some potatoes to go along with it, and I can rustle up some bread from this morning if you like. Say, aren't you two a little young to be carrying around those weapons and armor?" the serving man asked, raising one dark eyebrow with humor in his eyes.

"Never you mind how young you think we are! Just get us some food and wine right now and do what you are told like a good servant!" Griefold snarled, puffing up his chest to intimidate the serving man.

Placing a restraining hand on Griefold's right shoulder, Bernella said, "We are more than old enough to be wearing armor and our weapons. Have you never met an Ameristan? You seem to be a nice man, so I will give you a chance to think over what you are going to say next and answer really carefully."

Smiling slightly at the two shorter Ameristans, the serving man said, "You can drop the intimidation act. I have seen it before, and I have never been scared by it before, especially by such small warriors as you. As for wine and doing what I am told, we don't have wine, and I will get you the food like I said. The price of the food is included in the price of the room for the night, so don't worry about that. As for meeting Ameristans before, I have never had the pleasure of hearing about your people, but I have never met any. Your people don't travel much, do you?"

Sensing an opportunity to learn more and maybe narrow down the search a little, Griefold asked, "What have you heard about us? Is anyone else in this village that you can point out to us who may know more? We are looking for some of our countrymen who came this way fifteen winters ago, and we don't know where to look for them."

"Well," the serving man said as he scratched the back of his head, "you could try asking around the far side of the village at a place called the Dragon's Roost. They tend to deal with more outsiders and travelers than we do here. The owner has been there since the dawn of time and loves to talk up a storm once you get him started. Getting him to stop again is a real chore. I would say that you can start asking your questions there and find out what you can hear from him; his name is Chintal. Can't miss him. He takes a little too much to the ale he sells and has gone too far too fat to move too much anymore. His mind is still as sharp as ever, so he may be able to remember if any of your people traveled through here before."

Nodding their thanks, Griefold and Bernella walked over to the table that Arten had secured for them. It was oaken and scarred but sturdy enough to hold the ales that were presented to them, as well as the platters of steaming food. Without a word, the three began to dig into the food and eat in companionable silence for several minutes.

After most of the food had been consumed, Bernella said, "Well, we have a lead to check into at another inn called the Dragon's Roost. We were told to contact the owner by the name of Chintal and ask him about other Ameristans who may have come through here. Did you find out anything useful, brother?"

"No, nothing. Other than the price of the room for the night and use of the bathhouse outback, the owner had nothing to say to me. He almost seemed happy to have our custom for the night." Arten replied before taking a deep swallow of the ale.

"What do you mean one room?" Griefold asked, frowning, "How am I supposed to rest if we are still sharing sleeping space? We just spent the last two and a half moons together in one small winton; how are we going to make one small room work!?"

Letting loose with a tinkling laugh, Bernella said, "Easily, you take the floor with my brother, and I take the bed for myself. How else could we work out sleeping in the same room? It won't hurt you to share more space with us while we are on this journey. As it is, we have limited funds, and I am sure that Arten did his best to get us the best deal on the room for the night. You need to get this idea that you are better than us out of your head, Griefold. We are in this together, and together, we will have to sleep together again."

With his face turning red from embarrassment and anger combined, Griefold said, "I never said that I was better than you. I only wanted to have some peace and quiet when we were trying to get some sleep tonight. Besides, what if I find someone to keep me company tonight, and I have to bring her to the same room as you two? That would put a serious crimp in my night."

Laughing out loud, Arten spit ale out as he said, "YOU! Find a woman to spend the night with you! I have known you for almost your entire life, and I have heard stories about how you would cringe away from the Dantorin women when they approached you late at night."

Growing even redder, Griefold spluttered, "I...I...I don't know what you are talking about. There were many times that I spent a wonderful night with many a Dantorin woman, as well as many a warrior from among the Amertalla living in the city. I have more than enough experience with women, and I feel that I could easily find company tonight if we had separate rooms."

Turing as red in the face as her hair from laughter, Bernella said, "I, too, have heard the stories about your *prowess* among the females, Griefold. To say that you have experience is going much too far, more like a severe lack of experience, would be more to the truth of things. But that is all right; you don't have to worry about company tonight. Like I said before, we are sharing a room. If you want company, I am sure my brother would love to keep you company tonight. I could always find someplace down here to sleep on the floor, I am sure."

"I don't need him to keep me company!" was Griefold's shouted response as he rose quickly from his seat and stormed out of the common room of the inn and once again into the village.

Bernella made it as if to rise to go after the fuming warrior when Arten stopped her with a hand on her arm, saying, "Sister, you have to let him be for a while. I think that we might have hurt him a little with our joking. He is sensitive; it seems that he lacks experience and is trying to make it seem he is more worldly than he really is. Griefold will come back to us after he has cooled down, and I think that he will be more than a little embarrassed about how he acted."

Sitting down in her seat again heavily, Bernella sighed and said, "I did not mean to hurt him like that. I only wanted to deflate him a little bit so that he would be more relaxed around us and let go of some of his determination that he was so much better than we were. I wish that he would open up to me a little more and share that part of his life with me instead of trying to wall himself off behind the story he has created about himself."

"I understand what you want, and after the past couple of moons, I feel that he is definitely more interested in you than he would ever be in me. I hope for the best for you, and I will have to salve my heart with the knowledge that my sister is going to find her heart's desire, even if I don't."

Smiling to herself at the prospects that her brother brought up, Bernella straightened up a little more. Slowly, she reached for her ale and drank deeply from her tankard, deep in thought about the future possibilities.

After an hour, the shamefaced Griefold returned to the inn and quietly asked for directions to the bathhouse. A young boy showed him how to get there, and he spent a long time soaking away his aches and pains in the hot water of the bath. While bathing, Griefold had plenty of time to think about what the siblings had said to him about his lack of experience with the opposite sex. Every time a female approached him while he was growing up, he always backed away from them, afraid of what to do or say. This had not gotten any easier when the more aggressive Dantorin women had made their intentions clear to the young man in recent winters. The more time he spent with the ambassador and his entourage, the more women who served the ambassador tried to spend time alone with Griefold. He knew that they were only doing this on orders from the Fanteth to try and get more of a lock on him and to get more sway with Petralis. With the thought of getting more sway, with his brother being the sole reason for their attentions, Griefold found himself pushing all women away from him. Despite the innate desire to get attention from his peers and feel that he was a part of the crowd. That desire is what led to his creation of fiction, which is that he was so worldly when, in fact, he had never known the touch of a woman. Now, here he was, trapped with a very attractive woman whom he once had feelings for, and he could not share them with her. Bernella was next in line to lead the Griffonara, and that was something that she had talked about since they were children. Leading the defenders of her Tallantanar was her only goal, and she could not do that and had ties with himself at the same time. Feeling as if he had solved none of his problems other than the immediate need to clean himself, Griefold rose from the bath and dried himself quickly before returning to the common room.

With plans to spend the night deep in drink to forget what he had been thinking about while bathing, he was disappointed to find out that was not going to happen. The common room of the inn was completely empty except for Arten and Bernella, both of whom were apparently waiting for him.

Walking over to them casually, Griefold said, "So, what are the plans for the night? Some drinking and maybe some singing or even some dancing from Bernella? I would really like to see you dance."

"That is not going to happen now or ever," Bernella growled, face growing as red as her hair again, "I DO NOT dance for anything or anyone, so get that thought out of your head. As for drinking, we have already spoken to the servers. They understand that if they give you anything more than one tankard of ale with your dinner, they will not receive the three copper pieces that were promised to them. Your night will be spent alone, not drinking or carousing with the locals since they do not frequent this particular inn for those sorts of things. Why do you think we chose to spend the night here instead of somewhere else for the night?"

Arten smiled and said, "Sorry to destroy your glorious visions of a night spent acting the fool and enjoying yourself like you were with Ambassador Fanteth. We are here for a very important reason, and we are tasked with keeping you in line by your brother."

"Alright, if that is how it is supposed to be, then I might as well eat something and then maybe get in some practice with you before turning in for the night," Griefold replied as he sat down again.

To practice that night, the pair of men pushed aside the tables in the common room and made a large, cleared circle in the center of the room. With the fire roaring in the fireplace behind them, they gave off an unsteady light, stripped to the waste, and drew their great swords. With the razor-edged blades glinting in the firelight, they faced one another in preparation for a sparring bout. With a sudden lunge, Griefold launched himself at the more heavily built Arten without holding back his strength. With the ringing sound of metal striking metal, Arten swept the approaching blade away from his stomach so that it passed over his shoulder without leaving a mark. In a fast riposte, Arten then lunged at Griefold, and in return, with another ring of steel on steel, the lunge was turned aside harmlessly. In a matter of moments, the sparring session began to move from simple lunges and blocks into a deadly whirlwind of flashing blades. Neither man gave quarter nor barely held back from landing crippling blows upon one another while they twirled across the floor in a dance of death.

Watching from a safe distance from the sparring men, Bernella felt her heartbeat faster as she watched the rippling muscles of Griefold. Each riposte, each lunge, each exchange, she saw a different flash of his well-muscled body moving through the fight. Feeling heat beginning to rush to her face, Bernella had to catch herself several times from jumping to her feet and rushing in to intervene. She watched with trepidation each time a lunge or swing of the sword in Arten's hands came close to reaching Griefold's skin.

Watching over the tendays as Griefold went from a soft loafer to this hardened warrior did not make it any easier to see him risking his skin. She felt the desire to reach out and touch him intimately increasing with each passing day and knew that she was losing herself to him. She was fine with that. If only she could know how Griefold felt about her in return, then she would know whether she was wasting her time and hopes in him.

The sparring session lasted less than an hour before Arten called for a halt to the fight so that they could relax before turning in for the night. When Griefold had left to go to their shared room, Arten sat down next to Bernella and sighed heavily.

She said, "He has improved greatly in the Dominance over the last several tendays. He is almost as good as you are."

"That he is, Bernella. I almost had to call it a few times before he scored a hit or two on me and drew some blood for real. I do not mind a training scar or two, but I don't want to offend our hosts tonight, and I don't want to give Griefold the wrong impression of his ability. Besides, I saw your abortive attempts to intervene a few times while we were sparring. Do I detect something more than just general interest in our young friend, or were you afraid to see me hurt?" This last was said with a self-satisfied smile on Arten's face. "You know, you could just ask him how he feels about you, and then it would be all out in the open. I know that he is not interested in me in that way for sure now, so why don't you take the chance and just ask him."

Her face flushing, Bernella said, "I can't do that! What if he laughs at me when I tell him how I feel?! What if he doesn't return my feelings and wants nothing to do with me after I tell him?! I couldn't live with the shame."

Chuckling evilly at his sister's distress, Arten said, "I could always tell him for you and let you know how he reacts. Would that make it easier for you?"

Jumping to her feet and reaching for one of her daggers, Bernella said, "If you do that, I will castrate you!"

Dancing backward with his hands held out before him placatingly, Arten replied, "I won't say anything. I swear by Amerton! Just relax, little sister; I am sure that he would not shame you in any way if you shared your feelings with him. Put your dagger away and calm down before you do something that I will regret."

Bernella slammed her dagger home in its sheath again and glowered at the slightly taller Arten before saying, "Just remember that the next time that you decide to try and share things with Griefold without my permission. You let one word about how I feel about him slip, and the next thing you know, you will be sacless, you understand me?!"

"I understand you very clearly, Bernella; I won't utter one word to Griefold as long as you promise to say something to him yourself before too much time passes. He deserves to know the truth, and you deserve to share your life with someone. Don't be like father after mother died; don't let yourself be alone just because he has been for so long."

"I swear I will tell him how I feel when the time is right. NOT BEFORE!" Bernella shouted before turning herself to the stairs at the back of the room and heading upstairs herself. She left a chuckling Arten in the common room to finish rearranging the tables and benches before turning in for the night himself.

CHAPTER 8

Rising with the sun the following morning, the trio made their way to the common room once again to start their day and prepare to continue their quest. It was only after a breakfast of watery porridge that they decided to set out in search of the inn called Dragon's Roost.

Setting out from their inn, they followed the directions given to them the day before by the helpful serving man. It took almost an hour of walking and searching through the various other buildings in the village to find the Dragon's Roost. It was a building made entirely of stone, a rarity to the Ameristans, and was three stories tall. Quite an impressive sight for those who were used to living in single-floor longhouses and wintons. As a group, they approached the front door of the inn and entered the large stone-lined common room. Here, the tables and benches were carved with loving care and attention to detail, unlike the inn where they were staying. Just by looking at the common room, it was obvious that this was a much finer establishment and would be more to Griefold's taste. Unfortunately for him, they were only there to gather some information and prepare to set out again as soon as they could.

Once they entered, the three warriors split up to look around for the owner, who was supposed to be able to help them with their questions. Arten was the first to find the owner, Chintal, a grossly fat man with a fringe of white hair surrounding the crown of his head. He was sitting in a chair clearly made to support his great weight at the end of the bar nearest the fireplace, dozing quietly. He wore a tunic of grey homespun wool with brown trousers, all of which strained at the seams, seeming about to burst apart at any time. Arten motioned for the other two to come to him where Chintal sat.

As he approached the other two men, Griefold said, "So, this is Chintal? He is not much to look at. I only hope that he can share the information that we need and that we can get on with our search in a timely fashion."

A gravelly rumbling voice said, "Aye, I can help ye' if what you be looking for is information that I am willing ta share." Chintal's eyes opened, showing that he was far from dozing despite his appearance. "Pull up a seat and tell me what you want to know about young ins."

Bernella said, "We were told that your inn is the place to come if you are a stranger and only passing through. We have some kin that passed this way fifteen winters ago, and we would like to know if they passed here on their way. They would look like us with a pair of twins and a small boy with dark hair about two winters old or a newborn girl with them at the time. Does that bring back any memories?"

Squinting his eyes at the three young Ameristans, Chintal said, "Aye, I do remember the group that you described to me. They passed through here about fourteen winters back on their way south. Never did get their names or where they were going just got the impression that they were in a hurry to get south and wanted to be left alone. They stick out in my memory, though, because of the big man that was with them. Not as big as the pretty boy with ye, but he was a big un-ta, be sure, and he carried the biggest bearded axe I ever saw in my life with him, too.”

Feeling his excitement rising in him, Griefold asked, “Do you remember anything else about them anything that sticks out in your mind about the child perhaps?”

Shaking his head slowly, Chintal said, “No, other than the boy crying a lot and the twins trying ta comfort him, they did not really say much else. They stayed for a few days while they planned to travel south like I told ye, and the entire time, the little boy could not stop crying. It was like he had lost his best friend and family all at once. Well, unless ye want to be askin for a room for the night, we got nothin’ else to be discussin’ here then.”

Bernella thanked Chintal for his time and effort and swiftly led the other two from the inn. Waiting until they were out of hearing, she said, “At least we know Blackston came through here with his protectors at about the right time. Now, we just have to head further south and see what we can find on the way. We should get more provisions and leave right away. Time is of the essence here.”

“I agree with you, Bernella,” Arten said as he began to quicken his pace, “the faster that we get on the trail, as cold as it is, the better we will be in the long run. We need to move on this information and find out what other villages or cities lie to the south of here and where they could have gone.”

“Let’s get a map, or some kind before we leave the village. Surely there must be one somewhere that someone is willing to part with for us to use.” Griefold said hopefully.

"I will head out to look for one while you two settle up with the inn owner," Bernella said.

They then split up with the two young men, heading back to the inn to pay the inn owner what they owed and to gather their scant belongings. The trio met back up again at the inn, with Bernella triumphantly waving a rolled parchment.

Taking a quick look at the map, they saw that there were no significant villages of any size south of their current location. The only place of any size to be found south was the capital city, Dracolia City, which is about a ten-day travel away. There was no discussion needed between the three since they knew that their next destination was going to be the capital. Due to the size of the city, they also knew that their search was going to be that much harder. How would they narrow down their search for one young man among the many thousands who would have passed through the city over the winters? Their task, which such a short time ago seemed to be coming to a quick close, was suddenly made nearly impossible by that simple fact.

Deciding to waste no time, they set out through the southern gate on a fast walk, hoping to put as much distance behind them as possible before the sun set. They spent the next tenday walking higher into the mountain passes that led to Dracolia City with increasing woods and dropping temperatures. Summer was nearly over and autumn was fast approaching, much faster than they were used to seeing being so high in elevation. The trees that surrounded them slowly gave way from those shedding leaves to the pines and evergreens of the higher mountains. The ground went from being firm underfoot to the softer loam of fallen pine needles. This change of footing made the nightly sparring sessions between Griefold and Arten more challenging and interesting. During these sparring sessions, Griefold managed to score a minor hit on Arten's right shoulder, which drew a small amount of blood. Causing the wound, Griefold thought that their sparring would end and said as much to Arten the following night.

Arten replied, "This is only a minor scratch and no reason to stop practicing at all. Once we are in a battle for our lives, a small wound such as this would be nothing to stop us from continuing on. You have to be prepared to keep fighting until the bitter end and be prepared to take a life when it becomes necessary. I know that father taught you that when we were children, but I think that you have forgotten your lessons. From now on, we are going to practice harder and longer. You need to prepare yourself to fight harder. Like your life depends upon it, which it will if we ever have to fight for our lives."

Nodding her head in agreement, Bernella said, "There are times when you have to make that final blow and end the life of someone who you are facing. That is the hardest thing that I have ever had to do, but I have done it when called upon to defend our people."

Griefold rubbed his stubbled blond-haired head and said, "I hear you; I hear you. I spent my entire life learning how to lead our people into battle and to fight for our people. I just never thought that I would have to shed blood in person, and I thought that since I hurt you, Arten, you would not trust me with a blade anymore."

"I trust that you know what you are doing with a great sword in your hands. After all, we did train together as children. Just because you scratched me only shows that your skills are improving after going to waste for a few winters."

"I guess that I am going to have to work that much harder on my skills, and I am going to have to get used to shedding blood. I only hope that I don't do any serious damage to you in the process." Griefold said to Arten.

Stripping off his shirt and brigandine armor Griefold rubbed his sweaty hands on his leather trousers and drew his great sword. Circling the fire that they had started for the night, Arten did the same without showing any sign that his wound was bothering him in the slightest. In a matter of moments, the two fighters were once again facing off with whirling blades in a dance of death and steel.

Watching from her position outside of the firelight, Bernella found herself once again trying not to jump to her feet to come to Griefold's aid. This feeling of wanting to help him was leading to more complications than she thought would be possible. If she leaped in to help him in a sparring match, would he thank her, or would he think that she thought him too weak to fight for himself? This made watching a joy and a chore for Bernella at the same time. She wanted to share her feelings with him but feared what his reactions would be. Unsure of what to do, she simply continued to watch and hold herself in control.

The following morning, as they began their trek once more, Griefold noticed a large bird of some sort that he had never seen before in the sky. It seemed to be following their progress through the mountain pass, never getting close enough to be identified. Griefold thought about saying something to his travelling companions but said nothing, fearing looking like a fool. Why would a bird be following them through the pass? It just had to be a coincidence.

Later that day, they neared the end of the pass that would lead into the valley that held Dracolia City, and Griefold noticed the bird again. It was stooping toward them from a great height, intent upon something on the ground. Griefold was about to say something to Bernella and Arten when Arten spoke up first.

"If I didn't know any better, I would say that that is the same bird that I have been seeing since we entered Dracolia. It is always there following us from a great height, and I cannot tell what kind of bird it is."

"I noticed it this morning when we started out from our last campsite. I think it is getting closer to us, though I cannot say for sure." Griefold said.

"I don't think that it is a bird," Bernella said, drawing her dagger. "I think that it is something a lot bigger than a bird; it is bigger than a griffon, too."

Reaching for his sword, Griefold said, "I agree with you. I don't think that is any kind of bird and whatever it is. It is getting closer!"

As Griefold, Arten, and Bernella moved back-to-back and watched the flying creature approach, they noticed its details. Instead of fur or feathers, the creature was covered in scales that were so iridescent black that they absorbed the light. This very large creature let out a roar that seemed to echo back on itself as it came closer to the three warriors. With fear in their hearts but determination set in their faces, they prepared to fight to the death against whatever this creature was. With a backwash of wings that snapped like thunder, the creature landed, and a man could be seen sitting on its back.

The stranger said, "Who are you, and what are you doing this close to Dracolia City? Why do you carry weapons and armor into a peaceful empire?"

Taking the lead, Griefold tightened his grip on his sword and slowly stepped toward the taller stranger. He noticed that the man was taller than himself, as usual with Ameristans, and covered in chain mail armor and a steel helmet. Griefold approached the beast that the man was riding and stopped a sword length away before he said anything.

"We are merely passing through the area and looking for some fellow countrymen that may have come this way in winter's past. We mean no harm and are only armed for our own defense." Griefold said as he spread his hands placatingly.

Removing his helmet to show a shock of brown hair and fair skin, the stranger said, "That may be what you say now, but why do you approach our capital like thieves sneaking through the night? What do you mean you are looking for countrymen that passed through here winters ago? How would you know that they came this way at all? Drop your weapons and prepare to be searched!"

"If you think that I am going to drop my weapons and let you lay one hand on me, then you are going to be in for a big surprise. You may just leave this situation with one less hand if you so much as try to touch me without my permission." Bernella said, drawing a second dagger from the small part of her back.

Arten grunted his agreement as he moved slightly to get a better view of the stranger riding the strange animal. Just then, he heard a loud snort behind him, which caused him to spin around in place and see a second creature and rider wearing chainmail come out of the woods. With a shouted warning to his companions, Arten stepped forward angrily and prepared to attack these new enemies.

As the new stranger removed his helmet, they were mildly shocked to see that it was a woman on the new beast. She said, "Roberton, don't be such an ass. They are obviously not carrying anything more dangerous than the weapons we can see. Besides, how much danger can three people pose to the empire? They may just be doing, as they say, passing through and looking for some missing kinsmen. I say let them pass and let us get on with our patrol. We have spent more than enough time following them for no reason as it is."

"Arella, I am in charge of this patrol, and I say that these strangers are a possible danger to the emperor and empire and, as such, must be held until they can be searched properly." The first stranger replied with heat coming to his voice.

Laughing at her patrol partner, Arella said, "If you want to waste your own time and get yourself hurt in the process, then go ahead. As for me, I am taking my dragon and heading back on patrol. They are obviously not a threat and no danger to anyone who leaves them to their quest." Saying this, she returned her helmet to her head and lifted the reins to her mount, then took off into the air again.

Slamming his helmet back onto his head with obvious frustration, Roberton said, "I will let you pass for now. Just remember that while you are in the Dracolian Empire, you are always being watched; we Dragon Riders are everywhere." Then he leapt onto his mount, lifted his reigns, and, with a snap of the dragon's wings, took off into the air again after his partner.

Watching the two black dragons disappearing into the distance, Griefold let out a sigh of relief as he said, "I was afraid for a minute there that we were going to have to fight our way out of that situation. I have never seen a dragon before. I have seen wyvern carcasses that were brought into the city to feed the griffons, but never a dragon. They are much bigger than a wyvern, aren't they?"

"That they are," Arten agreed, sheathing his sword and letting out a deep breath of his own before saying, "They are obviously watching us and have been since we crossed the foothills into Dracolia. They are going to be watching us, so let's not disappoint them and get on with our search. We are doing nothing wrong, and if they want to follow us all the way to the capital then I say let them. It wouldn't hurt for some extra eyes on our quest this way, we will have advanced warning of anyone trying to get too close to us."

Bernella nodded her assent as she too, sheathed her weapons and took a deep breath before continuing down the trail towards the city. They could see the wall surrounding the city from a great distance, proving to them that the stone walls were tall and thick. Circling over the city were many more black spots that they assumed were more dragons and their riders keeping watch. This did not bode well for their mission to seek out Blackston and his guardians if they were watched so closely. They had come to the city only to pass through and then move on to a more easily concealable village. With this in mind, they set out for the city at a faster pace in order to try to find the possible direction to look next.

It took most of the day for them to approach the city and to find a gate with which to enter the city. As they walked, they saw more evidence of the Dragon Riders in the air, as well as a wingless variety patrolling the outside walls of the city itself. The wingless dragons were just as large and just as black as the winged dragons that they had encountered so far. The only difference that the travelers could see was the fact that they lacked wings. Instead, they had stronger-looking legs and tails. Both varieties had clawed feet and black iridescent scales giving them the look of taking in all of the available light. When the pacing dragons passed through shadows, they seemed to disappear into the darkness of the shadows completely. In the dark of night, they would completely disappear and be a true terror to try and defend against.

With this dreadful thought foremost in his mind, Griefold said, "Where do we even begin to look in Dracolia City if all travelers are treated the way that we were? Would they have completely avoided the area and kept moving south, or would they have risked the Dragon Riders and passed through the city?"

"I think that the people to ask would be the ones who are watching all strangers who pass through this area. Why don't we ask the Dragon Riders themselves about our quarry? They may have ideas about where the guardians took Blackston and how we can find him now. What do you think, Arten?" Bernella said.

Arten's reply was, "I think that you are right. We need to find where the central command for the Dragon Riders and see what information they will be willing to share with us. They may know exactly where to locate Blackston and his guardians and how to get to them. The way that they were following us since we crossed the border, they may do the same to all travelers."

Griefold said, "How do we find their central command if they even have one? Do we just walk into the city and start asking questions about where the leaders of the Dragon Riders are?"

With a laugh, Bernella said, "That is exactly what we do. We go through the gate and start asking questions about where to find the leader of the Dragon Riders and hope that whoever that person is, he or she is willing to talk. Once we do that, it should be a simple matter of finding out which village or city or wherever Blackston and his guardians are. We could finish this and return to The Holy City by the time the snow flies."

Griefold said, "I just don't believe that it can be that easy. They have been in hiding for so many winters now and for us to just find them like that. What if there were more assassins coming after him? Would they have easily found him as that, just asking for strangers passing through and getting directions? I think that we are following a false trail by going to the Dragon Riders."

Arten said, "We will at least try to find them this way. If we are wrong, all we are going to do is waste a few days looking around the city and talking to a few people. If Bernella is right, we can end this soon. At least this part of our quest, that is. We still have to find your sisters and they could be much harder to find. Why not take the chance to get some good news and hope for the best?"

"Alright. I will go with your plans for now, but I want you to know that I do not think that they will be found that easily. Why else go into hiding to be found so easily?" Griefold replied with a heavy tone of sarcasm.

As they discussed their options, the trio neared the main gate to the city and saw that a dozen wingless dragons and riders guarded it. The guards all wore chain mail armor and swords at their sides with shields hanging from their backs. The dragons were all nearly the same size, larger than a full grown auroch, and easily taller at the shoulder than the riders themselves. They snapped and hissed at one another while the riders spoke quietly among themselves near the brazier in the shadow of the gate. With the cool weather coming on, the brazier must be a welcome site to wait out the hours on duty. Griefold and his companions approached the gate slowly with their hands hovering near their weapons, ready to defend themselves if necessary.

Seeing the approaching strangers, the lead guard said, "Hold there, what business do you have in Dracolia City?"

Griefold replied, "We are merely passing through and only seek shelter for a few days and some answers about others who may have come this way before."

"If that is so, then you are welcome to pass through the city. If you have questions, we can help you find your answers. Do you have a place to stay in the city? If not, can I recommend a few places that are not too expensive?"

Smiling at the obvious ploy to get them to stay at a friend's or family member's inn, Arten said, "We have someplace to stay, and it's already picked out. We could use some help in finding where your commander can be located. We have some questions for him about other travelers from winters back."

"If you want to speak to the commander, then you have to go to the palace and speak to her there. It will only take you about a year to get into the palace, and once you do, you have about a chance to see the commander. She doesn't take to talking to visitors much and not to mention she doesn't like outlanders much either so you have about no chance of seeing her at all." The lead guard said.

With Griefold shaking his head in dismay, they entered the city proper and began to walk down the main road. Once again, there were vendors everywhere hawking everything from pins to grilled meats to all interested passersby.

Without stopping, Arten and the other two went on with their search for a place to stay while they conducted their search of the city. They knew that it was going to take many days to get through all of the possible places that the others could have stayed, and it had been many winters. This time, they were not going to get lucky and find one of the only places to stay in the city and find the one man who would remember their quarry from winters ago. This change of plans would only add to the time that they needed to search for Blackston and make it that much harder for them. To deal with this, they quietly decided to divide the city into three parts and start asking questions at every inn and hostel in the city. This could possibly take many tendays, but they had no other choice except to try and approach the Dragon Riders commander at the palace, with the information given to them about how the commander felt about outlanders. Add to it the fact that it could take even longer to get into speaking to her, and that seemed like a closed-off option for them.

They eventually found an inn to stay in for a reasonable price while they were in the city and to act as their base of operations for the foreseeable future. It was located in a wooden building that had seen its better days near the heart of the city and the palace itself. It was not as fancy as most of the surrounding residences and places of business that catered to the nobility and upper classes, but it worked for them. They knew that they were going to be there for several tendays at least, so they made arrangements for separate rooms to stay in. At the same time, they decided to use part of the stables in the back as a sparring area for the three of them.

CHAPTER 9

One tenday into their search of the city, they were meeting dead end after dead end; no one remembered seeing the previous group pass through, or they refused outright to share information. This was proving to be very frustrating to the searchers, with every avenue they searched being closed off them. It was becoming more obvious with each passing day that they would have to approach the palace. That prospect did not bode well for them, and the time they were willing to spend waiting in Dracolia City. The second tenday in their stay at the inn came to a head, with Bernella losing her temper at her latest failure to get any information.

She said, "I think that we have no choice left but to approach the palace in the morning and try to get in to see this commander. We are running into dead ends with all of the city's inns and hostels, which is quickly becoming a waste of time. I say we go to the palace tomorrow and try to see this commander and do whatever we have to get the information that we need from her."

Arten replied, "I agree with you, little sister. We have been at this for two tendays now, and we have gotten no closer to finding even a trace of them. It is time that we approach this commander like you said and take our chances with her dislike of outlanders."

Griefold nodded his head as he said, "We are out of options at this point, in my opinion. We have to go to the commander and see what we can get from her about

Blackston and his guardians. We have to hope that they have some memory from that time and are willing to share it with us without too much delay."

With all of them in agreement, they decided to turn in early for the night and set out for the palace at first light in order to try to get an appointment with the commander. Following through with their discussion the previous night, they shined their armor as best they could, along with their weapons, before setting out for the palace. It took them less than an hour to reach the palace gates and to find a line already forming for entrance to the palace grounds. They ended up spending most of the morning waiting to get into the gates before even having a chance to speak to anyone. After entering the palace grounds, they were shocked to see that the palace was like a city unto itself. Everywhere they looked, they could see hundreds of people running about, rushing from one section of the grounds to another. The buildings were astonishing to the trio since they were all made of stone and marble, something rare to the Ameristans, who primarily used wood, leather, and sod in their construction. The expense of these buildings must have been staggering, and the time needed to create them must have been winters in the making. This astonished the Ameristans so much that they stood gaping at the structures around them as people shoved around them. After several minutes of staring at themselves in awe, they started to move forward again and began to look for someone who was officially looking to help them. They found one such person who was wearing fine linen robes and gold chains around his neck, showing much wealth and evident authority.

Arten and the others approached the official-looking man with a shining shaved head and said, "We are looking to speak with the commander of the Dragon Riders. We have business with her, and we would like to know when we can speak with her."

Huffing at the trio in exasperation, the man said in a gravelly voice, "Commander Alicia only sees people who have appointments with her. Do you have an appointment to see Commander Alicia?"

"Unfortunately, we do not have an appointment with the commander at this time. We would like to try to get one with her as soon as possible. Can that be arranged?" Arten told the official-looking man.

"I cannot make the appointments with the commander; to do that, you have to see one of her lieutenants and make the appointment with them. I will gladly take you to see one of them now. Will you please follow me?" the man said as he turned and began to walk away swiftly.

They followed him for several minutes through several paths and then down several other corridors inside one of the marble-covered buildings. The walls were lined with granite and held torches every few feet down the hallway. There were no windows to be seen in the building, giving an oppressive and dark feeling to the trio, who were used to the open plains of their home. Only after traveling in the building for many minutes and giving the Ameristans a shaking feeling of the building closing in on them did they come to a door.

Without knocking, the official opened the door and walked into the room without announcing himself as he entered. In his gravelly voice, he said, "Tynela, you have some visitors. They want to see the commander, and I thought it best to bring them to you instead of letting them wander around the palace grounds like lost little lambs."

Upon following the so far nameless official into the room, the Ameristans saw a tall, dark-haired woman sitting at a table covered with parchments. She was busily sorting through the many parchments and did not bother to look up from her task as she spoke in a lilting voice, saying, "Might as well show them in, Pentar. I am never going to get any of this done any time before winter hits at this rate. Let me see what I can do to get the commander to see them; it will give me a break from all of this work for at least a little while."

Pentar motioned for the three to fully enter the room and made short introductions, saying, "This is Tynela, the Chief lieutenant of the Dragon Riders. Tynela, these are the three strangers who want to meet the commander."

Raising her black eyes from the parchments in front of her, Tynela took in the sight of the armed Ameristans for several seconds before she said, "You will have to disarm before you are able to see the commander. We don't let strangers go armed into the palace itself. I hope that you can understand that."

With a look at one another and a shrug of compliance, the three quickly divested themselves of their assorted swords and daggers, carefully laying them in neat piles at their feet. Once that was done, they all turned their light-colored eyes expectantly to Tynela and waited for further instructions.

Tynela said, "Come with me, and I will take you to the commander. Keep up and keep your hands to yourselves as we go into the palace properly. I don't want to have to search you three before we return in case you decided you liked some pretty bauble." Then she turned and quickly brushed her way out of the office and into the hallway.

Yet again, following another official without knowing where they were really going, they quietly followed their guide, hope rising in their chests. Griefold and his companions were finally making some headway in their search since they were going to speak to the commander today and not in a year as they were originally told. Hope was fleeting to them, though; they had no idea if they were going to learn the information that they were seeking or if they were just wasting more of their time.

It was only a matter of a few minutes, and they entered a different granite-walled building. Only this time, the floors were covered in fresh rushes, and the walls held fine tapestries. Continuing down the great hall of the building, the three could only marvel at the sights around them and be astonished yet again. The obvious wealth that these people displayed so openly spoke volumes about how they saw themselves. At the same time, the materials were all made of wool, marble, and other stones, with some precious metals and rough-cut jewels adorning them.

Eventually, they came to the throne room; it lay near the center of the palace and had large windows near the ceiling open to the late autumn sun. At the far end of the room was the throne, a large ornately carved chair inlaid with the same rough-cut jewels that glowed in the light. Down the center of the room were three large fire pits, currently in use, with small piles of wood merrily burning away. Sitting on the throne was a large man who would have towered over the Ameristan trio if he had stood up. He was wearing finely woven woolen robes, a rich purple in color, along with a golden circlet about his head. His hair was kept short to his shoulders and was as dark as a moonless night. Griefold and his companions assumed they were in the presence of the Emperor of Dracolia.

Tynela waved for them to stop where they were and continued to walk towards the small crowd of people standing near the throne. She approached the crowd and addressed the shortest of the women standing there. The woman that she approached wore no armor nor a weapon of any sort, only wearing a dark black tunic and trousers to show her status as the commander. After several minutes of close discussion, the woman Tynela was speaking too made a sharp cutting gesture with her hand and turned away.

Tynela returned to the waiting party and said, "Commander Marinella will see you after his Imperial Majesty has finished with the court for the afternoon. You can return with me to my office until she is ready and wait there with me. In the meantime, I will bring some food to us so that you can eat while we wait. It should only be a few hours until court ends."

Again, turning sharply, Tynela led the three armored warriors out of the throne room and back to the closed confines of her small office. There, they waited impatiently for several hours and waited for a relaxing meal later for Commander Marinella to appear.

When she finally came to the office, she entered without fanfare and, in a husky voice, said, "What do you strangers want from me? I am a very busy person and have other things to do with my time other than dealing with outlanders who don't know any better than bothering me with complaints about my Dragon Riders. Well, out with it, what do you want?"

Griefold stepped forward and said, "We are not here to complain about your riders or to take much of your valuable time, Commander. We only have a few questions about some strangers who came through here about fifteen winters ago. Is there some kind of record of them coming through here from the north and passing through the city for somewhere else within your empire?"

"Many strangers come through here all of the time; most of them do not bother to check in with me or my riders as they pass through. How could I be expected to remember some people from fifteen winters ago?"

Griefold said, "They would have stood out. There would have been three adults and a young boy with them. They also would have been moving quickly through the area and kept moving south. Also, they would have been armed like we are; we have seen that only your Dragon Riders go about armed. Does that help?"

Scratching her chin in thought, Commander Marinella said, "If I could remember such a group, why would it matter to you, and why would you be looking for them in the first place."

"They are family, and we are trying to find them and bring them back home. The little boy is my brother, and we have been looking for him for a long time now. All we want is to bring my brother home again so he can be with his family. Do you remember such a group passing through here more than ten winters ago?"

"What would it mean to you to bring your brother back to your family? I lost my brothers in battle with Zealots winters ago, and it didn't matter to me any when they died. Why would your brother mean so much to you that you would travel so far to find him? What can you do for me if I help you find him? What good will come from it for my people if you are given my help?" Commander Marinella said angrily.

In his most placating tone, Griefold said, "We have some pull with the leader of the Ameristan people. We could petition them to begin trading with you for goods and luxury items that you don't seem to have here. Would that help your people?"

Nearly snarling now, she said, "I am to believe that you have sway with your Tallantanar?! The same person who won't take an ambassador from my emperor for some unbelievable slight that supposedly happened centuries ago?!"

"For over a thousand winters, we were raided for slaves by other nations, and you expect us to forgive and let you have your way with us now. Of course, there are hard feelings, and they are not going to be stopping any time soon. If you want to talk about how we can fix those problems, then you can simply send an envoy to the Tallantanar and ask for an audience. That is what the Dantorins did fifteen winters ago, and we are now willingly trading with them for the good of both people. Why don't you just try asking instead of just getting angry with me?" Griefold replied hotly.

"Who are we to ask for anything? We are the Dracolian Empire. We have no need to ask for permission to speak with some jumped-up clan leader of some nothing nation. If we wanted to speak to you, we would tell you as much, and you should feel proud to have been asked in the first place. Now, what do I have to do to get you out of here and away from my people?" Marinella responded.

Tynela stepped in between them and said placatingly, "We Dracolians never raided for slaves. We have always tried to live peacefully with other people. The only ones we fight are the Zealots who try to make it through the passes into the other nations. Commander, why not just share with them what they want, and then they will leave like you want them to?"

Taking a deep, calming breath, Griefold said, "I feel that maybe I should tell you that I am the brother of the Tallantanar, and I carry a lot of weight with him. We are not aware that the Dracolians did not raid our people. We never stopped to ask who was attacking or where they came from.

I will tell my brother the truth and share the fact that you helped him. If you are still willing to help us, find our missing brother. We are sorry for the misunderstanding. I hope that you can see how, after many hundreds of winters without open communication, things can be misunderstood. Please just let me find my brother, and we will leave you alone."

Visibly calming herself, Commander Marinella said, "I am sorry for being so short with you. We have been having increase attacks from the south by the Bostowlians, and that has been making it very difficult for my Dragon Riders lately. I am aware of the strangers that you mentioned. There was a report made many winters ago about them, and they stand out because they never left Dracolia City. They are still here, and I can show you to them if you are still willing to speak with your brother about opening negotiations with my emperor."

A large smile spreading across his face, Griefold said, "Of course, Commander, if there is anything that I can do to make it easier for your Emperor and my brother to open negotiations, then I will. I only ask that you keep the fact of who I am between us. We do not want the fact that we are bringing our family back together again to get out. The assassins that killed our parents are still out there, and we do not know where they came from as of yet."

"I understand what you are saying, young man. I will show you where your brother and his guardians are staying and then let you decide what to do after that." Commander Marinella said. She then turned about and led the way out of the building once again. This time, the trio followed with their hearts beating fast, knowing that they were nearing their goal for the first time.

The path that Commander Marinella took them led form the palace complex deep into the city itself. The entire time, Griefold felt himself growing more excited about the prospect of being reunited with his brother for the first time in so many winters. What had changed with him? Would Blackston remember his family? Would he even know anything about his people after all of these winters apart in a different country with such different customs? All of these thoughts and many more were running through Griefold's mind as they approached the carpenter shop where his brother was currently living.

Once they neared the carpenter shop, they were stopped by a small group of Dragon Riders who were standing guard outside the building. Commander Marinella waved for the group to stop where they were and wait while she spoke with the leader of the small group of guards. After speaking with the guard for several minutes, she returned and tried to hide a smile that was forming on her face.

Commander Marinella said, "Well, it looks like your brother is currently at home entertaining a guest and cannot be disturbed. We could come back in a little while and check again to see if he is still busy."

Confused, Griefold said, "Who could he be seeing that there have to be guards to protect them and keep people away from the house?"

Unable to control herself anymore, Commander Marinella busts out laughing as she says, "Apparently, the rumors about the Imperial Princess finding herself a betrothed are true, and she is sealing her…. commitment with the young man today."

Astonished, Griefold said, "Are you serious? Do you mean to tell me that my brother is in there with your princess right now? You cannot be serious; how would they even have met? I mean, she is the princess of your country, and he is just an Ameristan living quietly in your city. Why are the guards even here? What are they supposed to be doing if they are not protecting her from strangers like he should be to her?"

Marinella continued laughing as she said, "Well, she is the youngest of the royal family and has always been headstrong. She is also the only girl, so she has been given a little too much freedom her entire life, so she has many friends outside of the palace complex. Besides, she is young, and so is your brother, I assume, since you are not exactly an old man yourself."

Griefold was fully stunned into silence by this declaration of how open the Dracolian people were with such things. In Amerista, it was not that they were close to relationships, even between two people of the same sex, but such open displays of affection were unheard of. At the same time, he was trying to find a reason not to laugh out loud at the absurdity of the situation that he found his brother in. To have come all this way to find Blackston, hoping that he was still alive and all right, only to find that his brother was now betrothed to the Imperial Princess of Dracolia. Things could not have gone any better now. All they had to do was get Blackston to return with him, and then life could get that much easier. With his hopes rising, Griefold and his companions agreed to return to the inn where they were staying until the next day, and then they would seek out Blackston once again.

***

Upon returning the next morning, the trio noticed that there were still some Dragon Riders standing guard outside of the carpenter shop where Blackston was supposed to be living. As the trio walked up, surprisingly, they were allowed to pass without being stopped by the guards this morning. Knocking on the wooden door to the building, Arten muttered something about how the guards were doing a poor job of protecting their princess from strangers.

A large Ameristan man with typical blonde hair and light-colored eyes opened the door for them. Before he could ask any questions, he looked at who was waiting for him, and his jaw dropped open in shock. Falling back several steps and stuttering out the question, "How did you find us? We have been hidden here for many winters, and no one has found us yet."

Arten said, "Be at peace, warrior. We found you because it is time for the family to be reunited and for you and your companions to return to Amerista. The High Priestesses told us to look in Dracolia, and eventually, we found you hereafter some looking and asking around. The Tallantanar has decided to have his family come home, and we are on a quest to do just that. Here is Griefold, the second brother, who is coming to bring Blackston home."

The Ameristan said, "Please be welcome in our home. My name is Carlton. Blackston is in the back having breakfast now, and the Priest Pair is with him, trying to council him out of this betrothal. We have tried for the last two winters to keep him away from the princess, but they are young, and they think that they are in love. Blackston is just as headstrong as his father was when it comes to what he wants from life. Now that the Tallantanar is bringing the family back together, he is going to have no choice but to abandon this betrothal. Surely, the princess will not willingly leave her people."

Griefold said, "I am sure that Blackston will be more than willing to break it off once he learns that we are here to bring him home again. Does he remember his people at all? Does he remember his family?"

Leading the trio into the home attached to the shop, Carlton said, "Of course, he remembers his people and his family. We have made sure that Blackston would remember where he came from and that his family loved him greatly. Tristan and Bertel have worked hard to keep the memories of our people alive within him these many winters. Blackston is a very astute student of the priest pair and has worked hard at mastering all that he could from them and from me. Blackston is a capable warrior. He is untested in battle but capable, and he is a good man, too. He has been ready to return for many winters now, and we have begun to run out of reasons to keep him out of Amerista."

Griefold said, "It is good that he is ready to return home. We have a lot of catching up to do, and I hope that he is ready."

A voice came from the back of the house saying, "Ready for what?" The voice was accompanied by a dark-haired Ameristan walking from the back of the house. He bore a strong resemblance to Griefold, so strong that it was obvious that the young man was Blackston. He had the strong build and barrel chest common to the Ameristan people, along with the same light-colored eyes. His hair was halfway down his back and dark as night, giving him his name from birth, and held in a Minnertalla braid. The fine herring bone steel chain in his braid showed obvious signs of long-term wear and polish in its shining links. The young man came to an abrupt stop upon seeing the three warriors who had come to find him. It took several seconds for Blackston to get over his shock of seeing the three warriors from his home nation before he said or did anything.

Rushing to Griefold and embracing him in a fierce hug, Blackston said, "I can't believe it is you! I never thought that I would see anyone from home again, and here you are, Griefold. I can't believe it. You got here just in time. I just got betrothed last night, and here, my big brother has come to wish me luck in my marriage!"

Griefold smiled ruefully as he said, "Actually, I am here to bring you home, Blackston. Petralis feels that it is time to bring the family back together again, and you are the first one that we have been able to find. The twins are evidently somewhere in Dantorin and Iristia, respectively. Your being here in Dracolia just made it that much easier to find you. As for being betrothed, we heard something about being betrothed to the Imperial Princess yesterday. Surely that is just a joke, right? I mean, how would her family allow you to marry her? Don't they like to keep with their own kind?"

Waving his hands dismissively, Blackston said, "Don't worry about that. She is the youngest of her family, and all of her brothers have already been married off or betrothed to the nobility of Dracolia. Princess Amelia has no such obligations; she is free to marry whomever she wants to marry; besides, we are in love. I am sure that I can talk her into coming back to Amerista with us. She has nothing to keep her here without me."

Griefold shook his head and said, "How are you so sure that she will be willing to leave her people and everything that she knows to be with you in Amerista? She is still young, and you have much to learn about each other before you can say something that is going to make such a drastic decision."

A calm voice came from the back of the house, saying, "That is because we have already discussed it before. We had already decided to leave Dracolia City before the snows fly and will find a small village to live in away from the royal court and all of the ceremony that I have grown up with." A beautiful young Dracolian woman came from the same area that Blackston had come from just a few minutes before. She had long dark hair as well and was wearing a brocade dress made of finely woven wool. She approached the Ameristans with confidence and pride in her carriage and smiled deeply at Blackston while taking his hand. Without breaking eye contact with Blackston, she said, "I am Princess Amelia, and I welcome you to Dracolia City, Griefold, my betrothed called you? I assure you that my family will be glad to have me marry someone of importance, even if it is to a member of a family outside of Dracolia. If what my aunt told me is true, then you are both brothers of the leader of the Ameristan people, and that is a lofty enough position for me to marry into. Aunt Marinella told me last night when I...finished speaking with Blackston about the family connection between all of you and how important it would be for father. She spoke with the Emperor, and he decided not to object to our marriage, provided that I correspond regularly with him. This can only benefit both of our people. With my family connections and Blackston's, we are sure to have strong ties for trade and mutual benefit. At least that is how my father put it in his message to me."

Shaking his head in disbelief, Griefold said, "I cannot believe that this is happening. I was sent to find our brother, and I succeeded in that. I also succeeded in securing another sister for the family. You are welcome to the Minnertalla of Amerista. Princess Amelia, be welcome, little sister to the Talla. How long do you think it will take you to prepare to depart? We want to be back to the Holy City before the snow flies and the plains become all but impassable with the winter storms?"

"I have only to send for a few things, and we can leave within the tenday if you so desire. I have nothing that I wish to take with me other than Blackston and a few cherished items from my rooms. Other than that, I am ready to leave already. We had planned to leave soon, as I had already told you. I will have to inform my father and mother and then see what they will demand to send with me while we travel to the border. Undoubtedly, they will insist on a guard detachment to come with me in the least."

Arten said, "That makes sense. You *are* a part of the ruling family, and the fact that they may want to keep you protected seems reasonable."

Nodding her agreement, Bernella said, "I have to agree with my brother; the more eyes watching our backs while we travel will make things that much safer."

Carlton cleared his throat before saying, "Excuse me, but the priests and I will be coming back with you as well. For too long, we have been away from our homes, and we are more than ready to return to our people. We can be ready to depart in a matter of days."

With his head spinning from all of the sudden changes to his half-thought-out plans, Griefold was finding himself at a loss for words. He never gave any thought to the protectors for his brother and sisters and how they would hopefully want to return to Amerista as well. Not only that, but they were going to have an escort to the border to help protect them from any prying eyes. This was only coming out to be a much better plan than he had originally thought about, simply taking Blackston and running as fast as they could back to the border. The larger the group, the safer they would be from any attacks, but at the same time, the more likely they were to be noticed. Yet, with a royal entourage, they would look like some kind of embassy on their way to Amerista. This would be the first from the Dracolians, so there would be some eyes on them, but they would not be looking for the few Ameristans in the group and not know their significance of them. This would work out far better than Griefold had originally planned.

CHAPTER 10

It took eleven days before the original trio of Bernella, Griefold, and Arten closed out their business with the inn and prepared to meet with Blackston. They had made arrangements to meet at the carpenter shop shortly after sunrise to begin their trek out of Dracolia City and then home. With a soaring heart, Griefold led his small party through the heart of the city to where his brother and guardians were packing their things to leave as well. Due to the early hours of the day and the lack of a large number of people on the streets, they arrived within minutes of their planned time.

Before they could so much as knock on the door to announce themselves, the wooden door swung open before them, and Carlton exited, weighed down with a large travel pack. In his hands, he carried a great bearded axe fully as long as the man was tall, with the blade nearly covering his enormous chest. The bearded axe shone dulling in the early morning light and had the look of long disuse about it, looking as if it had not seen the light of day in many winters. Even though the blade itself showed signs of disuse, the edge gleamed in the wan sunlight from a fresh sharpening and oiling.

Upon seeing the waiting trio, Carlton said, "I am ready, as are the priests. Blackston will be ready shortly. He is just finishing packing his travel pack with the last of his belongings. Fortunately, he has a few things to go through and to pack. We have always been prepared to move on if we needed too."

Arten replied, "That is good. We still have to meet up with the Imperial Princess and the guards that her father is going to be sending with her, so we need to move out very soon. We have only a few tendays until the snows fly, and we need to make as much distance as possible before then." Blackston then appeared in the doorway with the priest pair, and Blackston said, "I am as ready as I will be. Amelia said to meet her at the city gate, that she would be ready there, and that she would make sure to bring along supplies enough to see us to the Holy City."

After saying this, he hefted his pack and picked up his weapon from the shadows near the door. The bearded axe was another great axe, just like the one that Carlton carried and many Dominance users carried in Amerista. The only difference was that the bearded axe head was shining brightly in the sunlight, reflecting a rainbow hue in the metal. It was obviously his mother's former bearded axe made by his father during Patralin's time of grief after that raid. Unlike Carlton's axe, this one showed heavy signs of use in the handle and the blade itself. This was a weapon that had not sat idle for the intervening winters and saw daily use by its wielder.

Looking with some small bit of envy upon the Amersteel weapon, Griefold said, "It is good that you still have mother's bearded axe and have taken such good care of it over the winters. I have one of the Great Swords' father created back in the Minnertalla longhouse, and I am waiting for when we return. I left it behind so that I would not draw too much attention to our group as we travelled at Petralis' insistence. I hope to test you in the sparring ring while we travel to see if you are worthy of carrying such a fine weapon." Griefold then smiled and said, "Of course, that is if Arten does not beat me to the match with you first. He must be getting tired of facing me after all of this time."

Arten also smiled and said, "I am looking forward to someone else giving Griefold a challenge, and I am sure that Carlton would love to spend some time sparring with us as well."

Carlton readily agreed with this as he closed the door behind him and started to walk away from the shop he had called home for many winters. Blackston looked back for a few minutes, taking in the sight of the only place he had called home for the last fifteen winters. He sighed before he turned and began to walk away.

As they made their way to the north gate of the city, the crowds grew larger in the city streets, slowing the group as they went. When they reached the gate, the group was surprised by the number of guards and people waiting for them there. Each of the guards was a Dragon Rider on the winged variety of the creature, each as black as night and sitting restlessly for the group. There were over a dozen riders, Princess Amelia, and a small number of riderless dragons waiting for Griefold and his companions.

When they approached, Princess Amelia rushed away from the guards and threw herself into Blackston's waiting arms, saying, "I have been waiting for this day for my entire life. I am finally leaving the city, and I am leaving with the man that I love by my side. Could this be any more perfect? Father sent enough riders and dragons to fly us to the border and assured us that they would keep watch from his side of the border until we were out of sight. This will make our trip that much faster, Blackston. We could be with your family in a matter of days instead of moons like I feared."

Holding her to himself tightly, Blackston said, "I am grateful to your father for the ride, but I do not know how to ride a dragon, let alone any other kind of animal. How are we going to mount them? Never mind riding them."

Amelia let loose a tinkling laugh as she said, "Do not worry about that, my love. We brought the older dragons, who are used to training the new riders, so they are gentle, and they will not fly that far from the treetops. It is perfectly safe, and this way, we can spend more time together."

Amelia then turned and began to show Blackston how to mount and secure himself to one of the riderless dragons. In short order, all members of the party were mounted and soon flew over the treetops away from Dracolia City. They flew for several hours that first day, covering many miles before stopping near sunset to make camp for the night and to rest their mounts. They travelers who were new to dragons then learned that they would have to rest their mounts for the next two days. This was no problem for the travelers since they had covered enough miles in the one day of travel that would have taken at least four days on foot.

When they made camp for the first night, Arten cleared a large training circle and prepared to begin sparring. He said, "Blackston, enter the circle. I want to see how well you are trained and if you are really ready to fight."

Nodding his head in acceptance, Blackston stripped off his traveling leathers and picked up his bearded axe from where it sat on the ground next to him. Stepping into the sparring circle and loosening his shoulders, Blackston set himself in a ready stance to begin sparring. Arten approached him with his sword drawn, swinging it at a low angle and facing off against his opponent. With a shout, Blackston rushed towards Arten, his bearded axe whistling through the air only to stop mere inches from connecting with Arten's head. With a small smirk, Blackston stepped back again, waiting for Arten's response. Not making a sound, Arten rushed forward and began to swipe his blade at Blackston, moving his blade so fast that it blurred in the firelight. The blade was stopped once it made gentle contact with Blackston's neck without drawing a single drop of blood.

Stepping back again and returning the smirk, Arten said, "Now that we are done showing off to the crowd and your heart-mate, maybe we can get down to some serious sparring."

With a laugh, Blackston said, "Fine, I will take it a little more seriously if you insist; I just wanted to show you what I was capable of and how good I really am."

Arten nodded his acknowledgement and then began to spar with the younger man in earnest. Within minutes, the two were whirling their respective weapons in blurs of reflected fire lights glinting off the blades. Both men were breathing heavily, and sweat was running down their faces when Arten signaled for a stop in the sparring so that they could rest. As they exited the sparring circle, Arten motioned for Griefold and Bernella to take the field and begin to spar against each other.

This was not the first time that they had sparred against one another, but it was the first time that they had sparred in front of an audience. With his heart beginning to pound in anticipation, Griefold found himself facing off against the one woman who really mattered to him. His hands began to shake with a slight tremor as he drew his sword and set himself to face off against Bernella. Across the sparring circle from him, Bernella drew two of her many daggers and spun them in her hands expertly, smiling brightly at Griefold. Giving no warning, Griefold rushed at Bernella, his sword swinging at her midsection in a move that would normally bisect an opponent. With a slight step back and a bend at the waist, Bernella dodged the attempted strike and made a move with her dagger to cut across Griefold's lead inner arm. Only the sudden snap of his body away from the incoming blade prevented his blood from being spilled on his opponent's dagger. They quickly began to spar in earnest, spinning about one another as each strived to at least touch steel to skin. This went on for several minutes without either scoring a hit on the other, and their movements began to slow. With a mutual nod of assent, the two combatants lowered their weapons and stepped from the sparring circle.

Bernella smiled at Griefold as she said, "That was exciting, Griefold. I thought that I had you there at first when you tried to cut me, but you were just too fast this time.

Maybe next time, I will give you a scratch or two and show you who the better warrior is, or maybe you will score a touch or two on me instead."

Griefold replied, "I will touch you yet, Bernella. It is just a matter of time before I have my way with you."

Her face flushed slightly. Bernella whipped her body about and then left the firelight. Griefold was unsure what exactly he had said that made her so flummoxed all of a sudden and why she left so abruptly. Shrugging his shoulders in confusion, Griefold sheathed his sword and, too, turned from the circle to find a place to watch the Dragon Riders each enter the circle to spar. After several hours of sparring, the entire party turned in for the night, with the Ameristans all entering their wintons and the guard forces the tents that they had brought along. To his surprise, Bernella was not in the winton with Arten, who was sleeping soundly. Griefold did not know what to make of it.

CHAPTER 11

The cycle of riding for an entire day and then resting for several days repeated itself for the next tenday. Each night, the travelers would each take to the sparring circle that Arten had created at the campsite where they had stayed. With the priest pairing along to heal, any wounds that the combatants took were healed right away by their magic. During the entire trip, Bernella would not spar with Griefold again and did her level best to stay away from him, going as far as to sleep with the priest pair in their winton.

This left Griefold confused and a little frustrated since he thoroughly enjoyed sparring with her. At the same time, Griefold wanted to spend more time alone with her and began to doubt that she would be receptive to his feelings. All during their travels together, Griefold was certain now that he cared deeply for the red-headed warrior. He wanted to share his feelings with her, but with her refusing to spend any time alone with him, how was he able to tell Bernella about this? Frustrated beyond all measure, Griefold resigned himself to keeping his feelings to himself for the time being and working out his frustrations in the sparring circle against all comers. This increase in his sparring led to some minor injuries that were quickly dealt with by the priests, and most of the party refused to spar with him. It only led to more frustration in Griefold, who threw himself into his sparring with more vigor, a vicious cycle with no end in sight.

Seeing the frustration and anger boiling up in his older brother, Blackston took it upon himself to try to find the source. He approached Griefold one morning and said, "Griefold, whatever is eating at you is making you too dangerous to spar with. Why don't you tell me what is wrong, and we can try to work it out together like brothers?"

Griefold said, "I cannot tell you what is wrong because I have nothing to share with you, little brother. My problem is one that can only be dealt with by one person who is doing their best to avoid me at all costs. I will have to find a way to work it out and approach the problem on my own when I have the chance. Maybe after we cross the border tomorrow, we will be travelling in a smaller group."

"You do not have to wait to share what your problem is; sharing your problems with others can release some of the problems. I am sure that you truly want to share what is eating at you with me. After all, we have been apart for so long. We need to share things with one another." Blackston replied, placing one bulky arm around Griefold's shoulder.

Hanging his head in shame, Griefold said, "I know that I should not say this, but I care very deeply for Bernella. More deeply than I do for anyone else, and I do not know how to tell her that I care for her without costing our friendship in the bargain. I do not want her to distance herself from me even further and lose her respect for me as a fellow warrior. I have spent too many winters playing the fop and fool for the Dantorins, trying to place myself in their good graces. Now, I have started to earn the respect of our people again, even if it is only with Bernella and Arten for now, to risk losing it. I will tell her how I feel about her after we cross the border and have less of an audience to witness my shame when she laughs in my face."

"I do not think that you will have to worry about that at all, Griefold. She does not seem like the type of person to laugh in the face of someone who expresses their feelings to her. I am sure that you are exaggerating what will happen, and to prove it, I will make you a deal. You share your true feelings with Bernella, and I will take you to the sparring ring. I will even use Carlton's bearded axe to spar with, and we can see who the better warrior is. How does that sound?"

Griefold smiled at his brother and replied, "I will take that deal. I share with Bernella how I feel and then fight you in the ring to show you how much farther you have to go to best me in a fair fight." Smiling at each other, the brothers then parted ways to prepare for the final leg of the trip to the southern border of their homeland.

It was the following day that the combined group of Ameristans and Dracolians reached the unmarked border of the two nations. While the Dragon Riders were going to stay for a few days to let their mounts get the needed rest, the Ameristans and Amelia began to trek onto the Ameristan plains. The weather was turning colder by the day, and it was quickly advancing into mid-autumn on the plains. The grass that was waving like a bright green ocean just a few tendays earlier was now turning brown and barely moving with the wind now. There was little animal life to be found during the first few days of the trek, so the travelers were forced to rely on their cold travel rations. Griefold was not the only person to regret the fresh meat that the guards had brought along for the journey and regretted the fact that they were back to dried or smoked mutton. Remembering his promise to Blackston, Griefold tried in vain to find Bernella alone for more than a few minutes at a time to speak with her. She kept away from him and would not allow Griefold any attempt to share guard duty with her either. Bernella kept sharing the winton with the priests and would refuse to spar with anyone now that they were traveling alone. This frustrated Griefold even more and forced him to keep his thoughts to himself in a more despairing manner than before.

After nearly a tenday of travel, Amelia, who was sharing a winton with Blackston each night, became fed up with the near constant grumbling from him about Griefold not keeping his word. She decided to corner Bernella and talk with the other female about what was going on. She also decided to find out why she was avoiding Griefold so stridently.

It was during Bernella and Amelia's turn at night watch that Amelia turned on the red-headed warrior and said, "I have had enough of this. Blackston has been complaining for days now about Griefold not keeping his word about something that has to do with you. Why won't you give him a chance to speak with you in private or even with the rest of us around? He clearly wants to share something important with you, and you are not making it any easier to do that, are you, Bernella?"

Bernella sighed heavily and whispered, "It is because I love him, and I don't want to lose him. I am afraid that he wants to tell me that he does not care for me and wants to break clean with me before we get to the Holy City."

Amelia laughed aloud as she said, "You two are so foolish, you know that. It is obvious to anyone who watches you two that he is as deeply in love with you as you are with him. Every time that you would spar with another warrior in the ring, he would all but jump to his feet to come to stop the fight. He spends all of his time watching every move you make with his heart in his eyes, trying to get you to notice him. Griefold is far too much in love with you to want to break things off before they have even begun."

Shocked, Bernella said, "How can you be so sure? Griefold is so quiet about his emotions now; he is a perfect Ameristan warrior like that. You cannot tell what he is feeling or thinking. He is a total blank even when in the heat of battle, and when he made that comment about having his way with me…...surely, he was only joking."

Still laughing, Amelia responded, saying, "I can tell because I look at Blackston the same way that Griefold looks at you, and Blackston does the same to me. As for the comment, I do believe that his tightly kept feelings were slipping out just a little, and he was showing how he cares for you. If you would only let him share with you how he feels, then you would know, and this charade could be over with. When he comes to relieve us, you stay here and talk to him for once; do not let your fear overcome you and destroy your chance at happiness."

Nodding her head in acceptance, Bernella stared out into the night and let her thoughts drift off into possible futures with Griefold. She was so focused on those possible futures that she nearly did not notice Griefold approaching her from the camp. Bernella spun around onto her feet with her hands reaching towards her daggers before she saw who it was.

Griefold came up to Bernella and took a deep breath before he said, "Bernella, I have to share something with you. It is important, and I need you to listen to me and let me finish what I have to say before you try to stop me. You see, I need to tell you how I feel about someone, and I am afraid that they will not share my feelings in return…."

Before Griefold could finish his sentence, Bernella placed a delicate finger on his lips and said, "I know, and I love you too. I have been afraid to tell you how I feel and that you would not return my feelings back. After all, you do have a reputation back in the city with the Dantorins, and how you spent so much time with them left an impression for which you had already spoken."

"I never did anything with any of them," Griefold responded, blushing, "I only let them think that they were going to get somewhere with me. I only did it to keep people at a distance since so many people wanted to have me speak into Petralis' ear in their favor on so many things. It made it easier for me to let them think that they would get what they wanted from me and keep them distant from my brother."

"Well, it worked. Everyone thinks that you are a drunken fool who would do anything to keep the Dantorin women and the ambassador pleased."

"I am glad that is the impression that I have given everyone. It makes it easier to keep them away from Petralis and let him deal with them on his own terms to help our people better. Sometimes, I went too far with the wine and let some of what they said go to my head, and I have done and said things that hurt Petralis and our people. For that, I cannot ever make amends." Griefold said, hanging his head in despair.

Bernella wrapped her arms around Griefold and held him to her tightly. She placed her lips on his in a gentle kiss. This was the first time that anyone had kissed him since his mother had died, and it shocked him to the core. Feelings of passion for Bernella began to sweep through Griefold as he leaned into the kiss and deepened his response to her. It was like sparks of lightning between the two of them as their hands began to roam over each other. Before they could do anything further, they were interrupted by someone clearing their throat loudly from the camp.

Snapping their heads to the sound with guilty expressions writ large across their faces, Griefold and Bernella saw Carlton standing with his back to the camp watching them. Carlton said, "If you two children are done, I believe that Griefold and I have the watch for now and that we should be watching and not doing whatever it was you were doing. Don't you agree, Griefold?"

Blushing furiously enough to match the rising sun, Griefold sheepishly separated himself from Bernella and said, "You are right, Carlton; it is time for Bernella to get some rest as it is, so we will continue our discussion at a later time. Sorry to keep you from your rest, Bernella. Please get some rest for now, and we can talk some more tomorrow." Without saying a word, Bernella turned and, as fast as a thought, ran to her winton to turn in for the night. Once she was out of sight, Carlton smiled broadly as he tunelessly whistled his way out of the firelight and into the shadows surrounding the camp.

Despite the silence that was kept between the three warriors about what had happened during the night, the secret seemed to get out to the rest of the travelers. Within hours of setting out with the rising sun, sly comments and looks were passed between all members of the party as they walked across the plains. The snickers and looks were more than enough to cause the two young people endless amounts of embarrassment throughout the day. By the time they stopped for the day, the party was so tired of smiling that their faces hurt from it. At the same time, the two members of the party who were the subject of so much fun were flushed from head to toe with embarrassment.

Before they even had a chance to set up camp for the night, Blackston grabbed Carlton's bearded axe and said, "It is time for us to spar, Griefold. You have put it off long enough. It is time to see which one of us is the better warrior and settle this once and for all. Into the circle with you now."

Griefold drew his sword, stripped off his armor, and wordless entered into the hastily made circle for sparring. He waved for Blackston to enter after him and waited patiently for his opponent to prepare himself for combat. This fight was going to be a rough one for the two brothers since they intended to fight until one or the other yielded to the better warrior. Since both young men were so head strong, this could likely lead to some bloodshed between the two, and the spectators were hoping that it would not be too much.

Within seconds, the two brothers were fighting in earnest, asking and giving no quarter as they swung and struck at one another. Shortly after the battle started, there was small cuts on each of the combatants, slowly bleeding and making the fight that much more intense. While they were not out to kill or maim one another, they were doing their level best to fight for all they were worth. Blackston's black hair whirled around his head as he swung his borrowed bearded axe in a deadly arc directed at his brother. Griefold dodged easily, returning the strike with his sword and leaving a small cut on Blackston's brow that quickly began to bleed into his eyes. This minor blow was enough of an edge for Griefold to end the fight in short order in his favor. The blood flow hindered Blackston from seeing what was coming next as Griefold leaned in and planted a solid kick to the back of Blackston's knee.

When Blackston fell to his knees, Griefold placed his sword against Blackston's neck and demanded, "Yield, Blackston! I have you!"

Blackston dropped the bearded axe and slowly raised his hands, saying, "I yield, brother. I never thought that you would be able to take me in a fight. I see now that I have much to learn about using dominance against you. Someday, I may be better than you, but that is not today. So, how did Bernella react when you told her how you truly feel about her? Is it true that they had to hold you up to keep you from falling flat on your face?"

The spectators all began to laugh at the look on Griefold's face as the priest pair moved in to heal the brothers from the combat. Bernella said nothing, only flushing again, this time turning so red that the heat radiated from her face.

When they turned in for the night, Griefold had the first watch with Bernella. They spent the entire time trying to avoid eye contact with one another to better focus on the job at hand. The two warriors kept sneaking glances at each other, only to look away when the other started to notice. This shy eye contact and the nearness of the one that they cared for so much drove them to distraction. Both were more than happy to return to their respective wintons when the watch changed.

The group decided to give Griefold and Bernella more time alone while they traveled, but to keep them separated during the watch. This, in turn, led to the two young warriors spending many hours with each other while they walked. The time that they spent talking and simply looking into one another's eyes for hours on end. The looks that they gave one another were so sweet-looking and of such a level of happiness that the remainder of the group did not know what to do. There were a few who wanted Griefold and Bernella to just get on with their courtship and do something to get it out of their systems. The other members of the group simply wanted to watch the two show expressions of their love for one another. Blackston and Amelia fell into the latter group due to their own devotion to one another and wanting to see Griefold and Bernella happy. Carlton and the priests were of the former group, getting sick of the sight of the looks and the obvious sweetness that was evident. Arten was just happy to let Griefold and Bernella just be as they were since both were his friend and sister, respectively, and he wanted them to be happy while they could. Arten knew that they lived dangerous lives, having served on the front lines in many a battle, and knew that even a little bit of happiness could be fleeting.

For several more tendays, they traveled through the dormant plains of Amerista. The grass continued to brown, and the wildlife was nowhere to be found, having moved onto their own wintering grounds. Each morning, there was more of a bite to the air, and on some occasions, there was even frost on the ground. The weather continued to cool, and the days shortened as they continued to march further northward. The few trees that were to be found on their trek were almost entirely bare of leaves and losing what leaves there were as the company watched. Wishing that they had brought along warmer clothing for the trip, the entire group would turn into their wintons earlier each night to try and save what little warmth they could.

It was nearly a moon and a half left of their travels before the first snow started to fly late one morning. The snow did not stay around for long, but it was a definite sign that winter had arrived and their time was running out with haste. If they did not reach the Holy City within the next tenday or so, they were going to have to fight their way through snow drifts and freezing weather. This was not a pleasant prospect for the travelers since they were beginning to run low on supplies and were having trouble trying to find food to sustain them. Griefold was not the only one to grumble about having a near-empty stomach on more than a few occasions during this part of the trip. They each took such grumbling in stride as part of traveling during such a harsh time of the year.

After nearly six moons of travel to and from Dracolia City, Griefold, Arten, Bernella, and the rest returned to the

Holy City. It was a most welcome sight for the travelers as they saw the wooden palisade surrounding the city come into view early one afternoon. All the travel finally came to fruition for the group, and for the first time in many winters, Blackston, Carlton, and the priest pair returned to their people. Amelia was just as glad to finally see the city and know that their long travel was finally over.

As the group neared the city, the gates were opened for them by the waiting Griffon Riders manning the gate that day. They were welcomed home with much enthusiasm by the people who were not busy at the time, and they were greeted with loud cheers and much celebrating. The sounds of the crowds cheering for the wayward travelers spread through the city like wildfire; soon, Petralis and greatly pregnant Mirta found the travelers.

Upon seeing his brother for the first time in many moons, Griefold broke free of the crowds and rushed to Petralis. Griefold said, "Petralis, I have found Blackston. He has returned with us and has brought us a new sister as well. They were to be wed before the first snow flew in Dracolia City, but they decided to return with us to Amerista before that happened."

Blackston broke free of the crowds himself, Amelia in tow, and approached his oldest brother, saying, "Petralis, I barely remember you, but I am glad to be here. Let me introduce my betrothed…heart-mate, Imperial Princess Amelia of the Dracolian Empire. Amelia, my love, let me introduce you to my oldest brother, Petralis II Tallantanar of the Ameristan people."

Amelia smiled at the blond leader of the Ameristan people and curtsied deeply before saying, "I am so glad to meet you. My father, the Emperor, wishes to share his greetings with you as well, Tallantanar Petralis. I have come here to Amerista and your Holy City not only to wed your brother and join our families but to open negotiations with you on behalf of the Dracolian Empire. My father wishes to send an ambassador here to treat with you and to open talks on many things that will be beneficial to both our nations."

Petralis was taken aback for a few seconds by all of the introductions. He said, "I am pleased to meet you, Princess Amelia. I am more than pleased to know that you are going to be my brother Blackston's heart-mate. Blackston, please excuse the crowd, but our people are more than happy to finally see you after all of these winters. I want to introduce you to my heart-mate, Mirta. She is pregnant with our first child, as you can see."

Mirta stepped forward and embraced Blackston, then a shocked Princess Amelia said, "I am the mate of Petralis. Please call me Mirta. I am so happy to meet you both. Please be welcome in our home."

Amelia said, "Thank you, Mirta. I was not aware of how to address you and your…. mate. I am used to addressing my father as Your Majesty, but I am not used to the informal use of names that you have here. It is going to take some getting used to for me to address you in such a way. I see that you are pregnant. How long will it be until the happy day of your first child?"

"It will be moons yet," Mirta replied, smiling happily, "I only hope that he or she will be healthy and strong."

"I can understand that I am the youngest of eighteen in my family, and we were all healthy at birth, according to my mother."

While the two women continued to make small talk with one another about the vagaries of pregnancy and life as part of a ruling family, Petralis took Blackston and Griefold off to one side to talk. Petralis said, "Blackston, it is so good to finally see you after all of this time. I hope that you are all right after traveling so far this time of the year. We are about to have the Tallanta meeting in a few days. They will be proud to meet you and to see that you are well. As for the impending, what did you call it…wedding? We can make arrangements with the Aunts for them to perform the mating ceremony. First, let me take you to the Minnertalla longhouse so that you and your heart-mate can settle in and warm up. We will have a lot of catching up to do during this winter."

Griefold only listened with half of his mind on what his brothers were saying. He was focused on Bernella as she tried to ease her way out of the crowd. Only the fact that her flaming red hair was so rare among the Ameristans was the only way for him to track her. Leaving his brothers behind, Griefold followed Bernella. She left the others behind and made her way to the longhouse that was set aside for the Griffonara. He had never entered the elite warrior's longhouse and almost hesitated to do so now out of respect for them. However, he wanted to speak with Bernella and was not going to be dissuaded from this decision.

Without even stopping at the door, he followed her in and said, "Bernella, I want to ask you to come live with me in the Minnertalla longhouse. It is only Blackston, Amelia, and me now, and I do not want to be apart from you ever again. I love you, Bernella. I cannot stand the thought of you being away from me anymore, and I don't want you to live as if you were not a part of my life."

Bernella turned and smiled at Griefold, tears forming in her eyes. She said, "Of course, I will come with you to your Talla's longhouse. I want nothing else than to spend all my time with you; only you have to make room for Harton, my griffon. We have been apart long enough now, and I need to reassure him that I still care for him and keep him from going feral."

"Arrangements can be made for you to care for your griffon. I will do anything to keep you close to me, Bernella." Griefold replied. "There is no one living in the longhouse but me since Petralis assumed his role as Tallantanar a few winters ago. It needs a good airing out, and I need to clean it up a little bit. I am ashamed of the way I was living there and having the ambassador and his entourage nearly every night."

Bernella said, "I will help you with that. Just give me a couple of hours to get my things ready, and then we will be able to settle in. As for the time that you spent with the ambassador, that will be something of the past, and there is no need for you to fall back into old habits."

With a guilty smile playing across his face, Griefold only shrugged his shoulders in defeat and then turned to head to his family's longhouse. Once he reached the Minnertalla longhouse, Griefold began cleaning and airing out, which was long overdue. Pleasant thoughts of the near future kept running through his head, keeping a smile on his face. With things beginning to work out for him in his personal life, Griefold felt that maybe he could change and become a better man. One that would make his father proud of him.

CHAPTER 12

Tendays passed as things began to settle into the winter season for the Ameristan people. They had come together as they always did in the Holy City for the winter when trading commenced between the Talla. As well as the few Dantorins who made the perilous journey through the Ocean of Fire during the winter storms. Once again, this winter, the Iristians had sent a trade delegation to the Holy City to trade their goods for steel. The Iristians had not sent a trade delegation for a few winters now, and the chance to receive the fabric that could only be found among the people from across the Sun's Dagger Mountains created a high demand. The cotton and silks that the Iristians used for trade were also in high demand by the Dracolians, who had sent their own trade envoy this winter for the first time. The trading by the three nations was brisk and helped to ease the tensions between all those attending for the first time in many winters. This season, the Ameristan people had more reasons to celebrate, with the return of Blackston and the impending birth of the next Tallantanar in the coming moons. Things seemed to be finally going right for the Ameristan people; their overall hopes for a brighter future seemed to be coming true.

Griefold and Bernella settled into a comfortable life together, living in the Minnertalla longhouse. They spent many hours together getting to know one another in all ways that a mated couple could. Even though he asked her many times, Bernella refused to go through the mating ceremony to make them a bonded pair. Bernella kept making excuses that were perfectly reasonable to Griefold, yet he was still insistent that they become a pair. This was the only point of contention between the two and sometimes put a strain on their relationship. Rarely did a day pass that did not end with the pair having a heated discussion about it, but they always calmed down and settled the argument before they went to sleep each night.

It was late into the winter, nearly spring before Petralis and Mirta were presented with the birth of their first child, a girl that they named Bealdhild. She would be the future leader of the Ameristan people, taking her place as Tallantanar when the time came. She was a healthy babe and was the apple of the eye of every Ameristan. They were proud to have another Minnertalla child added to the nation and the continuance of the line of the Tallantanar. While the High Priestesses were happy about the recent birth of the next Tallantanar, they were concerned about how little effort the brothers were putting into finding their sisters.

Several days after the birth of Bealdhild, the High Priestesses called the Minnertalla clan to go to the temple of Amerton for a discussion. Once there, the three young men seemed to be not paying attention to what the discussion was about. Each one had their thoughts on the women in their lives and what they were going to be doing in the future.

The High Priestess waited patiently while the young men talked about the new child and how their individual relationships were doing. After several minutes of senseless chatter, the twins said, "We did not bring you here to talk to you about your relationships with your mates, or in Griefold's case, his lack of a mate. We called you here to find out what your plans are for finding Arista and Aristin. The girls have been separated from their people for most of their young lives. It is imperative to find them and bring them home. We have already told you that they were in Dantorin and Iristia. What are you going to do about it then, wait until they are old and grey, having known nothing of their people or their true family?!"

The three brothers just sat there dumbfounded by what their aunts said to them about waiting to look for the missing twin sisters. All three men exchanged sheepish glances between them and then looked at the High Priestesses with the same looks.

Petralis looked at his brothers and then at his aunts and said, "Sorry, aunties, I have just been so excited about the birth of Bealdhild that I have completely lost track of important things. I will try to focus more on our people and do what is necessary for the betterment of our people. Once the spring thaw is upon us, I will task Griefold and Blackston with trying to find the girls and do what we need to get them home at long last."

Both nodding their agreement, Griefold and Blackston began speaking at once, trying to assure their aunts that they would be working hard to find their missing family. The two of them spoke rapidly at one another and to their aunts, and no one could get in a word between them.

Raising their right hands in unison, the High Priestesses interrupted the young men and said, "Come this spring, it will be time to head out and begin the search where it left off. We would recommend trying to get to Dantorin first since we have established trade with the Dantorin people. They sail their ships on the seas instead of trying to fight their way through the jungles of the Bostowlian zealots. There should be at least one captain who will agree to take you to their homeland and return with you and whichever of your sisters you find. This will be a much safer trip to take, according to the Dantorin Ambassador, once the winter storms have stopped and the sailing becomes safer. It is a journey of many tendays from our shoreline to the Dantorin coast. Griefold and Blackston, you will be travelling as escorts for the new Ameristan Ambassador to Dantorin. Once she has arrived, you will be free to do what is necessary to find your sister and bring her home again. In the meantime, Petralis will work on the Dracolians to put some further pressure on the Zealots and work on ending the raids. Do you have any questions for us at this time, nephews?"

Rising to their feet, the young men shook their heads in the negative about having questions and then began to leave the temple. Petralis turned to leave as well when he was stopped by the High Priestesses and was told to wait a few minutes. Leading Petralis deeper into the temple, the twins took him into the private areas that served as living quarters for the priests and High Priestesses.

Once out of sight of anyone else, the women turned on their nephew and, speaking in unison, said," Tallantanar, we need you not to go on this search for your sisters. The first time your brother left, you stayed here for the birth of your daughter and the safety of your mate. This time, you must stay here to be on hand to deal with the new Ambassadors from the Dracolians. This is much too important to be left to your mate or any of the Tallanta who are willing to step forward. We have seen either disaster or peace for the people of Amerista depending upon this one turning point. Amerton has spoken to us, and you have to make the right decisions with repercussions for many winters to come. We know how much you want to bring your family together again, but your place is not searching for your sisters. It is with your mate raising your daughter."

Nodding in acceptance, Petralis turned to leave after his brothers and said, "I understand what you are saying, aunts. I just hope that they are ready and able to find our sisters before too much longer. I want to save our family since we are all that is left of the Minnertalla. It is time to show the rest of the world that we are not going to be so easily cast to the winds of time and forgotten."

Having said that, Petralis left the residential area of the temple and began walking to the longhouse of the Tallantanar, where his small family resides. He was determined to do his best to keep his word about working with the new ambassador from the Dracolian Empire as well as his brother's new mate. Since Blackston and Amelia had moved into the longhouse of the Minnertalla with Griefold and Bernella. Not willing to let the two young women be alone in the longhouse for the many tendays of travel for their mates coming upon them, Petralis was going to ask them to come with him and his family in the Tallantanar longhouse. They had the room, and being close to those closest to his brothers would help him deal with the stress of being a leader for many people.

Petralis knew he would have to be very firm with Bernella about not going south with Griefold. The fact that they shared a bed and the fact that they were not mated yet had to be thought of as well. While he cared for Bernella like a sister, there had to be no distractions for Griefold and Blackston while they searched for their sisters. If the brothers brought along the women that they loved and something were to happen to them, there would be no telling what the men's reactions would be. Arten would accompany them on this part of the quest. Meanwhile, Petralis would have time to send some Ameristans to Iristia to look for rumors about his sister. The small delegation of traders that were to follow the Iristian traders back to the desert was also tasked with finding any rumors or stories about the missing girl. Knowing the purpose of their search, the young traders were ready to leave and were excited by the prospect of being the ones who brought her home. Whichever one she proved to be.

Since this was the first time that the Ameristans had sent a trade delegation to the desert-dwelling people. This was, to be sure, the most exciting journey for the traders, being the first to see the endless plains of grass, oases, and sand that supported life in the desert country.

Since the winter trading season for the Iristians was coming to a close with the onset of spring, both parties were prepared to leave immediately. With the shortness of time that the Ameristans had to ready to leave, the Iristians were impressed. It took only a matter of minutes for the wintons to be packed away and the packs to be readied for the long journey ahead of them. With more than a few well-wishers coming to see the young Ameristans off, it was nearly midday before the two parties was finally able to take their leave. Little fanfare followed as the trading groups left the Holy City and headed for the hidden mountain pass to the west. It would be a long journey for all involved, yet they were optimistic about the chance to see another nation and help the family of the Tallantanar.

CHAPTER 13

With one party searching in Iristia, the second group to head was going to be led by Griefold and Blackston in the coming tendays. Once spring was fully upon them, the Griefold's group would be heading for the coastline in the east to find a ship with the Dantorins that would take them to their homeland.

Griefold spent days arguing with Petralis II about bringing Bernella with him for this part of the search. Griefold did not want to spend any more of his time without her by his side. He thought that Bernella felt the same, but when he tried to get the woman he loved to side with him, she declined, saying that it was not her place to go against the wishes of the Tallantanar despite her own feelings about it. This did not sit well with the lovestruck young warrior and made him feel that his relationship with the fierce warrior woman was only one way. The fact that she refused to become his mate made things hard for the young lovers, and it became worse. Griefold resignedly decided that his brother was right and that some time spent apart might be a good thing for their relationship.

While Griefold and Petralis fought over Bernella staying back, Blackston had to try to reason with his young bride for her to remain behind as well. It was obvious to many that the young couple were going to be expecting their first child in the coming moons. While Blackston and Amelia had not gone through the ceremony for the mate bonding of the Ameristans, they were still mated in their own opinion.

Despite her swelling belly, Amelia persisted in arguing that she would not be separated from her mate. This was their first point of contention as a mated pair, and it was not easy for either one to give in. Both had their own opinions about what Amelia should or should not do while she was carrying their first child. Blackston was more concerned that the time that they had to spend at sea could endanger the child or Amelia. Amelia was more concerned about Blackston missing the birth of his first child. He was torn between familial obligations and what he felt was a higher purpose to find his hidden sisters. This was not going to be an easily dealt with problem. After several days of arguing between the two, Blackston decided to go on the search for his sister, and Amelia decided that she would stay. The risk to the baby was too much to deal with since she was learning how to be an Ameristan from her new family and acting as a temporary ambassador for her father. The permanent ambassador was due to arrive late in the spring and would need to be taught about the minutia of the Ameristan people. This did not sit well with the willful princess, but she hoped that it would work out the way that she expected it to.

If the new ambassador was on schedule with his staff and guards, then they would be in place in a matter of tendays. Once they had arrived, Amelia would have the chance to step back and allow them to take over. The baby would not be due for some moons into the summer. The passing over of duties would come at the perfect time. This small hope kept Amelia firm in Blackston's and her own decision for her to stay where it was safe. Disappointing as it would be for the first-time father to possibly miss out on the birth, something bigger had to take precedence. Reuniting the family was finally at hand. It would take some time, but the evil wrought that day so long ago was not forgotten and would be wiped from the face of the planet. The entire Minnertalla clan, what was left of it, were more than ready to find the Iramians and put an end to them. The Ameristan people were also eager to destroy such a grave threat and protect their people.

Despite the overall goal of finding the missing Arista or Aristin, the group that was preparing to set sail in a matter of days was anxious to leave. Griefold, Blackston, and Arten put aside any fear of going out upon the ocean with the drive to find the girls pounding through their hearts. While the search for the girls was of higher importance, Blackston was not taking the separation from his mate and future child at all well. The first couple of days, we traveled into the east, where the only safe harbor along the sheer cliff sides was to be found. The entire coastline of Amerista was sheer ragged cliffs and was home to millions of sea birds for the mating season. There was only one small inlet that led to the ocean and was sheltered by protruding rock spires that kept even the foolhardiest captain from trying to land ashore. The beach area where the group was headed hosted the small village of Ameristans, who worked as guardians on the first line of attack by the Iramians. While the Zealots always came from the south, and to the north was nothing but rugged snow-covered tundra, logic dictated that the Iramians had to have been coming for the sea. With the inclusion of the fortifications begun under Patrallin still taking shape, the guardians had not had any instances of Iramians trying to make it to shore.

The Dantorins were the only people to come by sea since the time of the previous Tallantanar, and they were almost entirely traders looking to do business. With no navy of their own, the Ameristans relied solely on the Dantorins to protect the surrounding waters. This was not an ideal situation to be in, yet the Ameristans had to hope for the best and prepare for the worst. The ten-day long journey from the Holy City was slow going since the group of travelers was weighed down with trade goods and thirty castrated aurochs that Griefold and his party were using as a cover. The hope was that if there were any spies looking for the searchers, they would overlook a small group of Ameristans trying to sell out their sword arms and livestock. It was under this guise that Blackston, Griefold, and Arten all wore their braids of the Himlatalla with the inclusion of gryphon feathers to further throw any observers onto another track.

Once the traders had made it to the small port village, the trio were more than a little anxious about how they were going to get the aurochs aboard the waiting ship. They had spent the last two days of travel arguing amongst themselves about how it was going to work. The idea that seemed to have the most merit was for them to somehow push the auroch into the sea and have ropes or something similar hoist the livestock up onto the ship. The other options were not thought out either since neither of the three had ever seen a ship, let alone seen the ocean before. If it proved too difficult to transport their livestock, then they would have to create another excuse for going to Dantorin. This option was not as popular amongst the three men, with each arguing, with each insisting that his plan had more merit and a greater chance of working.

Blackston, having grown up in Dracolia, had the idea that they pass themselves off as swords for hire, heading to Dantorin in search of work. This was *not* a popular alternative to being traders with the other two men. Being a sword for hire, even in name only, did not sit well with Arten or Griefold. They felt that any warrior who would fight for the highest bidder was someone who severely lacked any kind of honor. Neither Arten nor Griefold had a better suggestion to try and were at a loss to come up with an alternative. Finally, they came to an agreement that if the trio could not get the steers upon the ship, then they would do their best to look like swords for hire. Secrecy had to be maintained for the protection of the searchers as well as the young woman that they would be looking for in Dantorin.

Much to the surprise and immense relief of the trio, there were multiple Dantorin trading ships resting against a large wooden structure going from the beach into the waters with the ships tied to it.

Arten looked at the construction and asked, "What is that thing that the ship is tied to?"

The lead Dantorin trader said, "That my young friend is called a dock. They are used for ships to tie to and aid in the loading and unloading of cargo from ships. Since your people did not have any idea to do. Loading your livestock onto the ship will go very smoothly and quickly once they are ready to board."

"They are not our livestock. The aurochs are Amerton on earth, given to us to follow their ways and to protect. We only take what we need from the herds to sustain ourselves and allow the herd to grow stronger." Arten replied hotly.

Before further words could be exchanged between Arten and the Dantorin, Griefold laid a hand on each man's shoulder and said, "We all share desire for peace and prosperity between our people, and at the same time. If you let the trader have his beliefs that the auroch is nothing but simple animals, Arten, then you would know peace. Trader, if you allow us our teachings by Amerton and please do not refer to the holy aurochs as being owned by our people in our hearing, I believe that we can keep the bloodshed to a minimum."

All of the color suddenly drained from the Dantorin trader's face as he suddenly remembered all the stories. That the Ameristan warriors were known for their short tempers and deadliness with their chosen weapons, he quickly began to sputter apologies to the two warriors facing him and quickly backed away towards his ship.

After the trader was out of earshot, Griefold let out a loud belly laugh that he had been holding in upon seeing the trader's face change color so quickly. "Now, you see. If you had just growled a little more at him, you could have sent him scurrying back to his ship screaming in terror instead of just soiling his pants."

Tears of constrained laughter were forming in the corners of Arten's eyes as he, too, began to relax and realize how much of a fool he had been. Indeed, the look on the face of the Dantorin had been worth the admonishment from his friend. With barely contained laughter, Arten said, "Maybe

I should go make it up to him. He does have a pretty set of eyes. I have heard some stories about those Dantorin sailors and their bed habits that I would like to try out sometime if I were ever to get a chance." This last part was said to Griefold with a sly look in Arten's eyes.

Blushing, Griefold sputtered, "I wouldn't really know anything about that. I have tried to be as friendly as possible to our Dantorin guests in the past. I have nothing to say about their bed habits, as you put it. I only know that their women folk are extremely friendly and outgoing at all of the gatherings that I have been to."

Arten wrapped his arm around Griefold's shoulders and said in a low whisper, "Don't worry, your secret is safe with me. I know how you truly feel about my sister, and I know that she feels the same about you, well, most of the time. If you two would only get over yourselves and do something about it, then you would be a very happy couple."

Griefold roughly shoved Arten's arm away from him with a deepening blush on his face, and words muttered too softly to be heard clearly. He then began to walk to the most prosperous-looking Dantorin trader who was waiting on the dock to see who would be interested in hiring them all on to sell swords as well as take on their small herd of aurochs. The Dantorins were rumored for their desire to hire Ameristan warriors for their trade caravans and transport ships.

Griefold felt some trepidation as he approached the first merchant on the newly built docks. This would be the first time that he had dealt with the Dantorins as other than the potential next leader of his people. Ever since he had that eye-opening fight with Petralis about how he had been acting and the fact that there was new blood in the line of succession, Griefold knew he had been acting the fool for many winters. This would be the time for him to show Petralis that he could be a true warrior of the Minnertalla and stop bringing shame upon himself.

The first few merchants that Griefold approached would not even acknowledge his presence and walked away from him as he approached. He was growing nervous about finding a way to Dantorin by ship when he came upon the final merchant who was standing at the end of the dock talking with a ship's captain about trying to leave as soon as possible. The ship's captain was explaining to the merchant that it was impossible to leave as soon as the merchant wanted to since the cargo was not fully loaded yet and would take several more hours.

As Griefold approached the bickering Dantorins, the merchant said, "I hired you and your ship since you were supposed to be the fastest out of all the traders who ply these waters. I want to set sail today, not tomorrow or the next day. I have deadlines to keep back home, and this special order of auroch is to be delivered to our king, or I am going to be ruined. If the auroch dies in transit, there will be no way for me to ever recover from the cost of this trip financially. How long will it take for you men to finish loading the ship and get us underway?"

The frustrated ship's captain sighed heavily and said, "It is not a matter of how fast my men can load the ship. It is the cargo itself that is causing the problem. These aurochs are not like the pigs and goats we are used to ferrying in trade; they are much bigger and require much more space to keep healthy. What do you want me to do? Most of my sailors are busy helping the carpenter in the hold and making the necessary adjustments for your cargo, and the rest are too busy loading the provisions that we will need for the trip home. Unless you want to be drinking seawater instead of water or anything else, you will have to wait until we can get the cargo bay fixed to meet your needs, and then my sailors can move on to loading the rest of our cargo."

Seeing an opportunity, Griefold approached the two men and said, "Maybe my companions and myself can help you with both of your problems, captain and sir merchant. We are looking to book passage as we sell swords to Dantorin for personal reasons and would be willing to lend some strong backs in loading the provisions needed in exchange for passage and a little bit of coin. We also have aurochs to trade, healthy younger bulls that were culled from the herds."

Both men turned to look at the warrior before them and ran their eyes respectively over his large frame and blonde-haired head. The merchant had had dealings with the Talla of the Ameristans before when striking his deals with the leaders for access to the aurochs he was currently trying to ship. The merchant could tell that the broad-shouldered warrior before him was of the Himlatalla people and that the other three warriors who were waiting for their leader were of the same clan, or Talla as they called it. The merchant quickly searched his memory about this specific clan and for what the clan was known. The griffon feathers were from the mountains, and this was also a sign of Talla, which was made up of smiths and weaponsmiths. The Himlatalla were not known for being the best weaponsmiths; that used to be the Minnertalla, he believed the rumors claimed. It did not matter, though, that Ameristan warriors were strong, fast, and very, very deadly in a fight with their chosen weapons. These three warriors would go a long way in showing the king how he had favor with the Ameristan people and maybe earn him more sway in the court.

The merchant said, "My name is Lord Elmintareth. I would love to hire you three for guard reasons and pay you handsomely for accompanying me on this journey to my homeland. I have had dealings with several of your Tallanta in order to acquire some aurochs to grace my kings' holdings and table. I believe that you three are of the Himlatalla clan and that your people are known for their metal work and weapons creations, am I right?"

Griefold smiled tightly and calmly responded to the misconceptions that the Dantorin merchant had about what he had just said to the warriors standing before him. Griefold said, "We are Himlatalla, and you may have spoken with several of the Tallanta of our people for permission to take some aurochs, but since the aurochs are sacred to Amerton, the permission to take them can only come from the High Priestesses. The aurochs that would have been chosen to share out with you are going to be the old, lame, and infirm of the herds, as well as being castrated. Our aurochs are younger, castrated as well, but in better condition. Never fear though, I am sure that your, King is it, will enjoy the sight and taste of the flesh of the holy animals."

Before the merchant could respond to Griefold, the ship's captain stepped between them and said, "MY SHIP means that I choose who can and cannot board her. I do not agree with you bringing on these warriors without getting some kind of compensation for it. They are going to mean more mouths to feed and more freshwater. I want to see some more coin coming from you before I will even think about letting them come near my ship or my cargo!"

Lord Elmintareth turned to the captain and calmly said, "Of course, Captain Meltern, I will pay extra for these fine young warriors and provision them myself for the trip back to Dantorin. And did you not hear that they are volunteering to help load your cargo so that we can set sail before nightfall as we had originally agreed?"

Captain Meltern looked over Griefold and his companions with a withering eye and grumbled under his breath for a few moments before saying, "Alright, they can board the ship as long as they move fast and load the rest of my cargo and stay out of the way of my men. We have a lot to do to get underway before sunset like you want." Turning to look directly at Griefold, the captain said, "Well, what are you three waiting for? Get to loading my ship, check in with the bosun for where everything goes and get moving. I will get your names later, and the bosun will find you someplace to sleep after we get underway." He then turned on his heel, dismissing the three warriors without a backward glance, and began to bellow orders to his men, calling for the bosun to show the Ameristans what to do.

Griefold and his two companions were not sure what a bosun was and were waiting with lost looks on their faces until a man who was shorter than an average Ameristan, and nearly as wide as he was tall came up to them. The man shouted at the Ameristans, saying, "I am the bosun, and you will be following my orders, or you will feel the lash of my whip no matter how dangerous you think you are! Start loading those casks of water there into the ship, go down into the hold, and the men down there will show you where to put them. When you finish with that, come find me, and I will tell you what to load next! Don't dawdle, or you will feel my lash; now get moving!"

With a collective shrug of their shoulders, Griefold, Arten, and Blackston started to move the large casks of freshwater onto the ship in preparation for departure in the coming hours. The three spent several hours loading barrels and crates onto the ship as directed by the bosun without complaint. They knew that they were going to have to prove themselves to the sailors and the ship's captain in order to gain some respect. They also all knew that the merchant was only trying to take advantage of them as Ameristans for future dealings with their people. Griefold knew deep down in his soul that it was the only reason that the emissaries spent so much time with him while he was growing up. Looking back at what he had done and how he had acted around the Dantorins now gave him great shame and made it hard for him to look his people in the eye. Even though it had been more than a winter since the fight with Petralis in the longhouse, Griefold still felt that he had not redeemed himself in the eyes of his brother. Maybe if he were successful in bringing back his sisters, then he would feel as if he had redeemed himself. With this upcoming voyage to Dantorin, there would be a good chance for him to find at least one of the two girls. He did not remember them at all, considering how young they all had been when they were separated. All he knew was that there was at least one of the original griffon riders and a priest paired with her. Those guardians would have ensured that his sister would have been kept safe from almost any danger and that she was taught the ways of her heritage, he hoped. As Griefold pondered all of this, he and his companions finished loading the cargo that they had been assigned by the bosun and then were waiting for further orders.

After a short look around the dock, Captain Meltern said, "All aboard now, step lively. We have no time to waste if we clear this bay before sunset and get out onto the open sea."

With that, the bosun began snapping orders to the sailors to start preparing for departure, and the Ameristans stopped standing around, gawking and getting aboard the ship or being left behind. The three men turned to one another, shrugged their shoulders, boarded the ship with the rest of the crew and quickly got out of the way of the sailors.

CHAPTER 14

The first few days at sea for the Ameristans until the constant movement of the ship caused all of them to start to feel the effects. They all struggled as a group to keep what little food they could down and all of the water that they could manage. This lasted only a few days for Arten, who used to ride a griffon through the sky, was used to unexpected motions up and down and from side to side. It took the two royal brothers a few more days to find their own footing on the ship, keep their food down like Arten, and begin to relax into the voyage. The three did not stop working on the ship with the sailors. They were eager to learn everything that they could about how to sail and what it took to keep a ship afloat. Griefold remembered his father's oath from that fateful day when Patrallin had sworn vengeance on the people who had all but destroyed the Minnertalla. It was he who spent most of the time with the ship's captain learning what it took to make the ships, which the captain knew little about, but Griefold learned much more about sailing them. Captain Meltern admitted that the building of ships was the business of the shipwrights in Dantorin and that it was a complicated process. Meltern further went on to explain that it took multiple winters to lay the keel and to build entire ships, especially in his homeland, since there was little in the way of trees in Dantorin. Unlike Amerista, the great forests abound with trees, which would be perfect for the construction of larger sailing vessels. In explanation, Captain Meltern said that the larger the keel, the larger the ship could be once the wood had had time to season properly and could be worked with.

Griefold took to this idea with a fervor and quickly sought out his brother to begin to think of plans on how to acquire shipwrights of their own. He said to Blackston, "Imagine what we could do with ships of our own! We could find these Iramians, and take the fight to them! It has been many winters since they have darkened our shores and attacked far inland, but we finally may have a chance to take the fight to them and destroy them once and for all!"

Blackston turned a doubtful look upon his older brother as he replied, "I agree with you, my brother, but how are we going to find the funds for such a large project? We cannot simply become like the Iramians ourselves and start to carry off these shipwrights when we find them in Dantorin. We would have to find a way to pay them. I learned many things in my winters in Dracolia, and one of them is that other people outside of our own expect to trade in coins or gold. We are a simple people when it comes to trade. We trade the safety of our coasts with the Dantorins for access to the aurochs. We trade for safety from the raids of the Zealots with the Dracolians in steel and weapons. We need to learn new ways to deal with the outside world in order to make the most of ourselves. It is fine to have high ideals of destroying the ones who have caused so much damage to our people for all these centuries, but we have to be smart about how we do it." Blackston placed a calming hand on Griefold's shoulder and continued, "I feel the need for vengeance burning through my blood as well, brother! We have to plan and take the time to establish the right kind of alliances to make this plan of fathers come true. For all we know, the Iramians may well be the Dantorins or the Iristians that we have been trading with for all these winters. We have to take the time to find out the true home of the Iramians to destroy them forever."

Griefold could only nod his head in disappointment and agreement with your younger brother about what to do about the Iramians. Turning away from his fellow searchers, Griefold made his way to the bow of the ship and stared out into the rolling sea ahead of him, deep in thought.

***

The first voyage of the three Ameristans was mostly uneventful, with little in the way for them to do either on deck or below once they were underway. The sailors and captain all knew their jobs well and did them all with practiced efficiency of long winters at sea. With so little to occupy them, the trio worked on their arms, training on the deck whenever they could without getting in the way of the sailors. After the first couple of bouts, where the warriors fought one-on-one or two-on-one to first blood, the sailors began to take bets on who would win. The overall favorite was Arten, with his flashing blade and limber quickness. Each time that one of the brothers won over the Griffonara, it was a great victory for them personally. Being able to defeat an elite warrior was something to be proud of. While the brothers may have spent their entire lives learning the art of Dominance, the Griffonara had spent his entire life fighting for his life in the few raids that still happened. He had learned the hard way how to score hits on his opponents and how to quickly end a fight against multiple fighters. The brothers grew frustrated by the ease with which Arten was defeating them when attacking together, so they began to develop their skills to work better as a team. To attack from different angles and approaches, and the number of bouts won by the brothers began to increase.

Secretly, Arten was proud of the increasing skill of those he was supposed to protect; he had been given orders by Petralis himself to get them ready for any kind of danger that they may face. It was finally paying off in all of the hard work that Griefold and Blackston were putting into their training. It may have been winters since either brother had really been pushed by their trainers, but it was now time for them to become as dangerous as possible. For the coming war that the High Priestesses predicted was nigh, at least according to them. While the High Priestesses were yet to be wrong on a vision given to them by Amerton, the timing of the events could be more than a little vague at best. It had taken more than four centuries for the rise of Patrallin to the status of Tallantanar. So, it was more than possible it would be several lifetimes before the Ameristan people were to set out and destroy the Iramians. That is, if anyone could figure out where the Iramians were coming from in the first place, that problem had yet to be solved. It was true that with increased trade with the Dantorins, the raids had trickled to little more than one or two every moon or so, but they did still continue, While the Iramians and the Iristians that came to trade once a year at the Holy City were of a similar race, the Iristians always came from the Suns Dagger Mountains to the west of Amerista. It was easy to think that the Iramians would only then come from the sea like the Dantorins, but the Dantorins denied any knowledge of the Iramians and where to find them at all. This was not the first time some of their people had sailed upon Dantorin ships, but maybe if he got to know some of the sailors, then things would work out to his advantage.

It was a voyage of nearly two moons before the ship made landfall in the nation of Dantorin, and the trio of warriors got to see the almost barren landscape before them. The Ameristans were used to the lush grasses of the plains and the heavily forested mountains of their homeland. This land was more rock-like in appearance, with few trees they could see being stunted and twisted compared to the towering giants of the mountains. The animals that they could see were small and stunted, too, when compared to the mighty aurochs. These were the pigs and goats they had heard about from the sailors and merchants during the voyage. Due to their size and the stench of them, it was obvious why the Dantorin king would wish to have auroch served at his dining table.

Once the ship had been tied up at the dock, the bosun began shouting orders to the sailors and the Ameristan trio to begin offloading the cargo. Griefold and his companions set to removing the same casks and crates that they had painstakingly loaded those many tendays before starting their journey on the sea. It was faster going for them now that the casks were empty and the crates contained the food they had eaten. Now it was time for Captain Meltern to resupply his ship and give his men some much-deserved shore leave before finding another cargo for another trip to upon the sea.

Griefold, Arten, and Blackston bid their farewell to the captain and then proceeded to help Lord Elmintareth with the offloading of his precious aurochs. The process went smoother than Lord Elmintareth expected, with the trio helping since they knew what needed to be done to move recalcitrant aurochs. Soon, the merchant and his armed escort of Ameristans were making their way through the teeming city docks, heading towards the towering stone edifice that rose high into the air. It was a structure that had been built by the hand of man, but much, much larger than anything the Ameristans had ever seen before. The palace walls, for it could be nothing else, stood higher than they could have believed its walls rose at least thirty feet in the air. Inside the walls, some of the palace was even higher than that, reaching a height of about forty feet. While the Ameristans were used to the towering trees of their homeland that could reach hundreds of feet into the air, they could barely comprehend how man-made this structure was. Surely, it would have taken hundreds of men working for at least a hundred winters to construct such a thing.

Lord Elmintareth saw the looks of awe and wonderment running through the faces of his hired escort and began chuckling quietly to himself. He had hired several Ameristans over the recent winters for such voyages, and every time they saw the castle, the reaction was the same thing. This was, but one castle in Dantorin, and not even the most impressive, but the Ameristans were such a simple people to be overawed by such a structure. Grey granite block made up Dantorin Castle with only two soaring towers over each gate leading to the palace grounds themselves. With only the eight towers and the high wall surrounding the castle, it had never been breached in the two hundred winters that the royal line had ruled. The current king of Dantorin was still young and occasionally warred with his cousins for control of the inland ancestral Dantorin lands. Fortunately, the Ameristans knew nothing of the two inland kingdoms, whom each claimed to be the true ruler of Dantorin. Otherwise, there would be more demand for trade and a loss of control of the aurochs. Someday, his king would reunify the nation, and then King Alintarneth would take back the inner kingdom of Derinteneth, where the forests and grazing lands were controlled by Camineth. Once the two rebellious kingdoms had been brought back under proper control, the Dantorin people would become a great power again. He no longer having to rely on Ameristan warriors to escort him from their homeland when he brought the aurochs down. Soon, Lord Elmintareth hoped he would be able to simply travel to Amerista and take as many aurochs as he chose to bring to King Alintarneth. No more having to beg the Ameristan Priests Pairs for the old and infirm ones that were all they allowed outsiders to take away from the plains. Wealth and power would flow into his hands in time as long as he could keep the Ameristans on his side and keep supplying King Alintarneth in aurochs.

This plotting and planning was not exclusive to Lord Elmintareth; all of the Dantorin nobles from all three kingdoms had the same plans as their respective kings. Each thought that they were going to be the one noble to bring about the resurrection of their nation and become the power behind the throne. While this was not an uncommon occurrence among the nobles of almost any nation, it was more prevalent in the lands of Dantorin. The young king was only seventeen winters old and was just coming into his true power and trying to establish himself as a power to be reckoned with. Even though he was young, many of his nobles were still loyal to him due to his late father's reign and the prosperity he brought. There had been no open warfare with the other claimant kingdoms in recent winters, and King Alintarneth did not show signs of trying to continue the fighting. While those nobles who lived on the borders and desired to increase their lands were always pushing for more war, King Alintarneth desired peace. He had lost his own father at a young age to the fighting with his uncles before they, too, had died in subsequent battles for control of all of Dantorin, but the sons of the triplet kings had all decided to try peace.

Griefold and his companions were completely oblivious to the plotting of their temporary employer. They were more concerned with their true reason for being in this rocky nation, finding one of the sisters who was supposed to be hidden somewhere among the people. When Griefold and Arten were searching for Blackston, they had no idea where in the land to begin and who to ask questions of. Griefold knew he got lucky when finding his younger brother since Blackston was known to the commander of the Dragon Riders of Dracolia and was popular there. How was he going to find one young woman among the teeming masses that were before him? This thought was running through his head repeatedly as they made their way through the lanes near the docks, herding the aurochs where Lord Elmintareth had space set aside for them. There were thirty of the holy aurochs in this small herd, a much smaller number than Lord Elmintareth would have liked. The animals were in good shape after being on a ship at sea for nearly two moons, but they would need time on land to rest before they could be presented to King Alintarneth.

Thinking about what had happened in Dracolia, Griefold decided that the only way to find his sister was to start with the common people of Dantorin. They would be willing to trade information for coins or labor, much like the common people of Dracolia had been. While the nobles may have been a better source of direct information, Griefold had a deep feeling that these nobles would be less likely to share information from any source that did not serve them in some way first. The Ameristans had picked up more than a few details about the Dantorin nobles from the sailors during their voyage. The details that have not quite made it to the rest of their people yet were the most interesting. Like the fact that Dantorin was not one kingdom like in their grandfather's day, but instead three separate kingdoms all ruled by cousins. The different kingdoms all had different laws, and their nobles were always at one another's throats, vying for control of the entire Dantorin nation. While the respective kings of each little kingdom were content with the way things appeared, the nobles were the ones trying to fight an unnecessary war.

The trio wanted nothing to do with the internal struggles of the Dantorin peoples, yet how were they to search the disparate nations when there was always war looming on the horizon due to the nobles? While herding the lowing aurochs to the pen set aside for them by Lord Elmintareth, they quietly discussed what their next steps would be. Griefold and Blackston came up with a plan that seemed to have the best shot of working in their favor. Since their aunts were the current High Priestesses of Amerton, then there would be a good chance that the brothers could get a special agreement for the current kings of the three nations. After all, since the aurochs were holy to Amerton, then maybe the aunts could be persuaded to allow a larger number of aurochs to be sent south in payment for help with finding their missing niece. If it was truly time for the family to be reunited, maybe Amerton would forgive the loss of some of the herds for a good cause and the family.

Once the aurochs had been placed into the pen with fresh water and fodder, Arten turned to Lord Elmintareth and asked what he wanted them to do next. Lord Elmintareth said, "Now I will take you to see King Alintarneth so that he can greet you properly to his kingdom and show you the wonders that we have to share."

Nodding their heads in agreement, the Ameristans followed the noble as he began to lead the way through the masses of people. Here and there, among the teeming masses, the occasional Ameristan could also act as a guard for some merchant or another. These warriors were from the other Talla and could be easily identified. Fortunately for Arten and Griefold, neither of them was familiar with the few warriors that they saw, so their true identities were not revealed. Who knew what Lord Elmintareth would do with information that he had one of the leaders of the royal guard, as well as two of the royal family, with him?

From the information that they had learned on the ship, Griefold and Blackston were sure that Lord Elmintareth would do his best to keep them all captive as long as he could manage. They gained the advantages of constant access to the steel that only their people could produce, as well as the aurochs herds. The brothers were under no illusions that the nobles of these countries were going to do anything that they could to try and control them. The brothers felt that they had to find a way to speak to each of these cousin kings. Then, they try to find their missing sister and be on their way as soon as possible.

Arten was in agreement with them on this and was considering some method to get away from their escort that would allow them to speak to the king, maybe by presenting himself as one half of a priest pair, maybe claiming to be one of the Tallanta. That would be a definite path to get to King Alintarneth in order to make things move faster for the quest set to them by Petralis. In short order, the small party found themselves at the gates of the castle of the local king, waiting for permission from the armed guardsmen to enter. As skilled warriors, the Ameristans looked over the guardsmen and saw that for armor, they had poor-quality steel copies and that the weapons themselves were simple iron swords and spear points. Nothing that they could not deal with easily with their steel weapons and armor. It was obvious to the trio that the merchants had not been sharing the spoils of their trade with their king, at least for this kingdom, maybe the other kingdoms as well. Yet, another bargaining chip to work on when the time came. Door by door, gate by gate, eventually the group made their way into the castle and eventually the throne room itself with the king.

King Alintarneth was dark-haired like most of his countrymen and young for the throne as they had heard. He appeared to be in his late teens, the same age as Blackston. Yet for his age King Alintarneth was obviously in good health and strong. He carried himself with the air of someone who regularly worked with arms and armor and carried the bulk to show for it. The throne room was full of courtiers, much like the ones who had filled the Minnertalla longhouse under Griefold's control, with more young women than men. It was obvious that the nobles were vying for control of the young king through beautiful young women, and it seemed to be working.

Standing at the side of the throne of the king was a voluptuous young woman who appeared vacant and beautiful at first look. Yet, with closer examination, the vacant doe-eyed expression was clearly an act for the woman. With clear intent deep in her eyes, she stared away at any other young lady who tried to approach the throne. If looks were deadly, then every other young lady in the throne room would have died multiple times over. Among many of the male nobles as well.

Unbothered by the deadly looks being thrown his way by the young lady attending upon the king, Lord Elmintareth approached his young king and bowed deeply. He said, "Great and true king of Dantorin, King Alintarneth, I bring to you a gift from the north, a small herd of aurochs from the lands of the Ameristans. They are in good health and awaiting your pleasure to sup upon when you so choose. They are fresh from the ship and taken care of during the voyage by my guardsmen from the very lands of the creatures. My three escorts are from Amerista, and they are fine warriors who know how to care for animals. They have agreed to stay until all of the aurochs I present to you have done their service to you, my great king, and now may I present my guardsmen to you?"

King Alintarneth looked over the bowing nobleman and sighed heavily before responding. He said, "Lord Elmintareth, have you brought old and infirm animals to me yet again? I told you that while I do enjoy the taste of aurochs, I am growing tired of the old and infirm ones that all my nobles and merchants have been bringing me. The meat is tough and stringy as well and hardly something appetizing for nearly every meal I eat. I am not going to grant any kind of special dispensation to any merchant who brings aurochs to me. I am not my father nor my poor grandfather. May the gods bless their souls. I do not believe in giving rewards for anything; I believe in earning your own accolades, and I do not give my permission to any noble to take up arms against my cousin kings. The old, tired wars of our fathers are over as far as we are concerned, and we have all agreed to this on multiple occasions. For the last time, I *will not* allow any noble to take up arms against any other, no matter what king they may follow! It is time for peace for poor Dantorin and its cousin kingdoms! Take your guardsmen and depart. I do not want to see any more Ameristans unless it is someone who is a royal messenger or ambassador of some kind sent by their king!" King Alintarneth was red-faced and standing from his throne, nearly ready to draw his ceremonial blade from his side.

As Lord Elmintareth began to back away, mumbling words of apology to his king, Arten sensed his chance to step forward and implement the plan he and the brothers had worked out on their way to the castle. Arten stepped forward and bowed deeply to the young king, saying, "King Alintarneth, I am Arten. I came to your lands for several reasons that your loyal nobleman did not know about. I am an emissary from the Tallantanar of Amerista himself here on a mission. My countrymen and I are searching for a particular person who is from our lands and would have been sent here in secret many winters ago. We are willing to offer you guaranteed trade offers with our people that would bring better aurochs to your table and true steel to your guardsmen, unlike what they are using now to defend you. I could even see if my Tallantanar would be willing to allow Ameristan warriors to defend your person if you would prefer. All I ask is for some of your time to discuss this with you and your advisors. To determine the truth of my words. I ask for you to call upon your court-wise ones to cast a spell on me here and now to show you that I do not lie."

King Alintarneth's mouth dropped open in surprise at the words coming from the clearly armed and apparently peaceful Ameristan before him. Sitting deeper upon his throne carefully, the king said, "I see that you and your companions are armed. Why were you not disarmed before ever entering my presence?"

"No one asked for our arms as we were with your Lord Elmintareth, Your Majesty," Griefold responded calmly.

"If you would, but let us speak your majesty." Blackston said, "I am sure that you will see that we mean no harm to yourself or your people. I myself have spent many winters as an emissary in the Dracolian Empire and know the reputation that some of our countrymen have. Let me assure you that the stories are only true about those who raid our lands and seek to attack us without provocation."

The young king finally seemed to relax a little into his throne again and replied to the Ameristan warriors, "If you are truly here peacefully, then you all will not have a problem submitting to a truth spell by my court wizards. Ulan and Triyama come forth and see if these men speak true." Turning his attention back to the three, he said, "If you speak falsely and seek to harm me, then my wizards will kill you where you stand!"

Two middle-aged men wearing dark-colored robes moved their way through the crowd of court hangers-on. These men of magic were obviously not identical twins like the High Priestesses of their homeland, but they carried their power much like the former ladies. Their heads were cleanly shaved, but their beards draped down their chests, reaching to their respective waists. As the wizards approached the three warriors, it was clear that their shaved heads were covered in hundreds of small tattoos from where their eyebrows would have begun and all the way to the backs of their necks.

As with all magic users, they spoke in unison when using their powers and said, "Stand still and speak only the truth; if you speak the truth, then you will not be harmed. Lie to us, and the pain will be enough to kill all of you on the spot." Muttering quietly, the wizards moved slowly around first Arten, then Griefold and finally Blackston. As the twins passed around the Ameristans, a dark cloud began to grow from the ground and shroud them from foot to neck. Once the cloud had reached the respective necks of the

Ameristans, the wizards stepped back and spoke again in unison to their king, saying, "King Alintarneth, you may question them now and find the truth of their statements."

The king smiled very darkly while turning to look directly at the trapped Ameristans. He said, "So, tell me, are you here to kill me on behalf of my nobles or the nobles of the other kingdoms of Dantorin?!" One after another, the brothers and Arten responded negatively. "Are you here to kill any of my nobles or nobles in the other kingdoms of the Dantorin lands?!" Again, they answered in the negative. Finally, the king asked his final question of the Ameristans; it was obvious to all present that he was surprised to find that they had spoken the truth. "Are you truly here in search of a young woman accompanied by three adults from your land who came here fifteen winters ago and your offers of trade with permission of your Tallantanar."

Arten spoke first, "I can assure you that we are here for the sole purpose of looking for a particular young woman, as for trade that would be up to Tallantanar Petralis himself…"

Griefold spoke up, interrupting Arten, and said, "King Alintarneth, I can speak for increased trade. I am Griefold, brother of the Tallantanar, and I can speak for him on this matter. We are willing to open up true trade negotiations with you and you alone to allow control of the flow of trade within your lands. I have spent many winters dealing with your lords as they have come to trade and bring back goods to your people, but we have not often received trade in return."

As the Ameristans spoke, the black cloud that surrounded them began to lighten in color and then eventually disappeared altogether. The gasps of awe at the disappearance of the truth spell showed the obviousness of the words of the trio, which was astonishing. The courtiers were used to seeing the nobles and other outsiders put to the truth spell crushed to death by their lies; this was a first for many of them. Some of the nobles furiously paid out bets for how long the Ameristans would have lasted and so forth to one another. None of the bettors thought that the young warriors would have ever even told the truth to begin with.

Stepping down from his throne, King Alintarneth approached the trio and said, "I have heard of you, Griefold. I was always under the impression that you were going to be the next leader of your people. Why are you here looking for some young woman from your land when you should be preparing to lead your people?"

Griefold shook his head slightly and said. "I was only next in line as long as there was no one else to take my place. The Tallantanar's heart-mate delivered their first child some time ago. I am not in the line of succession anymore. Also, Your Majesty, I never truly should have tried to put myself into the place of being the heir of the leadership of our people. I can tell you we are looking for a very important woman to our people, and I would like to ask if we could speak in private. As my compatriot said, we would like to strike deals with you alone so that we know that we will be getting trade goods in return instead of just sending aurochs and steel to your nobles."

There was an outbreak of boos, hisses, and threats of death for Griefold and his companions immediately after this statement. The king raised his hand in a fist and suddenly dropped it again to his side; the entire throne room went deathly still. King Alintarneth said, "Guards, clear the room. Leave the Ameristans alone. Triyama, Ulan, bring me the rest of the royal council. We will take this to the council chambers to speak with these new emissaries." Looking the Ameristans in the eye, he then said, "Could I provide you with something to refresh yourselves before we begin trade negotiations? Wine, perhaps or mead. Would you like to bathe before we begin since you have so recently come from the sea, and I doubt that you have had much of a chance to freshen up."

Blackston said, "We would appreciate a suite of rooms, if that is acceptable to Your Majesty, for us to refresh and change into less intimidating clothing. It is true that we have been as a sea for many tendays. Also, we have not had a chance to even break our fast this day since Lord Elmintareth was in such a hurry to bring us to you. We would greatly appreciate the chance to have wine and something to eat while we prepare ourselves for meeting you properly in chambers with your council. We wish not to offend you and your nobles with our presence until we have had a chance to cleanse the scent of the sea as well as the scent of the aurochs we brought from the ship. If there is anything that we could do for you, your majesty, before meeting with your council, please do not hesitate to ask it of us. We are truly searching for both a young woman who is long missed, as well as a true friend in your lands."

Visibly relaxing and with a true smile spreading across his face for the first time, King Alintarneth said, "Of course it will be done. Let me call my majordomo to take you to some rooms so you can relax and refresh. We will all meet at the council meeting in a few hours' time. I will have a selection of food and drinks sent to your rooms as well as freshwater; I will see you all in the council chambers."

The court majordomo abruptly appeared and silently led the small group away from the throne room and deeper into the castle. It was not a far walk for them as they admired the decor and the stone walls surrounding them. The mere fact that someone was able to make such a large building from stone was still a mystery to the Ameristans, and they could not puzzle out how it was done in the first place. Blackston, having grown up in Dracolia, was used to shorter buildings made of much smaller stones, rarely above two floors in height, with the top floors being of wood. The majority of homes and buildings in Dracolia, as well as in Amerista, were single-story and built of wood with thatch roofs. Being surrounded by stone was stifling, and at the same time, it was interesting to them, such a new experience. The halls were all lit with torches, and arrow slits along the way helped to brighten up the halls so that it was not in complete darkness. The rooms that they were shown were not too small, yet obviously not the largest to be found in the castle. There were four separate rooms for sleeping around a central room that had a large hearth with firewood laid out ready to be lit. The sleeping rooms were not all that large, just large enough for a bed, armoire, and a small brazier to keep the room warm. There were several buckets of cool water waiting in the main room, and as they arrived, a maid brought in two more buckets of steaming water. In addition, there was a wooden tub set up near the fire, which the maid quickly set to light with flint and steel. With practiced ease, she lit the fire and swiftly left the room.

As the maid left, the majordomo finally spoke to them and, in a high-pitched voice, said, "Is there anything else I may do for you warriors?"

Blackston turned to him and bowed his head slightly while saying, "That will be all for now, Master……?"

"Majordomo," the majordomo replied, "I gave up my name for the title when the late king appointed me to the position eighteen winters ago."

Looking the man up and down, Griefold could see that he was slim to the point of emaciation yet in obviously good health. He had iron grey hair cropped close to his scalp, and his clothing was made of fine wool and silk. Obviously, this man had a lot of power in the castle, and his word carried weight with the king, or he would not have been so richly dressed when the king himself did not wear silks.

Determining that this was someone who had the most pull with the Dantorin king, Griefold said, "Majordomo, what would be the best way to approach your king about these trade negotiations? We are not merchants like your people, but we do know a little about barter since this is what we do among ourselves. What would be fair for us to ask for, and what would be fair for the king to expect to give in return for true steel weapons and armor? We saw what his guardsmen wear and carry unless there are better guardsmen we have yet to see, and they are in much need of better armament."

"My king will greatly appreciate the offer of better arms and armor for his guardsmen, but he will want to see proof of this. The few weapons and arms that the noble merchants bring back from your homeland and sell to the king are what you have seen. They have all claimed that these are the best of the lot and that they are the finest steel to be had on the face of Tarna. I have always had doubts since I have seen what they equip their personal armsmen with, but the king does not agree. Can you truly guarantee my king will receive the finest steel weapons and armor that your smiths can provide?"

Griefold said, "I can guarantee that we will offer the best that we are willing to trade. We keep the finest for our own warriors, of course, but we will be willing to trade with anyone who is fair to us."

A slight smile came across the majordomo's face as he replied, "It was worth the try. Well, I will escort you to the king's council chambers when you have had a chance to refresh yourselves and change into some fresh clothing. I am sure that there will be much to discuss when the time comes." The majordomo bowed himself out of the suite and firmly shut the door behind him for their privacy.

Arten turned to Griefold and said, "Are you sure that your brother would want us to agree to strengthen only one of these kingdoms down here and not the others at the same time? It could lead to problems in the future for our people and make our search for your sister much more difficult."

"What makes you think that I will only agree with one kingdom being able to trade with us?" Griefold asked as he began to strip himself of his travel-stained clothing. "I only said that we would be willing to trade with them, not exclusively with King Alintarneth nor the Dantorin people. From what we learned, there are two other kingdoms in control of these lands, and our sister could be among one of them instead of just here. We need to be flexible with our *negotiation* abilities. We may need to establish ties with all three kingdoms in order to get what we need."

"I see what you are planning now," Arten replied, "Yet you need to be careful what you promise where and to whom to prevent the wyvern from biting you back when they all find out that you have made deals with them."

"No fear, my friend. I plan on making it clear at each negation that I have to make with these cousin kings that they are not going to be the sole beneficiary of our trade. They may not like it in the long run; they may not even agree at first, but I am going to find our sister, and that is all that matters." Griefold said with finality.

The discussion quickly turned from trade to the best way to present themselves to the king and how to make the right impression. Obviously, the three warriors did not bring fine clothes like those they had seen among the nobles of the court when they were introduced. Also, they did not have any real trappings of the level of their true standing in their homeland since they were traveling in disguise. Griefold and Blackston did not have the traditional steel chain of the Minnertalla for their braids, and Arten did not have fresh griffon feathers for his. So, they made do with the worn feathers that they had been wearing for the trip and the cleanest and most presentable clothing that they had on hand.

It was less than an hour after he left that the majordomo returned to escort the trio to the royal council chambers. Griefold, Blackston, and Arten felt much better after having a chance to remove much of the grime and stains from their travels and a chance to change into clean clothing. Even if they did not make the same kind of impression that the lords of Dantorin did upon first sight, their appearance did not disgust people anymore. A seafaring people, they were very much objectionable to the scent of the sea upon themselves and people around them.

As they entered the council chambers, they could see who had made up the council for the young king. Without surprise, the two wizards were in the room, along with ten nobles, not counting the king himself. Each of the nobles wore fine linens, wool, or silk garments. Each tries to outdo the next in color or brightness of their clothes. All of the nobles wore clothing of dark blues and bright, brilliant reds. Only the king was still dressed in somber leather clothes that hid armor plates beneath the leather. The leather clothes were minor protection from small dangers and the armor plates that the Ameristans could discern would be protective for much larger weapons. The fact that the king felt the need to be secretly armed, even in the presence of his chosen council member, spoke volumes for the dangers of these three kingdoms to the Ameristans. Even deep in his own kingdom, King Alintarneth felt the need to be protected, and that was a sad thing for the Ameristans. While they were all warriors, they never felt the need to armor themselves amongst friends.

King Alintarneth said to them as they entered the chambers, "Please be seated, my councilors, and I am eager to begin negotiations with you." After the Ameristans took their own seats at the council table, the king continued, "So, I would like to know what you would like to receive in trade for your weapons and armor made of steel that only your smiths can provide. We can offer many things, such as wine, goats, pigs, exotic fruits, the likes of which you have never even heard of, or maybe something more intoxicating."

"Your majesty already knows what we are willing to offer as well as what we are seeking in trade at this time," Griefold said to him, taking the lead. "What we would be willing to open up for in addition to trade is some of your shipwrights coming to Amerista and teaching our people how to build ships. As well as some of your sailors and captains to train us how to use them. We have a desire to take to the seas ourselves and to discover what we can about them. As for what we can provide, I can guarantee that my older brother will allow me to assure you that you personally will receive true steel arms and armament. I can offer that each Talanata will be asked to send warriors to protect you until your guardsmen are each armed and ready to protect you. I will also speak to the High Priestesses to see if they could intervene with the great Amerton and allow some better stock of aurochs to be shipped to your lands."

The young king began to look interested and, leaning forward, asked, "How many warriors could I expect to get from each of your Talla? Two, a dozen, a hundred? I would like to know this before I settle on any kind of agreement about armed men from another country in my land who will be charged with protecting my person."

Griefold again took the lead and said, "That is something that each Tallanta would have to decide. I cannot speak for them as I would speak for myself or my brother. As for my Talla, there are no warriors to give in your protection, so you can see that it will be up to each one of them. The warriors will be vigilant in your protection until the terms of the trade negotiation are met, and then they will leave. Our people who come here will not take up arms against anyone except in the defense of yourself and any of your family or council members that you deem need protection. Would you be agreeable to those terms for my fellow warriors to come here? In exchange, we would like to seek permission to look among your people for our missing warriors and the young lady whom they were assigned to protect."

King Alintarneth looked amongst his advisors, and each of them gave him a nod in the affirmative after speaking quietly among themselves for a brief moment. He said in response, "That would be acceptable to me. Next, I would like to address the shipwrights; they are my subjects, but I cannot force them to leave their homes and come to your lands to teach your people to build ships. That is something that takes a lifetime in many cases to learn, but I can have my nobles sell your people ships or even have them hire out ships to you for a fair price. Is that agreeable?"

"That would be acceptable to my brother. It is much like becoming a master smith or weapons master. They are not something that you can do in the course of a few moons or even a year, but a lifetime of dedication. The prices will have to be agreed upon for each use as long as they are fair and not aimed at lining the pockets of certain nobles. Especially those who have taken advantage of my people in the past."

After quietly muttering with the council members and finally agreeing to nod to the king, the king says, "Those terms are agreeable. We would like a list of the names of those particular nobles assembled by you and have given to my majordomo in the near future so that we can make sure that they no longer trade with your people."

Griefold nodded his agreement, saying, "That would have to come from each of the Tallanta, as they have all had their own dealings with your nobles privately. We would like to offer better aurochs in trade for access to some of your wines and fruits to supplement our longhouses. My aunts are the current High Priestesses of Amerton, and I can speak directly with them about intervening with our God and allowing better stock to be sent. I do know that all of the stock sent here will be gelded since they are still holy animals, and Amerton's protection for his token animal does not extend this far from the plains. That is something that is completely non-negotiable."

Without even looking to his council, King Alintarneth said, "Those restrictions are completely understandable. Your God's power and your people's beliefs must be followed. You are not a subject to my rule, and your High Priestesses will have the final say. I will arrange for trusted merchants to come to your Holy City to make the final decisions about the amounts of wine and fruit in exchange for the number aurochs for trade. Will that be acceptable to you and your brother?"

"As I said, Your Majesty, I can speak for my brother, the Tallantanar, but I can only offer to speak for my aunts. They are the ones who would then, in turn, speak with Amerton. Yet, I do not see any problems with this deal." Griefold replied. Then he looked at his two companions and turned back to the king before saying, "Is there anything else that you would like to negotiate with us for now, or are you satisfied with our current situation?"

The Dantorin king looked thoughtful for a few minutes as if considering what to ask for next, yet he finally replied, "No, Prince Griefold, I believe that these few negotiated terms will suffice for now. It is something that will open the way to further negotiations in the future."

"As an outside party, who truly has no reason to favor any one of your kingdoms over the other since we are here to find a missing girl, maybe we three can offer to be negotiators for your kingdoms." Arten offered quickly. "We are more than willing to travel to the other Kings and offer to open talks in exchange for the ability to only seek the missing warriors and girls from our land. We will not offer anything of value to them that we have not offered to you already in exchange and promise under any oath to keep true to our agreements with your court."

King Alintarneth looked at the Ameristans incredulously, saying, "You would be willing to speak to my cousins and try to seek a consensus of peace between us with no reward for yourselves other than the right to search for the girl you are missing?"

"Of course, Your Majesty, we have no agenda here with yourself nor your people in general. We are were set a goal to achieve and only wish to achieve it in a timely manner so that we can return to our home and get on with our lives." Arten answered.

Griefold added, "It is our only purpose for being here, King Alintarneth. We are only looking for a young lady and her protectors who came here many winters ago. The fact that we were able to negotiate with you and your council is only something that came about with our chance of meeting you in your throne room. The ability to help negotiate with your fellow kings will only be to our advantage since we do not know where this particular young lady is in the three kingdoms. All we have to go on is that she came down here almost fifteen winters ago, and she was accompanied by three Ameristan warriors. If you could consult with your people on our behalf to let us know if any of that sounds familiar, please do so for us. We ask for nothing in exchange."

Blackston finally broke in to say, "We wish we could give you more information to go on for our search; all we know is that she would be young and blonde-haired. Other than that, we cannot say much about who or what she means to our people; there are other considerations to take into account."

One of the council members finally spoke aloud and said, "That information will help narrow the search somewhat; we do not have many Ameristans living in our lands. Other than the few warriors hired by our nobles and merchants as escorts, I cannot even think of many of your people here. I can send for the few of your people who live here permanently for you to speak with and to determine if they are the ones you are seeking."

CHAPTER 15

Of the sixteen Ameristans that they met with, none of them were warriors who were sent with one of the missing sisters. They were all warriors who had decided to stay with their Dantorin merchants permanently or had married into Dantorin families. None of the warriors that they spoke to knew anything of the group that they were searching for nor where to even begin.

The questioning only took one day, so they did not waste much time, and they began to make plans to journey to the next of the two kingdoms. Plans were being made to join one of the many merchant caravans that traveled frequently about the land that was not controlled by the nobles.

King Alintarneth explained that it would be easier to do it this way than trying to find trustworthy nobles from any of the kingdoms. He also revealed that secretly, each of the cousin kings was in constant communication with one another through their court wizards. The wizard twins of Dantorin were a guild unto themselves and stood apart from any of the infighting and bickering of the nobles or kings. They only answered to the Gods of Dantorin and acted as messengers and quasi-priests for the entire populace of the three lands. King Camineth and King Derinteneth were each awaiting the searchers in their respective kingdoms. Many of their respective nobles wanted war and to help lead their particular kingdom to the supremacy of the land. The kings themselves were dubious about more war and wanted to find a way to peace if it were possible in their lifetimes, at least according to the wizard's guild messengers, who were above questioning and reproach.

It was only a matter of days before Griefold and his two companions could find a merchant train heading to the kingdom of Cantorin and King Camineth himself. They would be walking as part of the hired guards for two tendays to reach the far inland kingdom northwest of Dantorin proper. With three separate kingdoms and bickering nobles across the whole of the lands, the roads were filled with bandits, and attacks on merchant caravans were quite common, so guards were always in demand. Mixing in with the other caravan guards was easy for them since several of the guards were already Ameristans who lived in Dantorin year-round or were part of the hired swords for the merchants from their homeland. Still, Griefold and his compatriots were not identified, which was good since they were still trying to keep the purpose of their search secret. No one knew what the Iramians had against the Minnertalla, and the fact that their people were nearly wiped out once, especially their own family, was something that terrified them.

***

It was more than two tendays of uneventful travel with the merchant caravan that finally got the searchers to the next castle. This time, they were expected by the royal court wizards for King Camineth of Cantorin at the city gates to escort the three companions to their appointed rooms. There, once again, they were greeted by the royal majordomo, buckets of fresh hot water, and tubs to clean themselves up with. This time, they were encouraged to dress in Dantorin-style linens and silks to be presentable to the king of this particular kingdom. They, of course, did as a bid of them; the Ameristans did not wish to offend the king who would aid their search in any way.

King Camineth was a man who also appeared to be very fit and used to the use of the sword he wore at his side when they were presented to him in his throne room. He was older than King Alintarneth by at least five winters and was as solidly structured across the shoulders as any Dominance master of Amerista. As powerfully built as he was, King Camineth was obviously not strong in his personality, unlike Alintarneth. He was dull-looking in the eyes and busy talking with his queen when the trio was presented to them. King Camineth did not even react to their presence once they were presented to him.

The queen was sitting on her own slightly smaller throne to the left of her husband and said, "Welcome, noble warriors of Amerista. If we are to understand you properly, you are here from our cousin King Alintarneth with wishes of good tidings and peace between our people. Guards, please clear the court so that our visitors and royal selves may speak with ease."

While the guardsmen were quickly clearing the throne room, Griefold assessed their arms and armament and came to the same conclusion that they all had in Dantorin proper. These men were equipped with the poorest of steel and mostly iron weapons and armament. They would not stand a sustained attack in a real fight with the kinds of weapons that the nobles had been trading for over the past winters. The royal families of two of the three kingdoms were in dire need of better equipment if there were to be another war for control. At this rate, they would be able to secure all of the help that they would need with a minimum give-in trade alone. Yet, this king did not seem to be the best and brightest; maybe the queen of this land was the true power behind the throne, and she would be the one to negotiate with. Time will tell.

Once the royal court was cleared and the royal wizards sealed it to outside listeners, the queen finally spoke to the trio before her. She said, "I am Queen Elyzabeth; as you can see, my poor husband is a bit under the weather and cannot really be of much help in the negotiations. I speak for our kingdom and am willing to offer generous terms on items that we can trade for and help you in your search. Our court wizards tell us you are looking for a particular Ameristan couple and their young girl who came here about fifteen winters ago?"

Arten stepped forward and said, "Let me introduce to you the brothers of the Tallantanar, Griefold, and Blackston of the Minnertalla. I am Arten, their bodyguard, and companion on this search for the young lady and her protectors from our lands. She is not their child by birth, but hopefully by heart since they have had so long to care for her and to protect her. Do you wish to start with trade negotiations, or would you prefer us to just begin our search and speak of trade another time? Of course, we could also open talks about what King Alintarneth wishes for peace with your kingdom and how to best achieve that."

"What would best serve to find lasting peace within our kingdoms would be for the nobles to be put into their places and kept there. Also, to find a way to heal my husband, king of this affliction that has overcome him in recent moons. He was a vigorous and proud man not that long ago, not this doddering fool who can barely sit on his throne. My court wizards are powerful in many ways, but they are not good about the healing methods that I have heard of from some of your people. For the ability to search for your missing people amongst ours, I would have to demand in return that one of your priest pairs come here and help to cure my husband of his illness. As for trade negotiations or peace talks for King Alintarneth, we can discuss them more easily. Let my attendants take my husband to his chambers to rest, and then we can begin to negotiate with my *trusted* advisors."

Griefold was especially interested in the way Queen Elyzabeth put emphasis on the word trusted when talking about her advisors. If the nobles here were more of a problem than in Dantorin with King Alintarneth, then they were going to have a much harder time trying to complete their search in Cantorin. The court wizards waved in unison and then, a moment later, nodded to the guards at the doors to allow the king's attendants into the throne room. They quickly lifted him and his throne as one and took him out into the dark halls of the castle itself.

Then Queen Elyzabeth said, "Follow me to the royal council chambers, and we will discuss your offers in trade and such and the offer for peace from our cousin king in Dantorin." She gestured to her wizards, and they led the way out of the throne room down another route leading deeper into the castle. It was a very short walk of a few minutes until they arrived at a sealed door that the wizards opened for their queen. Without further ceremony, she entered the room and took her place at the head of a large oak table surrounded by backless chairs. No other people entered the room except for the Ameristans and the wizards, with the latter again spelling the room from outside observation. Once again assured of privacy, the queen slumped into her full chair and sighed heavily before saying, "I am sorry for the royal front that I had to put up in front of my husband's guardsmen and nobles. He has been ill, as I said, but my wizards assure me it is not of a natural origin, and their powers do not lead to the ways of healing the body. The wizards of our lands are more martial in their training and tend to be less inclined to learn ways to heal. I want my husband back, but I am afraid that I am losing him more and more every day to whatever this illness is. As for the peace negotiations with Alintarneth, I am the one who will be speaking for my husband until he is healed of this affliction. What does Alintarneth offer in the way of peace, and what does he seek to end the hostility on the border with us?"

Griefold took charge and said, "For King Camineth, we can only offer to send to our aunts, the High Priestesses, for a healing priest pair to come and look into his illness. They are caring and will be swift to respond with help. I am sure we cannot assure you that they will be able to cure him, though. Personally, we know little about the healing method other than the simple binding of wounds that any warrior learns to save himself and his comrades in battle. King Alintarneth wishes peace and for the border fighting to stop as well as you do; it is the nobles on both sides of the border who are fighting against the orders of the king. Furthermore, he proposes a new style of governing the kingdoms so that there is again one kingdom but three rulers.

"When it comes to trade, we will make the same offers for food, wine, aurochs, steel, and warriors to protect the royal family until your guardsmen are all equally equipped. We will insist that all trade between our people and yours come through the royal family since we are tired of the nobles taking advantage of us. We have already provided a list of names to King Alintarneth of those who fall under his rulership, and we will, of course, give you the names of the nobles under your rulership. All the Ameristan people, and us in particular, ask is for the chance to search for the missing young lady from our lands and her guardians. The guardians would be a married couple to you, her protectors, and teachers, while she would be young and of blonde hair. We have noticed that amongst all the Dantorin people, dark hair seems to be the most prominent, so it should be easy to find her. We would hope."

"I can trade with Alintarneth for a fast ship to Amerista and an envoy to the Holy City if you would provide some kind of introduction for them, please. I beg you for your help with this!"

"That is something that I am willing to do for you without any other kind of consideration, Your Majesty." Griefold said with fervor, "I, too, am separated from my heart-mate, and the pain of the separation eats at me every day. It must be so much worse for you to be here and see your heart-mate falling to this illness with nothing that you can do to aid him. I will send my personal sigil to my aunts on your behalf, and they will know it came from me."

"That will be acceptable to me for you to have permission to seek your missing young lady among our people here in Cantorin. Most of the Ameristans who live within our land are employed here at the castle as guardsmen or as merchant guards, whom you would have met on the road here. We are too far inland for most of your countrymen, and the two guardsmen, we have a man and woman warrior pair who came here about the time that you would be looking for. They do have a daughter who is about the right age and has blonde hair as her parents. She is one of my handmaidens and is currently helping to care for my poor husband as we speak."

With his heart racing, Griefold said, "Your majesty, would you be willing to send for these guards and your handmaiden so we may question them with all due haste?"

Blackston and Arten could also feel their hearts racing in their chests at the thought of finding one of the missing sisters so easily and so quickly. Still, they had one more crucial stop to make before they could begin their trek back to Amerista, even if the girl was the one. They had promised to offer peace negations to Deltorin, the third of the Dantorin nations. So far, they seemed to have had some success with Queen Elyzabeth of Cantorin, yet the last king remained a mystery.

While pondering this thought, Queen Elyzabeth spoke, saying, "I believe we still have negotiations about wine, aurochs, steel, and arms before I will have Felinos and Zawar unseal this room, and you can question the young lady. Let us get to it, gentlemen."

It was hours of hard bargaining later when the Ameristans were adamant about limiting the trade to be equal to that of King Alintarneth. Queen Elyzabeth, sensing that the trio was eager to get on with meeting the young lady in question, was just as adamant about trying to gain any advantage over the other kingdom.

Finally, with a small smile of admiration for the trio, she said, "I have no choice but to agree. Your willingness to send for the healers who could help my dear Camineth outweighs any advantages I could get in trade deals from you at this time."

Smiling just as tightly, Blackston said, "I lived most of my life with the Dracolian people, your majesty, and you have the killer instincts of a she-dragon going into the mating season. I would not like to ever be on the other side of the negotiation table with you again."

Arten felt the tension in the room easing as he said, "Please don't forget the part of our reason for being here is the negotiations for peace with Dantorin, Cantorin, and even Deltorin when we arrive there. King Alintarneth would like to propose a council of Kings who would rule jointly with one another and all share power between themselves equally. He proposes that no king is above another and that all share power equally, with all trade being shared amongst the kings and tight control over the nobles, especially those who seek to cause war. How does your majesty feel about this proposal?"

Queen Elyzabeth leaned forward onto the table before her and steepled her fingers together as she looked deep into the eyes of each of the men before her. She said, "Would he be willing to state this under a truth spell by wizards from the guild of no court to assure me that he speaks the truth?"

"King Alintarneth was most willing to do so, Your Majesty, as long as all three rulers were to do the same with him at the same time. He truly wants peace in these lands and to end the fighting of the nobles. It is the nobles and not he who wish to conquer your lands and the lands of Deltorin; he is not willing to admit it, but even among his own nobles, there is a rising tide against him. We observed this ourselves when we traveled through Dantorin and saw how the noble keeps were armed for war with the steel they have been assuring us was being traded for their king these past winters. Tallantanar Petralis has assured us that we have the power to deny all trade with any Dantorin, no matter their homeland, without the express permission of their king." The last part was a minor lie, being as only Griefold and Blackston had said this, yet they felt assured that their older brother would agree to this restriction.

"I can agree with those terms. I will send it to Tapio and his wife, Atena, in a few minutes. As for Arista, she will be sent for immediately." Queen Elyzabeth said promptly, waving for Felinos and Zawar to lift the spell sealing the room and for them to call for the necessary people.

Recognizing the name of one of their missing sisters was all that the brothers could do to keep a calm façade about themselves. The two names of the Ameristans who were pretending to be the missing girl's parents were, in fact, the Velocity Master and one-half of the priestess pair sent to protect and train her. Arten was hoping that the other priestess, Melia, was still alive and could be found as well. It would be well for Ameristan people for the entire group to be able to return home like they had with Blackston. As Petralis had stated all those moons ago, it was time to start to bring the family back together and to heal their nation.

A young blonde-haired girl entered the room, followed by two Ameristans dressed as Dantorin guards. Before anyone could say anything, the girl said, "Your majesty, I do not wish to leave his majesty alone for long. He is feeling worse today than before and needs more attention. Melia says that there is nothing her potions can do anymore that will prevent him from growing worse."

The shock and fear for her husband were clear on Queen Elyzabeth's face as the blood drained from it. She said in growing horror, "Daveth is only five winters old. He will not grow into his majority for at least ten more winters and cannot take control of himself. The nobles would never stand for me to rule as regent! There has to be something that we can do to save my husband!"

Arten spoke into the quiet that came about after the queen's outburst, saying, "I may know of a way to help your king faster than waiting for the messenger to reach the Holy City and the High Priestesses. It would involve some use of some of your people and the admission to some deep secrets that the Tallantanar would rather not have revealed before the time was right. I have to get permission from Griefold and Blackston first, and with your permission, I will speak with them in private."

Queen Elyzabeth waved them away without even a thought as she turned to speak with the young handmaiden, who still had not been properly introduced to the trio. Arten said, "Do we break their secret and tell the Queen who the women really are? I do not know if they are strong enough healers to help the King, but they may be what he needs to survive long enough until help arrives. The problem is that we are not to announce who your sister is until she is safe from any possible attack by the Iramians, whom we still don't know anything about."

"The safety of this King and the possibility of good relations is a strong enough reason to share who our sister truly is. Besides, she obviously cares deeply for the king, or she would not be so worried about his health. If we can get him the help he needs, even temporarily, then she will be more willing to come home with us, I am sure." Blackston stated plainly.

Griefold nodded his head in agreement and said, "We have no choice but to do it the way that you suggest, Arten. She must be told of her history, and the priestesses may be the king's only hope for now."

They returned to the queen, and looking at the Ameristan guardsmen, Blackston said, "Topia, Priestess Melia, we are here to return our sister Arista to her proper place with our people on the order of the Tallantanar. My name is Blackston, third son of Patrallin, brother of Petralis II, brother of Griefold, and heart-mate to the Imperial Princess Amelia of the Dracolian Empire. The Tallantanar has declared it is time to bring back our family together and to heal our nation and people. Arista, you are my sister, and I am proud to name you, so it is time to take you home and find your twin, Aristin."

Arista looked shocked at the statement coming from the dark-haired Ameristan warrior standing before her. She said, "I always knew the day would come when I would have to return to my homeland. My adoptive parents always told me that I had a destiny to uphold and that I would have to leave Cantorin when the time came. I just can't believe that the time came so soon. I can't leave right now, though, with King Camineth in such a dire condition. It is all I can do with the powers of the wizards, and what little power I possess, we are barely keeping him alive."

Griefold then said to his sister, "Arista, your adoptive mother, and her sister are priestesses of Amerton. They have more power than you realize and probably have been keeping that power hidden for many years to prevent the danger that would come to you from using it. Isn't that correct, Priestess Melia?"

The female guardsman smiled slyly as she stepped forward and said, "We have kept our powers hidden away for so many years that my sister and I can hardly remember them anymore. But we know how to rekindle the health of the king if we need to. We have been working together to make the potions that have been sustaining him in these past few moons. We have feared reaching out too much due to the danger to Arista, but there was only so we could do it quietly. Together, Atena and I should be able to sustain King Camineth until a proper healing Priest Pair can be sent for and come stop the poison." Priestess Melia turned to Queen Elyzabeth and continued speaking, saying, "We are sorry for our deception for so long, Your Majesty, but after the king was poisoned, my sister and I started infusing the potions that the healers were giving him with our power to sustain him as best we could. We do not know what poison was used, but it is strong and slow-acting. It is something that we have seen before in the writings of past Priest Pairs in our training. It is a thing of the assassins of the Iramians who have attacked our lands in the past. Only a powerful healing pair can stop the poison and restore his majesty to health."

Queen Elyzabeth's face went from rage to shock, to anger, to resignation in a few short moments before she finally said, "I am grateful that you have been doing what little that you have to keep him alive. I love my husband dearly, but I do not know who would poison him like this. King Alintarneth speaks of peace and has sent the Ameristans as envoys seeking peace, yet he is the one who has control of the ocean shore and contacts outside of the kingdoms. It seems that he is the only one who could have the means to reach out to these assassins and poison my husband. I will not seek to have peace with him under these conditions! It is obvious that King Alintarneth is behind this attempt on my king!"

Sensing that Queen Elyzabeth was close to losing her temper and doing something that she could later regret, the Ameristan men standing there were at a loss for what to do. It was the young Arista who stepped into the situation and calmed the queen with soothing words, saying, "My queen, there is no proof of what you are saying and thinking about your cousin king. Think about it: he is the first one in a generation to reach out for peace and insists that the nobles be held accountable for what has been happening on the border. Please, Your Majesty, let wisdom prevail here. Your own husband has told us in his lucid moments how he does not trust his own nobles very much and that they are not to be allowed any more power. I have been with him almost more than anyone else since he has fallen ill and know that he blames his nobles for his illness, not his cousins. Please, Your Majesty, think clearly on this!"

Queen Elyzabeth visibly took control of her temper and calmed herself down, saying, "My dear handmaid, you are right. I let my emotions get the best of me with worry for my king and husband. I worry that the same thing could happen to my son and then what would happen to my people. Griefold, please make all haste with your mission to Deltorin and share with King Derinteneth that we, too, desire peace. I agree with King Alintarneth that the only way to stop these nobles is to have a unified ruling council. The only stipulation that I have for you is that the priestesses stay to care for my husband. I am sure that you would want them to accompany you on your journey, yet if it is within their powers to help him, then that is what I desire the most."

Melia said, "Your majesty, we would no more leave your husband than I would leave my heart-mate Topia behind. As you may not be aware, we have children of our own who would also suffer greatly if war were to return to our land. Topia, Atena, and I made the decision long ago not to return to Amerista when the time came for Arista to return to her family. We are here for as long as you will have us."

Nodding her understanding and gratitude, Queen Elyzabeth said, "Then it shall be so. I will provide an armed escort of my trusted guardsmen, minus Topia and Melia, to the boarder with Deltorin. I will have my court wizards send a message ahead to King Derinteneth to be waiting for you on the border with his own guardsmen. It is time that we all put these nobles in their places and show them once and for all who is truly the rulers of these lands!"

"We would like to leave within the next day or so if it is possible in order to keep ahead of the news that we have found our sister," Griefold said. "What would be the fastest way to reach the Deltorin border and then to return to our homeland from here? Time is of the essence, and trying to avoid the detection of the Iramians and other possibilities of assassins finding us is paramount."

Topia said, "I have patrolled the border with Deltorin many times for his majesty as a guardsman. Deltorin is the smallest of the kingdoms and shares borders with both Dantorin, Cantorin, and Bostowlia. King Derinteneth has the smallest amount of land but the largest standing army of all the kingdoms of Dantorin. He is under near-constant attacks by the Zealots like we were in your grandfather's time. They do not have the mountain passes of the Dracolian Empire to deal with like we do in Amerista."

"The prospects of peace on two sides of his nation and the ability to call upon aid from his cousin kings should be a large incentive for King Derinteneth, shouldn't it?" Blackston asked. He went on to say, "I mean the possibility of being able to call upon more warriors, with better equipment from our homeland if he agrees with our terms, would greatly aid in the defense of his lands."

"I feel that we should proceed with caution when it comes to approaching this particular king. He may not be as accommodating as Her Majesty or King Alintarneth have been." Arten added.

Queen Elyzabeth said, "I will have Zawar and Felinos reach out to Aafje and Anja. They are the court witches for King Derinteneth from the wizards guild. They are among the strongest members of the guild to be found, but they are old, and he does not always heed their advice because they are women."

Griefold replied to the queen, saying, "That may be, but we are wasting time discussing what may or may not be. We have to move fast to avoid the information that our sister has been found from spreading to our mutual enemies. We should leave as soon as the messages can be sent to Deltorin; the less time the information has to spread that we are on our way there, the better."

All of them quickly agreed to begin the preparations necessary for a quick departure from the castle that day. There was a tearful separation on Arista's behalf since she would be leaving the three people who had raised her as their own. The children that Topia and Melia had that she grew up with as brother and sister, she would be leaving them behind to go with virtual strangers. Growing up, Arista was told the story of what had happened to her family and the history of her people. Meeting two young men barely out of their teens who happened to be her brothers was almost too much. Arista was holding back the tears she felt threatening as she packed her few possessions into a travel pack and was preparing to leave.

It was when she was almost ready to leave that Topia came to her and said, "Arista, you have been a daughter to me your entire life. I am going to miss you dearly, but it is time for you to go with your true family and return to Amerista. I am going to give you something that your father made when your Talla was nearly destroyed all those winters ago. It is one of the Xiphos that your father made in his grief. It is the reason I was sent along to train you and protect you. I trained you in *Velocity*. Like your father, you are equivalent to a master of the art, and it is time for you to strike out on your own. Your brothers and Arten are masters of *Dominance*, so they will not be able to help you with your training regimen. You will have to work on that on your own and keep up with your training in order to be able to protect yourself. Remember, I care for you like a daughter, but it is time for you to move onto your own and become a warrior of our people."

Arista hugged Topia hard and then accepted the sheathed Xiphos that was presented to her with great solemnity. Pulling a few finger lengths of the blade free of the sheath, Arista could see the rainbow-hued metal that her father had forged. She, of course, knew the story about what had happened to the Minnertalla; she did not know she was of that nearly dead Talla until now. Sheathing the blade fully again, she strapped it across her back for a quick draw of her dominant left hand. She also proudly began to belt on her belt of daggers that she had always hidden under dresses and smocks that she wore.

Looking at Topia, she said, "You will tell Cathán and Iovita that I will miss them greatly. Maybe even give them a chance to come and see me when they are older in Amerista. I feel I may never be able to return here again."

Topia replied, "I am sure that your brother and sister will not forget about you, and when they are a little older, we will make sure that they each have a choice to return to Amerista. They should know more about our people, and maybe we can all come home when the dust settles here, and the kingdoms are at peace."

"Don't we all wish for that day to come soon," Melia said as she entered the small room that had once been assigned to Arista. She quickly hugged her foster daughter and continued, saying, "Once King Camineth is restored, we shall return to Amerista for a short visit, but this is truly our home now. There is nothing stopping us from visiting from time to time, though."

Arista smiled at her foster mother and then hugged her just as hard as she had Topia, showing the great affection that she held for both of them. Arista released her foster mother and then turned to leave the small chamber room that had been her own for a few winters. Though she was considered too young to be a woman in Cantorin, only being fifteen, she knew that in Amerista, she would be considered a woman and warrior by now. Many thoughts ran through her mind since she had never shaved her head like her brothers and given herself a warrior's braid. Maybe she should do that, but she would have to ask about why her brothers had griffon feathers in their braids and not the steel chains of the Minnertalla. There were so many things that she had to learn about her own Talla, as well as her brothers, in such a short amount of time.

CHAPTER 16

It was later that very day that the Ameristans and a handpicked escort of royal guardsmen left the castle and began the trek again to the border with the last of the Dantorin kingdoms. Deltorin was complete to the north of the other two kingdoms and was even rockier and more baren looking than the land they had traveled to before. It was only a hardy people who could stand living in this rough land, and it made for hard people who would be facing them. It took them only a few hours of travel to reach the border, and then the royal guardsmen stopped short of the border by hundreds of feet. On the other side of the unmarked border between the kingdoms was a large escort of over one hundred guardsmen in the livery of the Deltorin royal house. Each was armored in true steel in good condition and carried steel swords in equal condition. It was obvious that the nobles of Deltorin were not the ones who were directing the inappropriate deals with the Ameristan people. Given what they had learned about the attacks from the north from the Zealots of Bostowlia, it made more sense that the border guards would be better equipped than the nobles' guards.

With a minimum of fuss, the Ameristans passed the border, feeling the tenseness of the two sets of guardsmen. Both sides stayed well out of bowshot of the border, and no sound was exchanged between them. The Ameristans were careful to show no signs of reaching for their weapons or any kind of aggression at all. There was such a feeling of imminent violence that the guards from Deltorin were giving off. These guards were obvious veterans of combat with the scars on their bodies and the worn look to the armor upon closer inspection. These guardsmen were obviously rotated away from fighting recently in order to rest and recover before being sent back to the fighting. Combat veterans were going to be the more dangerous and on edge for the smallest thing that could lead to fighting. Arten was aware of this from his time fighting off the Iramians and occasional Zealot attacks.

Griefold, taking the lead for his small group of family, said, "I am here as the envoy from King Alintarneth and King Camineth searching for a consensus of peace with King Derinteneth. I can speak for the Tallantanar of Amerista for offers of trade and mutual aid against Zealot raids. I need to speak with your king to make the offers from his cousin kings as well as from my Tallantanar. We will allow ourselves to be disarmed when in the presence of your king and queen. Until then, we rely upon you for our safety. Do we have permission to cross the border and seek counsel with your king on his lands?"

A heavily scarred grizzled veteran came forward and said, "I am Captain Zotikos of the First Regiment of the Royal Deltorin Border Guards. I will take you to my king and give you my word that we will escort all four of you safely to the palace. King Derinteneth is awaiting you and your companions; he has received word of your coming from the royal court witches and your mission of peace."

Nodding in understanding, Griefold, Blackston, Arista, and Arten moved carefully across the border of the two nations from Cantorin to Deltorin proper. As the Ameristans crossed the border, they were quickly enveloped by the regiment of guardsmen and escorted away from the border. They were not allowed to step outside of the cordon of guards and were only allowed to speak with Captain Zotikos when they had questions about their route.

It was only a matter of two days before they were led to the royal palace, which was more of a squat castle than the others they had already seen, such as the palace of King Derinteneth and Queen Arleth. That was all that Griefold and his companions were able to learn. They were able to determine that they had been taken by a circuitous route to the castle and that they had doubled back several times by tracking the stars above. While not the stars that they were most familiar with for traveling, they were still able to determine that they should have been at the castle itself in less than a day of travel.

Speaking quietly amongst themselves under the cover of darkness, Arista was able to explain the reason behind the deception to the rest of the party. She said, "While they are the smallest of the three kingdoms, the Deltorins are the proudest. The late King Derinteneth I was the first born of the triplets and saw himself as the proper king of all of Dantorin and was the first to start the war to try and claim all of the lands for himself. When his brothers disagreed and stood against him, he took the castle at the border and tried to make deals with the Bostowlian priests for aid. They, of course, betrayed him, and he lost most of his land in the subsequent battles with his brothers and the Zealots. His son, King Derinteneth II, has since tried to hold onto what little lands he was left with and is trying to keep the Zealots out in order to save his kingdom."

Blackston said, "In Dracolia, where I grew up, the Zealot raids were a near-constant thing as well. They would come through the passes and attack the outlying villages of the Empire, looking for slaves as well as for livestock for their Tigre. If it were not for the constant work of the Dragon Riders in the past ten winters, the raids would be worse for the Dracolian Empire."

"Sounds like we need to make these negotiations quickly and get back home to start the process of sending the weapons and armor that these kingdoms need," Griefold said thoughtfully. "The sooner we get home and finalize the trade negotiations with these three kingdoms and can protect our Talla, the better off we all will be."

The other three nodded their agreement, even Arista, who was still coming to grips with the fact that she was part of the ruling family of a nation she only knew about from stories.

As they approached the so-called palace, they could see it was more of a castle designed for defense than for looks or splendor. Unlike the castles of Dantorin and Cantorin, this structure was low to the ground, barely standing above the rocks from which it was built. This structure also bore the scars of many battles on its outside walls and was heavily fortified from the outside by a sizeable regiment of guardsmen. While the regiment that had escorted the Ameristans from the border numbered around one hundred, there were several hundred guards surrounding and on top of the palace of King Derinteneth. These guards were not as well armored as the border guards regiment, but they were also obviously veterans of more than a few battles, and this showed in their bearing. These guards were steadier looking and sharper of eye in appearance than members of the First Regiment who had escorted them. They appeared ready for action at any moment, as did any warriors the Ameristans had ever seen. These were the elite warriors of Deltorin, and it looked like these guardsmen were ready for a fight.

Griefold said, "Keep your hands away from your weapons while we are here, and do your best to keep from saying anything that can be considered a threat while we are here. It is too obvious that these Royal Guardsman are on edge for some reason, and we don't want to give them any excuse to attack us."

"I agree with you whole heartedly on the fact that they are on edge and that we must tread carefully from here on out," Arten said quickly. "I wonder if they are expecting an attack to come from either of the kingdoms to the south or from Bostowlia to the north?"

"Why not both," Blackston asked, "if they are at war on all their border kingdoms, then maybe they are not sure who may attack?"

"Personally, I am more afraid that the Bostowlians are attacking more since the treaties we have made with the Dracolian Empire are pushing them away from our land," Griefold said. "With King Alintarneth and Queen Elyzabeth seeking peace, there would be no need for worry coming from the south. It must have been the Bostowlians attacking more and pushing for more land of their own. I mean, what do we really know of their lands other than that they are south of the Dracolian Empire and covered in jungle?"

Arista said, "The only people in the area who would have any knowledge of the Bostowlian lands are the Deltorins. I don't think that they are in the mood to share that information with us right now."

Before they could say anything further about what might be happening, the Ameristans were interrupted by Captain Zotikos, who said, "I will leave you here now. The Royal Guard will see you from now on, and they will escort you into the palace to see King Derinteneth when he is ready to receive you. I wish you well, warriors." With that, he turned on his heel, sharply motioned to his regiment, and led them back to the south in a direct line this time.

A Royal Guardsman approached them, and from his dress and demeanor he was obviously the Captain of the Royal Guard. He said, "I am Captain Medraut of his Majesty's Royal Guard, and I am here to see you disarmed and brought to see King Derinteneth. His majesty has expressed a desire to see you right away and to hear what words his cousin kings wish to share."

Royal Guardsmen quickly began disarming the four warriors and patting them down for concealed knives or daggers. The guardsman who was patting down Arista took free advantage of the chance to search her more thoroughly than her brothers, and Arten were being searched. This caused anger to flash across her face and the three others to clench their fists in preparation for a fight.

As her companions were about to lash out in anger, Arista quickly lashed out with a vicious strike of her own. She kicked the guardsman squarely between the legs so hard that he immediately crumpled to the ground, gasping in pain. She said, "I have more of the same for any other guardsman who feels free with his hands upon my person like this fellow. I will not allow it to continue if you can't keep your hands where they belong. I will gladly put your manhood where it belongs. *Up around your ears!*"

The remainder of the guardsmen dropped their hands to sword hilts in preparation to fight. Captain Medraut simply smiled at Arista as he casually walked over to the prostrate man. With no sign of concern or effort, he kicked the guard in the belly, flopping him onto his back, saying, "If you can't do your job correctly, then maybe you don't belong in my command. Get yourself on your feet and get out of my sight before I rearm this young woman and let her castrate you *to her heart's content*! Young lady, I am sorry for what happened just now. His Majesty did not want anything or anyone to offend you and your companions. He will be punished for his actions and sent off to one of the border regiments until he learns his manners again. As for the rest of you, take your hands off those hilts. These are envoys from at least one fellow kingdom and deserve more respect than has been shown to them."

With guilty expressions and shows of chagrin on their faces, the rest of the Royal Guard quickly moved their hands back to neutral positions. With the sudden drop in tension and the return to the normalcy of the guardsman stance of wary but poised for action, the Ameristans were escorted into the Deltorin palace. In this castle, unlike its counterparts, there were no rich tapestries hanging from the walls, nor was there any fine furniture to be seen. As they were escorted by a ring of armed guardsmen, they could feel that they were going deeper into the ground. Everywhere they looked, the lighting was crude candles and torches or murder holes cut into the ceiling of the castle to let in fresh air and sweep away the smoke. There was no beauty to this structure; it was designed entirely for defense, and it showed.

After several minutes of walking in what seemed to be the center of the castle, the Ameristans were brought to what appeared to be the throne room. Sitting on a massive, gilded throne was a young man of about eighteen winters and of a slight frame. This had to be King Derinteneth, yet where his cousins were large-framed and hard-muscled like warriors, he appeared more bookish. Sitting on a smaller throne to his right was one of the most beautiful women that any of them had ever seen. She had fiery red hair and a pale complexion; her belly was swollen with child, and she glowed with health. This had to be his wife, Queen Arleth.

Once they were brought to the throne room, King Derinteneth said, "So you are the envoys that my court witches told me were coming to try to broker this so-called peace with my cousins. Tell me, why should I trust you in any way? You are from Amerista, far to the north. You came through Dantorin and King Alintarneth's court, gaining his favor and offering him trade in steel and warriors to protect him. Next, you spent time in Cantorin with Queen Elyzabeth. Yes, I know my cousin King Camineth is a bit under the weather, but do you know who poisoned him? Is he his own majordomo? I do! You promised her the same things: steel and warriors to protect them, along with something else to make her reach out to me for some reason. I have a very good spy network, yet I do not know why you are reaching out to me. I have nothing to offer you. I control the smallest of the three kingdoms and have nothing worth trading for as far as your people are concerned. So, tell me why you are here?!" This last was said by the young king as he rose from his throne, his face turning redder by the second.

Queen Arleth reached out a calming hand to her husband and said, "Peace, my husband. Give them a chance to answer your demands and see what reason brings them to our court and why they are being sent as envoys by your cousins."

Visibly calming himself, King Derinteneth sat once again upon his gilded throne and said, "I will hear you out before I pass judgement upon you for coming to my court. As you can see, we are awaiting an imminent attack from our enemies, both my cousins and the Bostowlians. My guardsmen will keep us safe as they have done since my father's time at the separation of the kingdoms, and his rightful place was stolen by his brothers."

Griefold, sensing that this particular king was on edge due to the dangers, either real or imagined, decided to speak frankly and calmly with him. He said to the king, "I am Griefold, brother of Petralis II; this is my brother Blackston, our sister Arista, and my friend Arten. We were sent to these kingdoms in search of our sister Arista, who was residing in your cousin's court for some winters now. We only offered to be envoys of peace to King Alintarneth, to your cousin, and to yourself, your majesty, as a means to an end. We needed a way to travel and search for our sister, and we have heard tales and seen how the nobles of the other two kingdoms vied for control of them. It is obvious that in your kingdom, you are the one in control of your nobles and that they do not seek war with your cousins to the south of you. We will make the same offers of peace and trade with you that we made with your cousins. Trade in steel, aurochs, and warriors to protect yourself and your queen until your men are equally armed as your cousins and more. Also, we bring word from your cousin kings that both desire a lasting peace between your nations by forming a council of kings where each of you shares power. By ruling as a council, you would be able to call upon the forces of your cousins to help defend your borders to the north without having to defend to the south. We can offer warriors to help defend your northern border instead of yourself and your family if you so desire. There will not be many, but any warrior is better than no warrior. We have a treaty with the Dracolian Empire to keep the Zealots from raiding our lowlands in our south by closing the passes as best that they can. Maybe we can speak to them on your behalf to try and do the same thing on your northern border with the Bostowlians."

King Derinteneth said, "Unfortunately, we don't have mountain passes to keep the Zealot raids from coming. We share a more porous border with Bostowlia. Their jungles and grasslands lead onto what used to be our northern plains. In my father's time, we were able to keep them at the edge of the grasslands. Now, they have pushed us so far south we are facing imminent attack on a daily basis from the Zealots and their Tigre'. I have lost so many men in the last few moons that I am facing losing my kingdom entirely, and you say your solution is peace with cousins whose nobles seek to take my kingdom from me as well?"

"No, what I am proposing is that you ask for help from your cousins in return for letting us help you find a way to keep your people safer," Griefold replied hotly. "We are not your enemy; we only seek peace for the sake of peace. By forging an alliance with your cousin kings and our people, we may be able to persuade the Dracolian Empire to help stop the Zealots as a whole. Instead, each of our nations deals with the raids in our own way. Maybe, just maybe, if we were to work together as an alliance of people, we could take the fight to them. Try to find in your heart the truth that we are here to help you for no other reason than to help."

Queen Arleth said, "Husband, listen to them. Why else would they have come so far once they had found the girl that they were looking for when they could have simply turned around and gone home? They say that they are here for peaceful purposes and wish to help us with the threats that we face to the north. Listen to them. I am soon to deliver your child, and I do not want to do so under the threat of attack or death by the Zealots."

The king turned to his queen and said, "I will listen to them, my queen, if only for your sake and the sake of our unborn child. I am fearful, though, that the next attack may be the last attack that we face as a people with the dangers all around us. I will consult with Aafje and Anja, as well as the Captains of the Regiments, before making a final decision. Will that appease you, my love?"

Queen Arleth said, "Of course, my king, please be at peace and take council with your Captains and the court witches. I think that I will retire for a time. Young Arista, would you mind coming with me so that the men can talk and you can have a chance to relax with other young ladies? My king, my lords, please excuse me." Then, the queen carefully stood from her throne and held out a hand for Arista to accompany her out of the throne room.

Once the women had left the room, Griefold and his remaining companions tried to relax a little and breathed a sigh of relief. Hopefully, with his queen carefully resting, King Derinteneth would be more amenable to solutions and trade talks than when he had her sitting next to him and was worried about her condition.

King Derinteneth said in a calmer tone, "I can understand the reason behind your coming to my kingdom, yet I don't know what I have to offer in trade for your people."

Arten spoke, saying, "I am of the Griffonara, the Royal Guard of the Tallantanar if you will, and I can speak for the quality of our warriors. I have not met your warriors in combat or seen them in combat, so I can't say how good they are. I would suggest that my people are just as good as, if not better than, your own warriors. I have personally slain more than a dozen Zealots in the few raids that they attempted when I was on patrol, and I know just how dangerous their Tigre can be. I suggest that you let us send word through King Alintarneth to my Tallantanar for a push from the north into Bostowlian lands to relieve the pressure on your northern border. My father is the leader of the Griffonara, and I am on good terms with the Tallantanar, so my word carries some weight in the Holy City."

"I can speak on behalf of my brother and assure that any negotiations that we settle upon, whether they be for trade or mutual defense, will be held as solid as any possible pledge." Griefold continued as if Arten had not even spoken. He knew that the Griffonara was working to try to help him establish trust with this mercurial king, but he did not want to go too far in promises that his brother could not keep. While Petralis was the leader of the Ameristan people, he did not speak for all of the Talla or Tallanta. Each Tallanta would choose how many warriors he or she could spare, if any, to the defense of other people. There were always possible attacks by the Iramians, even though they had been infrequent lately, but the raids by the Zealots were still a consideration.

Each of the warriors knew that they had to take these and many other thoughts into consideration before agreeing to anything with King Derinteneth about mutual defense. Blackston spoke up, saying, "I am heart-mate to the Imperial Princess of the Dracolian Emperor; Emperor Ashvin and his Dragon Riders are more than an adequate force to help put pressure on the Bostowlians. That is, if he is approached correctly and valid reasons are given to him to put his warriors into the fight, I can speak on your behalf since I am like a son to him if you would allow me."

King Derinteneth looked thoughtful and said, "You all would do this for my people with no promises of anything in return for yourselves?"

"Of course," the trio said in near unison.

Each, in turn, then restated the reasons behind the offers that they had just made to the king and the purposes behind them. With a mutual enemy of at least three nations sharing a border, if all nations were to press, then maybe they could either cow the Bostowlians into peace or bring them to the negotiation table for the same purpose. No matter what, there had to be a consensus between the leaders of the nations to force something upon the Bostowlians to keep them under control.

King Derinteneth took a deep sigh and finally said, "I have no choice but to agree with you on this, do I? If I am to keep my people alive and drive the Bostowlians back to their own lands, then I have to agree to peace with my cousins, work with your brother, and work with Emperor Ashvin. My father would be spinning in his grave if he knew that I was acknowledging that my cousins were equal in power to me. You know, it was he who started all of this fighting for the throne of Dantorin and was finally pushed back by his brothers to this small strip of a kingdom by the other two. He was so sure that since he was born first of the triplets, he was the one destined to rule when his grandfather died. Father was a fool!"

"Don't lament the dead; we never know what the real reasons behind the choices that others make, and speaking ill of them only attracts their attention from the afterlife, according to the priests," Arten said.

Blackston and Griefold nodded their agreement as they relaxed even more now that the king seemed ready to negotiate in earnest. Once King Derinteneth summoned Captain Medraut, Anja, and Aafje, the negotiations began. His other regimental captains were either at the borders, on patrol, or otherwise involved in the defense of their homeland. Anja and Aafje used their power to reach out to the Wizard's Guild to send for more wizards to come in defense of Deltorin. Since they had come with assurances of the other two kings to control their nobles and have them pulled from the border, Deltorin was now not in as much danger. Speaking through their court wizards and witches for the first time in their entire lives, the three cousin kings began to hammer out the beginning of a true peace treaty amongst themselves. This was the best situation that Griefold could hope for since finding Arista in Cantorin and negotiating with Queen Elyzabeth.

The time to return to their homeland was quickly approaching, and then the search for Aristin was going to be the next thing they would do. Where she was hidden in Iristia, only the High Priestesses knew, and they would not reveal that information any time soon, Griefold and his companions were sure.

CHAPTER 17

It was without any ceremony that the Ameristans once again were on the move to their next destination. At least this time, their destination was going to be their homeland. It took almost two whole tendays to cross the two kingdoms to the capital and port city of Dantorin itself. Luckily, Captain Meltern was still in port awaiting orders from King Alintarneth to take the Ameristans home since he had one of the fastest ships when unloaded of cargo. The *Sea Spirit* was already fully provisioned, and since this time, the true identities of his passengers have been known. Captain Meltern was a much more accommodating person. Instead of letting themselves be treated as honored passengers, the men once again took to working alongside the crew just as they had on their journey south. With a good following wind and an empty cargo bay, the *Sea Spirit* made the trip back to Amerista in just over a moon. It was much faster than the original trip since they had the southern winds behind them, stirring up the storms that would slash the coasts of Amerista through the winter moons. Arriving ahead of the storms was a good thing since there would be little in the way of trade until spring, and the change in the weather allowed for safe passage again. This, however, would not stop the quick return of Captain Meltern to Dantorin in order to deliver the much-needed healer Priest Pair promised to Queen Elyzabeth. With time being of the essence for this particular promise, only warriors from a few select Talla were sent to protect the priest and priestess as well as to fulfill the deals that had been made.

The *Sea Spirit* set to sea into an incoming storm within a few days of arrival at the storm-battered coast of Amerista. In the meantime, the searching party turned their way to the Holy City. Arista was thrilled to be able to present herself to her last brother and the chance to have firm land under her feet once again. Like her brothers, she did not handle the voyage very well at first, and it did not improve for her as the trek went on because of the increasing storms.

While the coast was lashed with increasing storms and winds, the plains of Amerista were being covered by snow. This was a new experience for Arista since the Southlands of Dantorin never experienced this phenomenon, even in the coldest winters. The fact that the material fell from the sky and did not seem to stay long enough was at first fascinating to the young lady. Yet, as the winter weather started to settle in, she began to grow sick of the sight of snow. Her brothers and Arten, who have spent their entire lives living upon the plains or the mountain passes of Dracolia, relished the return to the cold of winter. Each of the travelers wrapped in furs and walking as fast as possible in the rising snow drifts, made their way home. During this time, Blackston and Griefold questioned Arista about her knowledge of their people and helped as best as they could to fill the gaps. This was done primarily by Griefold since Blackston, himself, had been raised away from his people and still had some areas that he did not know about.

It was during their three-day trek to the Holy City of Amerista that Arista was instructed in depth about her family history and the tragedy of their parents. After learning that she and her twin were sent away the very day of their birth and separated, she asked, "Why did our aunts separate me and my twin upon the day of our birth? I have had dreams of a sister that I have never met, but I did not believe that they were more than that; they were just dreams. Why separate any of us from one another? We are obviously stronger together than apart!"

Griefold could only shrug his shoulders in confusion as he said, "They are the High Priestesses of Amerton; he gave them a vision, they claim, that the separation of us as children was the most important part of keeping all of us safe from danger. Mother and father were both killed the day you were born, and I can only remember that day is blood and death. I remember the death of our father as he kept the assassins away from us children and the promise that I made to our mother to keep you and Aristin safe from any danger. Then the aunts came and took you two away from us; other than that, I can't remember much."

"I, too remember very little of that day, sister," Blackston said sorrowfully, "I was too young to remember much more than the oath I made to our mother to keep you and Aristin safe. She was adamant about that."

Arista was near to tears as she said, "But, I have a twin; doesn't that mean that I am also a Priestess then?! Shouldn't I have been raised with Aristin in the Holy City like Petralis and you, Griefold?!"

Griefold tried to put a consoling arm around Arista's shoulders to ease her discomfort for her to shrug him away in anger. He said, "That is a question that only the High Priestesses can answer for you, and I will support you in asking them. The aunts can be very difficult to talk to since they are so involved with the priesthood and speak with Amerton so often. At least that is the excuse I always got."

"That is not good enough for me!" She said, sniffling a little, "I am going to get answers from those two, no matter what I have done to them!"

"I wish you the best of luck and will do what I can to help you with that," Griefold said, "just be aware that they are also two of the most powerful women in our country, and even Petralis has to answer to them at times."

Arista moved away from the other three and continued to mutter under her breath for some time about interfering with people and such. It was obvious to her brothers and Arten that she was in no mood to be comforted or consoled about the separation from her twin sister.

For the remainder of the journey, Arista did not speak much to her traveling companions, still fuming over the facts that she had confirmed for herself. At the same time, the three men were concentrating on trying to teach her the significance of learning how to survive winter on the plains. Arista had grown up primarily in the castle of Cantorin as a handmaiden to Queen Elyzabeth. The trek through the snow and all of the walking was wearing on the young woman, and it was telling. It was little more than three days from their final destination when the travelers finally made contact with one of the roaming patrols of Griffon Riders who were in the area. With the Riders clearing a path in the deepening snow, the travelers were finally able to speed up their trek.

At first sight of the griffons, Arista was shocked beyond belief that such a creature could exist. She had seen the lions of the southern plains on occasion be brought in for presentation to the court. She had also seen many large birds of prey used for falconry by the king before his illness, but never a cross between the two. She was fascinated by the creatures and how tame they appeared. To say that she was enraptured was an understatement. The size of the griffons alone was what astonished her the most; the fact that each creature could carry a full-grown Ameristan easily, as well as fly with them, was shocking. She began begging for short rides with the Griffon Riders as they sped their trip. Each warrior was more than willing to share the thrill of the sky with the young lady. They did not know who she was in relation to the brothers, but each rider had an inkling that this was the missing sister of their Tallantanar and that keeping her happy would be a benefit to her. It was obvious that her spirits were low for the most part due to the travel, unfamiliar weather, and distance from all that she had known her entire life. It also was obvious that she was dealing with information that was difficult for her to hear, even though she would not share it.

When they were able to see the walls of the Holy City and the smoke rising from the many fires of the longhouses of the Talla, did Griefold put an end to the fun for Arista? He said to her, "It's time for you to be formally introduced to our brother and Tallantanar as well as to our aunts. Petralis will be more than overjoyed to finally see you again after all of these winters, but you have to be careful what you say to the High Priestesses. They may be the reason we were all separated, but as I said before, they carry a great amount of power among our people, and they are not used to being questioned."

Arista merely nodded her head in grim agreement and said nothing to her older brother as they approached the gate. At the gate, there was no ceremony. Griefold and Arten were recognized at once, and the Griffonara guarding the gate opened it with all due haste. While Arista looked around at the longhouses of her people for the first time in her life, Griefold and Blackston eyed the city streets, looking for their heart-mates. Blackston was certain that Princess Amelia would be at the gate waiting for him since they had such a short time together before he had left. Griefold was just as certain that Bernella would be waiting for him at the gate once word had been sent to the Holy City of his imminent arrival. The brothers worried that something might have happened to their loved ones during the moons of their search. As it was after clearing the gate and it closed once again behind them, the Ameristan people began to come from the longhouses into the winter air. Slowly, at first, the crowd quickly grew into the hundreds of thousands of warriors and such that made up the nation in their winter homes. The noise alone was near deafening as the shouts about the return of the brothers and Arista to their home were heard. The joyous crowds surrounded the four and escorted them to the Tallantanar's own longhouse, with the noise proceeding them. It was not until Petralis II himself stepped from the longhouse and raised his hands in a commanding gesture that the crowds began to calm themselves from the excitement.

Petralis had to shout over the loud murmuring of the assembled people as he said, "My people, my brothers, and one of my missing sisters have returned to us, as you can easily see. I have not had a chance to meet her yet, and your joy at her return is enough to warm our hearts. Let my Talla and my family have this day to meet one another and for my sister to meet my child for the first time. After this day, I promise that I will give all of you a chance to speak with Blackston and Arista and get to know them like you know me and Griefold. I am sure that they are just as eager to meet all of you in time and to get to know you all as their fellow warriors and friends."

The crowd shouted its agreement before slowly dispersing back to their respective longhouses to get out of the winter winds. Many still lingered here and there to get a sight of the young lady that had come from so far and was, by all accounts of the young men present, a true beauty. Having grown up amongst the most beautiful women of the courts of Dantorin, Arista was unaware of her allure. Her brothers only saw her as their sister, and Arten was indifferent when it came to women's concerns. Now that they were seeing her effect on the other young Ameristan warriors, Griefold and Blackston become protective of her. They felt that she was far too young for prospective suitors, even though they were only five and three winters her senior, respectively.

Arista was basking in the attention of all the many young males and even a few female warriors who were admiring her from afar. She began to blush in spite of herself and the resentment she felt towards her aunts. The attention was heady. She was used to not being seen and not being the center of attention, but for the first time amongst her own people, she was an outstanding beauty like her late mother.

Petralis, seeing the attention of the young warriors upon his younger sister and the over-protectiveness rising in his younger brothers, said, "Maybe it is time to bring you all inside to introduce you to your niece and reacquaint yourselves with your heart-mates and sister. All are inside and waiting where it is warm instead of braving the weather with me like sensible people. Come, come." Upon hearing that the people they were looking for were mere steps away from them, Griefold and Blackston rushed inside the longhouse, nearly knocking Petralis off of his feet. Inside, near the central fire, sat Mirta holding a sleeping infant in her arms with a contented smile on her face. Seated on either side of her were Princess Amelia and Bernella. Amelia was obviously with her child herself and struggling to get to her feet to greet Blackston. Bernella had no such problems jumping to her feet, rushing to Griefold, leaping into his arms, and knocking him to the ground.

The small family and group watched as the two warriors held each other tightly and struggled to find the words to share their love with one another. Blackson and Amelia, on the other, had come together with great gentleness on his part as he realized that she was pregnant. The look of joy and shock on his face was enough to bring tears to even the most hardened warrior's eyes, and Barten, who entered just then, started to shed a few tears. This was the most heartwarming event that the old warrior had seen in a very long time, and he cherished it greatly.

Barten spoke into the loud chatter of the reuniting lovers and returning family, saying, "I know that all of you are very happy to be reunited with your loved ones, but I think that it is time for the assembling of the council of the Tallanta to inform them of who has returned and to seek the council of the High Priestesses."

"Speaking of the High Priestesses, I would like to have some words with them before long, and I have some things to say to them about separating me from my twin sister!" Arista growled out between gritted teeth.

Petralis replied to her statement, "You may speak with them all you want, but I have no control over what they are going to say in response to your questions. I have asked them many times over the winters about why they sent the two of you to separate places when they split us up. All I ever got for an answer was they would reveal the answer sometime in the future. The aunts can be very difficult to deal with at the best of times, and when they choose to be stubborn, they are the worst beings to deal with on the face of the plains."

"I will see about that!" Arista said, still growling between her teeth. She then turned to the young infant and asked to hold her in her arms. She had some experience with infants and knew how to hold the baby without injuring her. Arista cooed lovingly at her niece and smiled at the looks of the baby returning to her. She held the baby for a few more moments before handing it over to her waiting mother.

Mirta said, "I am glad to meet you, Arista. I am also glad that you have had a chance to meet your niece while she was awake and not squalling for a change. She has quite strong lungs, and I swear she can be heard all the way back to the Sun's Dagger Mountains from here when she chooses."

Smiling like the proud father that he was, Petralis said, "Bealdhild is a strong daughter and will be a great Tallantanar when the time comes, and I pass onto the great plains with Amerton. In the meantime, I think that we will let you four return to the Minnertalla longhouse to refresh yourselves before the council. I want to introduce Arista to Tallanta and inform them of the deals that you negotiated with the Dantorins. Arista, I want you to try to relax and spend some time getting to know me and my family. I know you had some time to get to know Griefold and Blackston, but I think that you have a lot to learn about the rest of us. Come to me if there is anything that you want or need, and I will see to it immediately."

Arista nodded her head stiffly and said, "Just a few moons ago, I was just pretending to be the daughter of two of the guardsmen of Cantorin and two younger siblings that I care for deeply. Next, I found out that I have an identical twin sister whom I have been dreaming about my entire life and that we were separated at birth. Now you want me to come to you with any problems I may have or what I may need. How about you send me back to my home, reunite me with my missing sister, and leave me alone!"

"You were separated at birth because, as a budding priest pair, your powers are like a beacon to our enemies," came the echoing voices of the High Priestesses speaking in unison, "and they would have spared no expense in lives to kill the both of you. Amerton spoke to us in visions and told us to separate you from Aristin in order to protect you in the best way possible. Your attitude is childish. We have always known where to find you and how to bring you and your twin home again, just like we did for Blackston. We have had to work to keep your and your sister's powers at bay, even separated by such distances, for your own sake. This is not something that we did lightly, and yes, we do regret it to this day that it had to be done, but you five are all that we have left of our beloved sister, and we could not bear to lose all of you as well as her."

The startled girl turned suddenly to look for the first time upon the faces of her identical twin aunts who had caused the separation of her family. The anger she felt melted away from her countenance upon looking at them for the first time in her memory. They wore snow-white leather robes denoting their status as High Priestesses, but there was no other adornment. Instead, the very power that they carried about themselves fairly glowed about them, and even the most average person could feel their power.

Arista quickly bowed to the aunts that she had never met in the custom of the lands that she had grown up in and quickly started muttering apologies. She said, "High Priestesses, please forgive me. You are obviously ladies of power and prestige and deserve my utmost respect in all things. Please, please ignore the harsh statements that I made about you and forgive my ignorance of your abilities."

Moving as one, as the twins had done for many winters now, the High Priestesses walked forward from the doorway and embraced their niece in a comforting hug. Iriena and Aralla finally started speaking in sequence, finishing one another's sentences like they had done for most of their lives as they said, "Arista, you and Aristin are destined to be, if not as powerful as us, then very near that level. We had to separate you for your own safety and to protect your brothers in their youth. The Iramians are very powerful magic users in their own right, and their magic is based on death. We had to protect you girls most of all since the power that the two of you could control would be a very powerful incentive to draw the Iramians to our people more than ever before. Come to the spring thaw; we will send for your twin sister; she has been living with the Iristians across the Suns Dagger Mountains within their horse clans. She has been trained by her guardians like you have been and has been reaching out to you in her dreams as you have been reaching out to her. We can no longer keep you two apart; your powers are growing too strong for that. It is time to bring you two together and to begin to train you. It will take several winters before you both are ready to take your place among the priest pairs."

Petralis said, "Once my sister comes with the spring from Iristia, I plan on starting to work with the southern kingdoms on pushing back the Zealots as Griefold and Blackston have negotiated for us. I will fight to keep their word with the southern Kings in order to show that our honor is unquestionable. It is time for the Ameristan people to stop protecting just ourselves from danger and to show the world where we truly stand. I will seek the consensus of the Tallanta and seek the permission of Amerton in this, High Priestesses."

Iriena and Aralla continued speaking one after another, saying, "That is something that will have to be brought up with the council of Tallanta; we cannot give full support at this time. We must commune with the other priest pairs as with our God and determine if He supports this decision. Is that clear, nephew?" The last was said in the unison voice that they used when speaking as the High Priestesses.

Petralis nodded his head with reluctance. It was obvious that he wanted to prove himself to his people as more than just a figurehead. Even though his people saw him as their God's appointed leader, he had done nothing to show he was more than any other warrior. It itched at him that he had never drawn a sword in anger and that the only time he had drawn blood was in the practice ring or when he had fought with Griefold. Meanwhile, his Griffonara and Griffon Riders saw combat with the occasional Zealot raid or the even more infrequent attack by the Iramians when they attacked the plains. Griefold and Blackston also felt the need to fight for their people, but they were not as determined since they were not the leaders that their oldest brother was.

Mirta calmly said, "Perhaps it is time for everyone to retire to their own rest and for them to get reacquainted with one another properly. I know that Bealdhild will be wanting to feed soon, and I can assure you that I do not want an audience while I feed her. Petralis, why don't you come to sit with me and let us talk of more pleasant things while our daughter is calm? Griefold, go clean yourself up some before you even thing of spending any time with your heart-mate. I don't think she will appreciate the smell of your travels while you get reacquainted in a more intimate fashion. As for you, Blackston…"

Before she could say anything else, Blackston held up his hands, saying, "I know. Go get cleaned up and be very careful with Amelia. She is pregnant, and I do not want to injure her or the baby. I am so happy to finally be back with you and to see you in such good health, my love." This last said to the Dracolian Princess, who was leaning slightly away from her heart-mate and wafting her hand delicately across her nose.

Amelia said, "I will greet you properly in our room once you have changed your clothing into something not quite as fragrant from the sea and the long walk from there." Then she turned and walked to the small closed-off area that was given over to her and Blackston in the Tallantanar longhouse. They had a similar room in the Minnertalla longhouse where Griefold was leading Bernella, yet due to her delicate condition, Mirta had insisted that Amelia stay nearby for emotional support.

Griefold and Bernella quickly made their escape to the Minnertalla longhouse, which was a short distance away from the piling snow. While Arista was being taken to the temple, Blackston was being seen by his heart-mate, and Arten was updating his father about what had happened. Griefold was glad to see that the longhouse was empty of visitors from Dantorin at long last, with fresh rushes strewn about the cobbled floor. There were freshly laid logs in the central fire pit, which Bernella was quick to start warming the longhouse for him. He turned to the buckets of cold water and quickly set about scrubbing the road from his skin so that the smell of the sea and travel across the plains were removed.

Once he had cleaned himself and was preparing to dress into warm, clean clothing, Bernella approached him from behind and pressed herself into his back, saying, "Not so fast, my love. It has been many moons since I held you, and I want to spend some time with you while we are alone and before duty calls us both away."

Griefold spun himself slowly around in her arms to find her equally naked and more than willing to embrace her. Together, they sank to the floor slowly in a loving embrace and spent the next several hours making love to one another beside the roaring fire.

Early the next morning, Petralis called for the council of the Tallanta and asked for his brothers and sister to attend, as well as the High Priestesses. The other Tallanta all agreed to come and listen to what he had to say about the possibility of leading their people away from the defense of their homeland into war. While every Ameristan was trained from childhood to be a warrior, many of them never truly shed the blood of their enemies.

As the Tallantanar, he was first among equals, and while he could order each Talla to battle for the southern kingdoms against the Bostowlian Zealots, Petralis wanted a consensus. Each Tallanta was the chief of his or her Talla, and each warrior had the right to choose for themselves where they went and what they were willing to do if it came to fighting. This would be the first decision that would involve the entire nation of Amerista that Petralis made, and he was unsure of how it would be received by the people as a whole. In his father's day, the decision to work together and defend the land as a whole was a consensus, even if it was Patrallin's idea. The Ameristans as a whole were still stubborn people, no matter what outsiders thought of them, and getting the entire nation going in the same direction was a challenge.

It was only a matter of hours before the other Tallanta came to the longhouse of the Tallantanar for the conclave. Many of the Tallanta were still the same men and women who were the leaders in Patrallin's time. Only two of the Tallanta were younger than Petralis, and that was only by a winter or two. It was a good time for the gathering since it was winter, and instead of having to wait for the moons, it would take for each Talla to come from their various ranges. As they always had, the Tallas would gather in the Holy City for the winter, setting aside all arguments and infighting of the various people.

The Hentalla Tallanta was the first one to enter the longhouse; he was short like all other Ameristans and broad across the shoulders. His name was Holger, and he had white hair, and his face was a map of wrinkles. He was the oldest of the Tallanta living, and his braid carried the lambskin totem. He was accompanied by his daughter Periboea, the next leader of the Talla. She, too, was short but whipcord lean, unlike her father, and carried a belt full of daggers around her waist. Her face was twisted with a sour look, and it was evident that she was not pleased to be here for the conclave. While the custom was to come unarmed to a meeting of the Tallanta, everyone was willing to overlook a short-tempered young woman this time.

Next, Brennus, Tallanta of the Fortotalla, came through the doorway, shaking the snow from his elk skin cloak and smiling at the warmth of the longhouse. He said nothing, just like his counterparts, and came to sit next to Petralis near the central fire. He was one of the few and rare dark-haired Ameristan people that cropped up from time to time. In his braid, the elk horn buttons were evident, showing his Talla affiliation and place within his home Talla. You could not tell by his looks, but he was one of the deadliest warriors of all the clans. He stood undefeated for the last twenty winters in the sparring circles for either *Dominance* or *Velocity*.

Following Brennus were both Aenor and Neonilla, the female leaders of the Himlatalla and the Amertalla, respectively. Aenor, with the griffon feathers woven into her short warrior's braid, smiled warmly at the gathered Minnertalla. She also smiled at her fellow Tallanta, who had arrived and moved to sit next to Mirta. She silently held out her hands to hold Bealdhild. Neonilla smiled briefly and shook the snow from her cloak, saying, "I saw the others as I was coming through the city. They should be here before too much longer, Tallantanar Petralis." She pulled her hair free of her hood and shook it loose with the caribou hoof totems rattling. As with most of her Talla, she was not a warrior and more of a builder and worshipper.

Carolus of the Dentalla entered, following the two women, not bothering to shake the snow from his shoulders. He was older, and his hair turned white at the temples; he was one of the contemporaries of Patrallin when the original Tallantanar came to power. Intertwined in his warrior braid were small metal and stone sea lion carvings that tinkled and rang as he walked. He had a sour expression on his face as well and would not look any of the other Tallanta in the eyes.

Taking his seat next to the fire, he stretched out his legs and groaned with relief from pain.

Wawatam of the Centalla, followed quickly by Faro of the Partotalla, entered at last into the Tallantanar longhouse. Each of the older men shook the snow from their cloaks and smiled with some affection at the sight of the other Tallanta gathered for the conclave. Wawatam, with the wire-wrapped pieces of coal suspended from his greying braid, took his cloak off and hung it on one of the pegs near the door for that purpose. Faro also shook his cloak out and hung it next to Wawatam's. He rubbed his shaved scalp with the multiple strips of auroch's horn, holding his braid straight down the back of his head.

During the conclave, the few remaining members of the Minnertalla were finally able to show their own Talla affiliation. No longer were Blackston and Griefold forced to wear the griffon feathers and re-braid their warrior locks with the polished steel chains of the Minnertalla. It was at this time that Arista was also shown how to shave her head and braid in the same style chain as her Talla. This was the proudest moment of her young life since it was the first time that she got to show her true affiliation with her own people. Even Princess Amelia, though not an Ameristan, braided a steel chain into her hair in solidarity with her heart-mate. Bernella, Arten, and their father Barten were the only Griffonara present at the conclave.

By silent agreement, while the women members of the conclave were taking turns passing around Bealdhild, the men began to pass around a wineskin. When the wine skin made it to Griefold, he just passed it along to Blackston without touching it, remembering how he had acted before. Once Bealdhild and the wineskin had made a couple of rounds, the infant was returned to her mother, and the skin was again placed out of sight.

Before anyone could break the silence, the High Priestesses entered on a flurry of snow and wind, making the fire dance and Bealdhild cry out at the sudden cold. With a stern look to his aunts, Petralis tried to shush his daughter as she fussed in her mother's arms at his side. He said, "It would be appreciated if you would have timed your entrance for a more opportune time, High Priestesses. As you can see, you upset my child, and I am not pleased with that."

Speaking in turn, they said, "We are sorry to upset your baby, nephew, but we have a very good reason to be here, and we needed to be here before the conclave could start. The information you are going to discuss will have many repercussions for all, as you well know, but at the same time, it will affect your family more directly."

"Just how will these events affect my family directly?" Petralis asked with deep suspicion in his voice.

The High Priestesses continued saying, "Come spring, when the Talla prepare to return to their traditional lands, and the snow melts from the passes, then it will be time to move on the Bostowlians. It will also be time to send your brothers on their way to Iristia, where your other sister is waiting to come home. Arista will stay here to begin her training as a priestess. It is past time for her to begin and without her twin for now. Aristin has had some rudimentary training from the Iristian magic users and has made progress already. Amerton has shown us this."

"That may be well and good," Petralis said. "Does that mean that I am to lead our people into battle against the Zealots, or am I to wait here in the Holy City again and do nothing?"

"No, this time, you will lead your people and fight with them as you intend, Petralis." Was the response of the High Priestesses.

"And just how many of our people are going to be led to their deaths in this attack on the Zealots?" asked Neonilla hotly. "My Amertalla are a mostly peaceful people, and we do not desire to be drawn into a fight that could cost us many lives! Since we are not all warriors like most Talla. We will not fight unless it is to protect the Holy City and the people who live within it!"

The High Priestesses said, "None of the Talla will be forced to join in the attack on the Zealots, any more than any of the warriors are forced to give up their ways and join your Talla here."

Petralis added, "Griefold gave assurances that only those warriors willing to join the fighting will be going or even be sent south to protect the kings and others. Not one warrior from any Talla will be sent without his or her first volunteering; the weather is milder there, and the service will be short."

"The warriors of my Talla will be more than willing to defend our southern border and take the fighting to the

Zealots for a change." Said Faro smartly as he entered the conversation. "We are not afraid of fighting, and we, too, are tired of defending from the Zealots. It is time to take the fight to them on our terms. I say let us push into their territory and show them the might of our people firsthand instead of just in defense of our people."

Aenor of the Himlatalla said, "My smiths can work through the winter here in the Holy City to prepare the warriors for both going to the Dantorin Kingdoms as well as for fighting the Zealots. We need to work through the entire winter, and they will not be ready to fight as much as the other Talla, but we will do our part, too."

Brennus of the Fortotalla growled out, "My warriors are used to fighting the Iramians. Even though they have not been attacking as much lately, we are the most experienced warriors. I will send almost all of my warriors to Bostowlia to destroy the Zealots! Those few whom I do not send south will be kept to patrol the coast and to protect against the Iramians."

Petralis nodded his head in agreement and asked, "How many warriors can you supply to the invasion of Bostowlia? Hundreds, thousands?"

Brennus answered back with an evil smile, saying, "My warriors number in the thousands, and all of them are willing to fight no matter where the fight takes place. I can safely field about five thousand warriors for the Bostowlian invasion and leave a few thousand for the defense of our homeland."

Carolus of the Dentalla said, "We are more laborers than warriors in my Talla. We can spare about three hundred warriors for the cause, but they will be better suited to hard labor than to fighting. We are used to moving heavy iron ore around and driving the aurochs carts to the Suns Daggers to the smithing Himlatalla than to fighting."

Arista said, "In Cantorin, they use people who do not fight as well in their wars with the other kingdoms as supply lines. These people manage the wagon trains of supplies for the soldiers of the kingdoms and manage the siege equipment that is used. Will your warriors be willing to support the fighting instead of being on the front lines of the invasion?"

Carolus smiled at the young woman and said, "That would be where we serve best for our people in this war. We are not really fair in the training circles as well as some of the other Talla warriors every winter, and we need to do something to support our people."

Faro, the Tallanta of the Partotalla, added, "Many of my young warriors want to prove themselves since we are the primary Talla that have to face the Zealot raids each spring. My Talla is fed up with the attacks and is not going after them in their homelands since we don't want to offend the Dracolian Empire. They are the ones, after all, that control the mountain passes."

Princess Amelia said, as she passed Bealdhild back to Mirta, "My father is also tired of the constant Zealot raids. We have been dealing with them for just as long as you have here in Amerista. We deal with them more, though, since they share a direct border with the empire, where our mountains begin and their jungles end. Those giant red and black cats that they ride are voracious for any meat. Not to mention that those Zealots that ride them are somehow bound to them with magic, which makes it so hard to fight them. If you kill the rider, then the Tigre' goes insane and kills anything it can find until it dies or is killed. We have lost many breeding female dragons to the Tigre. Even after the battles, due to the insane cats getting to the wingless females. We have lost many generations of potential mounts for the Dragon Riders and have had trouble in recent years getting our Riders into battle."

"Do any of your people have any more information that they would be willing to share about the Bostowlians?" Blackston asked his heart-mate. "I grew up in the Dracolian Empire, but I know next to nothing about the Bostowlians that any other person could not pick up."

Amelia replied, "In my grandfather's time, we had diplomatic ties with the Bostowlian Priests. They were the real power in the country for a long time, evidently. Yet, we have not had any communication with them in my father's lifetime, and I am sure that if we had any information, he would be willing to share it."

The Centalla leader Wawatam said, "We know little more than the effects that killing the Zealot before killing his Tigre causes even more death during a raid. I think that all of us know what happens and know what the Tigre' are capable of doing when they are insane. The problem is trying to kill them fast, before the Zealot, and trying to stop the raid itself is going to be most important. I can send only a few hundred warriors to help since, as with the Dentalla and the Amertalla, we are not really many warriors. My warriors would be better suited to helping with supporting the effort along with Carolus and his warriors."

Petralis said, "As soon as it is possible, I will send an armed party south to the empire and Emperor Ashvin's court to get any information that he can share. I will also ask that he join in this attack with whatever forces that he can spare. It is time for the Bostowlians to learn their proper place and that they do not have the right to attack us to feed their Tigre or to force their beliefs on us."

With grumbles of agreement all around the central fire pit, the Tallanta each nodded their heads in turn, giving their assent. Before anyone could say anything else, Griefold said, "Am I to take it then that I am not going to be going along with the invasion and instead go to Iristia?"

Before Petralis could answer, Blackston said, "I am not leaving Amelia while she is with her child! I do not intend to be absent for the birth of my first child nor to leave her in this condition! I have been gone far too much already since our heart-mating, and I will not abandon her again if I can help it."

Petralis grimaced slightly and said, "I understand what you are saying, brother, which is why I did not come with Griefold or you when he went to find you, or you both went to find our sister. I am not going to ask you to leave Amelia this time. This time, I am going to leave my young family to lead our warriors in the invasion. You will stay here with your family to protect my daughter and heart-mate. Griefold will be sent to Iristia with Arten, Bernella, and Barten as soon as the pass is clear this coming spring. Arista will stay here as per the wishes of the High Priestesses to begin her training."

Griefold said, "I will go for Aristin, but do we have any specific city to go to this time, High Priestesses? As I searched the last two times, I ended up finding Blackston and Arista by mere chance, traveling to the correct city and finding the right people. I don't want to miss out on the invasion of Bostowlia if it is at all possible. I want to be able to prove myself as much as you do, Petralis, but what can I do to make this happen faster?"

"We will just have to have to wait for the spring thaw and the clearing of the pass to Iristia, Griefold," Arten said with resignation. "I, too, want to join in attacking the Bostowlian Zealots in their homeland and give them a sound beating to show them that we are not weak."

Before there could be further interruption to the conclave, Petralis said, "There have to be priorities set and followed by the ones assigned to them. You each have your instructions for the coming spring, and there is nothing that you can do about it in the meantime. I suggest that each of you prepare your Talla for the coming invasion or prepare yourselves for leaving for Iristia."

Griefold said, "It will be as you wish, Tallantanar." Then, he turned to Bernella and motioned for her to come with him out of the longhouse so that they could speak in privacy.

Once outside, Bernella turned to Griefold and said, "Come heart-mate, we should return to the Minnertalla longhouse and enjoy ourselves for a while before we have to make some kind of decision about our future."

Griefold held his arms out to her in a silent question for her to come to him, and she did. He said, "My love, I only wish to prove myself to our people as my brother plans to. I have found my brother and one of my sisters, yet I have not proven myself to our people as a warrior. You have been in a few battles with Iramians and Zealots, but I have not done it, and it rankles on my very soul. I have been training since childhood to be a war leader for our people. How am I to prove myself and redeem myself to my brother and to my late parents if I do not shed the blood of our enemies like others have?"

Bernella hugged her lover tighter and said, "Don't think that way, Griefold. You have done the impossible so far; you have traveled to the Dracolian Empire and found your missing brother. You have traveled to the Dantorin Kingdoms and negotiated peace with them, as well as established trade for our people. Who else can say that they have done that in our lifetimes, let alone ever in our people's history? We have always been treated by other nations as slave stock to be taken at any time that they chose. Or to be killed outright like your Talla was in your father's time. You have made a difference to our people without lifting your sword, and that is something to be proud of."

The pair made their way to the longhouse that they now shared and quickly entered the building, wishing that they had someone to tend the firepit for them when they were gone. While they shared the longhouse with Blackston and Amelia, there were no servants or other members of the Talla living in the longhouse anymore. Arista spent almost all of her time in the temple with their aunts, learning what she could do without her twin present to use her powers fully. Working together, they quickly lit the fire and carefully fed it until it began to warm the longhouse. Once the fire had done its job, they found themselves making their way to the alcove that was theirs alone and began to make love to one another again. It was many hours later when Blackston and Amelia returned to the longhouse, and they quietly made their way to their own alcove on the other side of the building. While his brother and Amelia made themselves comfortable amongst their furs and settled into their own solitude, Griefold dressed himself again and went in search of food for himself and Bernella.

****

So went the winter for the Ameristan people. Plans were made and decided upon, discarded, and then decided upon again. While the Ameristan people were all warriors to one degree or another, the strategy was not something that they had made much use of over their history. Working together as a unified people was going to be a difficult concept; yes, after the massacre of the Minnertalla just a generation before, they all started to work together to defend themselves. It was still a matter of defending their ancestral lands and working more as individuals. Working with ideas from both Blackston and Arista, who had seen the armies of other nations, the Tallanta began to work with each other as a whole.

It was during that winter that Amelia gave birth to her first child, a strong, healthy boy with dark hair like his father. They named him Blalas. The joy that was shared by the Ameristans as a whole was felt throughout the land. There was another member of the Minnertalla, and the family was once again growing.

Griefold and Bernella took that winter for the opportunity to share their vows and become mated in the eyes of Amerton. They were not the only couple to take their vows that winter; many couples, fearing that they would lose their loved ones in the coming war, took their vows. It came to be that hardly a day went by that there was no celebration being held for newly mated couples of both sexes. It was also a winter of many female warriors coming up with swollen bellies of pregnancy. Many young male couples going to war wanted to leave something behind to replace them in their Talla if they failed to return. Those female members of the Tallas who themselves were not warriors agreed to this, especially the female members of the Amertalla. It was their way of contributing to the war effort for their people without joining the fight directly.

CHAPTER 18

As the weather began to warm and, the first hints of spring began to show, and the early shoots of the spring flowers began to push through the melting snow, the Ameristans prepared for war? Instead of returning to their ancestral grounds, which they had trod as a people for untold generations, the nation, almost as a whole, began to move south. It was at this time that Griefold, accompanied by his heart-mate Bernella, Arten, and Barten, began to travel to the west. They were given the directions to the secret pass by Periboea, who insisted on traveling with them most of the way through the Sun's Death Mountains. While Griefold and his mostly new companions would be going to the Iristian people to search for his other sister, they had no set place to search. The Iristians were also a nomadic people, who, unlike the Ameristans, never stopped following the herds of horses and camels. As the herds moved across the scrub grass and plains of Iristia, the people that lived there would only set up their tent cities for a few tendays to a couple of moons at a time before moving on. For these nomads, life on the move in the more temperate lands of Iristia was everything. It could take many moons for the searchers to find the right clan that housed the missing Aristin. The High Priestesses were reluctant to share any more information than that with Griefold and his companions. The excuse that was given was that the Iramian magic users were beginning to focus on the Minnertalla again. It would take all of the power of the Priest Pairs not going on to the battlefields to obscure the presence of the Minnertalla and where each of them were. This precaution would be only one of many ways that the Minnertalla were going to be protected from the Iramians, according to the High Priestesses. This was little consolation to the Minnertalla as a whole. There were only eight of them in all of Amerista at the time. Finding Aristin and rebuilding their clan was going to be their priority after the war with the Bostowlians.

Using wintons to keep the worst of the weather off as they came closer to the still snowy pass, Griefold and his companions missed the warmth of the longhouses. While Griefold and Bernella shared a winton together, the others made do with their own winton during the trip.

Periboea's winton's walls showed her history much like the wall of the Minnertalla wintons. It showed her bravery in combat against the wolves that attacked the flocks of sheep as a young girl. The walls also showed how she became one of the strongest of her siblings and was chosen by her father for her position as next in line. While most Tallanta were chosen by birth order, if there were multiple children, sometimes they would fight for leadership in the sparring circles. Periboea had gone from being the last child born to the first among her eight siblings in succession to the Tallanta of her clan. This was impressive for the slim woman since she was a *Velocity* Master, and her siblings were known for their use of great swords, hammers, and great axes in *Dominance*. It was not often that a *Velocity* user, known for their quick slashes and short swords or daggers, was able to defeat a *Dominance* user. *Dominance* focused on the use of strength and larger, longer weaponry, forcing one's opponent to come in close for the fight. Periboea made use of her slight frame and the speed of her whipcord lean limbs to attack and retreat without getting hurt. She was one of the few warriors who had ever entered a sparring circle to leave the victor again more times than not.

Barten continued to focus on the training of the three other warriors as they neared the pass in the mountains. While his children were used to near-constant sparring sessions as members of the Griffonara, as well as being Masters of *Dominance* and *Velocity*, even they felt the strain. It was during these sparring sessions that Barten began to notice how Bernella was slower in her attacks, and her defense was not as robust. He looked more closely at his daughter one morning before starting the sparring sessions, and he finally figured it out.

Barten roared, "Griefold, what have you done to my daughter?!"

Griefold was shocked by what the leader of the Griffonara said to him. He had never even sparred with Bernella since admitting his love for her. What did Barten mean by 'doing something to his daughter'? All they had done was join each other as proper heart-mates and live together more openly.

Griefold asked, "What do you mean, Barten? I have done nothing more than love her and shower her with my affection! What do you mean I have done something to her?!"

Baren snarled back to Griefold, saying, "She is pregnant, you fool! You have gone and gotten my daughter pregnant, and it is affecting her ability to fight and defend herself!"

Griefold began to splutter a reply to the statement Barten had just unleashed upon him and looked at his heart-mate with astonishment. He stood shocked beyond belief and was unable to even breathe properly.

Bernella, blushing deeply, dropped her eyes to the ground without making a single sound as she sheathed her blades. She said, "I did not want him to know yet, father. I am not that affected by the baby yet, and I do not feel any different yet. How did you notice before I even started to swell I am not completely sure myself that I am carrying?"

Barten said, "I have been a weapons master long enough to know the subtle signs of pregnancy in a female warrior, as well as training you since you could hold a dagger. I have seen you fight in more sparring circles than I can count, and you have never been this slow. Either you are ill or with a child, and I know that you are not ill. You never get sick."

Griefold said, "You are carrying my child, and you did not tell me that you could be pregnant? Were you going to keep it hidden from me until you began to swell or until you were going to deliver our child? You should turn back to the Holy City now and the safety that can be provided for you while you are in this condition!"

With her head snapping to look Griefold in the eye, Bernella's face went from shock to pure venom as she said, "I hope that I did not just hear you correctly, *my love*. I surely did not hear you say that I am going back to the city and sitting safely while I am one of the Griffonara. I also am sure that you did not *imply* that I am suddenly too fragile or unable to be the warrior that I was only yesterday, did you?"

Arten stepped up to Griefold and whispered into his ear, saying, "My sister loves you dearly, brother of my heart, but if you *do not* shut your mouth right this instant and apologize for what you said, she will hurt you. Pregnant or not."

Griefold gulped in fear as he saw the anger in Bernella's eyes and decided to take Arten's advice, saying, "Bernella, please forgive my words. I spoke without thought, and I wish to take back what I said about you going back to the city for your own protection."

Bernella did not change the look on her face, saying, "I will take your words into consideration and think about this for a while. I think that for the next little while, I will ask Periboea if she minds me staying in her winton. I think that you need some time to think about what you said and what you feel about me as a mate and as a warrior!"

Griefold was about to protest this change in his sleeping situation, and his heartmate Arten stomped on his foot to silence him. With a significant look at Griefold, Arten shook his head tightly in the negative, giving a warning to his friend. When Bernella went off a short distance to speak privately to her father, Arten spoke quickly with Griefold.

Arten said, "Do you intend for her to cut you to ribbons while you sleep? Or worse yet, for her to simply cut your throat? Bernella is a proud warrior, just as proud, if not prouder than you, about the fact that you insulted her and said that she could not protect herself?! She may be a little slower and maybe a little more on the delicate side when it comes to fighting for a while, but she is still a member of the Griffonara!"

Griefold harshly whispered back to him, saying, "I only think that she needs to be protected from the dangers of this trip to Iristia. We don't know what we are going to encounter on the way, and who knows how many attacks we may have to fight off. How can she protect herself if she is pregnant with our child and already having trouble in just the sparring ring? Your father noticed before she was even sure of being pregnant herself and called her out on it. What am I supposed to do, let her go into a fight when she is already slowing down? What will she be like when she is swollen and hardly able to move?"

Without warning, Barten delivered a harsh cuff to the back of his head. He then said to Griefold, "I am the Weapons Master of the Griffonara, and we are the best warriors of our people. Do you think that I would let my only daughter, as well as my first grandchild, go into danger if I knew she could not survive? What kind of fool do you take me for, Griefold?! Even with a child, my daughter is one of the best warriors our people have seen since the death of your father. Bernella may be slowing slightly due to the changes her body is going through, but she is still fast enough to kill any opponent. The next time that you open your mouth and doubt her abilities to defend herself, I will cut you from crotch to throat for her!"

Griefold felt a sudden chill shiver through him as the threat of what Barten said sank through his mind. He had known Barten his entire life and had never known him to *ever* give a threat that he did not follow through with. Now, Griefold did not only have to worry about upsetting his heart-mate and what she was going to do to him if he misstepped, but now he had the warning from Barten as well.

It was a long tenday during which Griefold was shunned by the entire group of warriors for his statements about the condition of his heart-mate. Only a minimum of conversation was used when he was addressed, and was only barely tolerated at the communal fire at night. It was something that made the young warrior consider his words deeply and think for the first time about the importance of Bernella in his life. Yes, she shared second in command of the Griffonara with Arten, and yes, she was his heart-mate, but she was carrying his child. After witnessing what had happened to his own mother and the loss of her life during the birth of his sisters, he knew full well what could happen to a woman carrying a child. Bernella was strong and healthy. Yet, his mother was strong and healthy as well when she gave birth to his sisters. He could not help but feel the fear that he could lose his mate as well as his child if she were injured.

At the end of the tenday, it was a repentant Griefold that went to Bernella saying, "I was wrong in thinking that you are lessened in any way my heart. I only wish to protect you from what happened to my mother during the birth of Aristin and Arista and the death of my father. She was strong and healthy, like you are, and yet she died in childbirth, and I cannot help feeling that I may lose you and our child. I would do anything to keep you alive. I don't want to lose you for any reason to anything. I have so few people in my life that I can consider family, and I have made so many mistakes with them that I feel I am going to lose them at any time. I don't want that with you or our child. Can you please forgive me, Bernella, the light of my life, my soul?"

Smiling tightly at Griefold, Bernella said, "You are the light of my life and soul as well, my mate, but you have a lot to learn about being a warrior still if you think that I am going to stop fighting just because my belly begins to swell as I told you before I am of the Griffonara and one of the best warriors of our people and I am not going to stop being such just because I am with child. I may slow down a little, but I could still defeat you in single combat if I had to, and don't even think that I would go easy on you just because you are the father to my child."

Griefold merely nodded his head in agreement before asking, "So, do you forgive my indiscretions by assuming that you could not protect yourself and our child, Bernella?"

With the rarely heard tinkling laugh Griefold loved so much, she said, "Come here, you fool and hold me! Of course, I forgive you; just don't make that mistake again, or I will give you a few scars to show to our child, and you can explain how you earned them as a fool."

Walking the few feet that separated him from his mate, Griefold wrapped her in his arms carefully at first and then tighter as he felt her reaching for one of her daggers. He knew then that if he treated her any differently than before, she would cut him in places that he would never forget.

Barten shook his head, and his one eye gleamed with mirth as he said, "Alright now, children. Now that you two have made up, it is about time that we separate ourselves from Periboea since we are in the pass. She will turn back to join her Talla for the attack on Bostowlia while we will continue on into Iristia. Once we are through the pass, we will be on territory that is not exactly enemies, but we do not know their ways, and we could easily offend them if we say or do the wrong thing. I want you three on your toes and ready to defend yourselves at a moment's notice. We have never had a fight with the Iristians, and they have always traded fairly with us in the past, but this is different. Do you have any questions? No, good, let's get going!"

With that being said, the four warriors who were going to continue the search went into the small pass that was the only known way through the Suns' Dagger Mountains to Iristia. The pass was the lowest point in a saddle between the mountain peaks, still deeply covered by snow. While Griefold, Arten, Barten, and Bernella worked their way as best as they could through the deep snow of the pass, Periboea stayed behind, taking her time packing away her winton.

It was late in the day when they had reached the top of the saddle between the mountains and were forced to stop and camp for the night. While there for the night, the two wintons were open to the fierce winds of early spring. They all struggled to keep warm throughout the night and had to take turns feeding the fire to try and stave off the chill. By mutual decision, Bernella was given the extra woolen blankets and furs that they had brought along. She may be a warrior, but she was the one who was with the child and needed to be kept warmer than the others. It would only be a day or two in the pass, and then they would be coming down into the Iristian plains, where it was supposed to be warmer and free of snow, according to what they had been told. It was with growing haste that the party of warriors moved through the pass, trying to escape the last ravages of winter. It took more than two days, which they had originally been told, to clear the pass. There were three days, mostly due to the knee-deep snow and the fact that they were on foot. The men did their best to break a trail for Bernella, despite her continuing protests, so that she would be able to move easily through the snow. She complained every step of the way that she was more than capable of helping break a trail through the snow, but none of the three men would let her lead the way. She was still a warrior, but she was their family and pregnant, and they would take care of her the best they could without truly demeaning her.

Bernella fumed continually for the entire time they traveled through the pass and muttered threats to the three men who insisted on taking care of her. Even though she made threats and promises of retaliation to them, deep down, Bernella knew that they were going to take care of her no matter what she said.

After the third day travelling through the pass and the decreasing depth of snow, they began to move more swiftly, heading into the lands of Iristia. At first, they were astonished as the lush grasslands the Ameristans were used to were not to be seen. Instead, the plains that they were walking onto showed more scrub brush and low grasses leading into the distance. The temperature began to grow quickly as they came down from the pass to the point where it was uncomfortable for them. The travelers had to remove their furs by the first day of leaving the pass and eventually even began to wish that they could remove their leather clothing as well. The lower they went, the warmer the climate became. Instead of seeing the herds of aurochs and elk that they were used to seeing in their homeland, they saw the fabled horses the Iristians were known for. Taller at the shoulder than an Ameristan and long-legged, the horses were only seen in the distance running wild. No matter how hard they tried, the Ameristans could not approach the herds of horses, unlike the half-tame herds of elk or aurochs that they were used to dealing with. These fleet creatures were almost as fast as the elk herds, yet they were obviously larger and had flowing manes and tails. They were like nothing the Ameristans had seen before. Even though Griefold and Arten had spent some time in the Dantorin lands, they had never seen the horses that the warriors there were supposed to use. When they asked the guardsmen, they never got a direct answer, and they were told that the horse warriors were controlled by the nobles of Dantorin, Cantorin, and Deltorin. Since they had little to nothing to do with nobles while they were there, they had, of course, not seen the horses. Still, these animals were impressive with their speed and beauty as they raced across the scrub grass plains.

As the warriors traveled across the plains of Iristia, they saw no signs of the people who had made these lands their home. There were no trails through the grass, nor were there any signs of settlements, much like their own homeland with only a few established settlements of the mining Talla, the Holy City, and the single smithing Talla that still existed. Before separating from Periboea, she had given them the advice to keep heading west and that eventually they would find one of the traveling bands, or better yet, to follow the herds of wild horses to a watering hole and wait there until one of the bands came. That was the way to find a band, according to the Iristian traders who had shared the way through the pass and the information of how to find them. Following this advice, the four of them trailed after the horse herds that they could see and stayed well back from the strange animals.

It was two tendays before they came across a watering hole, and they were short on the water themselves by this point. In their homeland, there were often streams running through the grasslands. Here, water was an obvious precious commodity, and they had to struggle to find it. Only occasionally did they come across a stream worthy of the name, and then they had trouble filling their skins. Small game was plentiful, and they were able to keep themselves fed on the birds and small animals that they came across. It was reminiscent of the time that the original three of them had gone searching for Blackston just the previous spring. It was hard to believe that only one full winter had passed and the fact that they were quickly approaching the end of the quest set to them by both Petralis and the High Priestesses. It was obvious once they found the watering hole that there had been human habitation in the past. There was a small stone well off to the side that the horses could not foul with their droppings and stamping feet. There were no other people in sight of the place, but that did not mean any of the clans would come to visit this particular spot. After all, they had been told, the Iristian people followed their herds constantly. There may be a group some days behind this particular herd for all they knew. So, with this knowledge in mind, the four warriors set about making their camp and planned on spending some time in this particular camp waiting.

They did not have to wait for long; it was only three days before a group of a dozen Iristian warriors came riding slowly up to the watering hole. Being cautious about causing a fight that would lead to misunderstanding between the two groups, Barten took the first step and disarmed himself.

He said, "I am Barten, and I come from the lands of Amerista to the east of the Suns' Dagger Mountains. I come in peace, and we are here as a group seeking a young lady from our lands who came here many winters ago and wishes to speak with holy people with whom she would be living."

After speaking within themselves for some moments, one of the Iristians rode his black stallion forward from the group of fighters. Like the others, he was swathed in loose-fitting robes from head to foot, with his face covered, showing only his eyes. As he rode forward, he removed his shamshir, handing it to another rider, saying, "I am called Ivaaq, and I lead this band of outriders for my clan. We see that you have come to rest at this oasis and that you are willing to speak without violence to us. We are not a violent people, but we will defend ourselves as we can see you would do for yourselves. I will send a rider back to my clan chief to let him know the strangers who are making use of this oasis are peaceful in intent and that we can bring our women and our young ones in."

Barten then said, "I am unsure of your ways, but would you sit and join us in a meal? We have only some meat from the local game and some little travel bread left from our journey from our homeland, but we will freely share what we have with you."

Ivaaq removed the wraps from about his face, smiling broadly, showing white teeth against olive colored skin as he approached more closely. He extended his hands in a show of peace and said, "I can see that you and your companions have little in the way of supplies to share for now. I and my men will share out from our supplies if that does not offend you warriors? We know little of your ways and do not wish to give offense either, but the sharing of food is a universal thing, I think, between peoples."

Barten waved for his three companions to sit with him near the small fire, with a subtle sign to disarm themselves at the same time, while he added a few new pieces of wood. Griefold carefully pulled his great sword from the sheath at his back and placed it on the floor of his and Bernella's winton before approaching the freshly burning fire. Bernella was slower in disarming herself since she carried far more weapons than were obvious. The stern looks her father gave her every time she stopped after removing another blade from some place of concealment kept her going. It was more than an even dozen daggers and knives that she removed from about her person before she was done. Arten only smiled and removed his own great sword quickly.

It was with smiles all around and some looks of astonishment from the Iristian riders who were dismounting and disarming themselves. The looks of astonishment were sent the way of Bernella, who was something that they were obviously not used to. It would seem that female warriors were a rarity among the Iristians, and she would be so heavily armed. She had only begun to swell about her middle, and it was as obvious to the Iristians as well that a female warrior was also with child and ready to fight.

At the astonished looks being sent her way, Bernella said, "Yes, I am with child, and I am still a warrior. I can easily take any man or woman in a fight, and I am no less a fighter just because I am carrying a child. We are a warrior people, and I am one of the best warriors in my group. If you wish to test me, just say so, and I will prove to you my worth and ability."

The Iristians all unwrapped the clothes from their faces and smiled deeply at Bernella, and all declined her invitation to a fight. They all had dark hair and olive skin like Ivaaq, and each of them pulled out his own waterskin and some pouches of dried fruits and meats to share with the circle of people. In a short amount of time, a peaceful conversation established what would become friendship among the two different groups of warriors. Over the cold breakfast, they exchanged stories of battles fought against Bostowlians and Iramians. It seemed that the Iramians would attack from the western coast on rare occasions as well. Boasts of their abilities in battle were shared around the fire even as they shared their food that late morning.

It was after all had eaten their fill that Ivaaq said, "I will now send Aucaman back to my clan to inform my Chief that he can bring our people in. He is my swiftest rider, as well as my brother's son, so I know he will not delay and will tell the truth without embellishment. He is a good boy and a bit taken with Bernella, especially the fact that she is a warrior despite being a woman. It is best for him to be off for a bit before he says or does something that gets him in trouble with Bernella herself for some innocent mistake."

The young rider in question began to blush, darkening his face to the amusement of all others around the small fire, including Bernella. Muttering beneath his breath, the young man, more of a boy really, mounted his bay mare and rode quickly northwest as fast his horse could carry him. With chuckles filling the air of the reaming Iristians and the Ameristans, they easily relaxed and waited for the rest of the clan to arrive.

During the wait for the clan of riders, Barten explained who exactly they were looking for by describing what Aristin would look like in detail. Since she was an identical twin at birth, he only had to describe his sister to Ivaaq and his men to get the answer that they were seeking.

Ivaaq said, "I would know if we had a young woman among our clan who was pale of skin as well as golden hair. She would stand out like a flower alone amongst the grasslands as our people are darker in hair and skin than your own. We do not all come together once a winter as your people do; we can go for many winters without meeting another clan during our travels. So we have no way of knowing where to search for her. There is a small chance that our magic users can help you in this matter in ways that I do not know about."

Griefold leaned forward and said, "We will defer to your people's wisdom in this matter since this is your land, and you will know more about what will be best. I only ask that we be allowed to speak with your magic users in this matter. The young woman in question is my sister, and I wish to find her."

Barten hissed his displeasure at Griefold and growled lowly under his breath about the stupidity of a certain young man and how he kept putting his foot in his mouth.

Before anyone could say anything else to break the silence, Ivaaq slowly began to chuckle and then burst out in a full belly laugh. He said, "Young people in love and a young couple with their first child on the way are always too hasty in their decisions and actions. Think nothing of it, friend Barten. I know the passions that young Griefold feels. I have several wives myself, and when each of them was first pregnant, I was always overcautious of them, much to my detriment and their displeasure. Be at peace, Griefold; our sorcerers and sorceresses are a people apart. They answer to no one but themselves and the clan Chiefs and only to the Chiefs in matters of war. Our clan's sorceresses will help you if you ask them. It is within their own control to help you or not. The choice is theirs."

At a sudden sharp pain in his backside, Griefold grunted and spun his head around to see Bernella slowly replacing one of her many daggers, which she had not removed, into concealment. He ruefully shook his head and realized that he had just given him a warning that he was close to crossing the line about being overprotective again.

Barten scowled tightly at the young warrior and shook his head so slightly it was barely noticeable to anyone but Griefold himself. Turning back to Ivaaq, Barten said, "We would appreciate an introduction to your sorceresses if that would not be an imposition. How would we address them appropriately so we do not offend them?"

"We are a very informal people, friend Barten," Ivaaq replied, waving away the concern, "the only titles we give to anyone are our clan Chiefs. Do not fear giving offense. I will introduce you to our clan sorceresses personally when they arrive."

Making small talk amongst themselves about the best ways to hunt and the differences between fighting on foot compared to fighting on horseback, the small group passed the time. It was nearly several hours after Aucaman had left that they began to hear the thunder of hundreds of hooves coming closer. Ivaaq and his men made their goodbyes as they quickly retrieved their weapons and mounted again upon their horses. Once mounted, the outriders turned and went in the same direction that the thundering could be heard coming from, and they were quickly lost in the distance. The Ameristans did not have long to wait before the bulk of the clan came into sight, mounted upon their horses and camels. The camels, the creatures that matched what had been described to them, were two humped tan animals that walked amongst the vast clan descending upon them.

The clan members numbered in the thousands, and the Ameristans were astounded. Only the largest Talla numbered so, and there were only a few of them. According to what Ivaaq had told them, there were dozens of clans traveling these plains at all times, some even bigger than this one. The problem of finding Aristin just became so much larger than they had originally expected. Hopefully, the sorceresses of this particular clan would be able to help them find her before the seasons changed again, and they would have to wait for winter to pass again before going home.

Griefold held his frustration deep inside himself since he had so recently been on the receiving end of Bernella's not-so-gentle reminder to keep his concerns about her to himself. Yet it was Bernella who said, "I think that our search just got a whole lot harder and that we are going to be here a lot longer than we had originally planned. I am thinking that maybe I should have turned back at the mouth of the pass to have my baby in the Holy City instead of on these foreign lands."

The three men with her looked at her in astonishment at this statement from her and how casually she admitted that maybe Griefold was right about his concerns.

Before anyone else could utter a word, Aucaman came riding up to them again on the same horse he had raced off on hours before, saying, "Uncle Ivaaq has already spoken with Rosmunda and Priya, and they have said that they will speak with you, once their tent is set up and they are comfortable." Aucaman said swiftly, looking away from Bernella as he began to blush again.

Barten asked, "Could you come to lead us to their tent once the women are comfortable and willing to receive us? We are not at all familiar with your people and your ways and do not want to wander around your encampment without an escort."

Nodding his consent, Aucaman again blushed. He snuck a quick look at Bernella's frowning countenance. He quickly spun his mount about and rode back to the quickly rising encampment of tents and pavilions. The vast herd of domesticated horses was quickly led to the watering hole, and they were encouraged to drink and begin to feed on the fresh grass.

To the Ameristans, being able to closely approach the tame horses was astonishing and a thing of wonder. They had never gotten a chance to come this close to the wild herd they had followed as they were traveling, and now they were encouraged to stroke the heads of the affectionate creatures. It was in awe that Bernella approached the first horse that came within reach of her hands. She was used to dealing with her griffon and the aggressive nature of the creature when it was feeding or in training. These horses were smaller in size than a full-grown griffon and obviously grass eaters like the aurochs and elk. On the ground, they were obviously faster than a griffon, but the winged fighting animals were faster in flight. She would love to see which of the creatures could cover more ground in a race against one another.

Griefold was the first one to break the silence, saying, "These horses are amazing creatures. Could you imagine being able to chase down the Zealots on their Tigre?" We could move fast enough to keep them from even crossing into our lands in the first place! What amazing creatures these would make riding into battle beside our Griffon Riders and Griffonara. It is hard for the Riders to get at the Zealots. They like to strike out from beneath tree cover, but the griffons can't get to them as easily as they can on the open plains. We should see what we can do to learn how to mount our warriors on these beasts to help in the war with the Bostowlians. It may be too late this season, but who knows how many times we are going to have driven them back into their own lands."

Barten replied, "It is something to think about, my boy, it is something to think about. We would have to talk trade with the Iristians to see if they would be willing to agree to share some of their animals. We would also have to learn how to ride and care for the animals. They are nothing like our griffons or aurochs. The griffons prefer to eat the wyverns or other predators of the plains and mountains, while the aurochs and elk stay in the grasses of the plains. These horses seem somewhat like our aurochs in this as they seem to prefer the grasses here around the watering hole. How would we care for them, or would we even be able to take them through the pass into our plains and for them to thrive?"

Arten said, "I think that it is something that we are going to have to ask the clan chief about. If he is willing to negotiate with us for this, that is fine. Griefold showed himself to be a good negotiator when we were dealing with the Dantorin kingdoms, striking good trade terms for our people."

Barten grunted his assent to this statement and cautiously eyed the horses his young charges were gently petting with enthusiasm. His one eye scrutinized the herd guards as the young men took turns eyeing Bernella and the other Ameristans. He did not trust the young Iristians around his only daughter. Even though she was mated to Griefold, he barely trusted Griefold with his daughter. She was his only daughter, after all, and she always held a special place in his heart.

The following morning, Aucaman returned to the Ameristans and offered to lead them to the sorceresses within the encampment. It was not a short walk to the center of the encampment, where there were many larger pavilions set upon the ground. The smallest of the tents surrounding the pavilions were larger than even the largest longhouse to be found in the Holy City. The pavilions stretched even further than that in length, with sides rolled up, allowing the breeze to blow through.

Sitting inside the largest of the pavilions was a white-haired man of medium build with a long white beard to his waste sitting on a pile of pillows surrounded by eight women. All of the people in the tent had a hardened leather look on their faces as if they had spent most of their lives in the sun. The man carried about him the look of a man who had more years than many of his contemporaries. He carried his years well, but he was still a man who appeared to be young at heart and healthy for his years.

Upon seeing his visitors, he said, "I am Fabricius Clan Chief Sun Mountain Clan. I am happy to greet you here in my tent among my wives. I am told that you wish to speak to the clan sorceresses about a missing young lady from your own clan who came to our lands many years ago."

With a none to gentle nudge to step forward from Barten, Griefold stepped up and said, "I am Griefold of the Minnertalla, brother to the Tallantanar, Petralis II, brother to Aristin, the missing young woman who was sent amongst your clans nearly fifteen winters ago. We are seeking my sister to return her to our people and reunite my family. I formally request your sorceress's advice to try to find my sister. I am told that she is under training with some of your sorcerers in one of your clans. We were told by our own High Priestesses to come to your lands and to seek out a pair of your magic users in order to find my sister."

Fabricius replied to Griefold, saying, "I have no problem with you asking your questions about my clan sorceresses; they are not really under my control as they are. Aucaman will escort you to their pavilion; it is close by, but before you go, would you break your fast with me and my wives?"

Griefold set aside his impatience and decided to err on the side of caution with this clan Chief. Knowing how vital the trade with the Iristians was and how touchy some leaders could be when dealing with outsiders. He said, "We will sup with you if you wish, Clan Chief; we are glad to have been asked to join you and your wives."

Fabricius waved to his wives and said, "Fetch my guests some pillows to make themselves comfortable as well as airags to quench their thirst. Bring some meats and fruits as well to break our fast and cement our new friendships with these Ameristans."

The eight women began to rise and move about quickly, bringing in more pillows while others began to go to nearby campfires to gather freshly cooked meat and dried fruits. The meat was gamey and chewy but full of a salty flavor. It was something that the Ameristans had never tried before. The fruits, called dates by the Iristians, were covered in honey and were a perfect counterpoint to the salty, gamey meat. Not wishing to offend their host with questions about the food but desiring to know what they were eating, Bernella asked.

Bernella looked at one of the many wives as she said, "Could I ask what this meat is? I have never tasted anything like it before and wish to know what it is?"

The woman who had been addressed looked to her sister's wives before answering in a strong voice, "Goat. We travel with herds of goats and use them for their wool as well as their meat and milk. They are a good animal to keep since they can eat almost anything like the camels, but they do not drink as heavily."

"What is this airag," Griefold asked suddenly after taking another small swallow of the thick drink, "it reminds me slightly of mead or even wine, but it tastes different for some reason."

The same nameless woman replied, saying, "It is fermented mare's milk, a delicacy of the plains." Griefold was puzzled and asked, "What is a mare? A type of plant?"

Laughing at his quizzical expression, she said, "No, it is a female horse! We milk them after they have foaled and ferment the milk to drink. We use everything that we can find to survive, much like your people do, don't you?"

Blinking, Griefold said, "Of course, we use the herds of aurochs or elk for the most part, but we do not ride them like you do your horses. We do not keep them like you do your horses, so we are less tied to them than you are, apparently. We do not take the milk from the females of the aurochs herds, which would be a death sentence to try and get that close to a mother and calf."

All of the wives laughed at this, having never seen any aurochs or the danger that they could present; the wives just kept about sharing the food that they had brought. While the thick, intoxicating airag was not to the Ameristans liking, they drank it sparingly so as not to insult their hosts.

It was almost an hour of eating and speaking with Chief Fabricius before he declared that it was time for his guests to be shown to the sorceresses. Aucaman, who had been waiting quietly for most of the time, waved for the party of Ameristans to follow him. It was a few short minutes walk to the pavilion of the sorceresses Rosmunda and Priya. Aucaman stopped at the flaps of the pavilion and spoke softly to the people inside, saying, "Sorceresses, I bring the ones who wish to seek council with you about their missing clan sister. May they have your permission to enter your tent and speak with you?"

A mumbled assent came from within the dim light of the pavilion, along with a whiff of some kind of herb smoke.

Aucaman motioned for the others to enter the dimly lit tent and stepped away to wait outside after they had entered the pavilion. In the front room of the pavilion, there were piles of small pillows everywhere for people to sit on. Without thinking about it, Griefold held out his hand to help Bernella into a reclining position upon a pile of pillows. She glared at him at first but then sighed a breath of relief after she was able to ease herself into the pillows. She was definitely showing her pregnancy now, and the weight of the unborn child was showing itself when she walked for long distances.

After they had all been seated, there came a sound of movement from behind the partition that separated the front of the tent from the private area at the back. Two women who were about middle-aged came out from behind the partition. There were obviously sisters, but not identical twins. Each had the olive skin complexion of the Iristians that they had already seen, as well as long dark hair. Once they had entered the public area, the twins, in unison, said, "We are Rosmunda and Priya, the sorceresses of the Sun Mountain Clan. We have been told that you wish to speak with us concerning contacting another clan sorcerer to seek out a missing young lady."

Barten first spoke, saying, "We are indeed seeking one of our own people who came to your lands many winters ago. She is fair-haired and one of a set of identical twins. Her sister is under training with our own High Priestesses. The young woman we are seeking is said to be undertraining herself with a set of your magic users amongst one of your many clans. We were told to seek out a pair of magic users in any of the clans that we came across if possible. We humbly ask for your help in seeking out our missing people."

Rosmunda and Priya looked at each other for several seconds in silence and then, speaking in turn, said, "As with any magic users, even among your own people, we can reach out to one another and speak with some difficulty. The further away the others are, the harder it is to speak and receive an answer, but we can do this. We will speak with Chief Fabricius and ask him to stay with the moving of the clan. For as long as it takes for word to get back to us about your missing sister. In turn, he wishes to speak of trade with your people during the time that we have to spend waiting for a reply. It will take many days to reach out to all of the clans, for word to spread to all of the sorcerers and sorceresses, and for them to respond." Then, speaking out louder, they said, "Aucaman, please carry our words to Chief Fabricius so that he may know what needs to be done while we prepare ourselves for communing with the others." Aucaman responded in the affirmative and sped off to the pavilion of the clan chief with haste.

Griefold spoke up and said, "I will speak for my brother on the matter of making trade negotiations with your chief. All I ask is that we be given a fair chance and even hearing when it comes to the negotiations."

Smiling at the young warrior, the sorceresses said, "We cannot speak to what the chief will ask for. He is chief because he can keep the clan fed and safe. We can only advise on where to go for safe water and fresh grasses for the herds. Other than that, we are just women of the clan."

Keeping his disgruntlement to himself, Griefold nodded his understanding to the clanswoman and relaxed himself further into the pillows. He looked to his heart-mate and saw that she was again glaring at him for his not-so-subtle attempts to speed things along again.

Bernella sharply elbowed Griefold in the ribs once he had seated himself and harshly whispered under her breath, "I grow tired of your attempts to coddle and protect me from imagined dangers that are not present! How many ways or times do we all have to tell you that I am more than capable of protecting myself and our child!"

Griefold smartly held his own counsel in this matter and listened silently as Barten gave a detailed description of what Aristin should look like to Priya and Rosmunda. The twin's sorceresses listened intently and then asked for the Ameristans to leave them so that they could return to their privacy to work their magic.

Taking their leave, Griefold and his companions were once again led to Chief Fabricius's pavilion to begin the trade negotiations. Griefold was the one to take the lead in this situation since he spoke for his brother. Chief Fabricius drove a hard bargain to keep his clan in place for an extended period of time instead of moving on as usual. Griefold had to make major concessions to the clan so they could stay in place for the foreseeable future. The concessions would not sit well with Petralis, for there would be trade goods such as aurochs and steel that would be hard to come by. The Himlatalla were going to be hard-pressed to produce enough raw steel for the deals Griefold had struck between all the searches for his sisters.

It took nearly a full seventeen days for Priya and Rosamunda to call for Griefold and his companions again. Once again, Aucaman escorted them to the sorceress's pavilion, and they were asked to wait in the public area. While waiting, the Ameristans seated themselves on the pillows with Griefold again, easing Bernella down and causing her disgruntlement. Griefold ignored the evil-eyed looks thrown his way by Barten and Arten when he turned to sit himself next to his heart-mate.

A few moments later, the sorceresses appeared from behind the partition and addressed the waiting warriors. They said, "We have reached out to all of the clans, and we have heard from the sorcerers and sorceresses. Your sister will be here in the next ten-day with the Watcher Clan when they pass through the area. The sorcerers of the clan are happy to share that she is in good health and eager to meet you all."

Griefold heaved a sigh of relief as he heard this and looked around at his companions immediately after in chagrin, knowing what they were going to say to him later. He then said, "Thank you, ladies, thank you for taking the time to search out for us and to bring us this information."

With a mutual shaking of all of their heads, Griefold's companions gave him evil-eyed looks yet again and began to mutter mutually under their breath. Griefold ignored what they were saying and simply hung his head, knowing that he would receive cold comfort that night yet again.

The following wait put Griefold on edge with every passing day as the stress was growing with the impatience of wanting to get his heart-mate home. While she was growing more about her waste and was having more trouble getting about it with the same ease she used to show, This caused him to resolve to ask for a trade with the clan chief for a horse or two to carry Bernella home to the Ameristan plains. Learning how to ride the horses would be difficult in such a short amount of time, yet he hoped that her experience with her griffon would help.

It was just after dawn on the fourteenth day that the Watcher Clan of the Iristians appeared over the horizon. By the dust cloud that they produced coming over the plains, it was obvious that they were not as numerous as the Sun Mountains Clan. After a quick count of arriving riders, Griefold and his companions realized that this clan was numbered in the hundreds, much like the average Ameristan Tallas. This was proof that while the Ameristans were almost a single person, a warrior people, they were very much a smaller nation than their friendliest neighbors. Griefold also realized that it was going to be much harder to take the fight to the Iramians who had decimated his Talla in his grandfather's time and had sent the assassins who killed his father.

While the two clans spent several hours in complicated greetings ceremonies that occurred when different Iristian clans met, the Ameristan party was patient. There was much pomp and ceremony, with warriors from the two clans hosting mock battles between themselves. It was a heart-racing event for the watchers as the Iristian warriors raced at each other and clashed with their shamshirs as they rode by. The speed of the horses and the flashing metal was thrilling and reminded the Ameristans of the sparring circles of home when contestants would fight out their differences or show their prowess.

After most of the morning was spent in the ceremonies, the two clan Chiefs met in Fabricius' pavilion and invited Griefold and his friends to break their fast. Again, there was airag, honeyed dates, and grilled goat's meat. This time, there was also cheese made from goat's milk. Even though the tastes were not to the liking of the Ameristans, they did their best to eat what was offered to them by their mutual hosts. Primarily being ignored by their hosts, the Ameristans spent the time trying to listen to the speeches of the clan Chiefs as each tried to outboast one other about the size of their mutual herds. It was interesting to hear about the four companions since their people did not count the number of animals in the herds that they followed. It seemed to be a point of pride for the Iristians to know the exact number of horses, goats, and camels in their control.

After all of the boasting and sharing of airag, finally, the clan Chiefs got down to haggling about what supplies each was willing to trade for. During all of this, Griefold felt himself growing more and more impatient about finding Aristin and leaving for his homeland. When he was about to rise to say something to the clan Chiefs about the delay, he felt the sharp point of a dagger resting just above his right buttock.

With a whisper, Bernella said, "If you so much as try to interrupt them, I will give you another scar that you won't soon forget!"

In growing irritation, Griefold seated himself again amongst the pile of pillows where they were waiting for their turn to be heard. He thought to himself that the time it was taking for the Chiefs to boast and then strike their trade deals was taking far too long. He wanted to get his mate back to the plains as fast as possible. It would not be too soon to get her safely into the Holy City with the High Priestesses. Then, he got himself off onto the campaign in the Bostowlian lands with Petralis and the rest of their people.

It was an early afternoon when the two clan Chiefs finally turned to the waiting warriors and addressed Barten with Fabricius saying, "So, Barten, this is Clan Chief Shikoba of the Watcher Clan of the Iristians, please be welcome to our conclave of clans."

Just as Griefold was about to interrupt, he hesitated and glanced over to see Bernella's hand on one of her daggers, who was glaring at him. He shut his mouth and kept his peace. Barten glared at Griefold out of the corner of his eye, then said, "Thank you for inviting us to this meeting, Chief Fabricius; we are honored to be here and to meet Chief Shikoba of the Watcher Clan."

Chief Shikoba was young-looking, only a few years older, and Petralis's senior in looks with a short, close-cropped dark beard. His olive skin was darker than Fabricius's, and he had scars on his hands from what appeared to be dueling. This young clan chief was obviously a fighter and had earned his place among his clan the hard way.

Chief Shikoba said, "From what I have been told by Chief Fabricius and by my clan's sorcerers, you are seeking a young woman from your lands who was brought here many winters ago. My sorcerers also tell me that the guardians that came with her passed away a few winters ago due to illness. Chinweike and Praxiteles have taken her under their wing and seen to her continued training in the use of magic, as much as older men can teach a young woman. I will send it to her and my clan sorcerers so that you can speak with them. Would you like to speak with them in your own tents for some privacy, or do you wish to speak with them here?"

Barten said, "In our own wintons would be best. We need to speak of some things with the young lady that are private. We have to see what she knows of our people and test her in our own ways."

Chief Shikoba said, "It will be as you wish, my friends." Then, turning to one of his clansmen who had been sitting outside of the pavilion, he said, "Go and fetch Chinweike and Praxiteles as well as their young charge."

The unnamed clansman quickly turned to his bay-colored horse, leapt into the saddle, and then was on his way at a quick trot to the other clan's encampment. It was not a long wait before the rider reappeared and said from horseback, "My Chief, the sorcerers, and their charge are on the way to the stranger's tents. They said that they would wait there for the strangers, and the sorcerers wanted me to pass along the word that they would have words for you when they were finished."

Chief Shikoba nodded his understanding and then waved the rider away negligently. He then turned to the waiting Ameristans and said, "I hope to see you before you return to your lands; we can speak of trade and other things." That being said, he turned back to speaking with Chief Fabricius and started to discuss the breeding lines of the animals in their care.

Leaving the clan chiefs to their discussions, the warriors took their leave of the pavilion and made their way back to the area where they camped. While the three others took their time, Griefold was forced to slow his pace to match theirs for fear of reprisals from his mate. They all knew that Aristin and her escort would be waiting for their arrival. It was not a long distance from their encampment, and they did not have anything to block their path. Excitement at the prospect of finally finishing their quest was rising in all of their hearts as they approached the wintons. Standing outside were three people dressed in the head-to-foot robes of the Iristians in bright colors. They did not have their heads and faces wrapped. They were talking excitedly to one another with broad gestures and easy smiles. The two men were of later years, judging by the long white hair, but unlike all of the other male Iristians that they had seen, they were clean-shaven like Ameristans. The young girl that was with them was obviously an Ameristan. She had blonde hair bleached almost white by the sun. When she turned her head to in profile to the approaching party, they could see the immediate similarity to Arista. She was obviously Aristin as they had been told, and seeing her for themselves, in person, gave them all a rise in spirits.

Griefold gave up all pretenses of decorum and rushed forward to the trio next to the wintons, saying, "Aristin, is that you? We have been searching for you and waiting for you for such a long time. I know you don't remember me, but I am your brother, Griefold. Your twin sister Arista is with our aunts along with our other brother Blackston in the Holy City. The sooner we are finished here, the sooner we can be on our way home and back to the lands where we belong!"

The young woman turned to look at Griefold with a puzzled look on her face. In response to his statements, she said, "I do not know who you are, warrior. I was told to come here with Praxiteles and Chinweike to meet some strangers from distant lands who had something to share with me. I am not familiar with the names that you have told me, and I do not know anything about having brothers and a sister. My guardians told me little about my birth parents, only that my mother died shortly after birthing me and that I had to be sent away for my protection."

Bernella, having finally caught up, elbowed her mate in the ribs yet again and said, "We have much to discuss, and all of the time you need to learn and understand will be given to you. We have been sent by your oldest brother to find you and to bring you home in the long run. Your guardians were to teach you of our ways and about your family and what had happened to them. I don't know why they did not do so, what they were thinking when they did not share with you the parts of your life that you needed to know."

Before anyone else could say anything, the sorcerers broke in, saying in tandem with one another, "We put a block on her memory after the death of her guardians to that sudden illness that struck only them. We were afraid that the assassins who had taken your leader and nearly her life as a babe may have found their way here. We can easily remove the block; it will be painless, and she will regain all of the knowledge that is hidden from her."

Aristin looked to the two sorcerers in dismay and said, "What do you mean that you put a block on my memories? I remember my guardians, and I remember that my mother died. I even remember my training! I do not understand what this has to do with assassins and the like! The illness was just something that happened, like anything else, and it was unfortunate that Aulus, Cumhur, and Aroa all died. True, they were the only ones to catch the illness, but that is not unusual, is it?"

Praxiteles and Chinweike continued in their soft voices, "No child, not when we are dealing with our ancient enemies, the Iramians. Centuries ago, we Iristians were sent to the eastern shores of this continent to found a colony and to destroy or enslave all people we found there. It happened that during the journey to the coast, all of the priests died in flux on the ships, or so the stories say. Once our people came to the land of Amerista, we found the land rich with grasses and herds of animals we had never seen before. Also, we found that the land was occupied by your people, so the leaders decided to move on and leave these people alone. We as a nation wanted nothing to do with the death rites and slavery that had infested our lives for so many centuries. We turned our backs on the priests, burned their bodies with the ships, and turned west. Renaming ourselves Iristians as a group, we traveled far into the mountains and lost many in our trek until we found the only pass to these lands. We found the wild horse herds, along with other animals, and tamed them to our hands. We made a way of life for ourselves in this land vastly different than what we left behind. At the same time, the clan chiefs declared that we would not stay in any one place for very long to prevent our ancestors from finding us. We knew that as a people who had defied the priesthood, we would be subject to enslavement at best and death at worst. So, the clans never stop moving, always keeping their faces to the winds and being watchful for strangers. We know that your people, the Ameristans, are not friends with our ancestral people, and that is why we trade with them and why we took you in all those years ago.

"There is a prophecy that was shared with the priests leading the colonizers, but that was overheard by the man who would become the first clan chief. The prophecy says that the people from the continent would be the ones to destroy the line of the God Emperor and destroy the Priests themselves. Our ancestors wished to be free of the priests, and we demanded of our clan chiefs that we stay away from the eastern shores and where our ancestral enemies come from. Now, we have the occasional raid from the western shores of the sea, where the Iramians are seeking a foothold on this continent again. They are unaware we are the remnants of those colonists long thought lost to the seas. When the time comes to bring the awaited retribution to the God Emperor and the Priests, the Iristian people will be ready to assist those who are willing to try to sail the seas again.

"Now, we will take the time to remove the block on your memories that we put in place to protect you, Aristin. It will be painless and take but a moment of our time. Please seat yourself so that you are comfortable. The effects of the spell may be a little jarring." Having said this last, the sorcerers helped ease Aristin to the ground so that she would be comfortable. It was a matter of some moments while they were crafting the spell, with movements of their hands and softly spoken words.

Aristin sat still and then seemed to stiffen in shock before her head fell forward, and tears began to roll down her pale cheeks. She began to softly weep, and Bernella went to her awkwardly, kneeling down to wrap Aristin in her arms consolingly. It took some time for the young woman to sob out her sorrow of the lost memories and to bring herself under control again. Once she had done so, Aristin stood again and said, "I remember everything now, including what my guardians told me about my parents, my twin sister, and my brothers. I think that going home to my family is a good thing. How long before we can leave for home, Griefold?"

"We can leave in the morning if you wish," Griefold replied, "It would all depend on who you need to say goodbye to and what measures you need to take to leave. All we have to do is collect our things and start walking back to the east pass to Amerista. It will take us several moons to reach the pass and then to reach the Holy City. If we are lucky, we will make it there before next winter. It sounds like a long way, but we cannot move any faster due to Bernella's pregnancy. I do not want to put her at risk."

Aristin gave her brother a puzzled look and asked, "What do you mean walk? I have several horses of my own from the herd, as well as a cart to carry my tents and other items that I inherited from my guardians. We can easily make the pass in a moon from this watering hole. As for the distance to the Holy City, that will be a matter of a few days. If Bernella cannot ride due to her condition, she will be more than welcome to sit on my cart, and I can teach her how to drive it for me."

Griefold took a sly glance at Bernella and tried to hide a smile at hearing this. His concerns for her health and the health of their unborn child were being taken out of his hands by his newly located sister. Bernella would have to argue with Aristin about how she was treated instead of berating him whenever he overstepped in her eyes. He said, "That will work out just fine for us, Aristin. How long will it take you to get ready to leave again? What do you need to do to pack your belongings?"

Arista tinkled a laugh at her big brother as she said, "Since we just arrived today, I have not even had a chance to unpack anything. I can simply hitch up my draft horse again, retrieve my other horses from the herd, and keep on moving. I only have to tell Chief Shikoba that I am taking my animals so that he does not try to use them in the breeding stock plans he is trading for."

Griefold could not help but let out a loud guffaw at this statement from his sister. He ignored the looks thrown his way by his mate and her immediate family for laughing at the fact that he finally won. He was getting his heartmate home faster and safer before the baby should be born, and she had nothing to say about it. Bernella finally started to smile at him and snorted out a small laugh at her own expense for the situation.

By sunset, the party had increased by one, and they were ready to leave with the sunrise as discussed. They spent the rest of the day learning as much as possible about riding and caring for the horses that would be coming with them. Aristin had only a small number of horses to her name when compared to other members of the clan. She only had twenty. Most members of the Watcher Clan could boast fifty or more horses per person, with many more on occasion for some of the clan elders. All of the Ameristans, but Griefold, had experience with riding griffons and were easily taught how to ride the smaller horses. They all spent many hours laughing at the problems and the number of times Griefold found himself falling off of his chosen roan mount. It took more than a few trips to the ground and the laughter of his fellows before Griefold managed to sit his mount for more than a few seconds. Having had his ego and most of his body badly bruised and beaten by this experience, Griefold knew it was time to go home at last. Aristin made her goodbyes the night before, and as soon as the sun broke through the tops of the Suns Dagger Mountains, the party started out to the east and the rising sun. As the two clans began to stir in the dawn light, Aristin turned her back on the only family she had ever known.

***

The journey back to Amerista went much faster for the travelers, though it was painful for one of them. Riding an animal for hours on end in a hardened leather saddle was new to Griefold, and he felt the pain in his thighs and backside for the first couple of days. It was not as uncomfortable for the others, who were used to riding horses or griffons, who were used to the pressures that a saddle put upon someone. Though in pain, Griefold did not complain as he became used to riding the horse assigned to him by his baby sister. After a while, he even became fond of the mare and took her to feed her extra tidbits by hand to reward her for carrying him safely so far.

At the end of the moon of travel that Aristin had predicted, the Ameristans traveled through the pass of the Suns' Dagger Mountains. It was very uneventful, for which they were all secretly grateful. None of them wanted to see any serious fighting or threats, given Bernella's condition. She was swelling with her unborn baby more every day. It was obvious that she was further along in her pregnancy than anyone realized before. Griefold was afraid for her since she was not exactly a small person by Ameristan standards. He knew many women lost their lives in childbirth amongst his people. Yet he also knew better by now not to say anything about his misgivings to anyone, especially her, since she was determined to show that she was still one of the elite warriors of her people.

It was eight days after they had cleared the pass and only a few more days until they would have reached the Holy City that Bernella went into labor. She hid the pains at first from her travelling companions for as long as she could. It was Aristin who finally caught her out.

Aristin said to the group, "Everyone stops, get a winton or my tent set up right away! Bernella, why didn't you tell us you were in labor?!"

With speed, the men all stopped their horses and leaped to obey Aristin's commands, pulling a winton from the back of the cart and setting it up in record time. Without even having to be given further instruction, Barten began to detail off the two younger men to find water and wood or dried aurochs droppings for a fire. He knew from experience with his own two children that part of their tasks as men would be to keep out of Aristin's way. During their trek, he spoke with the young woman, and she explained that part of her duties of studying with the sorcerers was also learning how to help midwife the women of the clan. She was not an expert, but she was the only person that they had to hand who could do the job in the slightest.

Barten pulled Arten aside and whispered into his ear, "We may have to restrain Griefold during this delivery. Bernella is a new mother, and Aristin is inexperienced as a midwife. If something goes wrong, he may try to interfere, and we cannot have that. See if you cannot get him to disarm himself for a short while, and I will do the same. Bare hands will be our best option to avoid too much bloodshed."

Disarming himself, Arten turned to look at his friend and began to move over to him calmly. He said, "Griefold, my friend, why don't we drop our weapons and go in search of fuel for the fire? Father can surely find water for your sister and Bernella; we can move faster without weapons on us and spread out further."

Without a second thought, Griefold disarmed himself as well, saying, "I will head east and sweep south looking for fuel. You go north, then come back. I will not range far. I don't want to leave Bernella behind for too long in her condition."

Having said that, he began loping off into the east, eating up the distance between himself and whatever may lay out there as a source of fuel. Having grown up on the plains and knowing the lack of trees, the only source of fuel for fires was dried aurochs droppings. Having taken one of the empty sacks that were available, he quickly filled it and came back at a dead run to their campsite.

When he arrived, Barten had the winton set up, and he was standing at the entrance, refusing to let Griefold enter. Barten said, "You are to start the fire and keep it going. Do not enter the winton. You would only get in the way of what has to happen. Aristin is the best one trained and suited to help Bernella right now, and you will be a distraction. *YOU WILL STAY OUT!!!*"

Feeling sudden rage at being denied access to his heart-mate and helping her through such a critical time, Griefold launched himself at Barten. The old, scarred, one-eyed warrior sidestepped the lunge and delivered a sharp blow to the base of Griefold's head. It should have been enough to knock him senseless or at least put him to the ground efficiently. Instead, Griefold roared out his frustration and lunged again for Barten, this time death in his eyes.

Barten tried to calm the young man down, saying, "Be at ease, Griefold. I do not want to hurt you any more than you truly want to hurt me."

Griefold only growled deep in his chest as he turned away from Barten to enter the winton again, only this time to find Arten standing there ready for him. Arten did not waste time talking about Griefold staying out. He simply lunged at Griefold and encircled him about the waste, tackling him to the ground. As soon as the pair of warriors hit the ground, the older man jumped atop both of them and wrapped his arms around Griefold's kicking legs. With Arten on his chest wrestling with his arms and Barten pinning his legs to the ground, Griefold was quickly subdued.

Griefold roared at his captors, saying, "Release me now, or I swear that I will kill both of you when I am free again! I have to get in there to help Bernella. She needs me!"

Before the two other men could respond, Bernella herself shouted out of the winton, saying, "I am fine, you fool! Your sister is taking care of me. The pains are coming and going, according to Aristin, and that is normal. As for needing help, the only thing that you can do to help me right now is to be quiet so that I can concentrate on what your sister is saying. If you can't do that, *GO ROAST YOURSELF!*"

Griefold continued to wrestle with the other two men for a few more minutes before the fight left him, and he was forced to calm himself down. Griefold remained calm until the first scream of pain came ripping from Bernella's throat inside the winton. At hearing the woman he loved more than life itself scream in such pain. He began to fight with renewed vigor to get away from his captors and into the winton with Bernella and his sister for the delivery of the baby. Instead of calming himself immediately, Griefold was rendered unconscious by a well-placed blow on the jaw by Arten.

It was a few minutes later that Griefold came to from being knocked out by the hit. He found himself tied hand and foot lying on the ground. Try as he might, he could not get loose from his bindings, so he stopped trying to break loose and just started cursing vehemently.

Aristin, upon hearing this from inside the winton, said, "Enough of that, you fool! You are distracting me from what I need to do with your cussing. Either be quiet and let me concentrate, or I will have both of them out there knock you out again!"

Griefold began to cuss more quietly to himself, sure that Barten and Arten would gladly carry out his sister's threat if so ordered. He lay there on the ground, listening to the occasional scream of pain from Bernella and the soothing words coming from Aristin. This went on for over an hour before the screaming stopped, and then the cry of a newborn babe came out of winton.

Before anyone else could say anything, Aristin said, "Both are fine! Your son is fine, and so is his mother. She will need her rest, and we will have to wait here for a couple of days for her to recover. You can let him up now, Barten, just don't let him come rushing into the winton. He may scare the baby or trample his mate.

With a couple of quick jerks on the binds, Barten released Griefold, helped him to his feet, and then stepped out of the way. Griefold wasted no time rushing into the small domed tent to find Bernella covered in sweat and a newborn baby at her breast. He began to shake uncontrollably in both fear and relief at the sight of his mate and their new son. Without a word being said, Aristin left the winton for the couple so that they could spend some time alone with their new baby.

THE END